The Girl Before

The
Girl Before

RENA OLSEN

G. P. PUTNAM'S SONS
NEW YORK

PUTNAM

G. P. Putnam's Sons
Publishers Since 1838
An imprint of Penguin Random House LLC
375 Hudson Street
New York, New York 10014

Library of Congress Cataloging-in-Publication Data

Names: Olsen, Rena, author.
Title: The girl before / Rena Olsen.
Description: New York : G.P. Putnam's Sons, 2016.
Identifiers: LCCN 2016008051 | ISBN 9781101982358 (paperback)
Subjects: LCSH: Young women—Identity—Fiction. | Mind and reality—Fiction.|
Perception—Fiction. | Family secrets—Fiction. | Psychological fiction. |
BISAC: FICTION / Psychological. | FICTION / Thrillers. | GSAFD: Mystery
fiction. | Suspense fiction.
Classification: LCC PS3615.L731 G57 2016 | DDC 813/.6—dc23
LC record available at https://lccn.loc.gov/2016008051
p.   cm.

Printed in the United States of America
1   3   5   7   9   10   8   6   4   2

BOOK DESIGN BY AMANDA DEWEY

For Mom and Dad, who taught me to believe

Now

I am brushing Daisy's hair at the kitchen table when the front door crashes open. The sound of gunfire and men shouting and children screaming comes in a tidal wave through the open door. Dropping the brush, I grab Daisy's hand and pull her into the nearest closet, fumbling for the lever that will open the false back. We huddle in the small space together, and Daisy trembles in my arms.

Daisy cries as the door to the closet opens. I put a hand over her mouth to muffle the sound. Our hiding spot is clever, but not clever enough. Someone taps on the wall. "This is hollow!" he shouts, and his hands make shuffling sounds as they grope for a way in. It only takes a few minutes before the latch is discovered and we are revealed. Daisy screams and buries her face in my chest. I shield my eyes from the sudden brightness, swinging out with my other arm and coming into contact with hard flesh.

"Whoa, there," a gentle voice says. I peek at the source and see a man with kind eyes. I know it is a trick. How could he be kind when he has broken into our home? I lash out again, and he catches my arm. "A little help here!" he calls over his shoulder. His grip is firm, and I cannot retrieve my arm from his grasp. I wrap my other arm tightly around a sobbing Daisy and glare up at him.

The man is dressed in black from head to toe, a large gun strapped across his back. A woman pops up behind the man, her hair pulled back in a tight bun. She does not look as kind as he does, but she speaks in a quiet voice, holding her hands out in front of her.

"We're not going to hurt you, sweetheart," she coos, and I roll my eyes. I am nobody's sweetheart. "Just come out here so we can talk."

I want to protest, but I don't have many options. The man with the kind eyes tugs on my arm, and reluctantly I stand, pulling Daisy to her feet with me. She clings to my skirt, trying to disappear into the folds. Daisy has only been with us a few months, but we have already bonded. Daisy isn't her real name. I don't know what her real name is. When Glen brought her to me, he handed me a bouquet of fresh cut daisies. It seemed fitting. She is like my own daughter.

We emerge into the kitchen, and I sit at the same table as before. I place Daisy in front of me, retrieve the hairbrush from the floor, and resume brushing. Daisy sucks her thumb, but I do not scold her, even though we broke that habit two months ago.

"What is your name?" the woman asks, sitting across from me.

Brush, brush, brush. Long strokes through Daisy's corn-silk hair. It is almost halfway down her back now. Sometimes we go out and make dandelion crowns and she looks just like a princess. She wears those crowns until they are completely wilted.

The woman is still staring at me. "My name is Meredith," she says. "And this is Connor." She gestures toward the man. "Can you tell me your name?"

Can I? Certainly. I bite my lip, wishing for guidance. As if by divine intervention, there is a commotion from the back door, and Glen bursts through. His arms are pinned behind his back, and he is surrounded by men dressed in black. He sees me and his eyes widen.

"Say *nothing*, baby, okay? Don't tell them anything." He continues to shout as the men wrestle him toward the front of the cabin. "I love you, baby! Remember that!"

I blush at his declaration in front of these strangers. The man and woman interrogating me look at me with odd expressions.

"Is that your husband?" the man asks.

Brush, brush, brush.

"How long have you been here?" the woman wants to know.

The strands sift through my fingers.

The man's eyes narrow. He looks as if he is concentrating very hard on putting a puzzle together. I see the moment he comes to his solution.

"Is your name Diana?"

Yank. The brush catches on a tangle and crashes to the floor. Daisy yelps.

"Who is Diana?" My first words. My only words.

Then

"Clara! That damn baby is crying again!"

I am awoken by Glen's yell. Our newest addition, whom I have christened Jewel, whimpers quietly from the floor. She has been having nightmares, so I brought her into our room to be closer. Glen grumbled about it at first, but his chest soon rose and fell with his deep heavy sleep breathing. He tends to overreact sometimes.

Now, I slip out of the bed and stretch out on the floor next to the fitful child. She is not yet four, with dark ringlets and bright green eyes. She is quiet, but in unguarded moments, her smile could light an entire city.

As soon as I reach Jewel, she relaxes into me. I stroke her soft curls, murmuring nonsense words of comfort. She should sleep through the night now. She never has more than one nightmare. I tell this to Glen, who has come to stand over us. He nods, then gathers Jewel into his arms. He can be so gentle when he chooses to be. He leaves to bring Jewel back to her room.

I am already in bed when Glen returns. He climbs under the covers and reaches for me. His stubble scrapes along my skin and his breath has already turned sour in the night, but it is comforting and familiar. It is Glen.

Now

It has been three days since I was taken. I lie on my narrow cot and try not to fidget with the scratchy gown they have given me to wear. I want to ask what will become of all my beautiful things, but that would involve talking, and I must not talk. Glen told me to *say nothing.* I slipped up once when the man asked about Diana, and I forgot for a moment that I wasn't to speak. The man began an explanation, but I tuned him out. I didn't want to hear. I only wanted to see Glen again, but he was gone.

They brought us out to the front driveway and ushered us into the backseats of the many cars cluttering the space. The children tried to run to me, but were held back. They let me keep a hold of Daisy, but wanted my hairbrush. "Evidence," they said. I don't know what a hairbrush is supposed to tell them, but I gave it to them anyway.

They pulled up in front of a brick building and took Daisy. She cried and reached for me, and I whispered, "Be strong, be brave," in her ear. I don't think Glen would have minded that. It didn't really count anyway, since none of the uniformed men and women heard it. I was brought to another building, stripped and bathed, and left in this room. Three times a day they bring food, which I have not touched. The room smells like antiseptic, and the wail of ambulances keeps me up at night. Once a day they bring me into a room with a table and three chairs and sit across from me, trying to get me to talk.

I won't talk.

There is a toilet in the corner of the room, but I only use it when I am sure it is nighttime. I only know it is nighttime because they turn the lights from dim to dimmer. There are no windows here. They say it is not jail. It is a hospital. They are only holding me here "for now." They want to help me.

I will rot in this room before I tell them anything.

Then

"No peeking!" Glen is acting like an excited schoolboy. He has driven me hours out of the city, blindfolded the whole way. He has a surprise for me and doesn't want to ruin it. I can smell the fresh air and know we must be far away from the pollution-filled city. Glen helps me down from the front seat of his truck, and my feet crunch on gravel as they land. "Just a little farther," Glen says, sounding absolutely giddy.

He comes to stand behind me and whips off the blindfold. "Ta-da!"

I am standing in front of the largest log cabin I have ever seen. We are surrounded by a forest of evergreens, and I hear water rushing in the distance.

"Glen," I breathe. "It's beautiful!"

His face breaks out in a wide grin. "Come see the rest of it!" He pulls me forward toward the large porch that wraps around both sides of the house. Double doors lead into a giant foyer. There are separate staircases leading to opposite wings of the house, but what catches my eye is the wall of floor-to-ceiling windows on the other end of the living room. The Rocky Mountains look beautiful, like a postcard, and I am in love.

"What is it for?" I ask, my voice hesitant. Sometimes Glen likes to play jokes. I cross my fingers behind my back that this is not one of his silly pranks.

"For us, baby," Glen says, coming forward to wrap his arms around me. He kisses my nose. "For us and the children."

I look around. "All of us?"

Glen laughs and leads me to the window. Down the sloping lawn I see a cluster of smaller cabins. "The guys will live there. The children will live here. The house already has plenty of spaces for safe rooms. It won't need too much work." It doesn't surprise me that Glen has already thought of this. He has become obsessed with ways to keep us safe over the past few months. From whom, I'm not sure, but we practice what to do in case of a threat each time a new girl joins our family. "And over that way," Glen continues, gesturing beyond the tree line, "there is more land we can use to expand."

He has a point. Right now our apartment feels like it will burst. A small bit of hope blooms in my chest. Here, with so much room to spread out, there will be plenty of room for our daughters. Maybe here, in the fresh air, nestled among the trees, things will be different.

Glen watches me, eyes shining as he waits for my response. I haven't seen him this excited since before Papa G passed last year. The stress of taking over for his father has weighed on Glen, and with this house, that weight seems to have lifted.

"I love it," I gush, spinning in a circle to take it all in. Glen catches me by the waist and lifts me high.

"Really? Do you really like it?"

"I think it's the best house I've ever seen." I sigh as he sets me down, keeping me within the safe circle of his arms. "But can we afford it?"

Something flashes in Glen's eyes. I recognize that look. I have crossed the line. His arms tighten and I flinch. Glen closes his eyes, takes a deep breath, and when he opens them they are clear once again.

"You don't need to worry about that, do you, baby?"

I shake my head, clamping my mouth shut. I got caught up in the moment and the idea that he wanted my opinion on the house. I only need to know what Glen tells me.

Now

The metal chair is hard beneath me. I wish they would give me pants to wear with my medical gown when they make me leave my room. Or a coat. It is always freezing. The paper slippers I have been granted do little to warm my toes. I sip the lukewarm water in front of me. Water is the only concession I make. I have not eaten in four days.

Meredith sits across from me, her ever-calm façade in place. Connor paces behind her, suit jacket off, tie loosened. They look different than they did when they came to the cabin. More formal, but less scary.

"Diana, it is very important that you cooperate with us."

They keep calling me Diana. But I am not Diana. They are confused. This entire thing is one ridiculous mistake. They think I am Diana, and they think Glen is a criminal. I usually stop listening when they talk about his crimes. I will not listen to lies.

I know that the table has five hundred ninety-two scratches in it. Five hundred ninety-seven now, since I have made some new ones.

When Connor paces, he walks eight steps in one direction, pivots, and walks eight steps in the other direction. The clock ticks steadily until seven minutes before the hour, then it starts clicking and moving backward. At two minutes to the hour, it buzzes and returns to its normal rhythm. Meredith always tenses up when it begins clicking, and I get secret enjoyment out of watching her squirm.

"Glen has been talking about you, Diana." This statement catches my attention as I am trying to figure the best way to count the ceiling tiles. "He calls you Clara. Do you want to know what he says about you?"

I do. Desperately. But I only stare at Meredith. *"Say nothing."* Glen's words echo in my head. Why is he allowed to talk and I am not? Then, Glen is allowed to do many things I am not. I fidget as I imagine his reaction to my thoughts. A few days away and I am getting myself into trouble again. I remind myself that Glen cannot hear my thoughts, though at times it seems he can. Glen knows me better than anyone else.

"He says you are innocent, Diana." Meredith pauses. "Would you rather I call you Clara for now?" She asks this as if it is only just occurring to her, but I am familiar with this trick. Glen uses it often. She is pretending to be nice, expecting me to break if she shows me kindness. Trying to get me to drop my guard. I narrow my eyes at her. I am on to her. She will not get me to talk.

"Clara." Connor has come to the table. He sits next to Meredith. "Glen doesn't want you to be in trouble. He wants us to let you go. But before we can do that, you have to talk to us. Can you do that, Clara?"

Does Glen really want me to talk to them? Or are they just trying to make it seem that way? Glen doesn't change his mind. Ever. He said not to talk. I will have to hear it from him before I do. I lean back and begin counting the ceiling tiles. Connor sighs and signals for the guard to take me back to my room.

Then

The apartment is in chaos, and a client is coming. Joel brought in a new girl last night, and she is tearing the living room apart. Glen won't let me near her for now. I am tasked with keeping the other girls calm. Jill will be leaving us today if the client is pleased with her progress. I try to distract the girls from the commotion in the other room by having them help prepare Jill.

"Look at her beautiful dress," I say, smoothing Jill's skirt. She stands, still and quiet, as I put the finishing touches on her. Jill is barely fourteen, but could pass for older. She has been with us for three years. One of our long-term girls, and one of the ones passed from Papa G when he gave Glen a portion of his business. This will be his first big deal without any involvement from Papa G, and he wants badly to impress his father.

Jill's straight brown hair falls all the way down her back. We have placed a large bow on top of her head, as requested by the client. Her few belongings are packed in a small bag, waiting by the door. Her bed has already been stripped in preparation for the new inhabitant, the one currently destroying half the apartment.

All goes quiet at once as the doorbell rings. I signal for the other girls to take their places on their beds, and they do so obediently. I stand with Jill and wait to be summoned, my hand resting on her shoulder. I feel a slight tremble and give her a squeeze.

"Jill darling, you are perfect. You will be very happy with Mr. Jamison."

"Clara! Bring Jill!" Glen calls out. He is using his professional voice. He only uses it around clients, and it is much more pleasant than how he usually talks. I enjoy meeting clients with Glen just to see that side of him.

I lead Jill into the living area, which is miraculously spotless. I had expected it to look like a tornado ran through. I spare a quick thought to wonder what they have done with the new girl, but my focus is pulled to the interaction between Jill and Mr. Jamison.

Mr. Jamison circles Jill, asking her questions, to which she responds appropriately. I beam with pride, and I can see relief on Glen's face. Mr. Jamison walks over to Glen and hands him a thick envelope, waiting while Glen counts the contents. I give Jill one more look-over and smooth her hair. I always feel a little sad when I am saying good-bye to one of my daughters. But I am confident she will do well. She has not even moved to hug me good-bye, though tears glisten in her eyes. She is ever the lady, just as I taught her.

Mr. Jamison leads Jill out, and after the door latches behind them, Glen lets out a whoop and spins me around. "We did it, Clara! Papa will have to be impressed."

I smile at him. "He will be." Jill was the first girl who Glen and I handled completely on our own after taking over her training. It couldn't have gone better, and Papa has to be able to see that.

A crash echoes from the other room. Glen swears. "Can you do something about that tiger? Now that Jill is gone, I expect you should be able to deal with her."

I nod and hurry to the other room. There is an observation room outside the small bedroom where new girls are put when they first arrive. We need time to observe them and pinpoint areas for improvement. The men have managed to get the girl into the room, but cannot shut the door, as she has wedged herself into the space between the door and the latch. The adorable bedroom I decorated has been ransacked, and there is a decapitated doll strewn across the bed. The girl has wild eyes, and she screeches as I walk into the observation room. Her dark blond hair is a nest of tangles that will take me hours to smooth out. I shake my head.

My entrance is enough to distract the girl so the men can push her inside and close the door. The girl continues to destroy the room, but it is silent now. The room is soundproofed.

"Sorry about your room, Clare," Joel says, shaking his head. "This one's a fighter for sure."

I just nod and wave them off. Joel and his companion leave gratefully. My eyes are glued to the girl on the other side of the window. She appears to be at least twelve or thirteen, a bit older than the girls we usually take in. The girl cannot see me, but has tasked herself with trying to break what she sees as a giant mirror by repeatedly ramming herself into it.

A fighter, indeed. I think I will call her Passion.

Now

They are trying something new today. They have brought me outside to a courtyard of some sort. A picnic table, shaded by a large tree, is centered in the area, surrounded by sparse blades of brown grass. It has been a dry spring. I drag my feet as I walk toward the table. All my energy is gone. I cannot remember my last meal. Connor and Meredith sit on one side of the picnic table, plates of chicken in front of them. Another plate sits waiting across the table, and I collapse in front of it. It is a struggle, but I push the plate away from me and turn to stare at the tree. It is a sad tree. Alone. It looks dead, but small buds give evidence of dormant life.

"You are wasting away, Di—Clara," Connor says. He sounds concerned. More of his tricks. I am worried his tricks are starting to work on me, because his kind voice makes tears prick my eyes. I will not cry, though. I will show no weakness. Not by talking. Not by eating. Not by crying.

"They have located the parents of all the girls from your house," Meredith says. "The reunions will be on the news."

Parents? Those are my girls. Glen and I are their parents. I turn to say so but catch myself just in time. There is a spark in Meredith's eyes that says she knows she almost broke me. I must be stronger. Meredith and Connor take large bites of chicken and talk about some sporting event that happened last night. They pretend I do not exist. Maybe I don't. Not anymore.

Meredith pauses and looks at me. "Oh yeah," she says, as if she has just remembered something. She does this a lot. She slides a scrap of paper across the rough surface of the table and returns to her conversation and her chicken.

I consider ignoring the note, but I am weak. I pull it closer, eyes widening. One word stares back at me from the paper.

Eat.

It is Glen's handwriting.
I eat.

Then

Glen's parents' house is large, located in a gated community in a wealthy area of the city. Though I have been here many times, my hands tremble with nerves as we pull up in the circular driveway. Glen is tense but excited as he hops out of the truck and motions me to follow. A maid lets us in and leads us to a cozy sitting room. I clasp my hands in front of me, unsure what to do with them.

Mama Mae stands as we enter the room. She embraces Glen stiffly and gives me a kiss on each cheek. Papa G stays seated, his breathing machine tethering him to his chair. Glen walks over to shake his hand and takes the chair next to him.

"Come, child." Mama Mae takes my arm and leads me out of the room. "Let's have a chat."

We settle into a small parlor down the hall, and I am telling Mama about the children's progress when there is a loud bang from the other room. Glen stalks into the room and grabs my hand.

"We're leaving." His grip on my fingers hurts, but I dare not complain. As we reach the sitting room, I see that a table has been tipped. Papa G sits calmly in his chair and does not look up as we pass. Glen drags me out the front door, leaving it open in his wake. Anger rolls off him in waves, and he throws me at the passenger door. I quickly climb in and buckle up. I don't get involved with disagreements between Glen and Papa and know better than to ask what has happened. I know enough to suspect that Papa was not as excited about Glen's decision to expand the business as Glen had hoped.

Glen drives like the devil himself is chasing us, and I cling to the door handle to keep from sliding all over the seat. He drives to a state park and stops the truck in the shadows of the towering evergreens. He is breathing hard and grips the wheel like he is strangling it.

"Glen . . ." I begin, unsure how to help him.

Glen lunges for me, crushing his mouth against mine. I cling to him, trying to absorb the demons he is fighting, if just for a short time. The layers of clothing between us disappear. As he rises above me, his hands find my neck. His eyes blaze and stare into mine, and his fingers tighten. I cannot breathe. I cannot speak to tell him I cannot breathe. He moves faster and squeezes tighter and my vision begins to blur, black spots dancing over his face.

When I am sure I am dying, his fingers loosen and he falls on top of me, his face buried in my shoulder. I feel the wetness of his tears on my blouse as he shudders and stills. After a few moments, he moves his lips to my neck, kissing the tender skin gently.

The next day, Glen presents me with a silk scarf and a single red rose.

The bruises on my neck linger for a week.

Now

I am back in the familiar questioning room, but feeling stronger. Glen's note has made all the difference. He wants me to fight. I cannot fight if I am weak, so now I will eat. This morning I got up and did jumping jacks and push-ups in my room. I tried to jog in circles, but the space is too small. They will not give me a jump rope. At least they have given me loose pants and cotton shirts to wear. I feel almost human.

The door opens and Meredith strolls in. Instead of taking her normal seat across from me, she drags the chair around the table to place it next to me. The sound of the metal legs on the floor causes me to cringe, and I see a small smile cross Meredith's face. She enjoys watching me squirm as well. Connor is not far behind, wheeling a television on a cart into the space. He pops a tape in the VCR and perches on the edge of the table with the remote control in his hand.

The screen comes to life, and I lean forward as I recognize Daisy. She is running into the arms of two people, who scoop her up and embrace her as if they will never release her. All three are crying.

Jenna has run to another couple, who are inspecting her in disbelief, as if they cannot quite understand that she is real. Simone stands slightly apart from her people. She is a miniature of the woman who is trying to speak to her, but she stares past them. Somber Simone. That is how she got her name.

One by one, I watch as my daughters are embraced and taken away by these strangers. Finally, I see Passion. My wild child. Never quite tamed, at least not for anyone but me. No one has come for her. She watches with disinterest until the uniformed men close in on her again. Then she comes to life, kicking and screaming. The camera pans away, but I can hear her continued shouts. "Clara! Clara!"

The screen goes blank, and Connor turns to look at me. Beside me, Meredith shifts and hands me a tissue to wipe the tears I did not realize were pouring from my eyes.

Then

The sun stretches across the smooth floor of the library, and I scoot myself away from its searching fingers, pulling my pile of books along with me. The window is open, but there is barely a breeze today, and sweat soaks the hair covering my neck. I want to put it up, but Mama insists I wear it down.

Giggling voices float through the open window, and I glare at it. The other girls have been allowed to spend time outside today to escape the oppressive heat inside the house, but Mama assigned me a "special task." She says it's an honor and she only gives these tasks to the best girls, but it feels like a punishment. I sigh and lift my hair off my neck for just a moment, leaning back against the bookshelf and closing my eyes.

"So lazy," a voice taunts from the direction of the doorway, but instead of feeling guilty, I smile.

"Buzz off, Macy, I'm special." I open my eyes and grin at my friend.

Macy wanders across the room to the nest I've made for myself within the pile of books. "What are you doing, anyway? It's too hot to be inside."

Rolling my eyes as she plops next to me on the floor, I shove a stack of books in her direction. "I'm supposed to pick another language to learn, and one to teach."

"You're such a pet," Macy says, but not in a mean way. "How do you even learn those stupid languages?"

I shrug. "I dunno. It's easy. But now Mama thinks that since I can learn them, I should teach them."

"She knows you're eleven, right?"

"I think she thinks I'm one hundred or something. Not nearly as old as she is, though."

We look at each other for a moment before breaking out in giggles. I sneak a glance at the open library door, certain that Mama is going to jump out and punish me for saying something like that about her, but the hallway remains quiet.

"Ugh, it is so hot in here," Macy says when we have calmed down again. "Can't you just pick some and come outside?"

Shaking my head, I reach for the next book. "I want to pick the right ones. Mama got all these books and workbooks, and if I have to use them, I want to at least have fun with them."

"Only you would talk about lessons as fun."

I shove her shoulder, toppling one of my neatly stacked piles in the process.

"They can be," I say, restacking.

Macy reaches over and picks up a thick volume from a pile I

haven't looked through yet. "How about Mandarin?" she asks. "This shouldn't take you more than a week or two." Her cheeky expression shines at me, bringing a smile to my face despite the teasing.

"Maybe someday," I say, grabbing the book from her and placing it in the "No" stack. "But I don't want to outshine you too much."

The smile falls off Macy's face, and I worry for a second that I hurt her feelings. Even though I roll my eyes at Mama's "special" assignments, she makes no secret of the fact that I am her favorite. Macy, on the other hand, is always getting in trouble. Mama says she has too much spirit and needs to learn to be a lady. Macy is really smart, though, and her art skills are better than any of the other girls. I have overheard Mama and Papa talking about clients for her already. She will find a great place to be.

"Hey," I say, nudging Macy's knee with my foot. "Do you want to learn a language?"

She shrugs. "Mama hasn't mentioned it," she says. "I don't think she'd let me."

"Why not?" I ask, pushing a stack of French workbooks toward her. "Pick one. I'll teach you whether Mama approves or not."

Macy's eyes glint with mischief, as they always do if I mention breaking the rules. "Like a secret tutor?"

"Exactly."

"Sounds right up my alley," Macy says, flipping open the book at the top of the stack.

"Sure you don't want to go back outside for a while?" I ask after a few minutes. I start moving my book nest away from the growing patches of sunlight again.

Macy doesn't look up from the book she is looking through. "Nope," she says. "If you're in here, I'm in here. You're stuck with me."

I hide my grin behind the Italian language book I pick up next. I can't imagine anyone else I'd rather be stuck with.

Now

When they come for me the next day, I am still lying in my bed. I refuse to move. I refuse to eat. I have soiled my bed, but I do not care. I see Passion's face over and over in my mind. I see all my children running to strangers as if they had no other mother. As if I weren't enough. I will never see them again.

They bring someone in to clean me and change my bed. I do not help. I do not move. They dress me like a doll. I am limp in their arms. I hear Connor's voice.

"Clara. Sit up. Eat something. Glen wants you to eat."

It won't work this time. Glen did not see my daughters being given away. Glen has never understood my attachment to them. I can say good-bye when the time is right, when I have prepared. But not this. Not all of them at once.

The mattress sinks as Connor sits on the edge. He puts a tentative hand on my arm. I do not react. I do not have the energy to shrug him off. I do not have the energy to care.

"I'm sorry, Clara," Connor says, and there is regret in his voice. More tricks. "I thought it would make you happy to see that your daughters are being taken care of."

I turn my head so I can see him. This is the first time he has referred to them as my daughters. How did he know? I have not spoken. Has he talked to Glen?

Encouraged by my reaction, Connor continues. "The people who were parents for the girls before they came to you . . . they agreed to take care of the girls again. They didn't want bad things to happen to them. You don't want bad things to happen to them, do you, Clara?"

Very slightly, I shake my head. Connor's brows rise, but he goes on without comment about my communication. "To keep them out of group homes, we had to find families willing to take them. Since they already knew these families, it made sense."

Connor's words are logical. The best place for them is with me, of course, but as long as I am kept here, the girls need to be someplace familiar. I give a short nod, then turn back to the wall. Connor's hand tightens on my arm before he releases me and stands.

"We'll forgo our questioning for today, Clara. Meredith and I will see you tomorrow. I trust you'll eat something before then." Without waiting for a response, Connor walks out of the room. I am alone again. I close my eyes and imagine myself as one of the parents in the video, all my daughters rushing toward me, tumbling into my arms. And I smile.

Then

Muffled giggles follow me as I tiptoe toward the window. It's a gorgeous day today, but Mama has shut us into the library with the windows sealed tight. I am in training, learning to work with the younger girls on their studies, but even though I'm in charge, my heart is racing as I creep toward the sheer curtains. Even as I come within an arm's reach, I falter.

"Chicken," Macy coughs from the door, where she is acting as lookout. She has been helping me with the younger girls as well. Mama says it will be good for her placement, where she will be acting as a tutor for young children. She'll be leaving in a few months, but I try not to think about the house without her around. At least she'll be happy.

Scrunching up my face at her, I take a deep breath, straighten, and stride the last three steps to the window. Without hesitation, I throw back the curtains, slide the lock open, and raise the window, admitting fresh mountain air to the stuffy room. A collective happy sigh from the girls seated at the small tables makes me smile. Leaning out the window, I close my eyes and breathe in deeply.

A warm hand closes around my wrist and I shriek.

"Shh," Glen says, and I open my eyes to see his face inches from mine, mischief twinkling in his eyes. "You don't want Mama to check on you, do you?"

My heart thunders in my chest, but I can't help the butterflies that flit through my stomach at the sight of him. "What are you doing here?" I glance back. The younger girls are leaning forward, craning to get a better look at Glen, while Macy stands by the door, arms crossed and a smug expression on her face. She gives herself credit for my relationship with Glen and points it out at every chance. After all, she reasons, if she hadn't pushed me to break the rules and talk to Glen, we never would have ended up together.

"I saw a pretty girl leaning out of a window. I couldn't resist a Rapunzel moment."

"We're on the first floor."

He smirks. "Clara-punzel, are you going to let me in?"

Macy gives me a thumbs-up when I check with her again, and I move aside as Glen launches himself over the window ledge and into the library. I take a small step away from him, though I want to do the opposite. Even though we're already breaking all kinds of rules, I don't want to set a bad example for the girls on how to act around boys. Glen grins at my small step and mirrors my movement, leaning close enough that his arm brushes mine. Tingles run up and down my skin, and an involuntary sigh escapes me. I wonder if I will ever feel normal around Glen.

"You can't stay long," I warn, moving toward the tables to pretend to check on the work the girls have done. "Mama will be back soon."

"But I came to help," Glen says, shadowing me. When I bend to check on Rebecca's French translation, he does the same. When I hold Cassie's portrait up to show the rest of the girls, he claps along like one of the group. This goes on for about five minutes before I break down in a fit of giggles. He has thoroughly charmed each little girl in the room, and even Macy's grin has shifted from smugness to a shade of envy.

"What is all this noise?" Mama thunders into the room. Macy has been so distracted that she forgot her job, and her horrified expression gapes at me from behind Mama, who stands with hands on hips, looking between Glen and me. "You two are not supposed to be unsupervised." A rule put in place after our initial adventure.

"I came looking for Papa," Glen lies smoothly. "I had some ideas about the expansions we were talking about."

"Papa never participates in the lessons with the girls," Mama says, unconvinced. "There would be no reason for you to stay once you saw what was going on."

"Yes," Glen says, not missing a beat. "But in a few years Clara and I will be running things, and I thought this was a good opportunity to practice doing some things together. Besides," he continues, flashing his most flirtatious smile at the rest of the girls in the room, "it's not like we were unchaperoned. We had quite a large audience, actually, and I swear nothing happened."

Everyone is so entranced with Glen's antics, even Mama, that no one notices when Papa enters the room until the smile slips off Glen's face.

"What the hell, boy?" Papa says, his voice deceptively calm. This is the voice he uses right before handing down some sort of punishment. He has been using it more and more around Glen and me, no matter what we do. We are still being punished for our indiscretions, as he calls them. I hope our punishment will not last the rest of our lives. Or his.

"I was just looking for you, Papa, and—" Glen begins, but Papa silences him with a hand.

"I heard your damn circus act from down the hall. You will work on things with Clara when I say it is time. Not a moment before. Now get to my office, boy, and we'll see what *ideas* you have for me." He manages to inject enough venom into his words to shoot icy daggers of fear down my arms, and I glance at Glen, worried at his reaction.

Glen squares his shoulders, his jaw ticking. "Yes, sir," he replies, and I relax only a little. At least he won't be causing a scene here. I try to catch his eye, to give him reassurance, but the playful boy from a few minutes ago has gone, replaced by this angry man who has been showing up more and more often. A pit grows in my stomach as Glen follows his father from the room.

Before the door shuts behind him, Glen looks back once more. With a small smile, he winks, as if this is all one big joke, but both of us know the time for joking is quickly passing.

Now

Connor lied to me. They did not come for me the next day. Or the day after that. I am eating again, and the days are flowing into one another like sticky honey. I sit on my bed and stare at the floor tiles. I stare at the ceiling tiles. I stare at the two-way mirror on the wall and wonder if anyone is watching me. I wonder if this is how my children feel without me. Trapped. Watched. Squeezed.

Needing a distraction, I begin humming a happy waltz. My feet move in time to the quiet notes, and the bed creaks with the rhythm of their dance. I jump up, take my frame, and move around the room. My humming grows louder, morphing into the nonsense "BA-dum-dum BA-dum-dum" rhythmic notes, and I feel the smile creasing my face as the steps come effortlessly.

I begin to laugh, whirling myself around the room, twirling to the tune of the waltz only I can hear. My eyes are closed. Without warning, my shin bangs into the sharp metal corner of my bed. I collapse on the floor, reeling in pain. More acute than the pain in my leg is the pain in my heart. For just a moment, I forgot where I was. And now that I'm back, it hurts even more.

"Well, that was . . . interesting," an amused voice drawls from the doorway. I peek through my hair to see Meredith leaning just inside the door, a small smile on her face. "I didn't know you could dance. Or sing, for that matter."

I glare, angry at her for teasing me, angry at myself for getting caught up in my memories. I pull myself to my feet and hobble to the bed, favoring my bruised shin.

Meredith walks into the room. "Connor wanted me to come and get you," she says. "We decided it's time for you to see Glen."

Then

The first time I see Glen face-to-face, my breath escapes me. He is the most beautiful boy I have ever seen. Of course, my exposure to boys has been severely limited. Mostly, I see Mama Mae and my sisters, or the older men like Papa G. Glen grew up in the house, but was kept separate from us. When we were younger, we would try to catch glimpses of him without Mama knowing. I was sure I caught him watching me from time to time, too. When Mama Mae suggested to Papa G that they hold dance classes, Mama's bruises lasted for days. But here we are. With actual boys. If we had been allowed to giggle, I'm sure most of us would be overcome by now.

The boys come from the training program. Some of them will be trained as bodyguards or manual laborers, and others will be trained to stay on with Papa G. I learned this from Mama Mae. She was not supposed to tell me, I don't think, but I helped her with the baby last night, and she talks a lot more in the night.

Mama Mae raps her yardstick on the floor, gaining the attention of everyone in the room. Papa G stands to the side, a frightening look on his face, but he allows Mama to run the show. "These are the rules," Mama begins, her voice clear and sharp. "You do not speak to each other. You do not touch except where it is required by the dance. You keep your heads up, but look over the shoulder of your partner. These classes are for all of you to learn steps, not for flirting. Any broken rules will result in expulsion from the class and punishment chosen by Papa G. Am I clear?"

The girls murmur, "Yes, Mama Mae," in unison, while the boys nod, their expressions solemn. I sneak a glance at Glen, only to find that he is looking at me as well. He winks, and my cheeks flush. I am surprised he is in this class. He looks just like Papa G, except for his eyes, which could only come from Mama Mae. They are bright blue with mischief now, but I imagine they change color with his moods, as Mama's do.

Mama has begun pairing boys and girls off. The couples stand awkwardly a few feet apart from each other, looking everywhere but at their partner. When she reaches Glen, he whispers something to her. She swats him, but in a playful way, and nods. "Clara!" She motions me over. "You will partner with Glen." She begins to walk away, then stops. "I want you to remain in this class, Clara. Glen, behave yourself." There is a mixture of amusement and warning in her tone, and warmth rarely present, probably reserved for her son.

When the couples have all been paired, Mama instructs us to face each other, and demonstrates the correct placement of hands. Glen pretends to get them wrong, and his hands end up lower than is appropriate. I risk a glare at him and see that he is watching me, amusement glittering in his blue eyes. He knows the effect he is having on me, and it takes all my willpower to say nothing and follow Mama Mae's instructions. Glen's hand travels back to its correct spot before Mama Mae comes to check our position, but I cannot hide the flush in my neck and cheeks. I wonder if the blush will become permanent.

"It is not becoming to flush, Clara," Mama scolds. "A lady is comfortable with all situations. Perhaps this exercise will be beneficial for you in more ways than one." She moves on.

"It's benefiting me an awful lot," Glen whispers, low enough so only I can hear. I pretend I have not heard. "And that dress is benefiting both of us."

I fake a cough to hide my laugh. Glen is being completely inappropriate, and completely charming. It is dangerous to feel anything toward a boy who is not a client, and especially this boy. I am being groomed for a very special client, and I will not let Glen distract me. "Behave," I warn him, refusing to meet his eyes, glancing over to where Mama and Papa stand watching over the couples. My tone is not very convincing, but Glen follows my gaze and settles down, a slight smirk on his face.

The rest of the lesson goes more smoothly, and Glen only makes one or two more remarks. I feel his eyes on me the entire time, a fact that cannot be lost on Mama Mae, or Papa G, whose eyes are narrowed every time we spin past him. When Mama dismisses us, I line up with the other girls and march out, head held high, back straight. It is difficult to stand tall with the weight of three pairs of eyes boring into me.

Now

The first time I see Glen in his jumpsuit, my heart stops. He looks pale, and thinner than I remember, but handsome as ever. I fantasized about our reunion the entire drive to the prison where Glen is being held, and I do not know what to expect when I enter the room, but no one stops Glen as he rises and comes around the table to gather me in his arms.

He smells wrong, strong with the scent of bar soap and industrial laundry detergent. Nothing like his normal citrusy aftershave. Though the feel of his arms is familiar, there is something off. He feels less substantial, and he grips my body like a lifeline. He buries his face in my neck, and suddenly I feel as if I am the one holding him up. It doesn't last long.

As abruptly as he grabbed me, he releases me, and I stumble back. I become aware of the eyes on us from all around the room. Connor and Meredith stand in one corner, Glen's guards in another. I walk on shaky legs to a metal table and sink into one of the hard chairs pushed against it. Glen ignores the chairs on the other side and takes one next to me, claiming my hand in a tight grasp, staring at me as if he is seeing me for the first time.

Except, unlike when he really saw me for the first time, now there is desperation in his eyes. He looks at me as if he's already lost me. But I'm not going anywhere. When we work this all out, we'll go and collect our children, and we'll find someplace far away from here. Far away from anyone who would try to tear us apart. If we have to go without the children, though it pains me to think of it, at least Glen and I will be together. Forever.

I do not notice that Connor has taken a seat across from us until he clears his throat. I tear myself from Glen's eyes, where I have been swimming, feeling whole again, and glance at Connor. I put my other hand on top of Glen's, reassuring him that they will have to rip me away from him if they try to part us again.

"Glen," Connor says. "You have been reasonably cooperative so far. We are hoping you can convince Clara to cooperate as well."

Glen's jaw clenches. Not a good sign. Glen is not used to taking orders, even if they are worded as nicely as Connor's. He also doesn't like people talking to him about me. In fact, he prefers if people just pretend I do not exist as much as possible. Even most of his men rarely address me directly. Only the highest ranking of his group dare to approach me or talk with familiarity.

"I told you before," Glen says, a slight tremble betraying the anger underneath, "she has nothing to do with any of this. She knows nothing. She can't help you."

Connor smiles. "I very much doubt that. I think she could be very helpful." His gaze shifts to me. "Don't you want to help, Clara?"

I look to Glen for guidance. He shakes his head slightly, and I fix my gaze on the table, silent as ever. This is confirmation that I have been making the right choice. Anxiety stiffens my muscles as I consider Glen's reaction if I had been talking to these people. The tremor must have reached my hand, because Glen raises an eyebrow in my direction, questioning. Of course, I cannot answer. If they would leave us alone, maybe we could talk.

Glen has always had a special sense of my feelings. It is one of the things that drew me to him. He looks at Connor. "Give me twenty minutes with her," he says. "We'll work something out."

"Five," Connor counters.

"Ten."

A pause.

"Five." Connor stands and smooths his suit jacket. Without another word, he leads the group from the room. Soon, we are alone.

"Glen—" I begin.

"Shh," Glen whispers, just barely loud enough for me to hear. "We're being recorded."

My eyes widen. I do not know why I didn't figure this out before. Of course they are recording. They probably have been all along. I feel violated, though I haven't said anything to be recorded. I want to wrap my arms around myself, shield myself from further intrusion, but Glen holds fast to my hands, refusing to relinquish them.

"We don't have much time, Clare," Glen says, his whisper becoming more urgent. "You have to talk to them, give them something. You have to pretend to cooperate, make them think you have nothing to hide. It's the only way to keep you safe."

My mouth falls open. First he told me to remain silent, now he wants me to talk? I hide my surprise and nod. Even with people listening, I know Glen will not hesitate to punish me for questioning him.

"What should I tell them?" These are my first words. Though I said his name earlier, the words come out as if being forced through a pile of pebbles in my throat. My voice sounds strange to me, and I cannot keep as quiet as Glen. One of his hands shoots up to cover my mouth.

"Quiet, Clara," he scolds, and I know he is cross with me. I blink at him and he removes his hand from my mouth and moves it around to cup the back of my neck. He leans in, his voice barely a whisper, his breath disturbing the hair falling around my ear. To an observer it would look as if we are simply sitting as close as possible. "Tell them only that you cared for the girls. Do not mention the other branches. Do not mention Papa G or Mama Mae. And *do not mention South Dakota.*"

I never knew about Glen's other businesses.

I never knew Glen's parents.

And South Dakota never happened.

I memorize my new reality, each piece clicking neatly into place. A small smile curves my lips. "Of course." This time I master the quiet whisper.

Glen leans his forehead against mine. His breath is minty against my mouth. "We are gonna get through this, Clara," he whispers. "I can't be apart from you." He moves to press his cheek against mine. His words tickle my ear. "You have the power to save or destroy us, Clara. Make the right choice."

He kisses me, hard and hungry, and the door flies open. Glen's guards wrench him away from me, and he bites my lip as our connection is severed. I taste blood. He breathes hard as they drag him from the room, but does not say another word. His eyes speak volumes, and I stare into them until the ugly metal door slams shut between us.

Connor and Meredith come to stand in front of me. Meredith has remained quiet, and I think she is up to something. Meredith is never quiet. Connor crosses his arms, raising one hand to drag it down his face. His posture is stiff, and I can almost read his thoughts. He thinks this was a bad idea, that Glen has made it worse.

"I think I might be ready to talk. Tomorrow," I say. Connor's hand drops from his face and his eyebrows jump to his hairline. I hear Meredith gasp, and I smile a secret smile that I have managed to surprise her.

I stand. "I'd like to go back now," I say. Connor nods and raps on the door. It is opened from the outside and we file out.

It isn't until later that Glen's words sink in. I have the power to save or destroy? What does that mean? And even more important, how would it even be a choice?

Then

Glen is on a business trip and Mama Mae has come to visit. She comes more often since Papa G died. I don't mind her visits, because I know she is lonely in the big house with only staff for company, but I do wish she would leave the girls alone. She has them lined up in front of their beds, and she walks back and forth, doing an impromptu inspection.

Mama has a stern way about her, and she uses force where I use compassion. Mama trained me, but I learned that children respond more readily to a kind word than a sharp tongue. Of course, I will never tell her this. It would break her heart, and she has gone through so much already. She raps a yardstick along the wooden floors as she stalks up the row. The girls stand at attention, eyes trained on the opposite wall, while she looks for flaws.

"There's a wrinkle in this bed." *Rap.* I hear the stick hitting the back side of a pair of legs. I wince and close my eyes, thinking of the special care I will have to give my girls later. Perhaps a picnic outside as a treat once Mama has left.

"Your hair is not braided." *Rap.*

"Teddy bears are for children, not young women." *Rap.*

"Did you sleep in those clothes, dear?" *Rap rap rap.*

The bell rings downstairs, and I slip out, leaving Mama's judgment behind. Glen told me that many of Papa's girls were returned in the early years, and others were reported as runaways. I believe that girls treated roughly run away more often. My girls stay with their families because they are desperate to please them. They want to be loved, as I love them.

Joel is at the back door. I hesitate. Men are not supposed to be in the house while Glen is away, but Joel is in charge in his absence. I open the door and step onto the back porch. Joel takes a small step back, but not far enough for my comfort.

"Glen called," Joel begins without preamble. "He's run into some trouble and will be delayed."

My heart jumps. "Trouble?"

"Nothing to worry about. Just has to lie low for a couple days."

I nod, my mind already with Glen. His run was to Iowa this time. It should have been a quick trip through the barren plains back home to the mountains. There are always risks, though. Kids who don't understand what is going on. Others with similar businesses trying to take over Glen's territory. I have met some of his associates and competitors. They're not the nicest people. I shudder.

Joel angles his head toward the house. I realize the window upstairs is open, and Mama's sharp voice floats down to where we stand. "How are things going with the old bat?" he asks.

I glare at him. "You won't speak about her like that," I say, more authority in my voice than I would dare to use with Glen. But then, Glen would never say anything like that about Mama.

He shrugs. "You're much better with the girls than she ever was." A pause, then he grins. "You know what I remember?" he asks.

I raise my eyebrows at him.

"Dance class." He laughs. "I had my eye on you that day. If Glen hadn't snatched you up first, I might have gotten to . . ." He trails off when he sees my face. I am sure my disgust is reflected there. Anger flashes in his eyes before he shrugs. "Anyway," he says, backing off the porch. "Just wanted to let you know about Glen." He turns and walks away without another word. I lock the door behind me when I return to the house.

Now

It is quiet. The lights have gone down, but my eyes have adjusted to the dimness. Glen's words echo in my mind. *Make the right choice. Save or destroy.* My life is not about choices. I don't know what he means, and I toss in my bed as I try to figure it out.

The faces of my daughters rotate through the flip book that my brain has become. Each with her own personality, each with her own special flair for life. I spent time with each of them to find their talents, to uncover what made them unique gems. What were they doing without my guidance? How would their new families know how to talk to them? Would Daisy's new parents know that she likes to count the dots on her pajama pants before bed every night? Would Kathy's parents know to braid her long hair before she sleeps, so it does not tangle into an unmanageable mess by morning? What about Passion? Where is she now? Did people come forward to take her, or is she in a room like me, alone, unable to sleep, haunted by her lost family?

My heart beats faster and my lungs refuse to take in air. I'm supposed to talk tomorrow. What if I can't remember what to say? More important, what if I can't remember what *not* to say? What if I slip up? Is that what Glen was talking about? Will a tiny mistake destroy us all? And who else do they have? Where are they keeping the others? The men, the other women? Did they get to Glen's other businesses? Is everyone waiting, wondering if I will say the right thing to save us?

I no longer want to talk, even if that means Glen's wrath. I cannot have this pressure. I cannot deal with it. I sit upright, and I cannot tell if the black in my vision is from the darkness of the room or my lack of oxygen. I stumble out of bed, tripping over my blankets and sprawling on the floor. I cry out, and the lights flash on.

Momentarily blinded by the sudden brightness, I cover my eyes and curl into a tight ball. I cannot breathe, but I no longer care. I can feel my head getting lighter, starved of air, and I welcome the sensation. I want to escape, to leave this place, to be someplace where I do not have to talk, where I do not have to lie, where *remembering* doesn't hurt so much.

Hands grab at me, trying to pull me apart. I lock my muscles and refuse to let them break me. But with my breath failing, I am too weak to resist for long. I am pulled flat, and I hear frantic voices around me, their words flowing together like a rushing river, surrounding me, covering me, pulling me under.

I scream. My arm lashes out, hoping for any contact. The fleshy thud and following crack of a skull against the wall are satisfying. I open my eyes and use all my limbs to launch myself at the intruders. They should have let me be. They should have left me to sink into the peaceful place where thinking is unnecessary.

Strong hands hold me down. I feel a stinging in my arm, and coolness rushes through my veins. Soon, it is too much work to struggle. My arms and legs go limp. The blackness reaches out for me again, but it is not threatening. It welcomes me, and I gratefully surrender.

Then

My excitement is palpable. Glen has brought me along on this business trip to South Dakota. It is something Papa never would have allowed when he was alive, but Glen wants me here, and I was not about to argue about going on a trip. I bounce in my seat, craning my neck to try to take in all the sights at once. Glen puts a restraining hand on my arm, but his smile is indulgent. I have never been this far from home, have never been much farther than a couple hours from any of our homes, and I am intrigued by the views rushing past outside the windows. Everything is so big out here, wide-open spaces interspersed with rolling hills, everything covered with a colorful layer of fall leaves. Our van travels through charming towns, with people crowding the sidewalks for autumn festivals, and lonely villages, where most of the people spill from the open doors of the one bar in the area. Glen has promised me a tourist stop and romantic dinner after our business is concluded. Our stay is short, but I intend to enjoy every minute of my temporary surroundings.

I do not know the man at the wheel; he is not one of Glen's, but he is friendly, regaling us with tales of his twin toddlers. I laugh along with him, but a sharp pang in my heart reminds me of my little girls, left in the care of Mama Mae in my absence. I hope she is treating them well.

We have been driving outside the boundaries of civilization for quite a while now. Every few miles a house pops out from the wilderness, some lit up, warm and welcoming, others dark, surrounded with an air of abandonment. Wildlife flashes through the trees, almost too quick for my eyes to catch. I look forward as the van slows. We stop in front of a tall gate, idling as the driver punches a code into a small keypad by the entrance. The gate swings open, and we drive up a long lane. I gasp when the house comes into view.

Standing at least three stories high, the house is twice the size of ours. Multiple balconies poke out from faux log cabin siding. Outbuildings dot the meticulously manicured grounds. As we park and exit the vehicle, barking fills the air from what must be an army of dogs, invisible right now, but clearly aware of our presence. More car doors slam shut behind us as the second vehicle in our small parade joins us. The men Glen brought rode in that van, and they follow us up the stairs. My heart rate picks up as Glen pushes the small button by the door and chimes resonate within the large building.

I hear a quiet chuckle beside me. Joel covers his mouth with his hand when Glen shoots him a glare, but catches my eye and winks.

"Don't worry, Clare," Joel whispers. "No one in here will bite." He pauses, eyes twinkling. "Unless you ask nicely."

I narrow my eyes at him. Joel has been more informal with me lately, and it makes me uncomfortable. He may be Glen's top guy, but I don't like the way he looks at me, or the girls. If I weren't afraid of Glen's anger, I would ask for Joel to be banned from the house.

The others around us are familiar, but I cannot place names and faces. I have had little contact with the other men, even on this trip. I spent most of the past day in the lodge, reading books about the history of the area. I was surprised when Glen invited me along this evening. He wants my opinion on something. I smile to myself. I feel important.

Rapid footsteps announce someone's approach on the other side of the door. It opens just wide enough for us to squeeze through, and we are ushered in.

"Hurry, please," the man at the door says.

Inside, the air is stale. The entryway is tall, and sunlight streams in through high windows, cutting the clouds of dust. There are cloth-covered pieces of furniture in the rooms off the entry, and while outside the grounds were well-tended, the inside of the house looks abandoned.

The man who opened the door starts up the stairs. "Come," he says, motioning for us to follow. I grip Glen's arm and he glances down at me, raising an eyebrow. I loosen my hold and give him a reassuring smile. I will not let on how anxious I am, though I sense he already knows.

At the top of the stairs, we are led to a large room. A small group is gathered there, and the air is thick with smoke. I cough and try to hide the action behind my hand. Glen shoots me a warning glance. My behavior must be perfect.

"Hello, and welcome!" says a large man, stepping out from the crowd with arms extended. He comes to Glen and clasps his shoulders, then kisses the air on each side of Glen's face. Glen looks startled at first, but covers his surprise with a genial smile.

"Mr. Harrison, thank you for meeting with me," Glen says.

"Of course, of course," Mr. Harrison says. His voice is deep, his tone welcoming. "I knew your father well. I was very sorry to hear of his passing."

Glen nods. "He always spoke highly of you as well, Mr. Harrison. I hope you find your dealings with me to be just as pleasant." I do not see this humble side of Glen very often. He is deferring to the other man. He has already begun negotiations.

Mr. Harrison chuckles. "I am quite sure I will, my boy." He turns to me, looking me up and down in a way that makes my skin crawl. Glen's arm tenses against mine, but his face remains impassive. "And who is this?" Mr. Harrison asks.

Glen snakes an arm around me. "This is Clara," he says. "She has come to help with the girls."

What girls? Glen never told me the exact purpose of my presence. I try not to let my surprise show. Mr. Harrison steps forward and clasps my hand. His skin is dry and feels like tissue paper. He lifts my hand to his lips. "I am very pleased to meet you, my dear," he says, his breath stirring the sparse hair on my arm. He presses his lips to my skin, and when he raises his head, a thin string of spittle stretches between us. My hand spasms. Mr. Harrison's eyes narrow, and I try to cover my reaction. I giggle.

"That tickles, sir," I say, forcing my lips into a small smile. I can hear the fake tone of my voice, but it seems to appease him.

"Genevieve," he barks, motioning someone from the crowd. A tall woman emerges from among the men. Her hair is a burnished auburn, and she is dressed in a frothy nightgown that leaves little to the imagination. She would be beautiful but for the thick layer of cakey makeup plastered over her face and the fine lines webbing out from her lips and eyes that no amount of cover-up can hide.

"Yes, my love," she coos, resting her hand on Harrison's shoulder. Her long nails are painted black, and they dig into the fabric of the man's sport coat.

"Bring Clara to meet the other girls," he says. He leans in and whispers something in her ear that only she can hear. Genevieve runs her hand down his arm as she leaves his side, and he swats her on the rear before she is out of range. She squeals, making the sound delighted rather than disgusted, as I would have.

"Come along, Clara," Genevieve says, her eyes on Glen instead of me. "We will have tea with the girls."

I cast Glen a questioning glance, and he inclines his head, indicating that I should go with Genevieve. I am not sure we should trust these men, but I go. I am nothing if not obedient.

Now

There is an annoying shuffling in the room. A moment of silence, a cleared throat, then the shifting of papers. I want to sink back into the blackness, but the damn shuffling will not quit. I crack my eyes open, and the light stabs into my pupils. I take a sharp breath, and the shuffling stops. Footsteps click across the room, and I sense the light dim behind my eyelids. I pry them open again and release a relieved breath when the soft light washes across my vision.

"Awake at last," a voice says from my right. I turn my head to see Meredith pulling a chair closer to the side of the bed. The metal legs scrape across the tiled floor, and I wince at the noise. A piece of hair falls into my face, tickling my nose, and I move to brush it away, but my hands meet resistance. I look down, and chains rattle as I strain against the padded cuffs securing my wrists to the side of the bed. My heart beats faster as my brain becomes more alert.

"Calm down," Meredith says, her tone mocking. "You don't want another sedative, do you?"

I stare at her with wide eyes. They drugged me. Memory flashes of my midnight panic attack assault me, and I close my eyes, my head falling back to my pillow. Tears well up behind my eyes, but I refuse to allow them. Not in front of her.

Meredith sighs. "We're not doing the silent act again, are we?" She crosses her legs and taps her pen on a sheaf of papers perched on her knee. "I thought we were past this."

"Why am I tied up?"

She smiles. "You're not tied up, Diana, you're restrained. To keep from hurting yourself or others."

"I'm not going to hurt anyone. And my name is Clara."

"I'll decide whether you're a threat," Meredith says, and turns her attention to her papers. "If our conversation goes well, and you are cooperative, I'll see about having the restraints removed."

I glare at her. She has all the power. I have nothing for her. I am nothing to her. I do not understand why she is torturing me.

Meredith's foot wiggles and she studies the paper she is holding. It is an anxious movement. I realize that I do have something she wants. I have information that will help her. She thinks, they all think, that

I am the key to whatever case they are building against Glen. A sense of power rushes through me, and with it a feeling of supreme calm. I feel my lips curl into a smile, and my muscles relax.

Misinterpreting my sudden change in demeanor, Meredith returns my smile. "That's better," she says, confidence in her tone. Her foot stills, and she uncrosses her legs, leaning forward to rest her elbows on her knees. "Kidnapping is a very serious charge, Clara. Not as serious as some of the other charges against Glen, but still, stealing those girls away from their families seems almost worse somehow, doesn't it?"

Stealing them away? She thinks that we *took* those girls? We gave them a better life. Their parents gave them up. I want to scream at her. If only they would talk to the parents, all this would be cleared up.

A sickening thought intrudes on my confidence. Would the parents lie? I knew it had to be done in secret. What if we were being punished for the choices these parents made? What were they saying to keep themselves out of trouble? And what else does she know about Glen? Certainly they can't know everything. Panic curls in my stomach, but I am determined not to let it show. I won't give Meredith the satisfaction.

"And refusing to answer our questions, well, that's obstruction of justice. You don't want to stop those little girls from getting justice, do you? A little cooperation will go a long way, Clara." Meredith's smile is grim, and not at all reassuring, despite her words. "Now," she says, eyes glued to my face. "Give me the names of your biggest clients."

My mouth drops open in shock. She doesn't waste any time. Except she is wasting time. Glen never trusted me with any of that information. I only knew them by their code names. Mr. Harrison's face flashes through my mind. But Glen said South Dakota never happened. I stuff the face away and stare at Meredith, trying to decide how to respond.

"Names, Clara," she says, leaning back in the chair. "Easy. Just some names, and we'll get you unhooked and back on track."

She wants names. I don't have real names, but I can give her the ones I know. "Mr. White. Mr. Black. Mr. McDonald. Mr. Costello. Mr. Apple."

The papers drop to the floor as she stands. "Is this a joke to you?" she hisses. "Do you even *care* where those girls ended up?" She begins to pace.

She is insulting my devotion to my daughters. Of course I care. Our clients were selected very carefully. "Those are the names I know," I say.

"Those aren't real names," she says, her heels clicking across the floor as she comes to sit by me again. Her face looms close, and I shrink away as much as the restraints will allow. "Tell me, so help me . . ."

I begin listing names again. "Mr. Marlboro. Mr. Busch . . ."

"I liked you better when you weren't talking," Meredith says, and the spit from her angry words sprays my face.

"Maybe you should try it. People might like you better, too."

Slap.

My cheek stings where her hand makes contact, and tears spring into my eyes. Meredith's chest is heaving, straining the buttons of her prim blouse.

The door flies open. "Meredith!" Connor strides in, his face twisted in fury. "Out," he says, pointing to the door.

"But she—"

"Out!"

Connor keeps his voice quiet, though rage vibrates through every word. Meredith stomps toward the door and Connor catches her arm. "We will discuss this later. Take the rest of the day off."

Meredith snarls something in response and stalks from the room. Connor moves to my side and uses gentle, efficient movements to survey the damage. A guard comes in and unlocks the shackles. I sit up and bring my knees to my chest, rubbing my wrists.

"Are you all right?" Connor asks. His voice has regained its normal calming tone, and I nod. "Clara." I look up at him. "Are you really okay?" There is genuine caring in his eyes, and I feel the tears creeping up again for different reasons than before. No one has shown me kindness like this in my entire life. Without the expectation of anything in return. Not Mama Mae. Not Papa G. Not even Glen.

Snap out of it, I chide myself. He *does* want something from me. He wants the same thing Meredith wants. Names. Information. Something to use against Glen. I can't give in to my emotions now.

"I'm fine."

Connor looks at me a little longer, then nods. "Okay." He stands. "We'll skip the questions today," he says. "I'll have them bring you your lunch, if you're hungry. "

I nod.

"Okay." He is saying that a lot. "I'll see you tomorrow." He walks to the door. I almost don't want him to go. I am growing weary of being alone. "Clara?" He stops and turns at the door. "I'm sorry about Meredith. And I'm glad you're okay."

I smile slightly. He inclines his head toward me, and then he is gone.

Then

I am walking through the hallway outside Papa G's study, arms full of linens to put away, when I hear raised voices coming from the cracked door.

"She is the one I want, Papa."

"She's not available."

"You said whichever I wanted! My pick!"

It is Papa G and Glen. I don't know what they are arguing about, but it is rare to hear Glen angry. Every time I have encountered him since dance class he has been laughing and teasing. Now he sounds like a spoiled child, rather than the seventeen-year-old boy he is. I roll my eyes and continue down the hall.

"Clara is meant for a very wealthy client, boy. I won't have you ruining that deal."

I freeze. They're talking about *me*. I will be sixteen this year, and the end of my training is getting close. I am almost ready to move out. I had been excited until recently, when I began to look forward to my frequent run-ins with Glen. Has he been feeling the same? I haven't dared to dream that our time spent together meant as much to him as it does to me.

"You told me when I turn eighteen I could pick my girl. I will be eighteen in three weeks, and I pick her."

"There are plenty of other options, boy."

"Stop calling me boy, old man, I am almost an adult."

The sound of flesh hitting flesh echoes through the empty hallway. "You will not show me that attitude, boy. She is not for you." Papa G's voice is calm. "Now get out, and I don't want to hear about this again."

"Father—"

"*Go.*"

The door flies open before I can duck out of sight. Glen stares at me for a moment, then glances back into the room before pulling the door shut behind him. He puts a finger to his lips, grabs my arm, and drags me down the hall. I scramble to keep up and keep a hold on the linens in my arms. He stops, grabs the stack of fabric from me, and dumps it into the nearest closet, which happens to contain brooms. I start to protest, but the look he gives me silences me at once.

We continue outside, and the frigid air blasts through the thin cotton of the dress I'm wearing. The snow crunches under our feet as we hurry across the lawn and into a small copse of pine trees. There is little snow amidst the trees, and though the air is still cold, we are protected from the wind.

Glen stops and shrugs his jacket off, wrapping it around my shoulders. He grasps my biceps and looks me straight in the eye.

"Clara. How much of that did you hear?"

"N-not much. Just . . . the last part."

"The part where I told my father I wanted you, or the part where he smacked the shit out of me?"

"Both," I admit.

Glen smiles ruefully. "Ah. Then my secret is out."

I watch him carefully, unsure of what to say. He seems to be deciding something as well.

"My father won't let us be together, Clara."

My heart stops. I nod, trying to give him a wobbly smile, but failing as tears fill my eyes. Of course I knew it wasn't possible, but a part of me, the part that allowed daydreams before sleep, had been holding on to hope. All the stolen hours together, the conversations we had had. Glen told me things he'd never told anyone else, and more often than not I had found myself thinking of a future with him, instead of with the client to whom I was promised. I drop my gaze to the pine needle–carpeted ground.

"Clara," Glen says, lifting my chin with his index finger, forcing my eyes back to his. "I don't give a damn what my father says." He drops his hand. "That is . . . I mean . . . if you . . ."

I understand his sudden vulnerability. Despite his bravado, Glen is worried that I might not feel the same way. My heart feels as if it will burst. I wondered if I loved him before, but now I am sure. I reach for his hand. "I do," I say, my voice barely a whisper.

Glen's face breaks into a grin, and before I can react, his mouth is on mine. I have never been kissed before, and I am not sure what to do. He pulls away suddenly, laughter dancing in his eyes. "Oops." He doesn't look sorry. "That was your first kiss, huh?"

I nod.

"Let's erase that one," he suggests, moving toward me again, cupping my face in gentle hands. "This should be the kiss you remember." His lips are gentler this time, lightly brushing mine at first, then becoming more firm. I mimic his movements, growing more confident under his patient tutoring. I thrill at the tingles running up and down my body. I am kissing Glen! My daydreams never came close to the actual moment. I want to climb inside him and live, and never be apart from him.

I lose track of time, but too soon Glen's kisses gentle, and he moves away, keeping my face in his hands. My hands rest on his hips, though I am not sure how they got there. It feels natural, and he doesn't seem to mind.

"Clara," he breathes. "I've thought about this a lot. I've been making some plans. I went to my father today as one last attempt to reason with him." His jaw clenches, and he raises a hand to a spot on his cheek that is already starting to bruise. "We have to run away. You will go with your client in a few months, and we'll never see each other again. I can't let that happen."

"Okay," I say. I would agree to anything he suggested at this point. My pulse races, and I wait for my breathing to return to normal.

"It has to be tonight. Papa will be signing your final papers any day. Leaving now will give him a chance to find a replacement and smooth things over. I don't agree with him, but I don't want to ruin him, either."

So soon. But what Glen says makes sense. I want a good future for my sisters. "Okay."

"After the girls are asleep tonight, go to the cellar. There's a set of doors at the far end they never patrol. Wait inside, and I will come for you."

"Okay."

"You can't bring anything with you, Clara," Glen warns. "I'll stash a jacket and boots for you, but you can't be caught doing anything that will tip them off. And you can't say good-bye. We won't be back."

My heart squeezes as I think of my sisters. I would be leaving them in a few months anyway. And this way, I'll be with Glen. "Okay."

His smile warms me to my freezing toes, and he gives me one more quick kiss. "Go," he says. "Before they realize you're missing."

I tighten my fingers on his waist briefly, then remove his jacket from my shoulders, gasping at the sudden chill. I take quick steps back toward the house.

"Clara." His voice stops me, and I look back. "I love you."

"I love you."

Now

I only get one day of reprieve before they come to bring me back to the questioning room. I brace myself as I enter. My wrists are still sore from the restraints, and the red slap across my cheek has progressed to a greenish bruise. I can't believe Meredith would hit so hard.

Connor is the only one in the room when I enter. I sag in relief and sit, absently rubbing my wrists.

"Are you still sore?" Connor asks, glancing at the motion.

I shrug. "A little."

He sighs. "They were only supposed to restrain you when you woke if you were out of control. I apologize for Meredith's decisions."

"Is she coming?"

"No."

I nod. Good. I hope they threw her in a small room like mine, chained down by restraints and slapped at least three times a day. A slap to go with each meal. I smile at the idea. Connor looks at me strangely, and I rearrange my features to a more neutral expression.

"How is Glen?" I ask before Connor can ask his questions. I want to take whatever opportunity I have to gather my own information.

Connor continues looking at me for a moment, then leans forward. "He's fine. We told him you had some problems, but didn't mention Meredith. It's probably best not to bring that up."

I agree. Guards or not, Glen would find a way to get back at Meredith for causing me harm. He does not tolerate others putting their hands on me.

"I thought we'd start easy today," Connor says, stacking some papers and knocking them on the table to straighten them. "To celebrate your found voice and to ease you into this."

I give him a small smile, but inside I am a jumble of nerves. I don't know what to expect, and I still haven't worked out what Glen said. I recite the rules in my head. *No clients. No Mama and Papa. No South Dakota.*

"State your name."

"Clara."

Connor smiles. "Your full name."

"Clara Lawson."

The smile falters. "First, middle, and last, please."

I am confused. Then I picture the ID I was given for South Dakota. My brain feels like it lights up, and I laugh. "Oh! Stephanie Ann Caraway."

Now Connor looks confused. "Stephanie . . . Ann . . ." His voice trails off.

"Caraway," I supply. I look at his paper, waiting for him to write it down.

"You have been insisting your name is Clara."

"It is."

"But you said it was Stephanie."

"No, my full name is Stephanie Ann Caraway. That's what Glen said if anyone asked. That's what it said on . . ." My mouth snaps shut. Three minutes into the conversation and I've almost given us away. I cringe as I imagine Glen's reaction. He would make sure the other side of my face matched what Meredith gave me.

"On what?"

"I forget."

Connor sighs, more loudly this time. "Clara, I thought this would be an easy question to start with."

I want to cry. I have messed up and don't fully understand how. I place my head on the table, cooling my flaming face on the smooth metal surface. What is my name? Clara. Stephanie.

Diana.

I sit up. "Can we move to the next question, please?"

Connor purses his lips. "Fine. How old are you . . . Clara?"

I ignore the pause before my name. "Twenty-three."

"Your birthday?"

"October sixth."

"How long have you known Glen Lawson?"

"Since I was fourteen."

"Where did you meet?"

"Dance class." These questions are expected. I rehearsed the answers. I decide the shorter the answers, the better, but I can tell that Connor is frustrated with my lack of elaboration.

"Where was the dance class?"

I do not answer.

"Clara? Where was your dance class?"

"In the studio."

"Which studio?"

"The one where we met."

Connor's lips have thinned. I can only imagine Meredith's reaction if she were here. I am glad she isn't. Connor has always been more patient. But clearly his patience is running out as well.

"No, Clara, *which studio?*"

I tilt my head. "I don't understand."

"What was the name of it? Who was the teacher? What city was it in?"

Scratching at the surface of the table, I hesitate. I'm treading on dangerous ground. I should have made up some completely random answer as to how I met Glen, but now I'm stuck. I can't say which studio, or who taught it, because as far as Connor knows, I have never met Mama or Papa. My mind blanks, and I go with the easiest answer I can think of. "I don't remember."

"Like hell."

My eyes widen. Connor is angry. How did I anger him so quickly?

Connor stands and begins pacing. "I can't help you, Clara, unless you help me. This doesn't look good, you know."

I remain silent as I follow him with my eyes. Back and forth, back and forth.

"They want you to rot, Clara. They want to throw you in prison for the rest of your life. They think you are a part of all this, that Glen is only protecting you."

I shake my head, my mouth opening in silent protest. I don't even know what "this" is, but I know I haven't done anything wrong.

"Do you want to spend the rest of your life in a cell, Clara? Because

I promise you, it won't be as nice as the space you've got now. These are plush accommodations, but you can't stay in the psychiatric ward forever. Eventually you'll have to make a choice that will determine where you go next."

My hands begin to tremble.

"Meredith was all for throwing you in with the other inmates for a few nights, giving you a taste of what it would be like." Connor runs his fingers through his hair, scrunching his hands in the strands so they stand out when he removes them. It would be funny if the look in his eyes weren't so terrifying. He comes and leans his hands on the table, moving until his face is inches from mine.

"You wouldn't last a night in that prison, Clara," he whispers. "I don't want to do that to you. Please, don't make me do that to you."

I can feel the blood drain from my face, and the room begins to spin. "Clara!" Connor's voice sounds far off. I try to catch myself as I topple from my chair, but my arms don't respond. Fireworks explode behind my eyelids before everything goes dark.

My ears ring as I float back to the surface of consciousness.

"Clara." Gentle hands pat my cheeks. "Wake up."

I open my eyes and see Connor's face, his blurry forehead creased in concern. As my vision focuses, I realize I am lying on the floor, my head in Connor's lap, and my brain feels as if it is trying to escape from my skull.

"I'm sorry, Clara, I wasn't quick enough to catch you. You hit your head pretty hard."

I shake my head, trying to clear it, and spots dance in front of Connor's face. I feel sick.

"The guards are coming to bring you to the medical wing." Connor releases a long breath. "Please think about what I said. I don't want to send you away, but if you won't help me, I can't help you."

There is no threat in his voice, only quiet desperation. I believe he truly does want to help me, and through the nausea I am experiencing, I feel a pang of guilt. I cannot give him what he wants. Because what he wants is to send Glen away. He hasn't said it, but I have put the pieces together. They hope to use me for information to put Glen in prison. They want to put him away for things he did to help our daughters, to protect me. And I can't let that happen.

I cannot be without him. And I won't.

Then

The house is quiet as I creep out of the room. My sisters are all sleeping soundly, exhausted from the marathon cleaning we did today in preparation for a new client interview. We never see the clients, unless they are our own. I have met the client whom I am promised to twice. He is at least thirty years my senior and wishes to have a girl in the house to help with household chores and other duties at his second home, where he lives when his business takes him away from his wife and children.

My hands tremble as I turn the knob on the doorway to my bedroom, easing it open and slipping out into the dim hallway. I have been weighing this decision in my mind all evening. When Glen suggested we flee, it made perfect sense, but as soon as I was away from him, the doubt started creeping in. I have grown up in this house, learned so many things, and running away seems like throwing all of that in Mama's and Papa's faces. What will happen when we leave? Will my client accept a substitute? Will he be angry? I know my fee is substantial. Will they completely lose that money? My palms dampen, and I rub them up and down my nightgown as I falter in the hallway.

Though Glen said he has been thinking about this and preparing for some time, I wonder if he really knows how to survive on his own. Yes, he has trained under Papa, but he also grew up here, was taken care of, sheltered. This is all either of us knows. I shake my head as I near the stairs, already preparing a speech in my head to tell Glen that there must be another solution, another way we can be together and not cause problems. Some way everyone can be happy.

But I know it's not possible. Papa is stubborn, and his business is his top priority. And Glen and I do know more than just growing up in this house. We know something Mama and Papa could not teach. We learned how to love each other. We trust each other. I know Glen will not let me down, and together we can get through anything. Yes, this is the right decision. The only decision that really makes sense. No more thinking, I tell myself. I have made my choice.

The stairs groan as I place my weight carefully on each one. I know the spots that will protest the least, and use this knowledge to my advantage. There are no lights on, not even the slice of glowing orange under the study door that would indicate Papa G is working late. My feet are bare and chilled on the hardwood floors. The basement stairs prove more tricky, as I do not use them as often and am not as familiar with their structure. I stay on my toes and move as quickly as possible, reasoning that if I barely step, the stairs will have no time to register my weight before I am past.

The basement smells musty. A flashlight waits at the bottom of the stairs, and I click it on, the beam bouncing over old furniture and forgotten memories. I pick my way through the clutter, careful not to touch anything. A toppled tower of junk may give us away. I reach the doors Glen mentioned, and I wait. After only a few minutes, I hear the doors creak.

"Clare," Glen whispers. "You down there?"

"Yes."

A thump, and a soft lump hits my legs. "Change into those and hide the bag behind some of the junk. Knock when you're ready."

I open the duffel that has landed at my feet and riffle through. Pants, boots, sweater, and a heavy coat. I put on the outfit with quick hands and shove the empty bag along with my nightgown under an old stuffed chair. I knock gently on the doors, and they fly open. Glen reaches a hand down and helps me climb the steep steps up and out of the basement.

My breath freezes in the subzero temperature of the night. Glen closes the doors with a quiet click and turns to me. He places a stocking cap on my head and hands me a pair of mittens and a scarf. I wind the scarf around my neck and stuff my hands into the mittens. Glen stares at me for a moment. "Are you sure about this, Clara? We can't come back, remember."

I nod. "Absolutely."

He leans over and presses his lips to mine. They are like ice cubes, but I barely notice over the thrill that goes through my body that we are doing this. We are kissing and we are running away and we will be together.

Glen releases me and grabs a backpack from the ground, shrugging it onto his shoulders. A second backpack is loaded onto my back, and I stumble at the weight. "You okay?" Glen asks. "I gave you the lighter one."

I adjust the straps and hike it into a more comfortable position on my shoulders. Better. "Yes, I'll be fine. Really." I give him my most convincing smile, and he returns it.

"Okay then. Let's go." He takes my hand and leads me into the trees that surround the house. I cannot remember a time when I left the grounds of the house. Icy fear runs through me, down to my bones. I have no idea what to expect out there. I clutch Glen's hand tighter.

He squeezes in response, but says nothing. It occurs to me as we crunch through the snow that for all the work we did to cover our escape route, our footprints will make it pretty obvious which way we're heading. I mention this to Glen, and he shrugs.

"They won't catch on right away. They'll assume someone was patrolling. I walked around a lot out there while I waited for you. They won't be able to tell which set is which."

The boots he has given me are the same as the men all wear, if a smaller size. Glen has done his best to cover all the bases and make a clean getaway. We trudge through the woods, cutting through thicker groups of trees to leave fewer prints. As we head in the direction of the road, I hear loud music and shouts of raucous laughter. I stop.

"What's that?"

"Nothing, ignore it," Glen says, tugging my hand, urging me to continue.

"I didn't think there was anything out here for miles. We haven't walked miles, have we?"

"No, Clara, we're still on Papa G's property. Which means we have to *hurry*."

"Then what is that?"

Glen sighs. "One of Papa G's other businesses."

"What is it?"

"Why are you so curious?" Glen yanks my arm again, and I yelp in pain. "Sorry," he apologizes. "Can we just go?"

I extricate my hand from his grasp and cross my arms. "Tell me what it is, Glen." I don't know why I've become so stubborn or so bold, but I don't like that Glen is keeping things from me. This is not a good way to start our lives together.

Glen comes close. "You want to know what it is?" He grabs me and propels me toward the noise. We come to the edge of the trees and I see a one-story log building, every window lit up from inside with dim, smoky, neon lighting.

"It's a bar?" I guess. I know a little about bars. Papa G likes to talk about meeting clients there, taking them for a beer. He always comes back smelling foul and stumbling around.

"Not just a bar," Glen whispers. "Are you sure you want to know?" At my nod, he leads me around to the back of the building. We stay low to the ground, crouching as we run. The first window we peek into is a giant room. Tables are scattered throughout the room, and all chairs face a small stage with a pole. A woman is dancing on the stage, but it is nothing like the dancing we learned in Mama Mae's studio. Along the walls, a few other girls gyrate in steel cages, while men with glassy eyes stare at them with slack-jawed expressions. None of the women are wearing tops, and their bottoms barely qualify as clothing. Even as I watch, a man and woman stumble together toward a hallway at the back, hanging off each other and laughing like children. Revulsion rises in the back of my throat. I turn to say something to Glen, but he is on the move again. He looks back over his shoulder at me, but does not meet my eyes.

"Are you ready to get out of here now?" he asks, his voice rough.

"Yes."

Determined to focus on what's ahead, I turn my back and disappear into the woods, leaving Papa G's "business" behind.

Now

I don't have a concussion, but my head is still swimming. I beg Connor for the rest of the day off, and I can tell he wants to refuse. He hasn't gotten the information he needs, and he is growing desperate. In the end, he concedes. I lie in bed the rest of the day, thinking of Glen, wondering how I am to answer these questions and follow his rules. I try to devise a plan to help him, but I am lost. I try to invent stories I can tell Connor to appease him, but I fail. I have never been a good liar.

When Connor comes for me the next day, I immediately notice the grim set to his mouth. Instead of going to the room as usual, he leads me outside to a van. He gets up front with the driver, and I am placed in the backseat. There is a wire cage separating the front seat from the back. There is room for at least ten more people in the van, but we are the only riders. The empty seat belts click against one another as we bounce over the road. Connor has not said a word. I want to ask if we are visiting Glen again, but I am afraid to speak.

We go a different direction than when we visited Glen, and soon we are beyond the city limits. My heart rate picks up as the van approaches a tall chain-link fence, topped with razor wire. An imposing concrete building rises behind it, and there are high towers stationed across the area.

"I don't know how to get through to you, Clara," Connor finally says from the front seat. "I don't want to send you overnight, but you need to understand what's at stake."

"What is this?" I ask, my voice small.

"The women's state prison."

Panic floods my veins. We pull up to the guard station, and after the guard confirms the identity of the driver, the gate creaks open. As it shuts behind us, my lungs stop taking in air. I cannot breathe.

"Put your head between your legs, Clara," Connor says, his voice calm and even. "Try to take deep, slow breaths."

"She okay?" the driver asks.

"She'll be fine," Connor responds.

"Should I pull over?"

"No, keep going."

I unhook my seat belt and lean over. Spots dance in my vision. It is not helping.

Finally the van halts. The side door flies open and Connor is there. "Breathe, Clara, come on," he says, patting my back. His presence is a comfort, and I find my breath. Tears fall on the carpet in front of me. I cannot do this. I cannot be here.

"I knew it would be too much," Connor mutters to himself. I pretend not to hear.

Soon I am breathing normally again, but no amount of deep breathing will calm the shaking of my hands. I lean heavily on Connor as he helps me out of the van. He releases me and makes me walk on my own unsteady legs toward the squat brown building leading into the prison.

A guard stationed at the door looks me over and then glances behind me. "Pick her up at three," he says. I look back and realize that Connor is still by the van. He nods and takes out his phone without giving me another glance. I feel abandoned. I feel lost. My legs start to give out again.

"Whoa there, little lady," says the guard, catching my elbow. "Don't let them see you like this. You'll never make it if you do."

Them? Who? Make what? I don't want to make it here. I want to go back to my private room and curl on my narrow mattress and scream into my thin pillow. I want to run and find Glen and have him gather me up and tell me everything will be okay.

I remember how Glen clung to me when I visited him. He has been in prison this whole time. For the first time, Glen looked to me to be strong. I stand up straighter. Glen trusts me to do what I need to in order to get us out of this. He is counting on me not to give in, not to let them break me. One day. I can do anything for one day. And if I do well, perhaps they will let me see Glen again. I position his face squarely at the front of my mind as I take the final steps to the door, which a guard holds open for me.

I wink at the guard and stride forward into the building, leaving him behind with a baffled expression. Good. I stop short when I enter the building, unsure of where to go.

"You here for the day?" a plump woman with tightly curled hair asks.

"I-I think so?"

She points to a door. "Through there. They'll process ya."

Process? I take a hesitant step toward the door. "Will it hurt?" I ask, turning back to the woman. There is a chuckle from one of the people sitting in the molded plastic chairs. I scan the room, but cannot figure out who finds me funny.

The woman eyes me. "Only if you don't follow directions. Can you follow directions?"

I nod.

"Then you'll be fine. And you'll be glad to be leaving at the end of the day."

I take a deep breath and walk into a nightmare.

Then

I dread Thanksgiving every year, and this time is no exception. Mama tries to make it festive, a time for the family to gather and enjoy one another, but there is a constant underlying tension between Glen and Papa, a push and pull that never quite lets up.

We sit at the enormous table in Mama and Papa's large home. They bought the house after things picked up with Glen's business and Papa retired. Well, he said he retired, but he still has fingers in all aspects of the business, and even insists on accompanying Glen on trips, which is a source of constant frustration for Glen.

"I said I would take care of the Smith situation," Glen says now, his tone conversational, but tight. "There was no need for you to get involved."

"He's an old friend," Papa says, the warning in his tone less disguised. "I called in a favor. Don't make this a big deal, Glen."

Glen slams a fist on the table. "It *is* a big deal." I place a hand on his knee, but he moves away. Mama notices the interaction and sends me a sympathetic look. "Your old colleagues can't assume that you will step in on all of our deals. How are they supposed to respect me if my daddy undermines me at every turn?"

"Watch your tone, boy," Papa says, his breathing growing ragged. He has been having more difficulty lately with his lungs, though he refuses the oxygen the doctor has suggested. The struggle becomes more pronounced when he is agitated, which is often around Glen.

Mama reaches toward Papa. "Take deep breaths," she says.

He swats her hand away. "I'm fine. Don't be a nag."

I look down at my hands, twisting together in my lap. I feel a tap on my foot below the table and look up to meet Joel's eyes. He sits across from me, as he has every year since we began our little family tradition. His eyes swing back to his plate, and he remains silent, but the corners of his mouth are tipped up in amusement. Instead of becoming uncomfortable in these situations, Joel seems to thrive. It is unnerving how much he enjoys seeing others implode, and I have suspicions that he helps the process along whenever he can.

Glen seethes beside me, but even he can see how an argument would affect Papa's breathing. Papa may not back down, but Glen always will, if only to keep his father breathing a few days more. Though they bicker, there is plenty of mutual respect between the two men.

"So, Clara," Papa says. "I hear you have some good news to share."

I shoot a look at Glen. We were keeping it a secret this time, until I started to show. The last time we announced the baby, we lost it within a week. I do not want to jinx it. Glen gives me an almost imperceptible shrug. Some things he has no problem keeping from Papa. My secrets, however, are fair game.

"Yes, sir, we are expecting around June or July of next year. I have not been to the doctor yet, so it's just an estimate."

Mama beams. "How exciting. Although I don't think we're old enough to be grandparents." She nudges Papa, who gives her a grudging smile before turning his laser gaze back to me.

"And how will being pregnant affect your work?"

My brow furrows. "It won't, sir. I mean, of course, when the baby comes, some adjustments will need to be made, but until then—"

"What sort of adjustments?"

This time it's Glen's hand that finds my knee, giving me comfort as I fumble for an answer. I want to swat him away, as he rebuffed me earlier. I am only in this position because he could not keep our secret. But, as usual, I cannot shy away from Glen's touch. I lean into him, and his hand moves from my knee to loop around my shoulders.

"During the pregnancy, I will be training Passion and at least one of the other older girls to help with some of the more important tasks."

Papa scoffs. "Passion. That little pet of yours should have been gone long ago."

"She's only fourteen," I say.

"She's untrainable."

I sit up, ignoring the increased pressure of Glen's hand on my shoulder. "She does everything I ask her."

"Yes," Papa says. "Everything *you* ask her. But she is downright belligerent to anyone else who tries to give her an order. How do you expect a client to take that on?"

"If a client could not handle her, how could we have possibly gotten rid of her?"

Papa raises his eyebrows, taking a bite as he waits for the answer to come to me.

My heart stutters. "You can't put her there."

"They could tame her."

"No."

He shrugs. Glen clears his throat and I jump. I had forgotten anyone else was there. I am surprised that both Glen and Papa let me speak so forcefully for so long. I will pay for it later, I am sure.

"Clara has a tight hold on the girl," Glen says. "She is quite helpful, and I see no reason to get rid of her, especially with the baby coming. I have every confidence that she will be helpful both with the other girls and in helping with the baby when Clara is . . . indisposed."

I swallow hard, understanding his meaning. My thoughts race as I try to figure out how Glen will deal with me while I carry his child. We will have to come to an agreement. I must protect this baby.

"Glen," Papa begins. "I really think—"

"It's not your call, Father," Glen says, picking up his wineglass and taking a large drink. Topic closed.

"Very well," Papa says, leaning back in his chair. I can tell from the look in his eyes that this conversation is far from over, but I know I will not be witness to the rest of it. I have already overstepped.

The rest of the meal is finished in silence. I help Mama clean while the men have an after-dinner drink, and then we join them. Mama fixes me a special tea that she tells me keeps nausea away. She made it last time as well, and I resist wrinkling my nose before taking the first sip. I remember the bitter taste, but I hide my disgust and drink the entire cup. She hands me a tin before we leave, reminding me to drink one cup a day. I know she will check next time they are over, and it does seem to help, so I accept the gift with a smile.

Our drive home is silent, and I am surprised when Glen only kisses me good night and turns off the light. No lecture. No punishment. Maybe this baby will be good for us in more ways than one.

Good things never last. This is what I have learned. When I wake up in the middle of the night two weeks later, stickiness running down my thighs, the metallic smell of blood in the air, I already know my baby is gone.

Now

My lip curls as I study the food on the tray in front of me. If it can be called food. A river of grease runs from the pile of meat, pooling at the corners of the compartment. Rubbery green beans give off a questionable odor, and I can see flakes of something unrecognizable in the mashed potatoes.

"Big day today, meat and potatoes! They always roll out the big guns for the vizzies." A large woman drops into the seat next to mine. She leans in. "And you better eat it, or you may not make it home this afternoon in the same condition you got here."

I jerk my eyes toward her. She motions in the direction of the kitchen, where an imposing woman stands, watching me. It is possible this woman is messing with me, trying to scare me, but I don't want to risk it. I take a tentative bite, controlling my gag reflex as I swallow the chewy meat. I manage a smile at the woman in the kitchen. She smiles back. I keep eating until she turns her attention elsewhere.

My lunch companion laughs. "Nice work, vizzie."

"Vizzie?"

"Visitors. Short-term ladies. Although"—her eyes scan my body—"I wouldn't mind if you stuck around."

Her gaze makes me uncomfortable, but I try not to let it show. "I'm Clara," I say.

"Marge. I killed my husband."

I choke on the soupy potatoes. Marge laughs as I lunge for my milk, washing the obstruction from my throat.

"That's . . . nice," I say, unable to think of a better response.

"It really was," Marge says, a dreamy look taking over her face. "I'd do it again, too. Bastard."

I nod, trying to look sympathetic.

"Those your girls?" Marge asks, indicating the group of teenage girls at the next table.

I shrug. "I guess." The girls were from some "scare 'em straight" program and had been with me since the morning. We were "processed" together, which consisted of being strip-searched, fingerprinted, photographed, and given the standard gray jumpsuit that would be our uniform for the day.

The warden had given us a tour of the facilities, and then set some of the inmates loose on us. They walked us through work detail, screaming the entire way. I spent the morning with Glen's face at the forefront of my mind. He was the reason I was doing all this. I would go through this every day if I could protect him.

"You're a little old, ain't you?" Marge asked.

"I'm not with their program. Just along for the ride."

"What'd they get you for?"

"They want me to give them information."

"What sort of information?"

I shrug. I've said enough. Marge doesn't push, and we finish the meal in silence. As I scrape up the last of my potatoes and force them into my mouth, there is a commotion at the table behind us.

"You think you can go behind my back and talk shit about me?" A woman with wild blond hair towers over a petite woman with dark coloring.

"Oooo," Marge whispers. "You picked a good day, vizzie. Things gonna get crazy."

"I ain't said nothing," the petite woman replies, calmly taking another bite. "You need to check your source of information."

The blonde grabs the front of the other woman's shirt, yanking her off the bench. "You need to check the shit pouring out of your mouth before it gets you in trouble." Spittle flies into the other woman's face, and she flinches as the drops bathe her skin.

Everyone in the room has gone quiet. The other women at the table edge away from their comrade, unwilling to fight this fight for her.

"Your breath smells like shit." The smaller woman wrinkles her nose in distaste.

Blondie laughs and drops the other woman back onto the bench. "You're right, lady. Maybe I'll go give my teeth a good brushing." There is a dangerous quality to her voice. She walks away, giving Marge a significant look as she passes.

"Stupid bitch," mutters the dark-haired woman, wiping her face with a napkin.

"All right, ladies, time to move on," says the guard. We're going to spend the afternoon on work detail again. As I stand to leave, Marge grabs my arm.

"Stay clear of the east bathrooms this afternoon," she says, then gets up and walks out before I can respond. A chill runs through me. I shake it off and rejoin the group.

The afternoon is more of the same. I'm stuck in the laundry room for a while with some of the teenagers, who spend the time gossiping. They don't seem the least bit scared. One of them brags that this is her third time going through the program. I can't help but shake my head and think how much more respectful my daughters are.

"Hey, you," one of the inmates says. I look up to find her pointing at me.

"Yes?"

She shoves a stack of sheets into my arms. "Take these up to the medical wing and see if they need someone to scrub the floors up there." The corner of her mouth quirks up. "You look like you'd be good on your knees."

I flush and turn my gaze to the blindingly white sheets in my arms. I have no idea how they get them so clean, especially considering some of the stained sets I saw go into the washer. Ignoring the laughter of the other workers, I follow a guard out the door and through the labyrinth of hallways to my next assignment.

I am halfway through cleaning the medical wing when there is a flurry of activity from the doors. A group of men enters, carrying a woman and putting her on one of the beds. I cover my nose as the stench hits me. It smells like she was swimming in a sewer. She isn't moving. I see blood.

"Where's the nurse?" the guard barks.

"She-she ran to get more supplies."

"Radio her," he commands another guard.

I inch closer. I recognize the petite woman from the cafeteria. She is covered with a brown substance, and the blood is coming from her stomach. A strong hand pulls me back.

"They got her in the bathrooms," he says. "Shoved shit down her throat and stuck her with a sharpened toothbrush. No one saw anything." He shakes his head.

My mouth drops open. Marge had warned me. I wonder if he knows about what happened at lunch. The guard is watching me with suspicious eyes. "You don't know anything about this, do you?"

I shake my head quickly. The woman on the bed moans, drawing his attention, and fresh blood seeps from her wound. I run to the nearest trash can and lose the contents of my stomach. It doesn't taste much worse coming up than it did going down.

Then

I am sitting in a parlor, surrounded by girls of different ages. Most are in their teens. They are fascinated by me. Genevieve sits off to the side, staring out a window at the rolling South Dakota Black Hills and puffing on a slim cigarette.

"You're just with one guy?" a girl asks, leaning forward.

"I, um, I am with Glen, and I raise our daughters."

A surprised look. "You have kids?" Her eyes rake up and down my body. I laugh.

"No, I don't *have* them. Glen brings them and I train them." I ignore the pang in my chest at the words. Of course these girls know nothing about the babies I have lost.

*Ahhh*s and *ohhh*s sound around the room.

"What about the other men?" another girl asks.

"I don't see much of them. I mostly stay in the house."

"You don't . . . service them, too?"

I'm not sure what she means, and it must show on my face.

"You don't fuck them?" A chorus of girlish giggles around the room, and my face heats.

"No," I say, "I am with Glen. Just Glen."

"How old are you?"

"Twenty-two."

This time the response is gasps, echoing throughout the room.

"But you are so *old*," one says. She is not being unkind. I would be unmarketable to private clients at my age, though several of the girls at Glen's other businesses are older than me.

Genevieve speaks up from her spot across the room. "So Glen took you over when you were no longer useful." Though she is trying to sound aloof, I can hear the curiosity in her voice. Genevieve cannot be much younger than me. I wonder how she has maintained her position in the house.

"I have never been with anyone but Glen," I admit.

"You're married?"

I laugh. "Yes. Of course."

"For now." Genevieve's raspy voice holds a finality as she turns back to the window, as if she knows her fate, and thinks she knows mine. But she doesn't know Glen. Glen and I will be together forever, like Papa G and Mama Mae. I choose to ignore her dig and go back to discussing my apparently fascinating life with these young girls. I keep the information general and do not name any of my girls. Glen did not prepare me for this conversation, and I do not want to say something I shouldn't. Mostly they are interested in my relationship with Glen and how we ended up together, so I tell them about dance class and Glen going to his father about me. I do not mention the fights, or the running away, and I can tell by their faces that they are completely caught up in my fairy tale.

We have been in the room for an hour or so when the door opens and a small group of men walks in. Glen is there, as is Mr. Harrison. I stand and walk to Glen's side, where his hand finds mine. I hear some wistful sighs from my new friends. Genevieve doesn't move until Mr. Harrison clears his throat. I see her neck tense and relax, and by the time she faces us, her mouth has curled into a small half-moon. She slithers over to Mr. Harrison and slides her arm across his shoulders.

He yanks her closer, his arm clamping across her waist, and she winces, but recovers with a flirty giggle.

I do not know what to think of Genevieve, but it is clear she is unhappy. I wonder what other duties she is bound to perform. She does not act like a mother to these girls, and though their attitude is somewhat deferential toward her, they mostly ignored her during the time I was with them. I shake off my morose thoughts when I feel Glen's eyes on me, and turn to smile at him.

"What do you think of these girls, baby?" he asks.

"They are very sweet," I say. "More experienced than my girls."

Glen nods. "I need you to help me choose five of them."

My brow creases. "Choose? For what?"

He grins. "They're going to help us expand the business back home."

I frown. "They are not trainable."

He shakes his head as a spark jumps into his eyes. "You won't be training them, Clare. Just pick five."

His grip on my hand has grown painful, and I know better than to question further. I look back at the girls, who are all watching me with hopeful expressions. I barely know them, and I'm about to change their lives forever. "Do you have any preferences?" I whisper to Glen, expecting backlash, but receiving only a small chuckle.

"Just pick a variety," he says.

I pick five at random, mostly younger girls, two redheads, two blondes, and the small brunette who was so interested in my relationship with Glen. After I whisper my choices to Glen, he nods at Mr. Harrison, who barks orders at the girls. They get up and leave the room on quick feet.

"They will be ready for departure in two hours," Mr. Harrison says to Glen, though his eyes are on me. "You may wait here or come back for them."

Glen pushes me behind him. "Joel will wait for them with the van. I'm going to take Clara back to the lodge. It's been a long day."

Mr. Harrison's eyebrows rise a fraction, but he only nods. "Very well, my boy. I hope this is the beginning of a profitable relationship for both of us." He comes forward and kisses the air by Glen's cheeks again.

"As do I, sir." Glen pulls me out of the room before the man can reach for me, and we move quickly down the stairs and out the door.

I am not sure what just happened, but it is a relief to be out of the house. Though the girls were nice, I felt stifled there, like the walls were closing in. As we drive away, I see a curtain on the second floor twitch, and I feel the weight of eyes on me, though I cannot see who is watching. I shift closer to Glen, and his arm comes around me.

"What do you think of South Dakota, my love?" he asks, nuzzling me under my ear. I smile.

"Right now, it's perfect," I say, and he pulls me closer for a kiss.

Now

I am in an unfamiliar room, curled up in the corner of a cushy couch. Sunlight streams through the window, giving life to the plants scattered throughout the room, but it does nothing for me. The chill I feel has nothing to do with the temperature. I still see the blood mixed with brown all over the woman's face. A woman whose name I never bothered to learn. I still see her deadened eyes, blank with shock. I wonder what put her there. How did she get to the point where she was locked up, fearlessly goading fellow prisoners? I don't even know if she survived. They rushed her out of there, and me soon after. There was so much blood . . .

The woman across from me adjusts her glasses and shifts in her seat. "Clara?" she says, her voice patient, though we have been sitting in the room together for twenty minutes and I haven't said a word. I have said nothing since the prison. When I started talking, things went bad. It's best if I stop, no matter what Glen said. If he knew about everything that has happened, he would tell me to go silent again, too. I am sure of it.

"Clara, this is a safe space." The woman introduced herself as Dr. Mulligan when I was brought in. She seems nice, but I know that no place is safe. No one is to be trusted. I started to trust Connor, and he put me in the prison. I haven't seen him since the brief glimpse I got as I was brought back to the ward. His face was white as they ushered me back into my room, and if I didn't know better, I would have thought his concern was for me. I know, though. I know he was only worried that I might have been hurt, and that would have hurt his case.

"What you saw yesterday, Clara . . . well, that couldn't have been easy." No kidding. I wonder if observations like that earned her a doctoral degree. My eyes skitter across the room and I catch sight of her desk. Framed pictures line the edges. A smiling family, laughing children, a wedding photo. Dr. Mulligan has a life outside of these walls. She has no idea.

Dr. Mulligan sighs and sets down her notebook. I catch sight of swirling doodles before she closes the cover. A small smile plays at my lips. I had assumed she was making all sorts of observations with her pen movements. Instead, she really was just waiting on me. I decide I like her just a little more. But I still won't talk.

"I need you to let me know that you're okay, Clara," Dr. Mulligan says, standing up and walking to a bookcase. "I can see that talking makes you uncomfortable." She selects something from the shelf. "Would you be willing to write some things down?"

She walks back and hands me a fresh notebook. It even smells new. The cover is a bright blue, and a thick spiral holds the pages in place. I pause before taking it, but cannot resist having it in my hands. I used to write. Before Glen took over for Papa G. Poetry, stories, adventures that I longed to take. Papa G found it one day and threw it in the fire. He told me that making up stories was not a useful skill, was nothing more than daydreaming, and forbade me from doing it.

I slide to the floor, positioning my legs under the small table in front of the couch. Dr. Mulligan hands me a pen. Black ink. The first strokes of pen on paper are bliss, and I feel the first spark of happiness since the last time I saw Glen. I start with swirls similar to those I saw in Dr. Mulligan's notebook, and the corners of her lips tug up into a smile.

"Guess I'm not so sly at hiding my doodles, huh?" she says, and lifts her notebook from the table. "I'll just continue my doodles here. You write what you want, and I won't disturb you unless you ask me to."

I nod, earning another smile, and return to my paper. So many words, begging to be released. I am not sure what I am supposed to be writing. She gave no instructions. *I love you, Glen.* It is the first thing that pops into my mind. *I promise I will not betray you. Even though you're not here to help me, I will be strong.* I continue writing my love note to Glen until Dr. Mulligan indicates that our time is finished.

I stand, hugging the notebook to my chest. Will I take it with me? Where will I keep it? Will the guards be as discreet? Will they try to read it? Panic begins to choke me.

Dr. Mulligan's eyebrows rise fractionally, and she regards my anxious stance with sympathetic eyes. She reaches her hand toward me. "Would you like to keep that here, Clara?" she asks. "I can lock it up tight in my cabinet, and no one will read it. Not even me."

I still don't trust her. She will open the pages as soon as I leave the room. She will laugh at my silly letter to Glen, where I talk about the first time I saw him, the first time he kissed me, the first time we were together. My cheeks heat.

Dr. Mulligan withdraws her hand. "How about this, Clara? I'll take this piece of tape and seal your notebook shut." She extracts a roll of blue tape from her desk drawer. "You can write something or draw a picture or sign your name on the tape, and you'll know I didn't open it."

It could work. I hand her the book and watch as she seals the pages shut. She hands it back to me, and I sign my name with a flourish, partially on the cover, partially on the tape, so I will be able to tell if it's been removed. She takes it from me and opens a drawer in her cabinet. The notebook earns a spot in the back, behind a bunch of folders. She closes the drawer and turns the key.

"There. Your secrets are safe."

For now.

Then

I stare at the human-shaped lump over on Macy's bed. If only it were a little more convincing, maybe my heart wouldn't be racing and my shaky palms might not be dripping with stress sweat. Mama is due to come for morning checks at any moment, and Macy has not returned. I tossed and turned all night, praying for the sound of the window sliding up, but all remained quiet and still. She has never stayed out all night before.

The sound of Mama's sharp voice carries up to our attic room. She will be here soon. Panicked, I toss back my covers, jump up from my bed, and rush across to Macy's. I toss the pillows and rumple the covers so it looks like her night was as sleepless as my own. Sprinting for the bathroom, I turn the shower on full blast, shut the bathroom door, and leap back into bed seconds before the tap comes at the door.

We are not to get up until Mama comes in the morning. It

discourages late-night or early-morning wandering. Of course, everyone breaks the rule, but we all at least pretend to abide by it. I think Mama expects some rule-breaking, which is why she is so strict. But even small infractions, if discovered, can carry heavy consequences. I do not want to think what our punishment will be if Mama discovers Macy has been not only out of her bed, but out of the house.

"Clara. Macy. Morning." Mama's clipped tone carries through the heavy door. The knob turns and she is there, filling the doorway, looking in confusion at Macy's empty bed. I sit up, rubbing my eyes, doing my best impression of a groggy teenager just woken from a deep sleep.

"Good morning, Mama." I yawn, stretching before rubbing pretend sleep from my eyes.

"Where is Macy?" Mama's words cut through my act.

I shoot a confused look at Macy's rumpled covers, then point to the bathroom. "She wasn't feeling well last night. Maybe she got sick?" My tone is innocent, but Mama's eyes narrow anyway.

Mama strides to the bathroom door and knocks hard enough that even my knuckles hurt. Of course there is no answer. "Macy?"

"Uh . . ." I fumble for an excuse. I kick myself. If I had left her bed, I could have played dumb. Now I have played an active role in deceiving Mama, and my punishment will be severe if she figures it out. I am so angry at Macy, I almost admit the entire thing, but I cannot do that to my friend. "It's really hard to hear through that door," I say. "I'm sure she will be out soon."

The look Mama gives me is dubious, but she turns and heads back to the door. "I'll be back in five minutes. Make sure she's out by then, and we'll have a reminder about out-of-bed rules."

Wiping my sweaty palms on my nightgown, I nod, thankful that Mama did not just barge into the bathroom. "Yes, Mama. I'll tell her."

She slams out of the room, heading back down the stairs to wake the rest of the girls. Almost as soon as she leaves, the window slides open and Macy tumbles through.

"Shit, Clare, just throw me under the bus!" she says, jumping to her feet. "Now I'm gonna get it for being out of bed."

"It was that or let her find your sorry excuse for a pillow person under your covers," I hiss. "I put myself on the line for you."

Macy sneers. "Wouldn't want to give Mama the impression that *perfect* Clara breaks *any* of the rules. I'm sure she'd be interested to know about your little visits with her precious son."

"You wouldn't," I gasp, blood rushing to my face.

"No, because I know what it means to be a friend."

Tears fill my eyes, but I can hear Mama making her way back toward the bedroom. "Get in the bathroom and get in the shower, quick. She's almost back."

Shooting me one last disdainful look, Macy disappears into the steam-filled room. I busy myself with making my bed and smooth the last wrinkle as Mama storms back in. This time she does not pause, but barrels straight to the bathroom and flings the door open.

"Ah! Mama, I'm almost finished," Macy screeches.

Mama crosses her arms. "Are you feeling better, my dear?"

"Yes." Macy's voice floats out with the steam. "Just a bit of an upset stomach. I threw up and then wanted a shower. I'm sorry I was out of bed without permission."

Gathering my clothes, I head for the bathroom as Macy slips past Mama wrapped in a towel. There is a heavy silence as Mama decides if she believes our story.

"Fine," she says at last. "Hurry and get ready. I need you to make breakfast. You should probably just have toast, Macy. God forbid you throw up on the laundry."

"Yes, ma'am," we both mumble. Mama leaves, closing the door behind her.

"That was close." Macy sighs, then remembers she is supposed to be upset with me. "Now she's going to make me eat toast all day. Thanks a lot."

"I saved your butt," I say.

"You saved your own ass," she throws back at me.

Without another word, I turn and slam the door to the bathroom, leaving Macy to rage at me by herself.

Stony silence hangs in a cloud of tension over the kitchen, punctuated only by the clatter of dishes and the splashing of water. My hands plunge into the soapy water with more force than necessary, soaking the front of my dress.

"If you keep that up, Mama's gonna make you wash the floors, too," Macy says, pointing to the small puddle forming at my feet before resuming her task of sweeping. These are the first words she has spoken to me all day, and I have only grown more angry with every passing hour.

"Like you care what Mama does to me," I say, throwing a glare in her direction. "You only care that *Macy* is happy and gets to do what *Macy* wants to do."

"And you only care that *Clara* doesn't get in trouble and ruin her perfect reputation. God, Clara, you are so annoying. Not everyone can be as angelic as you."

I roll my eyes. "I'm not trying to be angelic, I'm just trying to avoid the yardstick." I cannot believe she is acting this way. If I had left things as they were, she would have been in trouble, bigger trouble than she has ever been in, and I would have been guilty by association, even if I had tried to act like I knew nothing. Macy gets into little scrapes all the time, but being out of the house, especially to meet with one of the boys, is something that could get her sent away.

"You just don't want to screw things up with Glen," Macy says, and I whirl to face her.

"Keep your voice down!"

She makes a face. "I knew it. You really like him, don't you?"

"Shut up, Macy." I am even more upset because what she says is true. I like Glen much more than I should, and those feelings have led me to act in ways that I normally wouldn't. I should stay away from him, but I can't. If Mama or Papa find out, it could ruin my chances with the client they have found for me. More and more, however, the thought of leaving here and going to live happily ever after with Mr. Q sends stabbing pains through my heart. More than anything I want to be with Glen, but I am torn between my growing feelings for him and my sense of duty to Mama and Papa, who raised me for the chance to be with someone like Mr. Q.

Macy continues to talk, but she does lower her voice. "You need to let that go, Clara. You're too serious about him. It'll never work, you two together." She sighs as I turn back to the sink. "I know I told you to go for it, but I thought it would help you loosen up, have fun like I do. I didn't think you'd go and fall in *love* with the guy. He's Mama and Papa's *son*, for Christ's sake!"

Spinning, I raise my arm to point at Macy with the plate I am washing. With horror, I watch as the plate, one of Mama's nicest, used for a client dinner tonight, slips from my soapy grip and shatters on the floor.

Macy and I gape at each other as Mama calls from the living room. "What the hell was that?"

Propping the broom against the wall, Macy rushes to the sink, bumping me out of the way with her hip and shoving her hands into the bubbles.

Mama stomps into the room, her face clouding as she spies the broken china on the floor. "What. Happened." Her voice is the sort of calm that comes before a giant explosion, and my entire body begins to quiver.

"It slipped," Macy says before I can respond. "I'm sorry, Mama. Clara was washing, but my stomach was still tender from last night and sweeping was making it worse, so we switched."

My eyes widen, but I say nothing. I want to jump in and defend Macy, tell Mama that it was my fault, but then Macy will get in trouble for lying. The look she gives me tells me to keep my mouth shut.

"Clara," Mama says evenly, "please finish up the dishes, but leave the broken plate. Macy will clean that up later. You may go to bed when everything has been put away."

I nod, still not trusting myself to speak.

"Macy, please follow me."

Macy avoids eye contact as she follows Mama from the room. I stand, stunned, for a few minutes before mechanically returning to my job. I move as slowly as possible, waiting for her return, but when I finish, she is still gone. I tamp down feelings of dread as I tiptoe around the shards of china littering the floor and climb the stairs to our bedroom.

I am almost asleep when Macy comes into the room later that night. Neither of us says a word as she goes about her bedtime routine and turns out the light. I know she's not sleeping, and a short time later she rises from her bed, pads across the room, and climbs in next to me. I drape a careful arm over her shoulder, and her intake of breath is all the confirmation I need that her punishment was significant.

We find a comfortable spot, and I begin to drift off when, almost as if from far away, I hear Macy whisper, "I'm sorry."

"Me too," I say, and as unconsciousness finds me, I vow to protect Macy with everything I am from now on.

Now

I have been writing in Dr. Mulligan's office for half an hour when there is a knock on the door. "Keep going," she says, standing to answer it. I bend my head back over my notebook and return to my sketch of Glen's face. I am not a fantastic artist, but I do okay, and it's important that I preserve the subtleties of his features. I am beginning to forget. It has only been a few days since I last saw him, but it feels much longer. I draw him so I can look back and remember, at least a little.

Dr. Mulligan is conversing in urgent tones with whomever is at the door, and as their voices grow louder, I find it harder to concentrate.

"It's not your decision," Connor says, pushing past Dr. Mulligan as he strides into the room. I see anger flit across her face, a strange expression on her features. I do not picture Dr. Mulligan as an angry person.

I look up at Connor, closing the cover of my notebook, covering Glen's face. I squint my eyes at him to show my displeasure at his presence.

"Still silent, I see," he says. He looks rough, as if he hasn't shaved for a couple of days, and his normally crisp clothing shows telltale wrinkles of being worn long hours.

I open my notebook again, turning to a fresh page, and begin drawing swirls. Connor leans over to see what I'm doing, and instead of hiding my work, my scrawls turn into creative cuss words, just for Connor. Instead of getting angry, as I expect, Connor barks out a laugh. I make a face at him.

"Can I see that?" he asks, reaching for my notebook. I slam the cover shut and shove it underneath me, so I am sitting on it.

Dr. Mulligan has been watching the interaction with interest.

"Can I ask what you're doing here, Agent?" she says, her calm façade back in place.

"I just wanted to check on her," Connor says, watching me.

"Check on her?"

"On her progress, of course," he stutters, standing up straight and looking at the doctor. "We need to get her back into questioning as soon as possible."

"Let's step out in the hallway, Agent," Dr. Mulligan says. "You'll be okay, Clara?" she asks. I ignore her.

As soon as the door closes, I creep closer until their muffled voices become clear enough for me to understand.

"She needs therapy," Dr. Mulligan is saying.

"I know. But we need answers. We were getting somewhere until—"

"Until you threw her in prison to scare her into talking? Yes, I can see that worked well for you."

Connor's voice rises, tension radiating through his tone. "You have no idea the pressure we're under to get this case taken care of," he says. "If we don't have her testimony—"

"Then what? You've talked to all the girls. Some of the other men are talking. Why is her story so important?"

Connor's voice becomes muffled, as if he is covering his mouth while he speaks. "It just is. There's more . . ."

"More what?"

"Nothing. Forget it. It's not your concern." He pauses. "Your concern is getting her to talk."

"Maybe if you'd brought her to me first, before scaring her with questioning and agent beatings and prisons, we'd be a little further along." Dr. Mulligan has lost her even tone. I recognize a woman in protective mode. I have used it a few times myself with my daughters.

"We didn't deem it necessary at the time," Connor says.

Dr. Mulligan barks out a sharp, uncharacteristic laugh. "A clearly damaged and traumatized woman is rescued from a brothel training house and you don't think she needs counseling?"

I don't wait to hear Connor's reply. I grab the doorknob and fling the door open, startling them.

"Rescued?" I say, my voice shaking. "I wasn't *rescued*. I was *taken* from my home, separated from my husband and my daughters, and kept in a tiny room with only idiots to talk to. And you wonder why I've stayed quiet!" My voice has risen to a high-decibel screech. My chest heaves in anger, and my pulse races through my tightened muscles. I close my eyes and take deep breaths. Dr. Mulligan and Connor remain silent. When I open my eyes, I am calmer.

"I'd like to go back to my room now." I walk back to the couch and retrieve my notebook from the ground, handing it to Dr. Mulligan. She takes it from me, tapes it up, and returns it for my signature. I notice that she does not put it in its hiding spot while Connor is in the room, but clutches it at her side.

Connor tries to take my arm, but I resist, walking ahead of him. As I return to the doorway, I turn around. "Will I see you tomorrow, Dr. Mulligan?"

She nods and smiles. "Yes, Clara. Please come back tomorrow." She taps the notebook and gives me a small wink. Connor nudges me, and I leave the room. I really do like Dr. Mulligan.

Then

I am woken by an unfamiliar tread in the hallway. Glen is gone for a few days in North Dakota. I have been alone with the girls, but it doesn't bother me. The footsteps I hear are too loud to be made by any of my little girls. Mama Mae offered to stay with me, to help out, but I declined the offer. The steps are too heavy to be hers, anyway. Glen is due back tomorrow. Perhaps he has returned early. But the steps are too timid, trying to be sneaky. One of the guards must have come in. I will talk to Glen about it. They are to use the trees if they need a bathroom. The house is off-limits, especially in the middle of the night.

Soon it is quiet again, and I roll over to go back to sleep. A small sound catches my attention. One of the girls is up now, too. I throw back the covers and swing my legs off the bed, reeling at the sudden dizziness. No time to wait for the world to right itself, I stuff my feet into my slippers and wrap myself in my robe as I hurry to the door. I open it quietly, pausing to listen.

There is the sound again. A small keening, almost too faint to be heard. Then a shush, which I wouldn't have heard through the door to my bedroom.

"Girls," I say, keeping my voice low so the other girls don't wake. "Time to sleep."

I halt as I come upon the scene in the young girls' room. A man is on top of little Grace, one hand over her mouth, the other working the button on his pants. He has already hiked her nightgown up and removed her panties. Tears stream from Grace's terrified eyes.

"Hey!"

The man looks up. It is Joel. And I can tell from the bland look in his eyes that he is quite drunk. Even drunk, however, he could easily overpower me. I must be smart. I feel sick as I realize what I must do.

I walk over to him. He watches me, eyes wary, as his hand sneaks back toward Grace's bare skin. I shake my head and hold out a hand. "You don't want to do this, Joel," I say. "If Grace's client can tell, Glen will be furious."

"Stay out of this, Clara," Joel slurs. "Lemme be." He turns back to Grace.

I touch his shoulder. "Come on, Joel," I say. "You don't want her.

She's a little girl." I take a step back and beckon him with my hand. "I see how you look at me, Joel." His eyes spark with interest. "Glen's gone. Let me take care of you."

His response is immediate. He rolls off Grace's bed and is in front of me in seconds. He lunges for my mouth, but I put a finger over his lips. "Not here," I whisper. I take his hand and lead him from the room. As we exit, I see Passion creeping over to Grace. Of course Passion was awake. She sees everything.

I lead Joel back past the room I share with Glen, to one of the empty rooms saved for our rare guests. He stumbles several times, and I pray that he will pass out before I have to follow through. As soon as the door is shut behind us, he begins tearing at my clothes.

"Stop, Joel, slow down!" I say, trying to catch his hands.

Anger crosses Joel's face. "Slow down? *Slow down?*" He grabs me around the waist and tosses me on the bed. "You offer yourself to me and then tell me to slow down?" He is on top of me and backhands me across my cheek. I see stars.

"Now shut up and enjoy what you're about to get," Joel growls. His hands and mouth jump across my skin, leaving a slimy feeling wherever they touch. He seals his mouth to mine, and he tastes of liquor and vomit. He is drunk, but not drunk enough. Soon his skin is slick with sweat. I stare at the ceiling and try to transport myself anyplace but here as he finishes and collapses on top of me like a load of bricks.

His breathing eventually returns to normal, but he does not get off me. His lips find their way to my ear, and he whispers, "Bet you'll come back for more after that, won't you, baby?" And then he is snoring.

I wait a while longer to be sure he is completely passed out before shoving him off of me. I gather my clothes and return to my room, leaving the clothes in a pile by the door. I spend forty minutes in the shower scrubbing every square inch of my body until my skin is red and raw. I wrap myself in a towel and step in front of the mirror, wiping the steam away with my palm. My cheek and left eye are swollen and red, and a bruise is beginning to bloom.

I go back to the bedroom and dress, twisting my hair high up on my head. My first stop is to check on Grace. Passion lies with her, and Grace is sleeping, a peaceful expression on her face. Passion's eyes open as I peek in the room. Her eyebrows rise in question.

"Whatever you hear, keep this door shut until I come back, okay?" She nods.

I gather my torn nightclothes and slippers from their heap in my room and step outside into the cool morning air. The sun is just sending pink streaks across the sky. I walk to the fire pit and dump the clothes. From my pocket I produce a box of matches I snatched from the mantel, and soon the clothes are turning to ash. They look like I feel inside, shriveled and black, paper-thin and insignificant.

Back in the house, I unlock Glen's study and head to his desk, where I retrieve my target from the top drawer. I walk upstairs with purpose and shove the door to the guest room open with a slam. Joel sits up. "Clara!" He grabs his head. "What the hell?" He shakes his head and a smile curls his face as memories from last night return. "Back for more, baby?" he asks, and my decision is made.

I walk toward him and bring the gun out from behind my back.

"Whoa! Whoa, Clara, hold on!" Joel holds his hands in front of him. As if I would be going for his heart. He doesn't have one.

I level the gun at his head and, with a quick jerk, point it downward, firing a bullet directly between his legs. His scream is horrific, and music to my ears.

"You crazy bitch!" he screams as I walk from the room and shut the door behind me. He becomes more creative with his expletives as I return to my room. I am so tired. I put the gun on the nightstand and climb back under the covers, falling into unconsciousness in no time.

. . .

"Clara! What the hell?"

When I wake, Glen is standing at the foot of the bed. It is mid-morning, judging by the sunlight streaming into the room.

"Good morning," I say, sitting up. I raise a hand to my head and feel the hair matted to my cheek. I wince as I brush it away. Glen is across the room in seconds.

"What the hell happened?" Glen demands. "I come home and the girls are all still in their rooms, there's a fire dying down in the backyard that none of my guys set, and you're in here with a gun and a black eye."

I stretch, my brain hazy. Glen waits, though I can tell he is ready to burst. I hesitate. Glen will be angry. I still believe I made the right decision, but no man other than Glen has ever touched me. And I allowed it. I *suggested* it. I seduced another man, and there will be consequences.

"Please, Clara." Glen's voice is pleading, but intense. I don't have any choice but to tell him the truth.

I take a deep breath. One by one, I recount the details of the night. Glen grows more and more still, and the hand stroking my cheek leaves my face to curl into the blankets. The look on his face is dangerous. I have never seen his jaw so tight. His eyes glint, slightly manic.

"Where is he?"

I stand and lead Glen to the guest room. The door swings open, and there is Joel, lying in a pool of blood. Glen walks over to him. "He's alive," he says, no emotion in his voice. He nudges Joel. "Wake up," he says. Joel stirs. Glen reaches and grabs Joel where the bullet got him. Joel screams.

"Shit! Fuck!" His eyes widen when he sees Glen. "Oh man," he says. "Clara is a crazy bitch, man. She shot off my damn—"

"Shut up." Glen is dangerously calm. "Clara, why don't you take the girls on a walk?"

I nod. "We'll be ready to go in fifteen minutes."

"Good. See you for lunch."

I wave and back out of the room, closing the door. I hear Joel begin to beg as I go to get the girls ready for an outing.

When we return an hour later, Mama Mae is there and has made lunch. The girls sit at the table, and Glen grabs two plates, beckoning for me to join him. We walk upstairs to our room, and he leads me out onto our balcony, which overlooks the mountains in the distance. He sets the plates down and turns to me.

I have remained numb through most of the day, but now that it's just me and Glen, I feel myself starting to break down. I shove my shaking fingers under my body and try not to think about how Joel held those same fingers in his sweaty grasp. My entire body feels foreign to me, dirty. I wait for Glen's judgment as he watches me, the expression in his eyes unfathomable.

I am ready for punishment. I let another man use my body, and surely Glen will be angry. Instead of pain, however, Glen gathers me in his arms, wrapping them so tight that I find it hard to breathe. I don't mind. I would gladly suffocate this way. It would be a fine way to die. I am not sure how long we stand there, but when he pulls back, there are tears in his eyes.

"Glen?"

"When I think of what could have—"

"Shh, I'm fine," I say, finding it odd to be comforting him after what happened.

"Thank you," he says, and kisses me with fervor. "Thank you for protecting our daughters. I only wish I had been there to protect you."

Guilt. That is what those tears are made of. Regret for not fulfilling his promise to protect me. I shake my head in denial. "I did what was necessary, Glen. I just hope you don't hate me."

"Hate you?" His face is unbelieving. "That's not possible, Clara. You are the most important person in my life." He kisses me, and soon our breathing picks up and the air heats around us. He lowers me to the floor of the balcony and banishes all the demons Joel left behind.

After, I lay with my head on his chest, memorizing the beat of his heart. He is quiet. I turn to look at him. "Glen?"

"Hmm?"

I hesitate, and he raises his head to look at me.

"What is it, baby?"

"Joel?" I can barely squeeze the name through my throat.

His features, peaceful just a moment ago, cloud over. "You won't have to worry about him anymore, Clara," he says. "Ever again."

I nod. I cannot imagine what Glen is going through. He grew up with Joel. They have been best friends since childhood. He has always been Glen's right-hand man, by his side in the stickiest of situations. The level of betrayal must be overwhelming. I am almost overcome with guilt that Glen was put in this position, but amidst the sadness I find an inkling of joy.

Glen chose me.

Now

Before I can see Dr. Mulligan the next day, I end up back in the dreaded questioning room. Connor sits across from me, and next to him is a young man with bright, excited eyes. The difference between the countenances of the men is striking. Connor has aged in the short time that I have known him, and this new agent looks fresh as a daisy.

Even as I think the words, my heart stutters. Daisy. I wonder where she is now. If she's okay. And the other girls. They have not been mentioned since the day Connor and Meredith showed me the tape, and I am overwhelmed with guilt that I have not thought to demand information about them before now. I have been so focused on myself and on Glen that I allowed my daughters to slip to the back of my mind. Some mother I am.

"Clara, this is Jay. He is new to the unit and has asked to sit in. Is that okay?"

I raise an eyebrow. I did not know I had the option of saying no. If I had known that, I would have kicked Meredith out of the room that first day. Looking at Connor's face, I realize that I still don't have a choice. It is only a courtesy that he has asked my permission.

"Sure," I say, and I see the surprise on Connor's face that I have spoken and acquiesced so easily. "Just one thing."

The surprise leaves his features and is replaced with wariness. "Yes?"

"How are my daughters?" I look expectantly at Connor.

"The girls are fine," he says. "Adjusting well to their families."

"All of them?"

"Every one."

"Passion?"

"*Emily* is her name, and she is still in the custody of the state."

"Why can't she come stay with me?" I ask. "I can take care of her."

"In your room?"

I frown. "Why do you want to keep her from me?"

"She's not yours, Clara."

"She is."

Connor groans in frustration. "Okay, let's talk about Emily. How long has she lived with you?"

I clamp my mouth shut. I haven't gotten what I want. I will not answer questions.

"Is this that silent thing you said she does?" Jay asks, keeping his voice low as if I won't hear him.

"I'm right here, Jay," I say, and he jumps as I say his name. "I am perfectly capable of answering questions I *choose* to answer"—I shoot Connor a look—"so you can stop talking about me as if I am dumb."

Jay's mouth hangs open, and I see Connor smirk. Despite the situation, I find Jay refreshing. He seems so innocent, and I can tell his confidence is for show. If I wanted to, I could probably break him. The power in that thought surges through me.

"Okay. I will tell you about Passion—"

"Emily."

I roll my eyes. "*Emily*. I will tell you about her if you let me write her a letter."

Connor thinks for a moment, watching me. He has already witnessed my determination, and I know he is weighing how long I can hold out against how much he needs information. Finally he nods.

"Okay. Write a letter to her during your session with Dr. Mulligan, and I will deliver it to her."

"I'll talk after I get a response."

"No."

I sigh. I knew that was a long shot. Hopefully Dr. Mulligan will back me up and make sure Passion gets the letter. I cannot think of her as Emily. She has always been Passion. My Passion.

"Glen brought Passion to me four years ago," I say. Connor grunts at my use of her name, but says nothing as he begins taking notes. "She was thirteen years old. One of my biggest challenges, and greatest successes." I smile as I remember how much work I put in to Passion.

"Where did Em—*Passion* come from?" Connor asks.

"I don't know."

"What month did she come?"

I furrow my brow as I concentrate. "I don't remember. It was warm, though. Our air-conditioning went out, and she kept slipping out of my grasp because we were both sweaty."

"Sweaty?" Jay jumps in.

"I had to chase her around a lot those first few weeks."

"What, exactly, was your role, Clara?" Connor asks.

"My role?"

"Yes, your job, your title."

I am confused. "I was wife to Glen. Mother to our children."

"What does that mean?"

"You don't know what a wife is?"

Jay laughs. A look from Connor quiets him, but his expression remains amused. Connor clears his throat. "What I mean is, what did you *do* as wife and mother? What did your days look like?"

"Oh. Well, there were always chores to do. And private lessons for each girl."

"What sort of lessons?"

"Building up a special skill. Languages, drawing, a wide variety of arts." I smile. "My girls are very gifted."

"And you did this all on your own?"

"I wasn't on my own. The older girls took a lot of responsibility for the younger. We were a family. We helped one another. Took care of one another."

"Where was Glen?"

"He had a lot of meetings." I shrug. "When we moved to the acreage, he was around more, because everything was in one spot."

"And the other men? They were around, too?"

I shake my head firmly. "They stayed outside as much as possible. Especially after . . ."

"After what?" Connor leans forward.

I say nothing. I feel my skin heating up as I press down the memory.

"Clara?"

"I think I'm ready for my session with Dr. Mulligan," I say, standing. "Can you take me to her?"

"Sit down, Clara." Connor's tone is firm. "You forget that you are not in charge here."

As if I could forget that I am not in charge. I never have been. Not with Mama and Papa, not with Glen, and not here, with these agents. I feel my control slipping away, the spark of confidence I felt being snuffed out. I slump back into my chair.

"That's better," Connor says. "Now, what about the men?"

I push my emotions down. "They weren't permitted near me or the girls unless Glen was around. Even then, they were to keep a distance. Glen has grown more suspicious of them over the past year."

"Suspicious? Why?"

My shoulders rise and fall in a shrug. "I don't know. He doesn't tell me everything." I don't mention the incidents that precipitated his distrust. One would be breaking Glen's rules. And one might break me.

Connor keeps me in that room for another hour before finally relenting and allowing me to visit Dr. Mulligan. By the time we're done, I am drained, but I feel a small flame of victory. I still have not betrayed Glen. He would be proud.

"Jay will take you to Dr. Mulligan," Connor says, waving his arm at the younger man and bending over the notes he's taken.

Jay jumps up and rounds the table, indicating that I should precede him from the room. He chatters about nothing as we walk through the halls to the therapy wing. I can only concentrate on getting to my notebook and writing to Passion.

Then

The front door slams, and Macy and I straighten and stifle our giggling as we continue folding the laundry. Everything must be perfectly straight, crisp lines, no wrinkles in sight. After all, when we are assigned our clients, we will have chores to do. I am not yet sure what our other duties will be.

Mama bustles into the room, her breathing heavy, eyes bright with excitement. It is rare to see Mama excited, and I drop the shirt I am folding in surprise. Mama frowns, but says nothing as I snatch it back up and straighten it out with a snap.

"Clara," Mama says as I smooth the shirt onto the top of my pile. "When you are finished with those, please come to Papa G's study. We will be waiting."

I nod. "Yes, ma'am." I do not question the instructions, though I am burning inside with curiosity. After Mama has left, Macy leans over.

"Do you think they found one?" she asks in a low voice. "A client for you?"

"I don't know," I say, biting my lip. Except in rare circumstances, girls do not leave until they are at least fourteen, usually closer to sixteen. And those who go earlier are carefully selected before being put in training. I should have two more years of polish before a client even sees my profile.

Macy's eyes are shining. "I bet it's something big. I thought Mama was going to start skipping, she was so excited."

Taking a deep breath, I smile. "I'd better go see what they want."

Placing my neat pile back into the basket to be sorted into rooms later, I stand and tiptoe down the hallway toward Papa G's study. I have never been in the study. It is a mysterious cavern that holds secrets I am both eager and nervous to discover. I creep toward the door, which is cracked open, hoping to overhear something to prepare my reaction, but the voices floating through the air are too low to understand. I step forward and rap on the dark wood of the door.

"Come in, Clara," Papa booms. I can hear the joyful tone of his voice as well.

I push the heavy door and it creaks wider, revealing a room colored in rich tones. A massive desk takes up one wall, with a leather chair behind it, occupied by Papa G. Two wingback chairs face the desk. Mama Mae stands by one, handing a cup of tea to the occupant of the other. A slim, tanned hand waves the cup away, and the man unfolds himself from his seat, turning to face me.

"Clara," Papa G says, rising and rounding the desk to stand by the visitor. "This is Mr. Q."

The man in front of me must be at least forty. Maybe older. He is handsome, I suppose, with just a touch of gray peppering his dark hair at the temples. Thin lines surround his mouth, but not his eyes, which makes me think that he does not do a lot of laughing. His eyes are appraising, but not unfriendly. Expectant. I give a small curtsy and form my lips into a smile. "Nice to meet you, sir," I say.

Mr. Q's face breaks into a grin that doesn't reach his eyes. "She is stunning, Glen," he says, taking a step toward me. "May I?"

Papa sweeps his arm in my direction, gesturing Mr. Q forward. Mama hurries to close the door. The click of the lock causes me to jump. Mr. Q chuckles at the movement.

"How old is she?" he asks.

"Twelve," Papa replies. "But she is one of our most mature girls.

Already helping out with lessons for the other girls and taking advanced tutoring sessions on her own. Quite bright. Obedient."

Mr. Q nods, bringing a hand to his chin. "Turn around, child, slowly."

I do as he asks, pivoting on my toes. I wish I had worn a nicer dress, but Mr. Q doesn't seem to mind what I am wearing. He walks around me, lifting a strand of my hair and running it through his fingers.

"I have many business dealings with those in other countries," Mr. Q says. "She will need to be well-versed in at least three languages, preferably more."

"That will be no problem," Papa says, his tone proud. "Clara is a fast learner. She already knows Spanish fluently, and has a basic knowledge of French and Italian. Another language or two will be no problem by the time she is sixteen."

Sixteen? This man is planning for me to join him in four years. I have never heard of someone planning so far in advance. There have been murmurs of more long-term clients, but I thought they were just rumors. My fingers tremble, and I clasp my hands in front of me to hide the shaking. If the adults notice, they do not mention it, and move back to the desk.

"You may return to your chores, Clara," Mama says.

Mr. Q stops and turns back. He strides across the room until he is in front of me again. His long fingers caress my cheek and his muddy brown eyes are intense as they drink in my features. "I look forward to getting to know you better, beautiful Clara," he says, and leans down to place his lips against my cheek. My face grows warm, and he smiles as the blush creeps across the skin he just kissed. "Much better." He returns to the desk and I know I am dismissed.

"Of course you will have the option to use the Treehouse at any time during your wait for Clara," Papa is saying as I unlatch the door. Once again I make as little noise as possible, hoping to learn more. I am not sure what the Treehouse is, only that other girls live there. I have only seen them in passing. Girls who do not earn clients get moved to the Treehouse. Or those who are disobedient.

"Clara," Mama snaps. "Quickly now. Don't leave Macy to finish the laundry on her own."

"Yes, ma'am," I say, glancing back to see Mr. Q watching in amusement, a contrast to the stormy look that has overtaken Mama's face. I slip out the door and hurry down the hall, eager to find Macy to share my news.

Macy will be excited for me. I am the first of us to have a client. My future is set. As I climb the stairs, I ignore the doubts tickling the corners of my mind and focus instead on my growing excitement. After all, why wouldn't I be excited? Mr. Q is handsome and powerful. The perfect client from all appearances. I couldn't have done better. Certainty settles in my stomach like a rock. He is my future, and I will be happy.

Now

My letter to Passion is three pages long, and the one I receive back from her the next day is just a few paragraphs. They are taking good care of her. She has a nice roommate. She misses me. My tears smudge the ink on the paper.

"Do you trust me now?" Connor asks, his face smug at accomplishing his task.

"No," I say, and his face falls. "I don't trust anyone."

He thinks for a moment. "Fair enough. But you know I will keep my word."

"So far."

"Everyone has to start somewhere."

"True."

Connor opens the folder in front of him. "Are you ready for some more questions?"

I make a face.

He pulls out a glossy photo and puts it in front of me. Vomit bubbles in my throat as Joel's face glares up at me.

"I think she's going to throw up," Jay says. Connor runs to grab the garbage can, and soon my breakfast joins the bits of paper and empty takeout containers in the receptacle. Connor knocks on the door and hands the trash bin to a disgruntled-looking guard.

"Can we get some water?" he calls, and someone hands him a bottle. He walks back to the table and opens the bottle before handing it to me. I take grateful gulps of the liquid and place my forehead in my trembling hands.

"So you recognize him, I take it?" he says.

"Joel," I croak.

"Yes, Joel DeSanto, age twenty-five when his body was found in a ravine about fifty miles from your acreage. He was badly beaten and someone shot his genitals off." Connor says it as if he is commenting on the weather.

I close my eyes, willing the flashes of memory to disappear, longing for the healing of Glen's touch. Many nights I woke up screaming, long after I knew Joel was dead. I never stayed alone with the girls overnight again.

"How does Joel fit into your story, Clara?" Connor asks. He seems more put together today and is more like the gentler version of himself that he was when we first met. This is a Connor I can come closer to trusting. I push my emotions back, making them as tiny as possible, and I recount my dealings with Joel, general information at first, that he was second in command to Glen, that he headed up a lot of the training in the boys' camp. He was trusted by Glen. Never by me, but I left that part out.

"And how did Joel end up in a ravine, minus his balls?"

Taking one more deep breath, I tell them, detail by detail, what happened the night I found Joel trying to soil Grace. I remain emotionless, but I can tell the story affects them. I had hoped it would. They need to know just how far Glen will go to protect me, protect his family. Surely they can't find fault in that.

"He raped you, so you shot his junk?" Jay mutters. His fists are clenching and unclenching on the table.

Connor is sitting next to me, a comforting hand on my arm. "I think we're done for today," he says after a pause.

Then

The mood is somber as we enter the small country chapel. There are not many people who have come to celebrate the life and mourn the death of Papa G. He was a man with few friends, and those who are in attendance are here more out of obligation than connection. Many check their watches, estimating the time until they can leave without being rude, while others use the opportunity to network. All eyes are on Glen, no matter the chosen distraction. He is being watched, assessed.

Glen has been running the business for the past year, since Papa got very ill, but even though Papa was technically "retired," he was still at the helm. Even from his deathbed, he was able to strike fear into the hearts of those who would dare come up against him. Now that he is gone, Glen will have to prove that he is every bit the leader Papa was. Papa always called him soft, but I don't doubt Glen. I know what he is willing to do for things that are important to him. I am not worried.

We walk to the front of the small room, where the casket is set up, lid open. Inside, Papa sleeps, the hard lines of his face softened in death as they never were in life. The skin is loose and translucent. Even a skilled makeup artist could not cover up the evidence of the wasted man he became in his last days. Glen squeezes my fingers so hard, I cannot feel the tips. I brush my other hand over the top of our joined hands, and he relaxes. We turn to make room for others to pay their respects.

Mama Mae sits in the front row, staring at the large portrait of Papa G set up next to the casket. He is several years younger, his face filled in, his hair thick with no hint of the wispiness it developed near the end of his life. There are no tears from Mama. Glen takes the seat next to her, patting her hand as he sits. She glances at him, nods, and moves her hand away from his. Mama is not comfortable with displays of affection, and she has refused any comfort since Papa died three days ago.

A man in a long black robe steps to the front, and the hum of conversation hushes. It is a generic proceeding. We did not know this man before he was commissioned for this service, and we will never see him again after today. He reads a few Bible verses, extols the imaginary virtues we fed to him before the service, and within fifteen minutes we are part of the procession walking to the small cemetery situated behind the church. The burial is more of the same. We each toss a handful of dirt as Papa is lowered into the ground, and it is over.

The small crowd disperses, a few of the men stopping to murmur condolences and to inquire about setting up a meeting with Glen. He handles the condolences and the business requests with equal class. After all, Papa would not consider a funeral to be an excuse to alienate business partners. We are the last to leave.

I sit in the backseat while Glen drives Mama Mae back to the big empty house she will now live in alone. Glen has not discussed whether she will stay, but I know she will. She refused our offer to move in with us for a short time. She is a strong woman, never as dependent on Papa G as she pretended to be.

Their relationship was always a mystery to me. They never touched, and rarely interacted outside of stilted conversations, at least in front of us. She did not cry at all when Papa died, but I have caught her staring at nothing several times over the past few days, her eyes far away, expression empty. Emotions overwhelm me as I try to imagine losing Glen. Just the thought of being without him squeezes at my lungs, and I wrap my arms around myself. Glen glances at me in the mirror, his forehead creased, and I give him a watery smile. He has enough to worry about without dealing with my anxiety.

When we arrive at Mama's house, Glen and I follow Mama inside. She heads straight for the kitchen and begins clanking pots around. "Clara!" she calls. "Come help me with dinner." It is as if we are back to normal, having Sunday dinner together, Mama and me in the kitchen while Papa and Glen sit in the study and talk trade. Glen squeezes my hand and pushes me toward the kitchen. I look back and catch him staring at an old family portrait, looking like a lost little boy, a foreign look on him.

As expected, Mama shoos us out the door after dinner is cleaned up. She refuses Glen's offer to stay over, and insists we hurry home to make sure our girls behaved for the men we left behind to watch them. Glen drives home, his mood pensive. Through all the preparations, we have not spoken about what Papa's death means to Glen.

"Glen," I begin, but he shakes his head, clamping a hand down on my leg.

"No, Clara," he says, his tone firm. I close my mouth, but his hand remains on my leg, squeezing until my eyes water. I turn to look out the window so he will not see. I know he doesn't do it on purpose.

That night, his lovemaking is rough. I do not comment on the tears in his eyes that I glimpse before he collapses on top of me. In the morning, he leaves early. I examine the hand-shaped bruises around my upper arms and wrists and choose a long-sleeved shirt before stripping the bloody sheets off the bed.

I do not bring up Papa G again.

Now

I am surprised when the door to my room opens late in the afternoon. I've already gone through my daily questioning, which is getting repetitive, and my session with Dr. Mulligan. Usually I am left alone until they bring me dinner, but it is too early for that.

Jay walks into the room, his hands fidgeting more than normal. I look at him without speaking, my question in my eyes.

"There's someone here to see you," he says, not meeting my gaze.

"To see me?"

"Yes, in the visitation room. Let's go."

I stand and follow him from the room. We take a route that is unfamiliar, and outside a windowless door, he stops and turns. His face is apologetic. "I need to put these on you," he says, holding out a pair of silver handcuffs. They look shiny and new, not scuffed like the ones Connor used when I first arrived. I hold my hands out, and flinch as the locks click in place around my wrists. I take deep breaths to calm my sudden feeling of confinement. I realize I am being irrational since I have been confined all along, but this feels different.

Jay opens the door and motions for me to enter. There are a few tables in the room, but only one is occupied. Mama Mae sits facing the door, her face expressionless as I enter. I feel a smile tug at the corner of my lips, something that I would not have expected with Mama being my first visitor, but she reminds me of happier times. Almost imperceptibly, Mama shakes her head. She does not let any recognition show in her eyes. She stands, her back straight.

"Clara?" she asks, as if she doesn't know who I am.

"Y-yes." My answer is hesitant. What game is she playing?

She holds a gloved hand out. Mama and her silly old-fashioned gloves. "My name is Mae Lawson. I am Glen's mother."

I understand now. Glen told me to pretend I don't know his parents. I have avoided answering questions about my life before Glen and I met. Connor gets frustrated with me for this refusal on a daily basis, but I don't care. And clearly Glen has filled Mama in on the plan, since she's looking at me with the sort of disdain she usually reserves for untrainable girls.

"Hello," I say, keeping my voice quiet and my eyes downcast as I lift my linked hands to take hers. She grasps them briefly and releases. No comfort there.

"Please, sit." Mama gestures toward the table. I sit, crossing my legs and staring at the table, waiting for her to speak. When she says nothing, I can handle it no longer.

"How is Glen?" I ask, and immediately regret it. Mama's eyes narrow.

"He's in prison; how do you think he is?"

"I just . . . I just was wondering . . ." My voice trails off and I feel tears pricking my eyes.

"I just wanted to meet the hussy who is trying to send my Glen to prison for things he didn't do." Mama's voice is loud and accusing, and I stare at her with wide eyes.

"What do you mean?"

"I think you know exactly what I mean." Mama glances over my shoulder, then leans in.

"Clara, Glen has a message for you." Her voice is so quiet that I can barely hear her. I glance over my shoulder to see that Jay has left the room. I know they are watching, but probably cannot hear us. "I need you to react like I am scolding you."

This is not a hard instruction to follow. I place my face in my hands as she continues to speak under her breath, trying to concentrate on the rapid flow of words directed at me. "Glen says to stick to the plan, to stay strong, and to give them what they want, as long as it's not the whole truth."

I nod as she speaks. This is what I have been doing all along.

"Mama," I say. "I'm trying, but it's not working. They are frustrated with me. They brought me to a prison . . ." My throat closes as I remember my visit.

"You can do this, Clara. You're stronger than I ever gave you credit for." She looks over at the mirror. "Glen also said they are trying to turn him against you. They will lie to get what they want, Clara. Remember that, and remember who kept you safe all these years."

"Glen."

Mama nods. "Good girl."

I hear the door open behind me. I am not ready for her to go. She was not always my favorite person, but right now she is my only link to Glen. I want to launch myself at her and cling to her neck, but I hold my seat, my eyes the only window to my desperation.

"One more thing, Clara," Mama whispers, even lower than before. "Glen says he will always love you. No matter what."

My mouth drops open. The words are meaningful because they come from Glen, but even more so because Mama repeated them. She was never inclined toward the romantic and scoffed at my relationship with Glen being anything more than an infatuation, and then a convenience. Does this mean she believes our love will get us through this? Or is she just trying to give me the strength to continue? Either way, I am grateful.

"I think you've had enough time, Mrs. Lawson," Jay says as he comes to stand behind me. He takes my arm and pulls me to my feet.

"Very well," Mama Mae says, climbing to her feet as well. "I'd like to talk to her again sometime, if that's okay."

"That depends on whether you can remain civil," Jay says, his tone bland. "She appears very upset now, and we cannot have that in the middle of an ongoing investigation. This ward has very strict rules about visitors, especially those who cause patients distress."

"I promise to behave," Mama says, her face the picture of contrition. "Just look at her . . . She's hardly the monster I thought she was. I'd like to get to know her better."

I'm sure Jay is going to laugh in her face. The lie is so transparent, it's a miracle she can keep a straight face. I wait for Jay's reaction. He is quiet for a moment, but then agrees. "Okay. I'll talk to the boss about it. But call first next time, okay? Clara looks a little shell-shocked."

Mama nods, then turns and exits the room without another word. I slump against Jay.

"Hey, are you okay?" he asks, concern coloring his voice. "We don't have to let her come back."

"No." I shake my head. "It's okay. I was just surprised."

Jay looks at me for a moment, and then takes the keys for the cuffs out of his pocket, using them to free my wrists. "All right. But I'm adding an extra dessert to your tray tonight." He winks.

As he walks me back to my room, I begin to realize that good and bad are relative terms, and that my world, for now, is a constant shade of gray.

Then

The skin on the back of my legs stings with the memory of Mama's yardstick. She has taken to punishing me for the infractions of the younger girls, since I am to be an example to them. This time, Leslie stained the sheets when she washed them. I was supposed to be supervising, but Macy and I caught sight of some of the boys out on their daily run. I knew it was wrong to watch them, but ever since dance class, I can't seem to stop thinking of them. One in particular. I missed the extra work shirts Leslie threw in. She had been hoping to save time, but instead earned us both a punishment. I just hope Leslie's legs are not as sore as my own.

It is my favorite time of day, and as I relax on the porch swing and start the gentle rocking motion with my toe, I let the past hour wash away, close my eyes, and imagine the pain leaving my body, the red stripes fading, the yellow bruises never appearing. Rest time is the best time, I think to myself, smiling at my silly rhyme.

"Do you always smile like that when you're alone?" A husky voice startles me, and I leap to my feet, the pain rushing back to my yardstick-kissed skin. As if I conjured him with a mere thought, Glen stands at the bottom of the porch steps, hands stuffed in pockets, smug smile in place. He is pleased to have surprised me.

"You-you're not supposed to be here," I stammer, and mentally slap myself. Why am I even questioning his presence? Haven't I been longing to see him again? To spend more time with him? I dream about his eyes, piercing into mine, and his arms, wrapped around me, whirling me around the dance floor.

Thankfully, he is not offended, and laughs. "It's my house, too, ya know. I grew up here."

"Yes, I know. But you don't live here anymore." Shut up, Clara. Stop being stupid.

His shoulders lift. "The view is better here."

My face scrunches as I think. I have never been to the boys' cabins, but I know they are by the river and are sure to have a mountain view. Everyplace has a mountain view out here, though from the porch it is difficult to see more than the peaks above the thick trees. "I don't know what you're talking about. There are just trees around here." I make a wide gesture to encompass the surrounding forest, as if Glen has not lived here his entire life. As if he does not realize that there are lots of trees. Stupid stupid stupid.

His boots make slow, heavy clomps on the wooden stairs as he climbs them, coming to stand entirely too close to me. "I really like the view from right here."

Blood rushes to my cheeks as I realize his meaning. It is improper, but I am having a difficult time caring. I do not think about what Mama or Papa would say, or whether the other girls would tattle on me if they witnessed this moment. The pain in my legs has disappeared, and I'm sure my feet have left the ground. I float, lost in Glen's eyes.

A door slams inside the house, shaking both of us out of our stupor. Glen grins. "Want to sit?" He nods toward the recently vacated porch swing, still swaying from my abrupt departure. I do not trust my voice, so I only nod and move to reclaim my spot.

Instead of sitting on the other end of the swing, Glen sits toward the middle, so that as he pushes the swing into motion, it causes the fabric of his pants to brush against the bare skin of my lower leg. The touch is angel soft, and if I weren't so aware of every square inch of him, I might not even notice it. As it is, shivers rush through my body at the small contact, and it feels naughty and forbidden even to be sitting here in silence with him. It is probably both.

We sit like that for the entire afternoon rest period. Too soon, I hear Mama as she begins to rouse the girls to begin late-afternoon lessons. She will be out soon to fetch me. She knows where I like to spend my limited free time.

"You have to go," I say to Glen, reaching to push his arm, my hand lingering at the feel of the solid muscle hidden underneath the thin cotton of the shirt.

He doesn't budge. "Do you want to see something?"

"Now?" I ask, anxiety creeping into my voice. I can almost hear the seconds flying away, and I can only imagine what my punishment will be if Mama catches me out here with Glen. Of course, I could leave, too . . . but I don't.

"Later. Midnight. Up on the roof."

My mouth falls open. "You are not serious."

"I am. The hall outside your room has a small door, which leads to the attic. In the attic, there's a window you can climb out. I'll be waiting there at midnight."

"I can't sneak out." I don't dwell on the fact that Glen somehow knows which room I occupy.

Amusement flickers in his eyes. "You won't be sneaking out. You'll be sneaking . . . up. Besides, Macy does it all the time."

I flinch. Macy's nighttime activities are a constant source of worry for me. I dread the day she gets caught, but I don't ask a lot of questions. I do not want to know the answers.

"I can't."

"I can't leave until you promise to meet me on the roof at midnight."

"Glen . . ."

He leans back and stretches his arm across the back of the swing, creating an even more incriminating scene for Mama to walk out to. This spurs me to my feet. "Okay. Fine. Midnight. On the roof. But only for five minutes."

"We'll see." He grins as he stands and stretches. "I bet I can get you to stay longer."

"Just *go*," I hiss. Mama's footsteps have started down the stairs. She will be out the door in seconds.

"Until later," he whispers, hopping the porch railing and disappearing into the trees as the door behind me creaks open.

"I can't do this." I am sitting on my bed, watching Macy shimmy into dark clothes for her own midnight rendezvous. "I'm just going to go to bed."

"Nuh-uh," Macy says, pulling her hair back and checking her reflection. "You're going. This is *Glen*, Clara. For goodness' sake, you moan his name in your sleep now."

I launch a pillow at her, which she catches with ease, giggling. "Shh," I say. "Don't wake the others." Macy and I share the room on the top floor of the house. It is small and the ceilings slope so that we have to stoop to walk in certain places, but it allows us to have a room with just the two of us, and no younger girls to get in the way. "And I do not moan in my sleep."

Macy raises an eyebrow. "You just keep telling yourself that. But I'm the one who has to listen to it."

"Shut up."

Putting the finishing touches on her makeup, Macy eyes me in the mirror. "It's almost midnight, Cinderella. Are you going to be a princess or a pumpkin?"

I roll my eyes, but stand and join her at the mirror. My face is clear of makeup. When we turn fourteen, Mama teaches us how to use makeup and we are allowed to wear it as much as we like, though there are some circumstances where it is required. I rarely wear it, and Glen seems to like me just fine without it. Though I considered backing out many times, I have not changed into my pajamas. I adjust the straps of the light blue summer dress I am wearing. "Will I be able to climb up there in a dress?"

"You'll be fine." Macy looks at me with approval. "Besides, he might like it if you flash a little something his way. They're pretty *hungry* down at the boys' camp, if you know what I mean."

I do know what she means. Sort of. I shoot her a smile. "Okay. I'm ready. Wish me luck."

"With a bod like that, you don't need luck," Macy says. She pushes the window open. "I'm going to break my neck one of these times," she murmurs, gauging the distance from the window to the ground. There are plenty of handholds, and Macy has become an expert at climbing the walls, but I still get a flutter of anxiety whenever she slips out that window. "'Night, Clara. Have fun. Don't do anything I wouldn't do."

"I don't think you have to worry about that," I say, and she sticks her tongue out at me before she disappears out the window. I wait until I see her shadowy figure race across the lawn before I creep out of the room and inspect the small door just down the hall.

It's not that I haven't noticed the door before. I was just never curious enough to see if it would open. Truth be told, I was probably afraid of what I would find. Spiders, mice . . . dead bodies. I grasp the tiny doorknob and hold my breath as I pull. Much to my surprise, it swings open with ease. I snag the flashlight I borrowed from downstairs and follow the narrow tunnel, pulling the door closed behind me. Macy and I have created pillow people in our beds. Mama rarely checks in on us, but just in case, we are prepared.

The tunnel is short, and soon I am straightening as the beam of the flashlight bounces across an attic I never knew existed. Dust covers every surface, rising in small puffs as I step carefully across the floor. Old, broken toys are scattered throughout the space, along with stacks of boxes with illegible scribbles on the sides. I would love to explore more, but a cool breeze beckons me toward the window, already open, waiting.

Glen sits a few feet from the window, facing the moon, which has risen over the mountaintops, visible from the higher vantage point. His legs are drawn up, and the fabric of his shirt stretches over the muscles of his back as he hugs his knees to his chest. I pause there, watching him in the moonlight, admiring him in an unguarded moment, when he is just himself, not trying to prove anything, all cockiness washed away.

"Are you going to stare at the back of my head all night, or are you going to join me?" His tone is amused, and he does not turn around. "Not that I blame you. My backside does look ravishing in starlight."

I scramble out the window. "I'm surprised you were able to climb up here with all that ego weighing you down." As soon as the words leave my mouth, I slap a hand over my traitorous lips. I cannot believe I just said that to *Glen Lawson*. Surely that is worth a few new stripes on my legs.

Instead of getting angry, Glen throws his head back in a deep, genuine laugh. "That's why I like you, Clara. You try to act all perfect, but then you say or do these little things, and you're just so damn cute. I'd risk a lot to spend more time with you." He turns to look at me, eyes sparkling.

"Is there a chance we could get caught?" I ask, a sudden rush of nerves tempting me to escape through the window and to the safety of my room.

He shakes his head. "Nah. My parents' room is all the way downstairs and on the other side of the house. As long as we're quiet, we'll be fine."

I settle in next to him, leaving a few feet of space, which he promptly eliminates. I stretch my legs out in front of me, and his leg is flush against mine, so I can feel his body heat through his pants and the fabric of my skirt.

"It's just us up here, Clara," Glen whispers, his breath tickling my ear. "We don't have to pretend. Not here."

"Who's pretending?" I ask, breathless.

Glen chuckles. "I know you've been watching me, Clara." I open my mouth to deny it, but he places a finger over my lips. "I know you've been watching me, because I've been watching you. You've always been different. You should hear my parents talk about you." Traces of bitterness creep into his voice. "'Clara mastered another language today. Clara is years ahead of the other girls her age. Clara learned to walk on water.'"

"Glen, I—"

"I hated you for a while. I thought they wanted you to be their kid."

Is this why he asked me to meet him here? So he could tell me how much he despises me? Small pieces of my heart begin to break. I look down, away from Glen's eyes, but he continues speaking.

"That's when I started watching you. I was going to catch you doing something terrible."

My stomach is in knots.

"But there was nothing," Glen says. His voice grows warmer. "You were just as great as they said you were, and beautiful, and that's when I knew I had to know you better." He takes a deep breath. "I think I'm falling for you, Clara."

I turn to look at him, and for a moment I think he is going to kiss me. Without thinking, I move my head slightly away from his. I'm not sure I'm ready for that step. Glen smiles, then reaches down and laces his fingers through mine.

"Look up, Clare," he says, shortening my name to one syllable. A thrill runs through me at the sound of it coming off his tongue. I look up, and my mouth drops open.

Above us, hundreds of stars streak across the sky, slicing shining holes in the velvety texture of the night. I catch my breath, exhaling the word. "Beautiful."

Glen grins and tugs me back until he is lying on his back and I am lying with my head on his chest. I have never been this close with a boy, never felt this intimate. I am feeling things I do not understand, but all I know is that I never want this moment, these feelings, to end.

When the meteor shower is over, Glen starts to speak. He talks about what he would like to do, if he weren't expected to take over the business. Work with animals, maybe, or children. Go on adventures to other countries. Explore the world. Some of these things he will get to do. Papa has been all over the world for his business. Glen will have those same opportunities.

But there is wistfulness in Glen's voice, a hint that he is not as happy with his legacy as his parents would wish him to be. Sadness washes over me as Glen's words slow, as his breathing grows deeper. I do not want to think of anything past this moment, because when we talk of the future, we talk of a time when we will be living separate lives. I cannot help but feel warmth in my chest, however, that Glen has chosen me to share his secrets with. I know that no one else has been privy to the quiet wishes he whispered tonight. As I drift off, my thoughts turn to dreams, where Glen and I are traveling the world together, both of us free to pursue our own desires, both of us choosing the other for forever.

Glen stirs as the sun comes up. He kisses my cheek and lowers himself over the edge of the roof, promising to find time to see me again soon. The separation overwhelms me for a moment, and I wait until I am calm before slipping back through the window, down the passage, and to my room. Macy is asleep, snoring softly, looking as angelic as Mama and Papa believe her to be. Macy is a soul that will not be tamed. She goes after what she wants. I push my pillow person aside and drift off, wishing that I could be more like her.

Now

"I hear you had a visitor yesterday," Dr. Mulligan says about half-way through our session. I have been scribbling in my notebook for the last twenty minutes, feeling uninspired. I flip back to the page where I drew Glen's face. It is a poor reproduction.

"I want to see Glen again," I say, ignoring her statement.

Dr. Mulligan studies me for a moment. "I'm afraid that's not in my power. Why do you wish to see him?"

"He's my husband. Do I need a reason?"

"I suppose not. But why now?"

I slam the notebook closed and cover my face with my hands. I do not want to cry, but I haven't felt right since Mama Mae visited. I hate this. All of it. I want to go back home and be with Glen and our daughters and even Mama Mae. I want to brush Daisy's hair and fold laundry with Passion and help Jenna learn a new language.

"Glen's mother came to visit me," I mumble into my hands. I lower them and peek at Dr. Mulligan. "She says I ruined his life. Is that true?" Though it is only something Mama Mae said to preserve our story, the words have been weighing on me. Maybe it would have been better for Glen if he had let me go to my intended client all those years ago. Maybe his parents could have found him someone more suitable, someone who could help in ways I was not equipped to. Maybe he would still be free.

Something passes across Dr. Mulligan's face, an expression akin to pain. She lowers herself onto the floor across from me. This is new. She always remains perched in her chair, while I usually choose to sit in my spot between the couch and the coffee table. It seems odd to have her at my level, her expensive-looking suit picking up carpet fibers and dust motes. She doesn't seem to care, though, her eyes focused entirely on me.

"Listen to me, Clara." Her tone is different from normal. Dr. Mulligan speaks in low, gentle tones, nonthreatening, not directive. She is like my guide, following me through the tangled web of my mind, nudging me here and there, but letting me take the lead. But now, her voice takes on an urgency, and I sit up and pay attention. "You did not ruin Glen's life. Do you hear me? From what I understand, you only made his life better." She stops and closes her eyes, and I notice a small tremble in her bottom lip.

"But if he hadn't picked me, maybe his parents . . ." I trail off as her eyes snap open.

"What do you mean, Clara?" Her gaze is razor sharp.

"I mean," I say, groping through my brain for the safe answer. I am not supposed to know his parents, so how do I explain how we got together?

"Clara." Dr. Mulligan's voice is gentle again. "When did you meet Glen?"

The memory of the dance class flashes through my mind. "Dance class," I say. That is the story I gave Connor as well. "We ran away together." Not a lie.

"How old were you?"

This is beginning to feel like a questioning session with Connor. I open my notebook up and begin to doodle again. It isn't that I do not want to talk to Dr. Mulligan. It scares me how much I want to open up and spill everything. But I cannot trust anyone.

Dr. Mulligan sighs. "I know you can't tell me the truth yet, Clara," she says, and I can hear how she tries to hide the frustration in her tone. I feel bad for frustrating her, but my loyalty lies with Glen. She watches me for a few more moments, then stands, brushes herself off, and moves back into her chair.

We do not speak for the rest of the session, but I feel a little better. I know Dr. Mulligan cares for me, and I believe her when she says my presence in Glen's life made it better. I just wish I could see him and talk to him about it. Just a few minutes would help reassure me.

"Time's almost up, Clara," Dr. Mulligan says. We seal and sign the notebook, and after she slips it into its secret spot, she leans against her desk, arms crossed. "I want you to think about something between now and our next session," she says, her eyes appraising.

I nod. "Sure."

"There's a group that meets in this building every week. Women who have come from . . . difficult circumstances. I'd like you to consider joining them."

Difficult circumstances? I'm not sure what that means, but I nod again. "I'll think about it."

"Please do. I think it would be good for you to connect with some other women." She gives me a small smile. "Those who are not incarcerated."

I return the smile, taking deep breaths to calm the flash of panic that goes through me at the implied mention of prison. Dr. Mulligan will spring statements like this on me from time to time. She explained that avoiding that which frightens me will not help me in the long run. Her smile widens as she notices my use of breathing techniques to calm my anxiety.

"Good job, Clara." There is a knock at the door. "Think about the group," Dr. Mulligan says as she goes to open it, revealing Jay, ready to take me back to my room.

"I will."

Then

Some of the novelty from my great escape with Glen has worn off. It takes five hours on foot to reach a town, and the sun is fully risen by the time we spot the buildings in the distance. My feet went numb hours ago, but I trudged on, taking only a few of the breaks Glen offered. The numbness and fatigue are forgotten as soon as we see the first signs of civilization. I have never seen a town before. My memories are only of the house I've always lived in, with Mama Mae and my sisters.

"It's so cute!" I say, grinning at Glen. The sleepy town is nestled in a valley, surrounded by snowcapped mountains.

Glen returns my smile, cheeks red from the cold, eyes shining. "I knew you'd love it."

We head down toward the town, and as we stroll the streets hand in hand, I feel a sense of freedom that I didn't know was missing. I want to jump and dance and twirl. Glen leads me to a small building on the edge of town. The bus depot. He buys two tickets to the next largest city, and we don't have to wait long before the bus rumbles to the bench where we wait. Glen begins to fidget, checking his watch and glancing down the road. I begin to grow anxious as well. How long before they realize we are missing? How long before they guess where we have gone?

There are few people on the bus. It smells a bit like dirty socks, but to me it is miraculous. We take a seat across from an old man who is gently snoring into the window, each breath leaving a brief puff of condensation on the glass. I giggle and point him out to Glen, who chuckles with me. As soon as the bus pulls away, I feel Glen relax.

"We made it," he says, turning to look at me.

I nod, unable to hold back my grin. "The start of a new life, right?"

"The best life."

We pass the time on the bus talking about where we want to go and what we'll do when we get there. Glen talks of a man he knows who is willing to create fake documents for us and keep it a secret from Papa G—for the right price, of course. Glen will contact the man when we're safely away. We entertain ourselves by creating our new identities. My name is Delia, and I am eighteen. Glen is Brock, and he is twenty-one. We are newlyweds, fresh from our honeymoon, ready for adventure.

"Oh!" Glen says, reaching into the front pocket of his backpack. "I almost forgot." He pulls out a small velvet bag. "It's not much, but it's something."

I take the bag and turn it over, emptying the contents into my hand. Two silver circlets rest on my palm, one with a tiny diamond chip on the side. I look up at Glen.

"Wedding rings," he says. "Temporary, of course, until I can get you what you deserve." He takes the rings from me. "May I?"

My heart thunders as I allow him to slip the ring onto my finger. The reality of the situation hits me. We are on our own, living as a married couple. No Papa G or Mama Mae telling us what to do, but also no one to provide for us.

"And mine?" Glen asks, holding out the larger ring. I say nothing as I slip the ring onto his finger. I begin to feel light-headed. Glen lifts my hand to his lips and kisses the ring. "Mrs. Montgomery?" And with that small gesture, my heart calms, and all is right.

"Mr. Montgomery," I say, my lips curving into a small smile.

"Happy?"

"Yes."

"Good."

Once we reach the city, we head directly to the ticket booth to figure out where we're going next.

"California?" I ask. "You could become a movie star."

Glen laughs. "I was thinking someplace even farther. East Coast maybe? New York City?"

I consider that. Everything I've read about New York makes it sound very exciting. And huge. The perfect place to disappear.

"New York sounds fantastic."

Glen grins and buys the tickets. It will take several days by bus, but that's okay. We are together, and we have a lot of catching up to do. Most important, I need Glen to coach me in how everything out here works. I don't want to stand out.

We eat at a small diner for lunch, and I decide I could eat cheeseburgers for every meal and die happy. There are still a few hours left before the bus leaves, and Glen spots a movie theater down the road.

"Do you want to see a movie?" he asks, as if I might say no.

"Are you kidding?" I ask. "Yes!" I squeal and jump on him, more excited to see a movie in a theater than I was to eat a cheeseburger.

"Whoa!" he says, catching me around the waist and stumbling back a few steps. "I'm going to start thinking you're only using me to eat cheeseburgers and see movies."

He holds me securely against his chest, and I look down at him, full of love. I bend my head and kiss him, pouring my feelings into the action. Without breaking contact, Glen puts me down and pushes me against a wall. His lips urge mine to open and I am lost. Too soon, his lips slow, and he backs a few inches away.

"So, about that movie . . ." He trails off.

"What movie?" I ask, dazed.

Glen throws his head back and laughs. "Let's go, beautiful." He grabs my hand and we rush toward the theater, hurrying to make it since our detour put us behind. Glen picks a movie at random and we make it in just as the lights are going down.

The movie happens to be a love story, and I snuggle closer to Glen, thinking that there's no way there is a more romantic story than ours, now that we have run away together. Mama Mae made me read a story called *Romeo and Juliet* once, about two kids who fall in love and get married against their parents' wishes. I feel just like Juliet. A feeling of foreboding rushes through me as I remember how Juliet's story ended, but I shake it off and increase my pressure on Glen's hand. He looks down, his brow creasing in worry, and I take the opportunity to stretch up and kiss him again. We miss the rest of the movie, and I don't mind.

We are laughing as we exit the theater. We have plenty of time to make it to the bus that will take us away from here and toward our destiny. Our hands are linked, and our arms swing in time with our unhurried steps.

"Okay, kids. Playtime is over."

I freeze, and the muscles in Glen's arm go taut. His hand is crushing mine. We turn, and, leaning against a van, smoking one of his signature cigars, is Papa G. Glen backs away, pulling me with him.

"Don't make this hard, boy. Just get in the van." Papa's tone is unconcerned.

"No," Glen says. "Clara and I are leaving. You can take your business and give it to someone else. I don't want it."

Papa sighs and pushes away from the van, reaching into his pocket for his tool to cut the burning end of the cigar and replacing both after flicking the end away. "We've discussed this, Glen." Papa rarely uses Glen's name, and I feel Glen's reaction as he stands up straighter. "You are almost done with your training. There is no one else. You will return to the compound. You will take over for me. And you will let this girl go."

Glen is shaking his head in denial at every word Papa says. We continue to back up until Papa looks over his shoulder. His men are waiting for us at every possible escape route. We are sunk. I can practically see the gears in Glen's head turning as he tries to come up with a magical solution. Suddenly, he stills.

"You can bring us back, Father," he says. "But we'll leave again." Papa opens his mouth in protest, but Glen will not let him speak. "If you sell Clara, I will go after her. I will cause problem after problem until you're forced to get rid of me. I don't care what methods you use to keep me in line, they won't work. That is a promise."

Papa G stares at Glen, his eyes appraising. I know Glen has stood up to Papa in the past, but never so strongly. He usually gives in. Papa says nothing, though his jaw tightens as he waits for Glen to continue.

"But," Glen continues, "we will go back willingly, right now, if you agree to let us be together. Clara can be Mother's apprentice and prepare to take over with me when you guys retire."

"She's worth a lot of money to me, boy," Papa says, anger coloring his voice.

"She's worth a lot more than money to me," Glen replies, releasing my hand to wrap an arm around me.

People are beginning to stare. Glen and Papa have kept their voices low enough that no one could overhear, but it's evident that there's a confrontation going on. Papa realizes this first.

"Fine," he says. "Let's discuss it in the van."

"No." Glen's voice is firm, no fear apparent in his tone. "I need your word that you will not sell Clara."

Papa considers, the wrinkles at the corners of his eyes deeper than I have ever seen them. "You will have to make up the money for me. Her client will take another girl, but he won't pay as much. You will make up the difference, as well as what I would have gotten for the other girl."

Glen stares at his father. "You want me to *buy* her from you?"

Papa nods.

"Agreed." There is no hesitation in Glen's voice. "If I'd known that was an option, we could have avoided this."

Papa looks at Glen, and I catch a glimpse of something like pride in his eyes, there and gone before I can be sure, replaced with his usual derision. "Of course, you will both be punished for this little field trip."

Glen flinches, but nods. "Of course."

We get in the van, and though Glen continues to hold on to me, I feel my freedom forever slipping away as the door shuts us in.

Now

The first waves of nausea wash over me in the early hours of the morning. I do not recognize the feeling at first. By the time I realize what's happening, I am almost too late to make it to the toilet, where the contents of my stomach end up. I feel shaky and cold, and sweat beads along my forehead. I lean against the wall by the toilet and release a soft moan. I cannot move even to make my way back to the bed.

I am still there an hour later, when the guard comes to check on me. He calls for a doctor immediately and helps me back to my bed. I am feeling better, though still dizzy. I fall asleep while we wait for the doctor. When he arrives, the doctor takes one look at me and orders the guard to take me to the infirmary.

The guard wheels me to an unfamiliar area of the building. It is near Dr. Mulligan's office, but we take a few extra turns. I am poked and prodded and asked to pee in a cup, and then I am allowed to go back to my room to rest. I think vaguely of the group I was supposed to attend today, after some more prodding by Dr. Mulligan, but soon I am swept into a dreamless sleep.

Connor is sitting by my bed when I wake. He is reading a sheaf of papers, and it is reminiscent of the time Meredith sat by me while I slept. This time, however, I am not frightened. Though Connor gets stressed and overreacts at times, he has been patient with me, and I know not to fear him. I wonder where Jay is. I have come to enjoy my time spent in the company of the enthusiastic young agent. I borrow energy from him through long hours of the same questions.

"Hey," I say, my voice hoarse. Connor looks up from his papers, a ghost of a smile on his lips, but his eyes are worried. I think again that Connor has aged since we met. A little more gray hair, a few more spidery veins around his eyes and lips. Or maybe I am becoming more observant.

"Hey," he says, stuffing his papers into a folder. "How are you feeling?"

I shove myself into a sitting position and am surprised when I feel only the slight dizziness that comes from sitting up too fast. My head is clear, and my stomach feels fine. "Pretty good," I say, looking at Connor in shock. "You have some good medical treatment here."

Connor's smile grows a little wider. "It's not a miracle of science, unfortunately. Or fortunately," he adds, furrowing his brow.

I shake my head. He is still so confusing at times. "What are you talking about?" I ask.

He looks at me. "You feel up to talking with Dr. Mulligan?"

I groan. "Is she going to make me go to that group?"

Connor chuckles. "Not today," he says. "We have bigger fish to fry today."

I roll my eyes. "Let's go, then."

He rolls the wheelchair over. "Hop in."

"No way." I stand, smoothing my pants and shirt. "I can walk."

"You have no shoes."

I look down at my bare feet. "Oh. Yeah." I look around for my slippers, but they have disappeared.

"Just sit, Clara," he says, sounding exasperated.

I sit, and he wheels me to Dr. Mulligan's hallway. It is carpeted here, so I hold up a hand for him to stop. "Please?" I say, standing. He shakes his head, but allows me to walk the rest of the way.

Dr. Mulligan is waiting for us. I am surprised when Connor takes a seat on the other end of the couch instead of leaving. I raise an eyebrow at him, but he has his attention focused on Dr. Mulligan. With a sigh, I turn to face her as well.

"How are you feeling, Clara?" Dr. Mulligan asks. Her tone is careful this morning. Or is it afternoon? I have no idea how long I slept.

"Much better," I say. "In fact, I feel pretty good right now. But maybe not good enough to go to that group thing. I don't know if I'm contagious." I give a little cough to be convincing, remembering too late that I had a stomach bug.

"You're not contagious," Connor says from his spot on the couch, and Dr. Mulligan glances at him.

I look between the two of them.

Dr. Mulligan squares her shoulders and takes off her glasses.

"You didn't have a stomach bug, Clara. That's why we know you're not contagious."

"Food poisoning?" I guess. "The food is pretty terrible here."

Connor snorts.

"No," Dr. Mulligan says, ignoring Connor. "The food is fine."

"Clearly you haven't had their meat loaf."

"Clara, I need you to focus."

"I am focused." I am not focused. I had a weird dream before I got sick that I want to write down before I forget it. I wonder how I can get Connor to leave.

"Clara, you're pregnant."

Then

There is a hush over the house as I limp to my room. The lashes I have received will become infected if I do not find someone to help me tend them. I wonder if Glen is enduring a similar punishment. I have not seen him since they separated us in the driveway. I was taken to the back, where Mama released her rage on me without saying a word. I have never been whipped before. That is a punishment reserved for the girls who cause trouble, the ones who are sent away. I have never caused trouble. Until Glen.

I slip into my bedroom and am relieved to see Macy waiting for me, bowl and ointment ready. I remove my shirt and lie facedown on the bed. Macy has stripped the mattress bare. The naked surface is dotted in stains that I try not to think about as I bury my head in my arms. The first dab of the cloth sends pains shooting to my fingers and toes, but soon I am numb to it, as I was to the switch outside.

"Where did you go?" Macy asks after several minutes of tending to my back. I hear the curiosity dripping from her voice, and I know it has been killing her to wait this long to ask. And she deserves to know. Macy has been my confidante for as long as I can remember, and we keep each other's secrets. The fact that I didn't tell her about leaving borders on betrayal, though she does not appear angry. Yet I am still hesitant to tell her.

When I don't answer, she presses the issue. "I heard Glen disappeared, too."

"How could you have heard that? Mama wouldn't talk about it."

"I got out of the house and went to Josh's cabin." Macy pauses. "He said Glen took off last night with one of the girls and Papa came through on a rampage. Tore Glen's bunk apart."

"You went to his *cabin*? In the daytime?" I gasp, sitting up. The cloths on my back drop to the mattress and I hold my shirt over my chest as I gape at her. Nighttime outings are bad enough. I had no idea she was taking such risks while the sun was out.

Macy's mouth turns up in a sly smile. "It's not the first time I've been there during the day." She shrugs. "With your extra lessons with Mama, I've had more free time. My client isn't as demanding as yours." My client demands that I be as educated as if I had attended a private school, excelling in reading, writing, proper speech, and three languages. My heart drops as I imagine the amount of money he has promised for my years of training. I cannot feel too guilty, though, as Glen's face flashes through my memory. He is worth it. And he feels the same about me.

I shake my head, bringing Macy's face back into focus. Her eyes widen. "What will your client say when he finds out?"

"He won't find out," I say, returning to my position on the bed. "At least not the details."

"What details?" Macy's tone is ravenous, willing me to share information.

A knock on the door interrupts before I can formulate an answer. Macy's shoulders sag as she stands to open the door. Mama fills the doorway.

"You can go to your chores, child," she says to Macy, moving aside. "I'll finish up in here."

"Yes, ma'am," Macy says, looking at the floor, the picture of a demure teenage girl. I wonder if she has really fooled them as much as she thinks. Mama's eyes narrow as she watches Macy depart, before she steps in and closes the door behind her.

I remain still, waiting for any sort of directive. Mama crosses the room and her hands take over where Macy left off with cleaning and applying ointment and bandages. I flinch at the first touch, expecting Mama's usual gruffness, but I am surprised at the gentleness of her hands. Her swift fingers move across my back faster than Macy's had, and she soon motions for me to sit up.

"Get changed and come down to the parlor," she says, standing and moving toward the door. "We'll have a chat."

My shirt is ruined, but I toss it in the hamper anyway. I will try to get the stains out and mend it later. It is the shirt Glen gave me to wear to run away with him, and I do not want to part with it. I will have to hide it to keep it from becoming rags. Glen's shirt should not be used to polish furniture.

After I change into an understated skirt and top, I make my way downstairs, my feet dragging until I am within earshot of the parlor. Then I perk up and walk at my normal pace. No use putting it off any longer. I am anxious about what Mama is going to say. It was clear from the whipping she gave me that there was more than just punishment on her mind.

Mama is already seated in one of the high-backed chairs by the window when I arrive. "Close the doors, please, Clara," she says, not looking up. I push the French doors closed until they click, and then move to the seat across from Mama. "Please, sit." Mama motions to the chair. I sit, careful to keep my back away from the hard surface. The movement sends waves of pain through my body anyway.

It isn't long before the silence grows uncomfortable. I burn my tongue as I sip from the tea Mama has poured for me. I know not to speak first. I have been punished once already. Though talking out of turn would not earn me another lashing, there are other ways Mama could seek out her revenge.

"I was never meant to have a son," Mama says, still not looking at me. I follow her gaze out the window, but see nothing that would catch her attention. A glance at her face tells me that she is far away, someplace in the past where I cannot follow. "I was broken after my third girl. I wasn't to have any more children, and I had not left Papa with a successor. He would have been right to get rid of me and find someone who could provide what he needed."

I keep my face neutral, but inside my thoughts churn. I do not know of any girls who would be Mama's daughters, born of her body. There is only Glen. My sisters and I are Mama's only daughters.

"Papa G was the oldest of five brothers," Mama continued. "He expected to have his pick of successors. When we found out we were pregnant again, we were horrified, expecting a fourth girl. But the joy on his face was worth it all when we found out Glen was a boy."

Mama's eyes crinkle as her lips turn up into a small smile. It is a rare expression on her face. I hold my breath, not wanting to interrupt the moment. I am craving more information about Glen as a baby, Glen as a child. There is so much I do not know, so much to learn about him. My future has taken a sharp turn in the past forty-eight hours, and I am ready to soak up whatever knowledge I can, just as I do in all my lessons.

"When Glen was born, he was small, sickly. We weren't sure he'd make it. But he did. He grew to be stronger than the other boys, and he made his papa proud. He has always made his papa proud." She turns to face me, her eyes drilling into mine. "Until he met you."

She could just as well have stabbed me through the chest, so severe is the impact of her words.

"I don't understand," I say, my voice small. I am determined not to cry, and I clasp my hands together in front of me to hide the trembling.

"Glen was always meant to pick a mate," Mama says, still glaring across the table at me. "There are plenty of girls who would be suitable. You are not one of them."

I take a deep breath. Glen has already promised we will be together. If that is the case, I must be brave with this woman. "Why am I not suitable, ma'am?"

Mama's eyes flash. "You have been trained for more than that, Clara," she says, and my mouth drops open in shock I cannot hide. "You could be on the arm of a tremendously important man, and instead, you will be hidden away from the world, your talents wasted. You are, simply put, too good for him."

This is not what I expected at all. The opposite. Despite what Glen has told me, I assumed Mama was upset that Glen had not made a better choice.

"I love my son," Mama says, reaching across the table to cover my hand with her own. "But it will take him years to pay Papa back for you. And our reputation will be tarnished."

Of course. It is the money. And the reputation. Mama does not actually hold me in high regard. It is about the business. It is always about the business. That's why they are disappointed in Glen and angry with me. They believe his choosing me will damage their precious business. We will have to prove them wrong. I straighten my shoulders, shrugging off the weight of Mama's judgment.

"I love your son as well," I say, summoning my courage and returning her glare. "And my talents will be useful in helping the business to grow even further. You have taught me well, and I know you have much more to teach me. I am eager to learn and to take my place at Glen's side."

Mama regards me, her eyes distrustful. My speech has had little impact. She stares at me for a few moments longer. "So I cannot convince you to let Glen go and fulfill your original obligations?"

This is new. I feel as if I have a choice. If I wanted to, I could meet with my client in a few months as planned. I could bring money and prestige to the man and woman who raised me, and grow their business further. Or I could take Glen's offer and be with him and risk the entire operation.

It is not really a choice for me.

"I will always choose Glen," I say, standing. Mama does not protest as I exit the room.

Now

The sickness comes in waves now, unpredictable, but I am prepared for it. I have all the crackers I could want, and peppermints help as well. I only wish I had Mama's special morning sickness tea to keep the nausea at bay.

A doctor came yesterday. One who specializes in babies. She estimates that I am almost two months pregnant. A little late for morning sickness to start, but she points out other times I have felt sick and dizzy and attributes those episodes to the pregnancy as well.

I cannot believe there is a child growing inside me. This is the fourth time Glen and I have created a life together. Of course, the timing isn't ideal, but I refuse to complain. I close my eyes as I think of those who came before this child, whom I have christened "my little Nut." Those tiny souls whom I never got a chance to meet. A blanket of fierce protectiveness falls over me, and I cross my arms over my still-flat abdomen. Nothing will happen to this child. I will keep him safe. I am terrified and excited. This time will be different. This time I have a doctor watching over me. This time I will not let our miracle slip away. I confessed my anxiety to the doctor and told her about my three previous pregnancies. She assures me that all is well and the baby is healthy. I want to believe her. There is nothing I want more than to keep this baby safe, to carry it to full term, to give birth with Glen by my side. We've been parents for years, but never to a baby, never to a child we made. When this baby comes, my bond with Glen will be stronger than ever.

The doctor says we will not find out if the baby is a boy or girl for several more months, but I don't need an ultrasound to know. I am growing a tiny Glen inside of me. Even though Glen cannot be with me, he has left a piece of himself behind. He has made sure I will be protected, cared for, in case he is unable to do it. It is further proof of our love, of the love that the people around me are trying to question. They cannot question it now.

The door opens and Connor walks in, followed closely by Jay. Connor's face is tight with concern. He worries about me, but he does not need to. My Nut is with me now.

"Can I have some books to read, please?" I ask, and his eyebrows rise in surprise. I have not spoken much outside of our questioning times and rarely ask for anything besides the chance to see Glen.

"Of course," he says, retrieving a small pad of paper and a pen from his pocket. I've noticed that Connor is never without something to write on. How many thoughts must be swirling through his head to need to always be writing something? "What kind of books would you like?"

"Books about pregnancy," I say. "And maybe a couple novels? And some children's books to read to Nut."

"Nut?" Jay asks.

"That won't be his name when he is born, of course." I smile. "But it suits him now, don't you think?"

The men nod, but they do not understand. How could they understand the joy of sharing your body with a miracle?

Connor writes on his paper and slips it back into his pocket. "Clara, do you still want to see Glen?"

I perk up. "Yes." There is no hesitation in my answer. Glen will be so excited.

Connor nods. "I'm going to leave it up to you," he says. "But I want you to consider waiting to tell Glen about the baby. Maybe even hold on to the news until your next visit, until you see the doctor again."

I frown. That makes no sense. The doctor already said everything looks good with this pregnancy. "Why? He'll be so happy."

"Just . . . wait, okay? If it seems right, tell him, but wait at least ten minutes."

My brow wrinkles, but I nod. "Okay. How long will I have with him?"

"Twenty minutes."

My heart sinks. "Such a short time." But longer than our last visit, I suppose. If I'm cooperative enough, maybe we'll get a full hour sometime.

"Are you ready?" Connor does not respond to my despondence over his time frame.

I stand. "I've been ready since I last said good-bye."

Jay stands aside as Connor leads me out. They do not bother cuffing me in the van for the short drive to the prison. We take the same route as last time, and the room we enter is exactly as I remember it. Glen sits at the table, cuffed to a ring in the middle, head down. He looks up as we walk in, and I gasp.

Glen's face has stretched over the bones of his skull so his cheekbones are hollow, his eyes wide and their look bleak. They brighten as they focus on me. "Clara," he croaks.

I cannot move closer. I turn to Connor. "What have they done to him?" I hiss.

"Prison is not easy on people like him," Connor responds.

Tears prick my eyes. People like him? Glen is the love of my life. How can they treat him so poorly? I take a deep breath and turn to give Glen a wobbly smile. His guards move toward the door, unlocking his hands from the table as they pass. It appears we will be given privacy without even asking this time.

"Twenty minutes," Connor warns as he pulls the door shut behind him. "That's all. Think carefully about what you say." And then he is gone.

My feet feel like they are slogging through mud as I approach the table. I want to run toward him and away from him at the same time. I move around until I am standing by him, and I drop to my knees.

"Glen?" It is a question, because I need to know that he is still in there, that my Glen is within the depths of this emaciated figure before me.

He turns, and his hands rise to clasp my face. "Clara," he breathes, and bends, resting his forehead against mine. My eyes flutter closed, and I feel him. It is Glen. My Glen.

"Are you okay?"

"Do I look okay?"

"You don't want me to answer that."

"Dammit, Clara," Glen snaps, but there is a spark in his eyes that wasn't there before. I am drawing him out. He cannot be defeated. "I look like shit, and I feel worse."

We are quiet for a few moments. "What is it like, Glen?" I cannot believe how brave I am being, but I take my strength from Nut.

He closes his eyes. "I don't want to talk about it. I hope you never have to experience a place like this, Clara."

I do not tell him that I have. That I still have nightmares sometimes where I am covered in blood, a sharpened toothbrush protruding from my stomach. I wonder if even through those nightmares, Nut was trying to tell me of his existence, trying to hint that there was something there. I silently apologize for not knowing sooner and pray that the dream is not an omen of things to come.

"Have you said anything?" Glen asks, his voice low.

"Only the basics," I say. "Things they already know." I pause. "Mama gave me your message."

A small smile tugs at his lips. "I heard you put on quite a show."

"I learned from the best."

"She'll visit you when she can, Clara. I don't want you to feel alone just because I can't be there."

"I'm not alone."

His head jerks up. "You mean those agents you're always with? That tall one, I don't like the way he looks at you."

Glen is always jealous, especially since Joel. "Connor is trying to help me," I say, and I am surprised to realize I believe the words.

Glen's eyes harden. "None of these people are trying to help us, Clara. They're trying to separate us." He slumps in his chair. "I hate feeling like I can't help you. I don't like being away from you."

It's like he is shrinking before my eyes. I make my decision then. "Glen," I say, my voice sharper than it has ever been addressing him. "Do not give up. Do you hear me?"

His eyes are surprised, and I see a storm brewing. Good. I want to get him worked up, angry. Passionate. He needs to care again. I lean in.

"I found out this week, Glen."

He moves closer. "Found out what?"

I rub my stomach. "I'm pregnant, Glen. We made a baby, and he's alive in here."

Glen's mouth drops open.

I nod, a smile growing across my face. "So don't you dare give up. I will not let my son be born into a world where his father has given up. Promise me you will fight, Glen."

He sits up straighter, and I see fire in his eyes.

Connor chooses that moment to come in. When I see the disappointment in his face, I know he has overheard. I do not know how much, but I know that he wanted me to keep the baby a secret. As I watch Glen's strength grow before my eyes, I understand why.

Then

I sigh and lean back in my chair, my hands covering my stomach as I draw in a deep breath. The crisp autumn air sharpens my senses, which have been dulled by a rich feast of South Dakota's best cuisine. I laughed when Glen presented the steak and potatoes meal, since it's not much different from what we have at home, but in a way it is completely different, and the best meal I have ever had. I would continue eating, if only to prolong the experience, but there is barely room left for the dessert Glen and I share.

Glen scoops up the last of the custard and grins at me. "Happy?" he asks.

"Incredibly," I say, returning his smile. "Thank you for this."

He reaches for my hand, bringing it to his lips and leaving a sticky kiss. "Will you walk with me?" he asks, pulling me to my feet as I nod my agreement. He drops several bills on the table and leads me down the path behind the lodge. I can see the lake from where we ate, and there is a path beside it. We walk in comfortable silence for a while.

"Clare?"

"Hmm?" I ask, distracted by the play of the moon on the soft ripples of the water.

"Are you . . . happy? I mean, with how things are?"

He has my attention now. "What do you mean?"

"Just what I asked. Are you happy?"

I wrinkle my brow. "Of course I'm happy, Glen. I'm with you."

"You . . . you don't wish you had ended up with your rich client?"

"How can you even think that?" I stop and turn to face him, taking his other hand. "I love *you*, Glen, and I have since we danced together that first time. I can't imagine a life without you. And I wouldn't want to."

Glen's muscles relax. I hadn't even realized he was tense. It dawns on me that something very important has just happened. I never knew that Glen harbored any questions about my desire to be with him. He is always so confident, so secure in who he is. It gives me a slight thrill to know that I can bring that vulnerability out of him. I feel guilty for thinking that way, but can't help the small smile that comes to my lips.

"What are you smiling about?" he asks, tilting my chin up and searching my eyes.

"Just remembering our first dance," I say, hoping my lie is not obvious.

He studies me for a moment, then releases me and steps back. "Well then, m'lady, may I have this dance?" He bows, hand held out toward me.

I smile and curtsy. "Of course, kind sir," I say, taking his hand.

He sweeps me into his arms and we make slow circles in the moonlight. I release a happy sigh and rest my head on his broad chest. The steady beat of his heart relaxes me, and he hums a quiet tune just for the two of us. It is the most romantic moment of my life.

The moment is spoiled when the shrill sound of his beeper slices through the peaceful evening air. His chest vibrates as he grumbles his displeasure, but he gently sets me away from him and digs in his pocket for the device.

"It's Joel," he says, brow furrowed. "911." He closes his eyes and takes a deep breath I know is meant to calm him. When he opens his eyes, the playfulness of a few minutes ago is gone. "I have to call him."

In my most fanciful daydreams, Glen would take that beeper and chuck it into the lake, refusing to allow anything or anyone to interrupt our romantic evening. But I know my husband, and I knew as soon as the beeper sounded that our evening was over.

"Of course," I say, and take his offered hand, following him back up the path and into the lodge.

Glen asks to use the phone in the lobby to call Joel at the place they are staying, dialing the number and moving us as far as the cord will allow for privacy.

"What?" he barks.

I cannot understand the tinny words coming through the earpiece, so I lean into Glen's chest, appreciating the deep rumble of his voice. Almost immediately after Joel starts talking, Glen tenses up.

"When?" A pause. "Did he say why?" Another pause. "Did you get the girls?" A slight relaxing of his muscles. "Okay. Fine. I'll bring Clara back to our room and then—" His body goes rigid in response to whatever Joel has said. "What the f—"

I lean back and look up at him. His neck has gone a dangerous shade of red, a sure sign that he is angry.

"I want you with me on this, Joel," Glen says into the phone, his arm tightening around me. "Get Pete to get the girls and get on the road. We'll leave tonight. I don't like this." He tells Joel to pick us up out front, and we find a couch in the lobby to sit on while we wait.

"What's going on, Glen?" I ask. I usually don't engage with him when he is this angry, but my curiosity has gotten the better of me.

"Harrison wants to see us."

"Us?"

"Yes. Both of us."

"Why me?" I know now why Glen is upset. He doesn't like anyone taking any sort of interest in me. He is very possessive.

He groans. "I don't know." He turns to me and takes my hands.

"Clara, whatever happens, you don't leave my side, got it? *Do not leave my side.*"

I shrink back from the intensity in his voice, but I nod.

"Promise me, Clara. Say it."

"I promise." My voice is small but sure. They will have to drag me away from Glen.

Now

I am the first one to arrive to the new group Dr. Mulligan has signed me up for. Connor got me very early and has taken his spot in the hallway. He did not want to sit in. He was worried the others would not open up as much if he were there, but I know he is more worried about me not opening up if he's there. He doesn't need to worry. I don't plan on speaking up at all. I am only doing this to appease Dr. Mulligan.

I shift in the metal folding chair, one of the ten or so set up in a circle in the center of this room. There is drab green carpeting stretching to the walls, but it is thin and worn almost to the backing in many places. The air-conditioning is set too cool in here, and I shiver through the tissue-like fabric of my shirt. I cross my arms over my stomach as more girls file in. Some whisper to one another, their words too soft for me to understand, while others sit as silently as me, staring at various spots in the room, avoiding eye contact.

Since everyone is ignoring me, I take the opportunity to study them. Many of the girls appear to be around my age, some a little older, a couple much younger. Since marrying Glen, I have not spent much time with girls so close to my age. The brief interactions I had with women from Glen's businesses were uncomfortable, the women full of disdain for me, and I for them. They were jealous of my position with Glen. The last friend I had was Macy. I push her face out of my head.

A woman with bushy brown hair stumbles into the room, loaded down with a stack of papers. One of the girls jumps up to help her, while the rest of us watch.

"Thank you, Tori," the woman says, handing half the stack to her. "Just set those by my chair, please."

The girl, Tori, does as the woman asks. Tori does not look as tired as some of the others, and her eyes have a glow to them that is unfamiliar. She takes her seat as the other woman makes her way into the circle.

The woman sets her papers down, smooths her hair and clothes, and sits, smiling at the expectant faces around her. All conversations have ceased. She lets her gaze rest on each face, and when she gets to me, I feel the full force of her eyes. It is as if I am the only one there, and it reminds me of the feeling I get when I go to visit Dr. Mulligan. The woman's smile widens.

"Dr. Mulligan told me she was hoping to send an addition to our group," she said. "My name is Heather. You must be Clara."

I nod. I am not playing a game this time, refusing to talk. My mouth has gone so dry that I cannot fathom forcing words up my throat and past my lips.

Heather smiles at me, and I believe the kindness in her voice when she says, "I'm so glad that you're here, Clara." She instructs the rest of the girls to introduce themselves, which they do, some more grudgingly than others. I do not commit the names to memory. I don't know if I will be back or not. The only one I remember is Tori.

"Clara, do you want to tell us anything about yourself before we get started?" My opinion of Heather sours. I draw my knees to my chest and shake my head. Instead of pushing me to talk, as I expect, she simply nods. "No pressure here, Clara. If you just want to listen, that's fine. We're just glad you're here." She turns to the girl in the chair next to her, a girl with blond hair and wide, haunted green eyes. "Then Mallory, I believe you were ready to talk today."

Mallory takes a deep breath and looks around the circle. Everyone has leaned in. I am impressed at the concentration on their faces. Even those who seem surly are focused on Mallory, as if what she has to say is the most important thing in the world. Dr. Mulligan did not tell me much about this group, and I wish she had filled me in on how to behave. I lower my feet to the floor and turn toward Mallory. Her eyes shift toward my movements, and our gazes meet as she begins speaking.

"I was a sophomore in college." Mallory's voice is hesitant at first. She continues watching me, and I feel an urge to protect her, comfort her in the same way I do my daughters. I give her an encouraging smile and a nod as she continues.

"I studied a lot. I had a scholarship I needed to keep. My friends would make fun of me for not going out with them every weekend, but I preferred to hang out at coffee shops around the city." Mallory smiles. "I would pick a different one each Friday and spend hours studying my books and the people.

"One Friday, I was checking out another new coffee place. It was in a nice area of the city. I was tired and had just finished midterms, and I was also recovering from a fight with my roommate because I didn't want to go out dancing." Mallory shakes her head. "What a stupid thing, right? But I was feeling rebellious. So when Eric approached me, I invited him to sit down instead of sending him away like I usually did with guys.

"Eric was older, and seemed so worldly. He bought me coffee, and we talked until the shop closed at two in the morning. I was worried about catching the last bus, and he offered me a ride home."

Mallory pauses, and I notice my heart is racing. I have been watching closely as she shares. Her eyes are dull and her face is losing color. She is completely caught up in the story. So am I.

"It was stupid. But I agreed. He said he didn't live far from campus and invited me to hang out with him and his roommates for a while. My friends had been texting all night, so I sent a quick text telling them not to wait up." A tear escapes from the corner of Mallory's eye, but she ignores it. Her posture stiffens, and I see her walls go up as she relates the next part of the story.

"We drove in the opposite direction of campus. I laughed and asked if he'd had too much coffee, but he didn't answer me. I got nervous, but he wouldn't turn around. We went to one of the rougher parts of town and he pulled up behind another car. He told me to get out. I didn't. I begged him to take me home. Another man got out of the car in front of us and came to my door. Eric pushed me out the door. I tried to run, but the other man grabbed me and threw me on the ground. I hit my head and blacked out. When I woke up, I was in the trunk of a car. The music was blaring. I can still smell the smoke and rot. They had taken my shoes, and my hands and ankles were duct-taped together." Mallory closes her eyes.

I do not want to hear any more. I do not know what Dr. Mulligan was thinking sending me here. What do I have in common with Mallory, who was taken so brutally from her life? I want nothing to do with this story. I tense, ready to bolt, when Mallory's eyes open and find mine again, and I am rooted to my chair. I cannot leave when she is watching me, when she looks at me with such vulnerability. It's as if she is taking strength from me. I look at her and I see my daughters. I relax back into my chair, wiping the panicked look off my face. I mimic Dr. Mulligan, who is a master at looking neutral yet supportive at all times.

Mallory takes a deep breath. "I pounded on the trunk, but no one responded. I doubt they could hear me. There was no lever to pull to escape the trunk. I had read somewhere that if you were in a trunk, you should kick out one of the taillights and wave your arm. I kicked and kicked, but I couldn't dislodge the lights. It wasn't easy since I was taped up, and I think I broke a toe or two. I didn't care. I was in a panic.

"The car stopped, and when the trunk opened I was surprised that it was daylight. I don't know how long I was passed out. The man who had taken me was even more terrifying in the light. Scars on his face . . . and he was huge. He threw me over his shoulder like I weighed nothing. We were in the middle of nowhere, by a long tin building. I didn't see much. Inside, there were wide doors that opened like garage doors. It turned out they were storage sheds. There were many more men inside, and one of them opened one of the sheds. The man carrying me threw me onto a dirty mattress and left."

Heather leans over and clasps Mallory's hand. "Are you doing okay, Mallory?" she asks. "You can take a break if you need to."

Mallory nods. "I-I think I could use some water."

I need water, too. And space. Everyone moves back, some retreating into their private worlds, others lapsing back into conversation. I jerk to my feet. No one pays attention. Heather is murmuring softly to Mallory. Tori has gone to get Mallory some water. I step toward the door. No one stops me as I slip out.

In the hallway, I lean against the wall and slide to the floor. I hit my head against the hard surface in rhythm to the thoughts swirling through my head. I place my hand on my stomach, almost imagining I feel flutters, though I know it is too soon for that. As always, Nut calms me. No matter what is going on out here, I know he is safe and sound, and will never be away from me. He is mine.

"How's it going?"

I start. I forgot that Connor was waiting for me in the hallway. I don't know how I missed him when I came out here. I look over at him, and his forehead is wrinkled in concern.

"Why am I here?" I ask, ignoring his question. "This has nothing to do with me."

"You've hardly been in there, Clara," Connor says, his tone gentle. "Give these girls a chance."

"A chance for what? To tell sad stories? To try to get me to tell my sad story? What is it with everyone wanting to know my business? It's my business! My life!" I slap the floor for emphasis.

Connor doesn't react. He watches me for a few minutes. "You promised Dr. Mulligan you would try."

"I am trying."

"No, you're not. You're ready to quit."

He's not wrong. I want to go back to my tiny gray room, or to Dr. Mulligan's office, or even back to the dreaded questioning room. Anywhere but back into the room to hear the rest of Mallory's story.

"All you have to do is listen," Connor says. "Just listen, Clara." It is not a command. It's a request. I sigh and nod as Heather sticks her head out into the hall.

"There you are, Clara," she says, smiling. "Are you coming back in?" Another question, and an opportunity to refuse. Instead, I scramble to my feet.

"Yes." I follow her back inside, glancing back once to catch Connor with a pensive look on his face, which changes to an encouraging smile when he sees me watching. The door shuts behind me before I can acknowledge him again.

Mallory starts where she left off as soon as we are seated.

"I don't know how long I was in that dark storage unit. I cried until I couldn't anymore. I peed myself because no one came to take me to the bathroom. My feet and hands were numb. I hadn't eaten in hours. I thought I would die there on that ratty mattress, alone in the dark. Finally, the door opened. A group of women came in and turned on a light. They didn't talk to me, but they untaped me and undressed me, cleaned me up as best they could. They put a robe on me and helped me across the hall to a makeshift office. A doctor . . . examined me." Mallory pauses. Her entire body is locked up, and her knuckles are white. Heather doesn't interrupt, doesn't ask if she needs another break.

"Another man, Mike, was watching the whole time. When the doctor finished with me, he brought me to another area. It looked like a warehouse. There were three other girls there, naked. Mike took my robe and pushed me over to them. He sprayed us down. After that we were given short shirts to wear, and nothing else. They brought us back to the hallway with the storage lockers. I was put in one with two other women."

I feel a soft brush against my fisted hand. Tori has moved to sit next to me. She places her hand over mine, using gentle pressure to urge me to relax. My fingers release, and I see that I have left red crescents on my palm. One has started bleeding. Tori says nothing, but leaves her hand on mine, offering me comfort. I don't know this girl. But I allow it. I'm not sure why Mallory's story is affecting me so strongly. It has nothing to do with me. Still, I focus on Tori's warming presence and tune back in to Mallory's story.

"It was only a few days before they took me out for the first time. They had a special van for outside runs. Sex for delivery. There were several different jobs, but the first was always to a high-paying john who wanted a virgin. My first was at least fifty years old. We went to some posh hotel. I didn't even fight back. It hurt. And I didn't fight." Mallory hangs her head, tears falling unchecked into her lap.

"And you still feel guilty for that?" Heather asks, her voice low.

Mallory nods. "If I had fought, maybe I could have gotten away. Maybe I could have run for help. Maybe I wouldn't be living this fucking half existence now." She pulls her knees to her chest, sobbing.

I jump when Tori's voice next to me breaks the silence. "I tried to run away once," she says. "I mean, most of you know my story is a little different. They kept me in a house in the middle of a city." She looks at me, guessing that I am the only one who doesn't know this. "I passed up so many opportunities that I thought I could have escaped. Finally I tried it."

Mallory doesn't speak, but she has raised her head, chin resting on her knees.

Tori locks eyes with Mallory. "What did they do to girls who tried to escape?"

"Ice bath." Mallory's voice is mechanical. No more tears fall. "Hours in an ice bath. Girls died sometimes. But it didn't leave marks."

Tori nods. "The ones who took me didn't care about marks. They caught me and beat me until I wished I was dead. I got two days off before I had to service the johns again. You were right not to run, Mallory."

I can tell that Mallory wants to believe Tori, but the doubt lingers in her eyes. I feel like I've been through the emotional wringer. I don't understand why Dr. Mulligan thinks a group like this will help. My life is nothing like these tragic stories. I have a beautiful house. I have a beautiful family. I have Glen. I've traveled. I am not tortured. Only disciplined when necessary. There is a big difference.

"I think that's enough for today, ladies," Heather says, wrapping an arm around Mallory's shoulders. "Please stay and visit."

I stand, knocking Tori's hand away from my arm.

"Clara," Tori begins.

I give her a tight smile and stride toward the door. Connor jumps up as I slam out of the room. "Finished? Ready to talk to Dr. Mulligan?"

"No." I am vibrating with anger. "I just want to go back to my room."

Connor's smile falters. "I thought you had a session today."

"Not anymore." I never want to speak to her again.

Then

It is late afternoon, and the sun slants through the windows of the parlor. Glen is tense beside me as we drink tea in silence. The source of his tension is the imposing man across from us. Glen's parents insist on gathering us all together each afternoon. Our betrothal was announced to the house two weeks ago. I do not know what happened with my client, Mr. Q. Two girls were sent in my place, but I am unsure what other compensation he was given.

The discussions in the parlor usually surround our future, the hard work we will need to put in, how much training we both need for our respective roles. When we speak at all. Most of the time is spent in terse silence, the weight of Papa's judgment feeling like a ten-ton brick, pushing us further into submission.

And yet, even thinking the word "us" causes me to sit up a little straighter. Despite the judgment, despite being worked morning until night, the end result is the same. I will be with Glen. We do not have to be apart. Ever.

Papa is still glaring over the rim of his cup when the door bursts open. One of the older men, Scott, stomps in, dragging a girl by the arm. Her hair is loose, swinging around her face, and with her free arm she is struggling to hold a shirt in front of herself. She is otherwise naked. She looks up and our eyes meet.

It is Macy.

I jump to my feet, my teacup crashing to the floor, splintering into a thousand shards that could just as well be piercing my heart. What has she done? Glen's hand is on my arm, restraining me, but I struggle against him. Macy's grip on the shirt is slipping, and soon she will be completely uncovered. I can't let my friend be presented to Papa like that.

"Stop," Glen whispers, his voice harsh as he holds me back. "Do not get involved. Do you understand?"

Papa stands as well, though Mama continues to sit and sip her tea as if nothing is amiss. I wonder if I will ever adopt that uncaring attitude. I hope not. Papa's eyes narrow as he observes the pair. Two more guards step in behind Scott and Macy, each loosely holding the arm of a boy who is not struggling. Macy's secret boyfriend, Josh, appears unconcerned. His chest is bare, his pants unbuttoned. His long feet, shoeless, are white from lack of sun.

"What's going on?" Papa asks, his voice calm despite the storm I see brewing on his face.

"Found this *girl*," Scott sneered, "entertaining Josh during afternoon break." He jerked Macy forward. "From what I hear, she's been entertaining him pretty frequently."

I hear a small gasp, but when I look over at Mama, her face is smooth again, the slight shake in her teacup the only indication that she is rattled. And with good reason. Macy is promised to another important client. I had my suspicions about Macy's activities, but I had hoped she was just fooling around. Her client would not be happy if he found out she'd been making out with another boy, but it wouldn't be a deal-breaker. But if she's been having sex with Josh, if she is no longer pure, that is unforgivable, and could cast a bad light on Papa's entire business. Part of what our clients pay for, what they expect, is that they will be our first experience. A buzzing begins in my ears as the implications of the situation begin to sink in.

Papa's fists clench. He picks up the teapot and hurls it across the room. It smashes against the far wall, tea splattering over the furniture and wall hangings. I jump, and Glen squeezes my arm. I no longer struggle against him. I am frozen in place, terrified of what will come next.

Papa strides forward and grasps Macy's chin, forcing her face up. She whimpers, but maintains eye contact. "You want to be a whore, little girl?" Papa hisses. Now his voice has become angry. "You were meant for great things. But giving yourself to this boy has sealed your fate." He looks up. "Take her to the tree," he says, nodding at Scott. He turns to Josh, who still has a self-satisfied look on his face. "I'll deal with you later," Papa says. "Personally." Josh's smirk disappears as Scott yanks Macy out of the room.

My hand flies to my mouth. The tree is where they whip the boys. When I was whipped, Mama did it on the back porch, away from prying eyes. The tree is in the middle of the men's camp. Whipping is a spectator sport for them. Tears fill my eyes, and Glen's hand is cutting off the circulation to the bottom part of my arm.

"You two," Papa says, not turning around. "You will come down as well."

"Now G—" Mama begins.

"Mae." There is a warning in Papa's voice. "This is a part of it. These children think they are ready to take on all the responsibilities? They need to know what comes with it."

I do not want to go. I want to run away. I want to hide in my room. I want to find the real Macy and laugh over the mistake, cluck our tongues over the poor girl who made such atrocious choices. I want to huddle in the safety of Glen's arms, block out the terrible things that are about to happen.

"Now." There is no question of disobeying. Glen detaches his vise grip on my arm and claims my hand instead. We follow Papa outside and through the trees to where the men's cabins are located. I do not look at Glen. I am not sure what I want to see. Do I want to see him scared? Worried about Macy? Or do I want to see the strength, the resolve it will take to do what needs to be done? Glen knows what Macy means to me.

By the time we reach the tree, Macy has already been lashed to the trunk, her only article of clothing in a heap several feet away. Even from where we are, I can see her shoulders shaking, her barriers down. Papa stops at the edge of the circle and lifts his chin. Scott turns, raises his arm, and brings a branch down hard against the tender skin of Macy's back. The switch whistles as it falls again and again. I close my eyes.

An arm snakes around my waist, pulling me from Glen. Papa's other arm comes to my forehead, lifting the skin so it is difficult to keep my eyes closed. His breath tickles against my ear. "Don't you dare look away, Clara," he says, voice low enough that I'm not sure Glen even hears. "This could have been your fate if it weren't for my son. This is how we maintain order, stay in control. Without consequences, there would be chaos."

Tears stream from my eyes, but I cannot look away. After several minutes, Papa removes his hand from my forehead and calls for Scott to stop, and I wince as my eardrum pulses, but I sag in relief that it is over.

"Glen," Papa says. My head swings to look at Glen. I see panic in his eyes before he shutters the emotion and looks at his father with bored nonchalance.

"Yeah."

"Take over for Scott."

I see Glen's jaw clench, and his eyes dart to mine. I plead with him through my expression to refuse, not to inflict more pain on Macy, who has long since stopped making noise, slumped against the thick tree trunk. He looks back at his father, and whatever he sees in Papa G's expression seals his decision. He stands up straighter and, without another glance at me, strides out to take the branch that Scott holds out to him.

"Watch, Clara, as my son becomes the man he was always meant to be," Papa says, pride evident in his voice. "Don't you dare look away."

It is like seeing a horrible accident. I cannot stand to watch, and I cannot look away. I see my Glen, my sweet, funny, easygoing Glen, transform before me. His swings start out tentative but become more aggressive as he gains confidence. The look on Glen's face terrifies me, and for the first time I wonder how much I know about the boy I have pledged my life to. And the man he is becoming.

Now

The carpet in Dr. Mulligan's office looks like a forest up close. I study it carefully, just as carefully as I ignore the good doctor. She has been sitting quite patiently since I came in. I had not planned on coming back, but Jay showed up this morning and announced that I didn't get a choice. I may not have a choice to be here, but I do have a choice to speak. It's my old trick, but it has served me well. Dr. Mulligan disagrees.

"Are you playing this game again, Clara?" she asks, and I am surprised that her voice sounds just as calm as her face appears. "I know you're good at it, but it hasn't gotten you out of anything in the long run."

True. But for now it's the best I can do. I pluck a long blond hair from the carpet. It doesn't match mine or Dr. Mulligan's. It hasn't occurred to me until now that she might see other people. Of course she does. She does such a good job of treating me like the most important person in the world when I am in here. Certainly she cannot do that for everyone who crosses her threshold. I flick the hair away and sit up from where I am sprawled on the floor. My notebook lies on the coffee table, but I have yet to break the seal from last time.

I fiddle with the tape, pleased to see that as betrayed as I feel by Dr. Mulligan, she still hasn't read what I've written.

"Connor said you were upset after the group. I understand it's a lot to take in, but I think it will be beneficial for you to get to know those girls."

A laugh bubbles up from deep in my belly, but not a laugh of amusement. A lot to take in? She thinks it will be beneficial? A volcano of anger erupts after the laughter and I snap. "Beneficial? I am *nothing* like those girls. If you find a group of wives torn from their husbands and daughters and wrongfully imprisoned, I would be more than happy to attend."

Dr. Mulligan raises an eyebrow. "I'm sure you could find stories like that at the prison."

The blood leaves my face. I know it's not a threat, but the memory still bothers me. "I am nothing like them, either," I mutter.

"Then who are you like?"

What kind of question is that? "I am like me. I am me."

"Have you met anyone else like you? In similar circumstances?"

Genevieve's face pops into my head. My hands begin to shake. I shove them under myself, but Dr. Mulligan sees everything. It is why she is so good at her job.

"Who were you just remembering, Clara?" Her voice is gentle, curious.

I shake my head. I will not speak. South Dakota never happened. But it did. And Genevieve, who represented a future I may have had if not for Glen . . . I cannot finish the thought. The words are spilling out before I can stop them. "There was a woman, Genevieve. She was . . . special in her house. The same way I am special to Glen, except I think Genevieve was more a possession. We met once. She took care of her girls, though they were older. She was bitter, but there was a connection. Shared circumstances." I pause, sifting my thoughts.

"She was like the dark version of me. Who I could have been. Who I wanted to avoid becoming."

Dr. Mulligan should play poker. I watched the men play sometimes at the house. The biggest winners never gave anything away. I brace myself for a strong reaction. More questions like Connor might ask, about how or where I had met Genevieve. Instead, her expression smooth, she asks, "Where is Genevieve now?"

Without answering, I break the seal and open my notebook. The subject is closed. I will not answer any more questions, and Dr. Mulligan does not try to ask any more. I am proud. I managed to bring up a painful memory and keep my promise to Glen. I never mentioned South Dakota.

Swirling my pen around a fresh page of the notebook, I let my mind wander. My entire reality shifted when I learned I was pregnant. A pinpoint of light in the darkness of my present life. Every therapy session, every hour in the questioning room, has been focused on the past. Who I was. What I did. Beyond knowing that my future must include Glen, I have given little thought to what it will look like, how it might be different now that our baby will be there with us. My haphazard swirls begin to take the shape of words, and my pen races across the page.

At the end of the hour, I close my notebook. I finished a letter to Nut, and as I was writing, I realized that I don't want to give them any reason to keep me here longer than necessary. My son will not be born in captivity. I will cooperate and put on a shiny face. They will never know the difference. When Jay knocks on the door, I stand and hand my notebook to Dr. Mulligan. "I think I will go back to the group."

Then

I wander into the parlor a few minutes early for my training meeting with Mama. Today's lesson is to be on appropriate punishments, and I am dreading it. Though I have been taking a larger role in training, Mama still doesn't trust that I can actually control any of the girls. What she doesn't understand is that they don't need to be controlled. They listen to me because I listen to them. I wonder how Mama would react if I asked to give *her* a lesson. I smirk as I imagine what creative punishment she would find for such a suggestion. I long for the day when Glen and I will be married and have our own group. Things will be much different when we are in charge.

A tall figure blocks the window as I walk through the doorway, and I stop short. Papa stands, waiting, hands clasped behind him as he gazes out at the mountains. "Close the door, Clara," he says, and I comply immediately, stunned that he has addressed me by my name, something that has not happened since Glen and I became engaged.

Wringing my hands, I stand in the center of the room. A quick glance tells me that I am alone with Papa. It feels weird, wrong. Papa is always around, but Mama is always close by. We all know that Papa is in charge, but Mama serves as a sort of buffer, protecting us from the worst of him.

"Please sit, Clara," Papa says, shifting from his spot at the window. He hasn't looked at me yet, but his voice is pleasant, not the gruff bark I am used to. In some ways this version of Papa is more intimidating, because I don't know what to expect.

He moves to the liquor cabinet in the corner and pours himself a small amount of amber liquid. He is rarely without some sort of drink in his hand these days. Mama's face usually takes on a pinched look when she sees him drinking, but she says nothing. I force my eyes away from the glass before he turns to face me. Mostly we just pretend the drinks don't exist.

I lower myself onto the small settee, perching on the edge, ready to run if necessary. It would be stupid to do so, but I like to keep my options open. Papa takes his time swirling his drink in his glass before finally turning to me.

"I suppose you're wondering why I've interrupted your normal training time, Clara."

The sound of my own name is starting to grate on my nerves, but I only give a small smile and a nod. Always agreeable.

Papa takes my nod as agreement and makes his way to the chair Mama usually occupies. His large frame looks ridiculous on the spindly-legged chair, like a giant trying to sit on a child's chair, but I maintain my composure. I make a mental note to describe the scene for Macy later, but my stomach drops when I remember that Macy isn't around to share these things anymore. I usually do a better job of compartmentalizing this information, only taking it out and examining it in the dark hours of the night, when I can cry in the room we once shared with no questions or interruptions.

My distress must show on my face, but thankfully Papa takes it as anxiety over his presence here. I am brought back to the present situation as he speaks again.

"There's nothing to be worried about, Clara." I'm not so sure. There is always something to be worried about when it comes to Papa. "Mama Mae and I have decided that you are at the point in your training where you should truly understand where your sisters and future daughters come from, and why they have been offered the opportunity to train here for their futures."

My heart speeds up in my chest. We are forbidden to talk about our lives before coming to live with Mama and Papa. I've been here so long I don't remember my life before, but for the occasional flash of memory or feeling of déjà vu.

"As you know," Papa says, "the men and I go out on scouting trips quite often. We search for young men and women who are in bad situations, where they have been hurt or are unwanted. We rescue them and offer them a better life."

I lean forward. "Do . . . do they want to come with you?" I flinch, expecting to be berated for my question.

Papa chuckles. "Most of the time, no, Clara, and that is an excellent question. I know you've seen the girls come in here, kicking and screaming, wanting to go home." He pauses for a drink, contemplating. "These children don't know what's best for them, Clara. They fear what they don't know, and all they know is fear. That's where we come in. Mama, and now you, with your girls, and Glen and me with the boys. We teach them skills, give them chances they would never have otherwise. Our work is very important." He looks at me, waiting for my agreement.

I grow cold at his words, and I gnaw on my lip as I consider the question I am burning to ask. It will probably make him angry, and he has been so pleasant, I don't want to ruin it.

Setting aside his now-empty glass, Papa leans forward, the chair creaking under his shifting weight. "What is it, Clara? Do you not agree that we offer these young people a better life? A better future?"

I nod, a subtle lift of my chin.

"You aren't convinced." There's an edge to Papa's voice. He stands and walks to refill his glass.

"It's not that," I say, rushing my words to prevent an eruption. "You and Mama have given my sisters and me everything, and trained us well. I am grateful, and I know my sisters are as well."

He leans against the wall, swirling his drink. "But?"

"But . . . I just wonder . . . What about the other girls? The ones who get sent away from here? Who don't complete their training?" *Like Macy.*

A slow smile spreads across Papa's face as understanding comes to his eyes. "Ah. Yes. Those girls." He walks back to where I am seated, but does not reclaim his chair. "You see, Clara, sometimes we get children from families that are broken beyond repair. Poisoned. It's in their very blood, and it comes out eventually. We don't want to send them back to those families from whom they were rescued, but they are not suitable for our program here, either. So they go elsewhere."

"To do what?"

Papa's eyes slice to mine, heating. I am trying his patience, but I must know.

"What did Macy ever do, Papa? She worked hard. She made a mistake. She—"

The glass shatters against the door of the parlor, the remaining liquid dripping down over the glittering shards. Papa braces himself on the arms of my chair and leans in close.

"Macy was a little slut. We assure our clients that all girls come to them pure and innocent. Macy was none of those things. Macy went where you would have gone if my son weren't so idiotically besotted with you." His breath is hot on my cheek as I turn my face away, cowering as deep in the chair as I can get. "You will never mention that girl to me again, or ask any more questions about her, or you may find out firsthand what became of her."

The parlor door flies open, and Mama rushes in. "Glen Lawson, Senior, what on earth is going on in here?"

Papa straightens, smoothing out the wrinkles in his jacket that his outburst caused. "Just finishing up, Mae," he says. "I think Clara and I are on the same page now." He turns to me. "Any further questions can be directed to Mama." Without another word, he stalks out the door.

Mama bustles out of the room and is back in seconds with a broom. "Go get the mop, Clara. Let's get this cleaned up before the entire room smells like bourbon."

My limbs unfreeze and I force myself to stand and do as I am told. Mama and I clean in silence. She does not ask what happened, and I am not planning to volunteer any information. Even thinking about Macy hurts, and I know I must put her away in the darkest recesses of my memories, at least for now.

When we finish, Mama shoos me away to help the younger girls with their lessons, but I don't miss the concerned look on her face. I pray I have not ruined everything already.

Now

I am immersed in a book on giving birth when Jay walks in. I'm surprised to see him. The next group is not until tomorrow, and there was not supposed to be any questioning today. I raise an eyebrow at him.

"You have a visitor," he says, his voice cautious. "You can send her away if you want."

"Her?"

"Glen's mother is back."

Instinctively, I place a hand over where Nut grows. I wonder if Glen has told her the news. Of course he has. That is why she's here. I am not sure if I want to see her. I hadn't thought of this before. Will Mama try to have control over my son? I want him to know his grandmother, but only if that is the role she chooses to fulfill. There will have to be clear expectations about how much say Mama will have in our son's life. I'm not sure it's a conversation I'm ready for today, but the possibility that she will bring news of Glen is too tempting to dismiss.

I stand. "I will see her."

Jay nods and leads the way out of the room. I am not cuffed this time, not even when he drops me off in the visiting room. Mama and I are alone again. She stands as I enter and moves forward to embrace me. I'm shocked as her arms come around me. If we are supposed to be playing strangers, why is she hugging me on our second visit?

"It's all right, dear," Mama says, loud enough for those listening in to hear. "Glen told me about the baby. We are family forever now."

Forever. I had planned forever with Glen. Forever sounds so long when Mama says it, though I've always assumed she would be around. She always has been. I give her an awkward pat on the back, and we sit on the molded plastic chairs across from each other.

"Hello again, Mrs. Lawson."

"Please, call me Mae," Mama says, her eyes bright.

"Mae. What can I do for you today?"

Mama laughs. "I just wanted to come to visit my grandbaby." She leans back, studying me. "Are they feeding you enough? You look thin. I can't even see a bump."

I try not to be offended. I am more confused by this version of Mama. She seems more shrill than she did before, and I wonder if she has taken something. "My pants are getting a little tight, but there is no noticeable bump yet," I say. "The doctor says I will really start to pop when I reach the second trimester."

Mama nods. "I showed late with my babies, too."

I do not like hearing her compare herself to me. I smile anyway. "When did you talk to Glen?"

"A few days ago. He's looking better. He credits you for his recovery. He is fighting again, determined to get out and help you raise that baby."

Pride bubbles inside of me. I knew telling Glen about Nut was a good plan. My confidence grows. We will make it through this. We will be a family. They cannot take this son away from me as they have stolen my daughters. He is mine. "Is his lawyer good?" I dare to ask.

I see the disapproval in Mama's eyes. I am not supposed to ask these questions, but I do not shrink away. Mama holds no power over me in this place. She cannot say or do anything to reprimand me, and it is a perfectly logical question to ask the mother of the man I love.

"The best I could get," Mama says, her voice colder. "It wasn't easy to secure someone willing to defend him in a case like this."

My forehead wrinkles. Lots of people get lawyers to defend them for murder. And the kidnapping charges will never stick once they figure out what really happened. "A case like what?"

Mama laughs. "You are so smart, Clara, but so naïve."

I ignore her dig and press for more information. "Will he be released?"

"I don't know, child. I really don't know."

I want to know more, but instead I allow Mama to babble about baby clothes and the things I will need to stock up on before transitioning into stories about Glen when he was a baby. It should be a natural conversation from one mother to another, but it feels forced, and I am grateful when Jay walks in. "Time's up, Mrs. Lawson. Let's go, Clara."

Mama doesn't stand to give me a hug this time. She remains seated, a troubled look on her face. I notice the lines around her eyes have deepened, and for the first time I begin to question whether Glen will ever be free. Or if I will.

Then

Mama smooths the veil in front of my face and turns me toward the mirror. I gasp at the stranger reflected back at me. The veil is thin enough that I can see through it, but it casts everything around me into a dreamlike haze. My dress is simple, white, and lace-covered. It falls just past my knees. The sleeves are long, but the straight neckline leaves my shoulders uncovered. My feet will remain bare for the outdoor ceremony. My long dark hair cascades in a smooth sheet down my back. The veil is attached to a hat and falls just over the top half of my face. When it is lifted, a line of pearls around the rim of the hat will be revealed. Another strand of pearls is my only other jewelry. I do not even wear an engagement ring. I never received one, though that will change today. I find myself in the familiar green eyes shining with excitement from behind the veil.

Today is my eighteenth birthday, and the day I finally join my life with Glen's. Officially, anyway. For me, we have been joined since the night we ran away together. My entire body floods with delicious anticipation. Today we pledge in front of others what we pledged to each other more than two years ago. Today we move into our own small cabin, built by Glen and some of the guys. Tonight . . . I thrill at the thought. Tonight we become one in every sense of the word.

I am nervous and excited all at once. This is the day I have been dreaming of. Even before Glen and I ran away, Macy and I would stay up late, giggling and talking about what it would be like to get married, have a wedding, be able to be with a soul mate. Of course, we always realized how blessed we were that we would be well taken care of, but it was fun to dream a little.

The thought of Macy makes my heart heavy. I still don't know what happened to her, though rumors about where problem girls are sent run rampant through the house. She was carted off after her whipping. The one time I brought up her name to Glen, I was sure he would hit me. I think he was ashamed of what his father forced him to do. He apologized for overreacting, but I have never brought up the topic again, as curious as I am.

Mama snaps her fingers in my face, bringing me back to the present. She is trying to hand me my flowers. "What is wrong with you, girl?" she asks. It stings. Papa is the one who calls me "that girl." Mama has always been more tolerant. But today she has been a beast.

The ceremony is small, just my sisters and some of Papa's men and Glen's friends. His men, I suppose. The ones who will be in his future workforce. Joel stands up next to him as I walk toward him. We are saying our vows by the small copse of trees where Glen first kissed me. Of course, we do not tell his parents why we chose that spot. It is our secret.

I glance across from Glen and almost stop in my tracks. Standing by him in a simple peach frock is Macy. At least . . . I think it is Macy. She looks much older, and much thinner. Nothing like the bubbly girl I knew. Still, my face breaks into a smile. She smiles back, but it does not reach her eyes. I hug her as I come to the front of the group, briefly concerned over how fragile she feels.

"Mace," I whisper. "You're here." It's just like my dreams coming true, like what we fantasized about when we were younger.

"I'm here," Macy says, reaching a hand to run down my hair. "And you're getting married, just like we always talked about." Her eyes shine with moisture, and I am touched that she can be so happy for me despite her circumstances. It amazes me that even after being apart for almost two years, Macy and I are on the same wavelength. Soul sisters.

A throat clears behind me, so I pull Macy into another quick hug and then turn my focus on Glen. His eyes are shining.

"Thank you," I murmur, knowing that he is the one who managed this surprise. I also understand why Mama has been so testy today. Seeing one of her failures paraded in front of her cannot be easy. And she also considers me a failure, since I did not fulfill my original purpose. Still, it would be nice if she could be happy on her son's wedding day.

Glen smiles, squeezing my hand. We turn toward his father, who is officiating the ceremony. I find my attention wandering frequently to the man standing to my right. He has grown up so much in two years. Now twenty years old, he is in charge of his own mini operation, under Papa's careful guidance, of course. We do not talk specifics, but once we are married, I know he will open up more.

When the time comes, I hand my bouquet to Macy and take Glen's other hand. We recite our vows, and he slides a beautiful large diamond onto my finger. He will wear no ring, but I recite my vows and go through the motions of placing one on his finger anyway. The symbolism is beautiful. I belong to him. And though his finger remains naked, I know I have his heart. We kiss, and everyone else disappears as we languish in our small bubble of happiness.

We have a small reception. While Glen laughs with Joel on the other side of the room, I sidle up to Macy. "Hey, Mace." She jumps. "I've missed you."

Macy gives me a small smile. "I've missed you, too, Clare. You look beautiful."

The question burns on my tongue, but I am afraid to ask. Will they take Macy away if I ask? If she answers? I feel Glen's eyes on me, always watching. I paste a giant smile on my face and lower my voice. "Where have you been, Macy? What happened to you?"

Her eyes grow shiny with unshed tears, but she, too, stretches her mouth into a wide fake smile. "I'm not supposed to talk about it. We'll both get in trouble."

I laugh and glance toward Glen. The laser focus of his eyes makes me uncomfortable, as if he knows I am doing something I should not. I raise my glass to toast him and nudge Macy, as if we were talking about him. His face relaxes and he raises his glass in return, holding up one finger to signal that he will be coming over soon. "Quick, Mace, before he gets here. I have to know."

The pain in her eyes is clear, but she speaks, the words rolling over one another to get out of her mouth, so low that I can barely hear. "After the beating, they moved me to a building a couple miles away. Men come and pay for an hour of my time." Papa's brothel, the Tree-house. I have heard of it in passing as I have been learning more about the business side of things, though much of it is still a mystery. Macy shrugs. "That's it."

My face has lost its warmth, and tears spring into my eyes.

"There's my bride!" Glen's voice booms from my left. I take a large drink of champagne, coughing and sputtering as I choke on the bubbly liquid. An easy explanation for the tears and my inability to hold my grin. "Whoa, slow down there, Clare," Glen says, rubbing my back. He wraps an arm around me as the coughing subsides.

"Sorry," I say, taking a deep breath and smiling up at him. "You startled me."

He doesn't believe me, but he lets it go. He turns to Macy. "Macy, it's been a while. Thank you for agreeing to come. It means a lot to both of us."

I do not recognize the tone in Glen's voice. The words are nice, but the tone is almost mocking, with a hint of menace. Macy hears it, too, and shrinks under his glare. "I—I should probably be getting back."

"No, Mace, stay," I say, reaching toward her.

"I need to go," Macy says. She leans forward and gives me a quick hug, which is difficult since Glen does not release me from his grip, and Macy takes special care not to touch him.

"Macy . . ."

"Let her go." Glen's words are a command, and I watch, helpless, as Macy approaches two guards who are waiting for her and disappears into the dark. I do not know if I will see her again. Will I be allowed visits now that I am officially Glen's wife? Now is not the time to ask. "Let's dance, Clara." Glen leads me onto the dance floor and we sway to the gentle music. Thoughts of Macy move to the back of my mind as I curl my body into Glen's, allowing him to pull me close. I am safe here, at home, and happier than I've ever been.

The party doesn't last long. I dance with Glen and Papa, and Joel for one song, but he holds me just a little too close and Glen cuts in. "I think he has a little crush on you. But he's harmless, Clare." Gone is the menacing Glen from earlier. In his place is this teasing, light-hearted man. There is not even a hint of jealousy in his eyes when he mentions Joel having a crush. He seems to trust Joel implicitly.

We kiss Glen's parents good-bye and head for our cabin. *Our* cabin. Mine and Glen's. I hug myself with happiness. Glen grins down at me.

"Excited?" he asks, his voice husky.

"You have no idea," I reply, a coy smile playing at my lips. "I have been waiting for this night for two years."

Glen stops, pulling me to a halt and turning me to face him. He gathers me in his arms, bends down, and presses his lips to mine. It does not take long for the kiss to grow heated, and his tongue teases my lips. We are in the shadows of the trees, completely hidden, but it feels like we are out in the open. He backs me up until I am pressed between the tree and his body, and soon I forget all about where we are. We have gotten heated before, but Glen is more aggressive tonight. Tonight we will not be forced to stop. His hands roam every-where. I moan, and he leads me away.

Neither of us says a word as he grabs my hand and pulls me toward the cabin at a run. Inside, our clothes are gone in seconds. I am hit with a wave of nervousness. Glen has done this before, but I have not. I know the mechanics, but it is different to be here, to be experiencing it.

As he always does, Glen senses the shift in my mood, and he slows, whispering words of encouragement, of love. And when we come together it is as natural as breathing. As natural as being with Glen always has been. We become one, body and soul, and nothing can separate us now.

Now

My stomach flutters as I walk down the hallway toward the group room. The doctor claims it is too early for me to feel Nut moving, but I think he's telling me he is here for me. That he isn't going anywhere. My tense muscles relax. Connor follows, silent. He has been strangely subdued lately. I want to ask him how the case is going, but I'm afraid of the answer. I am starting to feel guilty for being so unhelpful. It's strange that I should want to help him when his goals and mine are polar opposites. Still, I wish there were a way for both of us to be happy. I have come to believe that he does want good things for me, that he does care about me. But I cannot help him.

The door is propped open, and a few of the girls are already there. I walk over to the refreshment table and grab a bottle of water.

"Hey." I jump when I hear a voice close beside me. I turn to find Tori smiling at me.

"Hello."

"Clara, right?"

I nod.

"I'm Tori."

"I remember."

My short answers do not discourage her. "I wanted to talk to you more last time, but you flew out of here pretty fast."

"I wasn't feeling well."

She frowns. "I'm sorry. I hope you're better now?"

"Much. Thank you." I toy with my water bottle, wondering when it is appropriate to leave the conversation and find a seat.

"Well, listen," Tori says. "I wanted to let you know that I'm here to talk if you need it. I mean, I know you're in therapy and all, but if you ever want to talk to someone who's been in kind of the same place as you, I'm here for you."

I raise an eyebrow. "I'm not sure what you mean by being in the same place."

Her brow furrows. "You know, why we're all here."

"No offense," I say—fully aware that I will probably offend her; that's why people say "no offense"—"but I really don't have anything in common with you all. I don't know what you've heard about me, or my husband, but we were happy until agents came and stole our lives. I'm only here because I am doing whatever I can to get out before my baby is born."

I wait for the backlash, for the yelling, for the harsh words. Instead, Tori gives a small smile. "Yep," she says. "I've been there, too." I watch her walk to the circle, which is now almost full. I am more confused than ever.

Heather runs in late again, taking a seat next to a stick-thin girl with a dark, pixie-cut hairstyle. "Good afternoon, ladies," she says. "I believe Erin is going to share today, unless there's something pressing anyone else wants to bring up?" She looks at everyone, but I feel her gaze heavy on me. I avoid her eyes, staring at a spot over her shoulder instead. "Okay then, Erin, are you ready?"

The pixie girl clears her throat. Tattoos snake up her neck and down her arms, and a spike protrudes from her eyebrow. She's dressed in dark clothes, and I realize for the first time that these girls are not kept here like me. I'm not sure how I missed it before. They must come voluntarily from the outside. A wave of jealousy hits me, followed by a new resolve to gain my own freedom. And soon.

"I'm not like y'all," Erin begins. "I wasn't kidnapped or forced to do anything. I knew exactly what I was doing."

Heather nods. "We all have different stories. But you're here for a reason, Erin, and you wanted to share, so I'm guessing there's more to it than that."

Erin nods. "I guess I should say I *thought* I knew exactly what I was doing. See, I didn't grow up in the nicest home. My daddy drank, and he was a mean drunk. I was the oldest, and as soon as I was tall enough I started standing between him and my ma. She wouldn't stand up for herself. When I was twelve, I'd had enough. I went after him with a knife. Nicked him pretty good, but he survived. Lucky bastard."

My hands curl into fists where they rest on my knees. The look on her face reminds me of how I felt when I shot Joel. Murderous and wistful at the same time.

"Anyway, I took off. I don't know what happened to either of them. They didn't come looking for me. I was on the street for a few weeks when I ran into a crew led by a guy named Brady. Brady took me in, gave me food. Even better, he gave me drugs. All the drugs I wanted. I was high for weeks. When I finally came down, it was hell. I begged the guy for more, and he told me that I had to earn it and pay him back for what I'd already used. And I was more than willing. I started sleeping with guys we knew, others in the crew, who would score me drugs.

Soon, though, Brady started bringing guys back who we didn't know. Or he would hand me a paper with hotel information on it and I would go there. As long as I was high, I didn't care. I got beat up more than once."

Erin relates all of this without emotion. Just the facts. I am not as drawn in by it as I had been by Mallory's story. It sounds like Erin deserved what she got. At least she had a home. She chose to leave. The street and drugs weren't her only option.

"What changed?" Heather asks. "You are also different in that you came for help yourself. You didn't wait to be rescued."

"Damn, girl, if I'd waited to be rescued, I'd still be sleeping with ten losers a night. No, I walked into a shelter one day for a meal. Brady usually provided food, but he was out on some errand and I was hungry. There were these people sitting with the homeless bums, just talking to them, listening to them. I sat near a guy and he was talking about his family, how disappointed they'd be with where he was. The lady listening to him asked what he would say if he could see them again. I don't remember his answer, but it got me thinking. What if someone cared that much about me? What if I had a family I cared about? Brady only cared about the money I brought in. I really only cared about the drugs. I walked up to one of the volunteers and asked for help. That was a year ago. I'd been doing it for three years."

A year? She looks so young. I do the math. She's probably only sixteen or so. Almost Passion's age. I feel sick as I imagine Passion doing drugs and having sex with strange men in seedy hotels. I would never let that happen. I saved her from that sort of future. I wonder if that's what will happen if they don't find a place for her to stay. I make a mental note to ask Connor about her again.

I am overwhelmed with sadness as Macy's face fills my mind. She was this girl's age when she was moved to the brothel. Sure, the brothel was better than the streets, but it still hurts my heart to think about her. It takes everything in me to move her out of my mind again.

Heather is asking Erin more questions. "Where do you live now, Erin?"

"Group home," Erin says, shrugging. "I'm a little old, but they're hoping to find a foster family to take me in. For now, I'm just attending these sessions and hoping to feel normal again someday. Or normal for the first time."

"What is normal?" Heather asks.

"Normal is . . . going to high school. Having friends. Not being beat up for making a mistake."

I cannot help it. I snort. I cover my mouth, but not quickly enough. Heather looks at me. "Did you have something to add, Clara?"

"No, ma'am."

Erin is watching me. "You think that's funny? To want to be normal?"

"Not at all." I shake my head. "But it's normal to expect a smack or two if you mess up. How else will you learn?"

They're all looking at me like I've grown a second head. Why am I the one needing this group when they all appear to be delusional?

"So being hit is normal?" Heather's voice holds no judgment, only curiosity.

"Well, yeah, if you deserve it. I mean, Glen would hit me if I spoke out of turn, but it didn't mean he didn't love me. Really, that's how he showed he loved me."

The looks change from disbelief to pity. I see the shift, and I feel it in the air. Even Erin, who had been scowling at me, now looks at me as if I am the child and she is the adult.

"Listen to me, Clara, and please believe me when I say I mean no disrespect," Heather begins, choosing her words carefully. "Being hit is not normal. Even when the person loves you. It's not okay. Healthy relationships do not include physical violence."

Her words are met with nods around the circle. Erin speaks up.

"I thought it was normal when I was little. But when I started going to friends' houses, when I saw that their dads weren't drunks and didn't hit their moms . . . that's when I started to get angry."

I don't know how to react. An angry denial is on the tip of my tongue, but I have no examples of other families to give them. I grew up in a home where we were disciplined by pain. It's all I know. It was always that way. So how can it be wrong?

Heather turns the attention back to Erin and her journey, but I hear little of anything else the rest of the hour. I don't even realize when Heather dismisses the group until she comes and takes the chair Tori vacated.

"Clara, thank you for speaking up today."

"Nobody agreed with me."

Heather shakes her head. "No, but that's why we have this group. It's for discussion."

I rub my forehead. "Is what I said wrong?"

"What you know is what you know. What we are exploring is whether what you know to be true is healthy or not, if it is helpful or not. What these girls have been learning is that not everything they have done is normal, that things that were done to them are not okay, and that none of those things take away from their value as a person. It helps to have the support of others on the journey."

"I don't think I belong here," I whisper.

Heather doesn't respond for a moment. "That's all the more reason that I believe you do." She pats my knee and stands to leave. I watch her go, still lost in my thoughts. Connor pokes his head in the room.

"Shutting the place down, I see," he says, smiling at me. The smile fades as he sees my face. "Everything okay, Clara?"

I shake my head. "Connor?"

"Yeah."

"Are you married?"

He chuckles. "No."

"Girlfriend?"

"Yeah."

I purse my lips. "When she makes you mad, do you hit her? You know, just to make sure she knows not to do it again?"

Connor's horrified look is my answer. "Of course not, Clara. Sure, she makes me angry sometimes, but I make her angry, too. We maybe yell a little, but then we talk about it. I've never laid a hand on a woman in anger."

"How about guys?"

His face stays serious, though his mouth quirks up at my question. "I've gotten into a fight or two. Not for many years, though."

"Do you buy your girlfriend presents?"

"Sometimes, yes."

"Why?"

Connor ponders the question. "Because I love her. Because she deserves to feel special."

"As an apology?"

"Rarely. I don't like the idea that things can be made better with gifts. Real healing comes from straight talking and real apologies, not trinkets."

I nod, still thinking. It is as if my brain is shifting, trying to make sense of the information. It seems obvious to the others that being hit is not normal. Everyone out here can't be doing it wrong, can they? But Glen is so ingrained in me, I am having a hard time wrapping my mind around a relationship where love is not mixed with fear, pleasure with pain.

"Do you need to talk to Dr. Mulligan?" Connor asks. "You're not scheduled until tomorrow, but I can call . . ."

"No." I need to mull this over myself. "I just need to sleep, I think. The baby is taking a lot out of me today." It is an excuse, but I do feel more drained than normal. My hand goes to my stomach, and I pray that Nut is safe and happy in there, even while the rest of me is a riot of emotions.

Connor is not convinced, but he takes me back to my room anyway. Sleep does not come easily, and my dreams are fraught with needles and panic and screaming.

Then

I roll over, reaching for Glen, but his side of the bed is empty. I sit up, confused. It is still dark, and the clock tells me it is hours until dawn. I don't bother with a robe as I tiptoe out of the room. It is our first night in our beautiful new house, and in the hallway enough moonlight streams in that I do not need to turn on a lamp. Piles of boxes are illuminated in every direction. I skirt them and peek into the girls' room. Soon the other rooms will be full as well, but for now, just four of the small beds are occupied. Passion has claimed the bed closest to the door, her normally fierce expression softened in sleep.

Downstairs, a slice of light shoots from the door to the study, which is cracked open. I tap the pads of my fingers across the smooth wood, and I hear Glen shift in his chair. "Clara?"

I push open the door, revealing a large room filled with more boxes. Glen has purchased a giant desk to fill the space, and he is seated in the plush chair behind it. Papers are strewn across the desk in front of him, and several of the boxes have been haphazardly opened.

"I woke up and you were gone." I take a few steps into the room, not wanting to interrupt if he is busy.

"I wanted to find some correspondence my father left," Glen says, watching me, but not really seeing me. His eyes are far away. It has been a year, but his father's death still eats at him. Their last conversation was not a happy one. I don't know the details, but Glen carries the guilt like an iron blanket.

Instead of asking more questions, I nod. I don't want to push my luck. Though Glen has been in a better mood since we bought the house and the land, he has been much angrier in general for the past year, quick to explode, quick to punish.

"Joel and the boys are patrolling. We begin recruiting next week."

Another nod. Glen doesn't always share that part of the business with me. I do not want to break the spell.

"Soon we'll be back at the size we were when . . ." Glen trails off, but I know where his mind is. Back when Papa almost lost everything. Back when we had to abandon the compound where I grew up. Back when Glen was learning the ropes and ended up having to learn the hard way.

I walk a few steps closer, around the desk, daring to enter his space uninvited. "Papa would be proud, Glen." I keep my face smooth, but my heart is pounding, in fear or excitement I am not sure.

Glen reaches for me, clasping my hips and pulling me closer. A wry smile crosses his face. "He would tell me it was about time I figured this shit out." He buries his face in my stomach, his breath hot through the thin fabric of my nightgown. His arms come around me and he pulls me closer, urging me down until I am straddling his lap. He pillows his head on the soft curve of my breast, and I run my fingers through his sleep-tousled hair.

We sit like that until the sun comes up. There is nothing sexual about it. I give him comfort, as I always have and always will.

Now

"I understand you had a difficult group yesterday." I am in Dr. Mulligan's office. My eyes are gritty from lack of sleep, and I am lying on the couch, curled up, staring at the diplomas on the wall.

"I guess."

"Want to tell me about it?"

"Not really." I know better than to hope that she will leave it alone.

"It might help."

"How would it help?" I ask. "How could you possibly help me? You have no idea what I'm going through."

"I might if you would tell me."

"Even if I tell you, you don't *know*. You can't know. My life is nothing like yours." I'm not really angry with Dr. Mulligan. I'm angry with myself. For being so unsure. For doubting. For disrespecting everything I have been taught in my life by questioning it.

Dr. Mulligan purses her lips. "Sometimes just saying out loud what's on your mind can help you process it. I may not know your life, but I am an excellent sounding board."

It gets really annoying when Dr. Mulligan makes sense. She raises an eyebrow, and I release a sigh.

"I don't feel like I'm normal."

Dr. Mulligan laughs, but it is not unkind. "What is normal, Clara?"

I shrug. That is the question that kept me up all night. "I'm starting to think . . . I'm starting to wonder . . . What if how I lived my entire life was not how I was meant to live?"

"What do you mean?"

I sit up, wringing my hands as I try to piece together my thoughts into coherent statements. "For so long I've been focused on the idea that love makes everything better. But yesterday in group, they told me that being hit for making mistakes is wrong. But that's all I've ever known. So how can my normal not be normal? If it is what has always been, isn't that normal? And how can that be wrong?" I have no idea if I am making any sense, but Dr. Mulligan nods.

"There are a lot of things in your past that many people would not consider normal, Clara. I spoke with Heather a bit, and she said that she told you how to identify whether things are healthy or unhealthy, whether they are considered normal or not."

"Yeah, I remember her saying something about that."

"So tell me. When Glen hit you, did that make you feel better or worse?"

I make a face. What kind of question is this? "Well, it didn't feel good. But it was for my own good."

"Explain that to me."

"It happened mostly when I was being nosy or questioning Glen."

"Can you give me an example?" Dr. Mulligan's face remains neutral, though this is the most I have talked in any of our sessions about my relationship with Glen.

"Like when I asked him how long he would be gone on a business trip. I was upset that he would be gone over our anniversary, and he reminded me that the job comes first. I got a little hysterical and he had to hit me to help me calm down."

Dr. Mulligan's lips tighten. "So when you expressed emotions he didn't like, he would hit you?"

"Yeah, I guess."

"And did it work?"

"Well, I definitely thought more about what I said to him. He had a look he could give me where I knew I was in trouble. If I could stop myself, I could make him happy and save myself some bruises."

"So your husband taught you, through hitting and intimidation, that you were not allowed to express yourself to him."

When she says it that way, it sounds terrible. I do not respond. Glen would not like the direction my thoughts are going, but for the first time I start to question him. Why did Glen not want me to think for myself? He always said I was smart and had good ideas, but if I shared out of turn, I was punished. If I looked at him wrong, I could be punished.

"Sometimes he would just be angry," I whisper. "It would make him feel better to have sex, but it was always rough. Then he would buy me presents. Connor said yesterday he doesn't like to buy his girlfriend presents after they fight. But he never gave her bruises, either."

"How did you feel when Connor told you that?"

"Confused."

"Why?"

"I always felt spoiled when Glen would give me presents, especially when I deserved to be hit, or when I had absorbed his sadness."

"Absorbed his sadness?"

"Glen puts on a good face, but I saw the real Glen. The Glen who was angry and sad and tortured by the thought of never living up to his father's expectations. When we would have sex when he was in one of those moods, I felt like I could take that from him. And it always showed up in bruises. But it was okay, because he always seemed lighter after." I draw my knees to my chest, holding them tight, holding myself together.

Dr. Mulligan's eyes look sad, and my fears are confirmed. I am not normal. My beautiful relationship with Glen is not right.

"I would like to write in my notebook now."

She nods and retrieves it. I don't speak for the rest of the session, but I do not write, either. The blank page stares back at me. I'm not even tempted to peek at the sketch of Glen's face.

Then

I throw what I can into the waiting boxes. Mama is across the room, wrapping her nice china and mumbling to herself. Over the past three days we have sent truckloads of boxes to an industrial area in the city, to an apartment building that will become our home. I pause and look around the room, memorizing the lines of the house I grew up in.

Glen and I have already cleaned out our cabin. We did not have much there to begin with. I wanted to cry over the loss of our first home, but any tears earned me a slap across the face and a stern lecture about being strong.

It was less than a week ago that Papa came home distraught. Glen and I had been visiting with Mama, and Papa burst into the room, lip bleeding, eyes wild.

"It's gone, Mae," he said, and it was the first time I had ever seen him look lost. He was always so in control, and I was frightened by this side of him.

"What do you mean?" Mama asked, standing and walking over to him. "What's gone?"

"Everything. Everything. I lost it all." Papa's voice cracked, and Glen's arm came around me to pull me close. He had never seen Papa that way, either.

It was the biggest fight I had ever seen between Mama and Papa. He was quite drunk, so even when he went to punish her for yelling at him, his strikes were ineffectual. Glen and I sat in the background, dumbstruck, as the story came out.

Papa took a big risk and messed with the wrong business partner.

He got drunk and made a stupid bet. Not that I know much about gambling, but the consequences speak for themselves. He lost the entire operation—his side of it, anyway. We were to be out of the compound in a week, when his partner would come to take over.

I glance at Mama now, trying to ignore the green and purple bruises scattered over her exposed skin. Though Papa was too drunk to punish her the first night, she had showed up the next day to bring us boxes, and she was covered. My guess is that Papa took out more than his frustrations with her.

The only saving grace is that Papa had already turned over a portion of the business to Glen, and that part he has not lost. We had already secured the building in the city, a building Papa's partner knows nothing about. It is an old warehouse with a large apartment on the top floor. Not ideal, but there is enough room for now. The girls on Glen's roster, the ones we are raising, have been moved to the apartment. Papa and Glen will have to build the business from practically nothing, but the seeds are there. I only hope Mama and Papa are able to find another place to live sooner rather than later.

Joel runs in, breathing hard. "They're here!" he shouts. I lock eyes with Mama, and we both scramble up. We were supposed to have another couple of days. Glen and Papa emerge from the study, loaded down with boxes.

Glen dumps the boxes into Joel's arms. "Hide these in the truck when they're not looking, then duck down in the backseat." Most of Glen's guys are at the new place. Papa's guys will be turned over to the new boss.

The front door slams open as Joel slips out the back. I cross my fingers that he will make it.

"Well, well, well." A tall man strides in, followed by a group of at least fifteen armed men. "I see I have arrived just in time to stop you from taking all my things."

Papa steps forward. "We were just trying to get the personal stuff. Mae's china, our mementos."

"I think you mean *my* mementos," says the man. He looks around the room. "I don't believe I've met your charming family. I am Neil. Neil Anderson. And you are all in my house."

"We're going." Papa says, gesturing for us to follow him.

"Not so fast," Neil says. "I need to make sure everything is here." He consults a list in his hand. "All the girls are accounted for?"

"Girls!" Mama shouts, and I am surprised at the strength of her voice. I'm not sure I could even say a word at this point. The girls we have been training, some for years, some only weeks, filter into the room, coming to stand in a line as they have been taught. They know little about what is going on, but they will adjust. My heart breaks as I look at their faces, knowing this is the last time I will see them, unsure about how they will be treated.

Neil walks down the line, counting. "Very good. All here."

One of Neil's men comes in the back. "All the men accounted for," he says, his tone brisk, businesslike. Taking inventory of the people who live here as if they are furniture.

"Excellent." Neil waves a hand. "You may leave my house now," he says. "Take nothing else."

We are not allowed good-byes. I lock eyes with each girl, trying to convey my feelings to them without words, and start to pick my way through the boxes and toward the door. I make a wide berth around Neil, but, quicker than I might have expected, his hand shoots out to grab my arm.

"And what of this one?" he asks, and I look at him with wide eyes. "She is not on the roster."

I try to yank my arm free, but his hold is secure. Glen starts across the room, his expression murderous. I am not sure whether I am more fearful for Glen or Neil.

"That is my son's wife," Papa G calls from the doorway. "She is not a part of my operation."

Glen has reached us, and I hold my breath. Neil looks me up and down, lip curling. "Pity," he says before releasing me. My arm throbs where his hand gripped it, but I am grateful he did not ask more questions. If he had time to look through the paperwork, he might see that I am still listed as collateral. Papa has not gotten around to getting rid of my paperwork, though Glen's debt has been taken care of.

Grabbing my hand, Glen pulls me across the room and out the door before Neil can second-guess his decision to release me. We jump into the truck, where Joel is concealed under a pile of blankets, and Papa guns the engine. Too soon, the house shrinks into the background, disappearing in the clouds of dust kicked up by the tires. Glen squeezes my hand, and I meet his gaze for a moment. Then, with one last look back, I say good-bye to my home, square my shoulders, and prepare for my future.

Now

It is questioning day. I no longer track time by the days of the week, but by group day, therapy day, questioning day, and the occasional visiting day, when Mama Mae comes to gush about how excited she is to become a grandma. Then there are the days in between, the rare days when no one comes for me. Those days I fill by reading my books about pregnancy and motherhood. I think I would like to try a water birth, and I wonder if I'm still here when he is born if they would be able to make that happen. Nut moves all the time now, assuring me of his presence with each gentle flutter.

The door opens and Jay and Connor both come in. Connor looks grim, while Jay fidgets as if he is nervous. I stand and follow them out of the room. There are no niceties today, and I do not need instructions to know where we are going. I am surprised when they turn the opposite direction of the questioning room and bring me toward Dr. Mulligan's office instead.

"It's not therapy day," I say, wondering how I could be the only one keeping track of the schedule. "That's tomorrow."

"I know," Connor says, not looking at me. "We thought you'd be more comfortable for the questioning today with Dr. Mulligan."

My brow wrinkles at his words. Questioning has been going okay. I have given them quite a bit of information, though nothing specific to Glen. I think Glen would be pleased with my answers. Just enough to be cooperative, but not enough to get anyone in too much trouble. Like balancing on the garden wall as we did when we were children. Falling off either way would be disastrous, but as long as I stay focused and centered, we will be fine. Mostly the questions have been about my part in things, in training the girls, the clients who we served, that sort of thing. Safe topics. They do not even ask about Mama's visits, though they must be wondering how much I could have in common with a woman I claim to have never met before. I do wonder about that. Connor and Jay are not stupid, and I know they suspect I have met Mama before. It makes me anxious that they have not pushed for more details on that relationship.

At the door to Dr. Mulligan's office, I stop. "Maybe I don't feel very well today. Could we do this another time?"

Connor's eyes are gentle, but his tone is firm. "There are some things we need to talk about, Clara. It's important. It can't wait any longer."

I chew my lip, contemplating a fainting spell, but instead I move forward, past Jay as he opens the door. Dr. Mulligan stands as we enter and gestures toward the couch.

"It's good to see you, Clara. I hope you weren't caught too much by surprise at coming here today." Dr. Mulligan knows that I have created a schedule in my mind. She knows more about me than anyone, except Glen. Or maybe not. She may know more about me than even Glen does now. It is an unsettling thought. I perch on the edge of the couch instead of sinking to the floor as I usually do. I sense this is an important meeting.

Connor rolls an extra chair over that has obviously been taken from another office, while Jay lounges against the wall, always watchful, but out of the way. The atmosphere is tense, and while I understand that they want to breach a tough subject in a place that is comforting to me, I resent that they have brought tension to the oasis of Dr. Mulligan's office.

"Clara, you have been with us for several weeks now," Connor begins. "And we have been going slowly with you. I understand this is all difficult." He looks at Dr. Mulligan. "Dr. Mulligan says that you have been making some good progress in therapy, coming to terms with some tough issues."

A flash of betrayal stabs through me, and my eyes shoot to Dr. Mulligan. How could she share what I have been saying with these men?

"Calm down, Clara," Connor says, and I drag my eyes back to him. "She didn't give us details, only told us that she is happy with your progress and feels you are ready to hear some things that we have been keeping from you."

I look at Dr. Mulligan with new appreciation. She really does keep my secrets, and she thinks I am strong. She's told me as much before, but this proves that she believes it, and it's not just something she says to make me feel better. I sit up a little straighter. "I can handle it," I say.

Connor smiles. "I know. But, Clara, this is going to be tough. That's why Dr. Mulligan is here. If you need a break, let us know."

A break? I've never been offered a break before, even at the beginning when the questions were so overwhelming that I wanted to crawl into myself and never emerge. I clasp my hands together, ignoring the moisture that has covered my palms. I nod. "I'm ready."

Connor retrieves a folder from his ever present stack of paperwork. He removes a glossy picture and sets it on the coffee table in front of me. A young girl with a missing tooth grins up at me. She has straight brown hair and dark green eyes that twinkle even through the photograph. I smile. "She's cute."

"Yes," Connor says. "Do you recognize her?"

I squint at the picture. She does look familiar, but as I riffle through my memory, I cannot place her. She is not one of my daughters. I remember each of them as clearly as if I had just seen them yesterday. Even when Glen's face fades, I can bring each child forward in my memory in sharp relief. "I don't remember her," I say, shaking my head. "I'm sorry. Should I know her?"

Connor's mouth is set in a grim line, and I resist the urge to cover my ears before he can speak again. "Her name was Diana."

Diana. That name. That is what they called me when they first took us, what Meredith insisted on calling me for days when I first arrived. Diana. My heart stutters and then begins to race. I think they are trying to suggest . . .

"You think this is *me*?" I ask, disbelief in my voice.

Dr. Mulligan leans forward. "It *is* you, Clara," she says, her gentle voice soothing my nerves. "Or it was you. You were six years old in this picture. It was taken about six months before you disappeared."

"Disappeared?" My mind is spinning and I cannot comprehend what they are telling me.

Connor is speaking again. "You were abducted someplace between your house and the neighborhood park when you were six years old."

I shake my head. "No, you're wrong. That's not true. My parents gave me away. They didn't want me. They wanted Mama Mae and Papa G to raise me."

There is a sharp intake of breath and I look over to see Connor's shocked gaze fixed on me. Jay swears under his breath. Even Dr. Mulligan's poker face breaks for a moment, her mouth opening slightly in surprise.

My heart stutters as I realize what I have said. It's over. I broke my promise to Glen. I was never supposed to let them know that I knew Mama and Papa. I have let them believe that I hooked up with Glen when I was older, and have refused questions about who raised me. This is huge. I can see it on Connor's face, and Jay is staring at me openmouthed.

"Mae? You mean Glen's mother?" Connor asks, careful to keep his voice neutral, as if I do not already realize what I have opened.

I clamp my lips together and stare down at the picture of the laughing girl on the table. Every muscle in my body is begging me to flee, but I stay as still as possible.

"Clara? How long have you known Mae Lawson?"

This can be salvaged. If I never repeat the information again, they still have nothing.

"She visited me for the first time a few weeks ago." It is not a lie.

"So we're back to this again. Evasive answers and half-truths. Dammit, Clara, we can't go backward. Enough is enough." Connor throws his papers on the table, and more photos slip out of the folder. The same girl from the large picture in front of me dances across the other pictures. In some of them she is alone, but in others, a blond girl plays by her side. Diana and the blonde with their arms around each other, eating ice cream, swimming at a lake. And one photo of a family. Diana sits in the lap of a large man with a kind face. A woman laughs as she looks over at them, and I feel an uncomfortable pang in my chest.

I reach forward, separating the family picture from the rest. The blond girl was hidden, but now she comes into view, nestled in the crook of the woman's arm. I can almost hear her laugh, almost feel the strong arms of the man, holding me securely in his lap. Is it possible?

I take a deep breath. "Who are these people?"

"Jane and Doug McKinley," Dr. Mulligan answers. "The older girl, the blonde, is Charlotte. That is your family, Clara."

My head is moving back and forth in denial before she even finishes. "That's not possible. My parents didn't want me. This family cannot be mine."

Dr. Mulligan moves to sit next to me, something she has never done. "It's true, Clara. They are your family. We compared medical records to be sure. And, Clara." She pauses. "They want to see you."

Then

I walk in the door, a basket of freshly dried laundry on my hip, and hear peals of giggling from the sunroom, overlaying strains of an old-fashioned waltz. Passion, who is in front of me, looks over her shoulder, eyes sparkling. A smile creeps across my face as I shrug. I left the girls doing lessons just twenty minutes ago, and I should be angry that they are goofing off instead, but it's such a lovely day, I can't really blame them.

"Let's go see what the troublemakers are up to," I say in response to Passion's unspoken question. She grins and follows me down the hall. As we draw closer to the sunroom, I turn and place a finger over my lips, and we tiptoe the rest of the way to the door.

My smile grows when I peek inside. Glen is in the middle of the room, surrounded by all of our daughters. He is taking turns twirling each girl around in time to the music. When I look closer, I see that he is letting them jump on his feet, allowing them to spin and whirl faster. It has been so long since I've seen Glen smile like this, and I hate to break the moment.

As if he senses his audience, Glen looks up, and his eyes heat. He works his way across the room, dancing with a few more girls before stopping in front of me. He holds out a hand and bows slightly. "Mrs. Lawson?"

I step fully into the room and do a small curtsy before taking his offered hand. It has been a long time since we've danced, but it feels as if no time has passed at all. We are back in dance class, and I am fourteen again, crushing on the cocky, unattainable boy. Except now the boy is mine, and he has grown into a handsome, confident man. Glen's eyes pierce mine, and I couldn't look away if I wanted to. Moments like this happen less often lately, which makes them even more special.

At some point, I tear my gaze away and realize we're alone in the room.

"Passion took the girls back to their lessons," Glen whispers, his voice tickling my ear. "I always liked that girl."

My arms twine around his neck, pulling him closer. "She's the best."

His mouth claims mine and we continue to sway together long after the record stops playing.

Now

Glen's face lights up when Connor ushers me into the room. He looks much better than he did the last time I saw him, when I told him about the baby. I am pleased that the news has rejuvenated him so. It worries me also, because of what I must talk with him about today. I don't plan on telling him about my slipup with Mama and Papa. He'll find out eventually, but just the thought of admitting to such an enormous mistake fills me with dread. I'm already uncertain about how he will take the news of my family. Will he be happy for me? Worried for me? Angry? After all, until yesterday, he was really the only family I needed. Him and my daughters. Will he feel betrayed if I tell him I am considering meeting the McKinleys?

Glen stands and rushes to the door to meet me, stopping short with his arms raised to embrace me when Connor clears his throat. Glen shoots Connor a dirty look but drops his arms.

"Hey, Clare," he says, and his voice is almost shy. I thought I had seen all the facets of Glen, but excited daddy is not one of them. I smile.

"Twenty minutes, Clara," Connor says before backing out of the room. There is censure in his tone. He's noticed the difference in Glen, too, and knows where it's come from.

As soon as the door is shut, Glen envelops me in his arms, holding tight for a moment before leading the way to the table. "Sit down, tell me how you're doing." His eyes are glued to my abdomen. On close inspection, there is a small mound beginning to form. He notices immediately, of course. Glen knows my body better than anyone, even in the baggy clothes they have provided. He places his hand over the bump, a grin creasing his face, melting away the years he has gained since being arrested. "That's our baby in there."

I nod. "And he's perfectly healthy."

Glen's grin widens. "It's a boy?"

Laughing, I grip his hand. "It's too soon to tell for sure. I just feel it."

"When can we find out?" His face is eager, and he reminds me of the boy I fell in love with.

"In a couple of months. Maybe we will both be out by then and can find out together."

Glen's face falls. "I don't know. They're gathering a lot of evidence against me. I think they're waiting for it all to come together." He pauses. "I think they're waiting for you, Clara. Be careful."

My heart races. "What do you mean?"

"No one is talking. My guys are loyal, and Mama, of course. I think some of the girls from the brothel have talked, but they're trying to get me on bigger charges."

"Bigger?"

"Don't worry about that now." His voice drops so low even I have a hard time hearing him. I lean closer. "They're going to try to trick you, Clara. Don't let them. I'm counting on you, baby. I want to be there for you, for our son." My heart surges with purpose. Glen is right. I have a family to protect. At the reminder of family, I feel the blood drain from my face.

"What's wrong, baby?" Glen asks, gripping my face. "You look like you're going to be sick. Do I need to call someone?"

"No," I whisper harshly, glancing at the two-way mirror. I hate being watched all the time. "No." Less harsh this time. "I just . . . Glen, they found my family. The ones I lived with before Mama and Papa brought me home."

His eyes turn dark. "What?"

"They . . . they want to meet me. These McKinleys. They want to meet the daughter they gave up almost twenty years ago."

"Don't be stupid, Clara."

I sit up in surprise. I have forgotten how quickly Glen's mood can change. His tone is fierce, almost mocking. "I am not stupid."

"You are if you see them. They're trying to fill your head with this fairy tale of a family, but, Clara, they are the ones who abandoned you. If they wanted you so badly, why didn't they come and get you?"

He makes a good point.

"They're probably out of the money they got for you and want more. Don't believe the lies. Believe in me, in us. We are the only fairy tale you need." He says it with conviction, his typical confidence in full force. I feel myself being pulled back to him, doubts piling up about the information I've gathered over the past several days.

I start to shake my head. "But Dr. Mulligan said—"

"Who, your quack therapist? She's with *them*, Clara. The ones trying to keep us apart, trying to put me away for the rest of my life. Don't let this happen. Stay strong. For us." His hand goes back to my stomach. "For him. For Glen the third."

"For little Glen," I repeat, placing my hand over his. Warmth rushes through me as I picture the three of us together. But the feeling disappears when I look up and see Glen's expression.

For a fleeting moment, I see Papa G in Glen's eyes. There and gone in a moment, but the sense of unease I feel lingers even into my dreams that night.

Then

Glen rolls away from me, breathing hard. "That was great, baby," he says, propping his hands behind his head. I snuggle closer, chilled away from his body heat. I listen to his heartbeat slow, and the perspiration cools on our bodies. Even after being together like this for several months, I am in awe of Glen and how he is all mine.

We stay like that, limbs tangled together, for countless minutes. Finally, Glen sighs. "I need to go check on the house, make sure Mama's secured everything." He swings his legs over the side of the bed and reaches for his clothes. I sit up and watch as he wanders, shirtless, into the kitchen of our tiny one-room cabin.

"Is Papa away on business?" I thought I had spotted him earlier, but Mama keeps me so busy during the day, I might have been confused.

Glen laughs. "No, he's at the Treehouse."

The brothel? I'm confused, and my face must show it, because Glen chuckles again and comes to sit on the edge of the bed. I sit up and raise the sheet to cover my nakedness.

"First," Glen says, tugging the sheet until it falls to my waist, "never cover up such beauty." He strokes my skin as his lips find mine, and my heart quickens again. My skin flushes.

"If you keep that up, I'm not going to let you leave," I tease. Glen's grip tightens for a moment. He leans back, a dark look flashing in his eyes, but he relaxes almost as quickly as he tensed.

"I would tie you to the bed before I would allow you to try to stop me." His words are light, but with a hint of warning. I am not to tell him what to do.

"Of course," I say, lowering my eyes. "I just want to stay near you."

He cups my chin, raising my face to look into my eyes. "I feel the same, Clara." He kisses me, a gentle brush of his lips. "But I'm also trying to prove to Papa that this whole thing isn't a mistake. So I make sure things run smoothly when he is . . . occupied."

"Still seems weird to have a meeting so late," I mutter, then look at Glen to make sure that wasn't over the line. He just smiles.

"He isn't at a meeting, Clara," he says, and his voice has the tone that tells me I am missing something obvious. It's frustrating when he uses that tone, because he so rarely explains things to me, and then makes fun of me when I do not understand.

I am preparing a good pout when he speaks again. "Papa often spends alone time with the girls over at the brothel." He looks to see if I understand. I shake my head. "They fulfill a purpose for him that he doesn't get elsewhere." Glen's neck grows red. I almost smile, but hold it back. I am not used to seeing Glen flustered. My eyes widen as the realization comes to me.

"You mean, he and Mama . . ." I understand now why Glen was

being evasive. It isn't comfortable to talk about his parents' sex life, or lack thereof. I feel sad for Mama when I think about what this means. "Does she know?"

"Of course she knows." Glen stands and grabs his shirt from the puddle of fabric on the floor. "She understands."

I move off the bed and stand behind Glen, wrapping my arms around his waist. His hands clutch mine and he pulls my arms tighter. I bite my lip, nervous to ask the next question. Nervous that I will not like the answer. Nervous that Glen will not like the question and will be angry. But I cannot stop the words from tumbling out. "Do you ever visit the brothel for those reasons?" I squeeze my eyes shut as Glen's ab muscles tense against my fingers.

He loosens my arms and spins to face me, staying within my embrace. I shiver at the friction between his shirt and my skin. "Clara. Look at me."

I open my eyes and lose myself in the deep blue of his. He cradles my face in both his hands. The look in his eyes is intense and it takes my breath away. "Yes?" I breathe.

"I have everything I could ever want or need, right here in my arms. Do you understand?"

I nod, as much as his hands will allow, and he drags my face to his. It feels like he wants to devour me, and I will happily succumb to him. We are both breathing hard when he releases me.

"We'll continue this when I get back," he says, then he turns and is gone with a rush of cold outside air.

I fall backward onto the bed, basking in the glow of my love for Glen and his obvious love for and devotion to me. I feel bad for Mama, that she doesn't have what Glen and I have, but she is clearly doing something wrong if she cannot hold Papa's attention. Thinking about Mama and Papa's sex life grosses me out, so I concentrate on reliving the past two hours with Glen.

My reverie is interrupted by the walkie-talkie that starts squawking from the table. "Lawson, you there? We have a situation that needs your attention. Lawson, Junior. Please copy."

Glen does not leave without his radio very often. He didn't plan to be gone long, and there typically isn't that much activity at this time of night. I stare at the radio as I try to decide what to do. I could leave it, but if it's important, it might need to be addressed immediately. And Glen might be angry if I don't let him know. Then again, he might be angry if I show up at the main house without his permission. He doesn't like me to be out on my own, especially in the dark. I am not sure why. With so many guards, I am safer here than anywhere else.

"Lawson, do you copy? We need a decision over here. Please check in."

I make a quick decision and throw a dress over my head. I shrug on a heavy coat and stuff my feet into some boots before grabbing the radio and slipping out the door. I turn the volume knob down, just in case anyone hears me. My feet crunch the gravel of the familiar path through the trees. There are few other sounds aside from the rustling of the trees and the occasional scurrying of a creature in the dark foliage. I am relieved when the brightly lit main house comes into view. I hurry up the steps to the back porch, but pause as I hear shouting.

"You are just like your father!" Mama's voice. I peer through the window and see their shadows.

"What do you mean by that?" Glen is angrier than I've heard him in a long time. Even when he's exasperated with me, he doesn't yell like that.

Mama stalks into view. She turns and jabs her hands in the air, punctuating her point. "You strut around here as if you are a god. I can handle some things on my own, Glen. Remember, I raised you."

"You were too busy with your precious girls to pay me much attention, Mother." Glen comes into view, fists clenched at his sides.

Crossing her arms, Mama smirks at him. "And you decided to go ahead and *marry* one of my 'precious girls,' didn't you? How long before you start visiting the brothel with your father? Just to 'check the merchandise,' or whatever nonsense excuse he uses. What will you tell Clara then?"

In a flash, Glen hits Mama across the face and pins her to the wall. Her expression is one of pure terror as he cuts off her air supply. "Never. Speak. Of her. Like that. Again." Mama's mouth and nose are both dripping blood, and tears leak from the corners of her eyes. She nods, the movement almost imperceptible.

"What are you doing?" I jump as a voice speaks from behind me. My finger flies to my lips to hush him.

Joel walks up the steps and peeks inside. "You better get out of here, Clara," he says, eyeing my scant outfit. "I doubt you're supposed to be seeing this."

I nod and scurry down the steps. "Clara?" Joel says from behind me. I turn around. "This will be our secret." There is a twinkle in his eye that makes me uncomfortable, but Glen trusts him more than anyone else. I don't like the idea of keeping a secret from Glen, but I also don't want him to know what I witnessed. I nod and slip into the darkness of the woods as Joel pounds on the door, saving Mama from whatever further damage Glen might inflict.

When Glen returns later, I pretend to be sleeping. He falls asleep without trying to wake me, but it is late before sleep finally finds me.

Now

My fists clench as I curl into a tiny ball in the corner of Dr. Mulligan's couch. I feel as if I have run an emotional marathon since she and Connor showed me pictures of my alleged family. After thinking about it, I am full of anger. These people, these McKinleys, they are just another trick to get me to cooperate.

"Clara, I can tell you're upset. Please talk to me." Dr. Mulligan is using her best soothing voice, but I am on to her tricks.

"Of course I'm upset," I say, willing my hands to release. I move my feet to the floor and cross my legs, smoothing imaginary wrinkles out of my pant legs. I look her squarely in the eye. "I almost betrayed Glen because you and Connor told me a fairy tale."

Dr. Mulligan's eyes widen slightly, but other than that, she shows no reaction to my statement. Her calm façade only makes me angrier.

"After all this time, I really started to trust you! But you have just been working with Connor and the other agents this whole time, trying to come up with a way to get me to spill. Trying to get me to turn on Glen. Well, sorry, lady, that's not happening. Ever."

"I see." Dr. Mulligan purses her lips. "Tell me, Clara, are you unintelligent?"

I frown. "No. That's why I know what you're up to. I figured it out."

She nods. "Okay. Have I ever treated you as if you were stupid?"

I consider the question for a moment. Of all the people I have encountered since being here, Dr. Mulligan has treated me the most like an adult capable of making my own decisions. "No." No doubt lulling me into a false sense of security, but I don't say that part out loud. She knows what she did.

"So why on earth do you think I would assume I could get away with telling such a wild tale, if, indeed, telling you about your parents was a trick?"

I think for a moment. "Say they are real."

"They are."

I scowl at her. "Say they are real," I repeat, and she remains silent. "Why would they want to meet me? Why now?"

"I'm confused, Clara. Why wouldn't they want to meet the daughter they haven't seen in almost seventeen years? Would your feelings change about any of your children after seventeen years? Why now? Because you were just found."

"*It's been seventeen years!* What took them so long? If I had the chance to see my daughters again, I wouldn't waste a minute. And I've been here for weeks."

"I confess that is our fault, Clara. We didn't think you were ready when you first came in. They were notified as soon as we suspected who you were, but we have been holding off until you seemed more open. Trust me, I've had my share of shouted phone calls from your father and tearful voice mails from your mother. Of course, I haven't even been able to speak to them, not even about whether I'm actually seeing you or not. I won't, not without your permission."

"You haven't talked to them?"

"No. They have called, but you're an adult. And I promised you that this is a safe place. Talking to parents you haven't seen in seventeen years or so without telling you would be a huge breach of trust."

"Yes, it would." I can feel my anger fading and my confusion rushing back. I thought I had figured it out, but Dr. Mulligan always finds a way to surprise me. "So they were angry? At me?"

"Oh no, Clara. Not at all. Your father . . . Doug," she corrects when she sees my expression, "he's frantic. They both are. They want so badly to see you, to see with their own eyes that you are alive and well . . . more or less."

The only time Glen yells is when he is angry. Papa was the same way. They would yell and yell until they became very quiet, and that was the time to get nervous. I wonder if Doug, my supposed father, is the same way.

"Clara?" I realize Dr. Mulligan has been speaking. I look at her. "Will you consider meeting with your family?"

My head begins a slow rocking back and forth, but I pause, raising my shoulders instead. "I think I won't be what they expect."

"I think all they expect is that you are yourself."

If only I knew who that was.

"I'll think about it."

She nods. "That's all I ask." A knock on the door tells me that our time is up.

I am about to open the door when I turn back. "Dr. Mulligan?"

"Yes, Clara?"

"You . . . you can talk to them if you want. I mean, just to tell them I'm okay. And thinking."

She smiles and pulls a sheet of paper from a folder on her desk for me to sign. I pause before writing my name, but scrawl "Clara Lawson" in the space.

Then

My heart beats an erratic rhythm as I light the candles and wait for Glen to return. I used Mama's special roast recipe to cook for him tonight. I want him in the best mood possible to ask him what I want to know. It has been a good week, with several new girls coming into the house, and he has been whistling, which is a sure sign things are going well.

I've been tiptoeing around Glen since I saw him get rough with Mama, but things are going well with them, too. We have dinner over at the house several times a week, and he dotes on her, as a son should with his mother. I smile and rub my belly. I hope to give Glen a son of his own someday. A little boy to follow in his footsteps. But that's for another time.

Glen's boots stomp up the porch steps and my shoulders straighten. Talk of children will come soon, but that isn't what tonight is for. Tonight I want some answers that I'm sure he will give me, now that I'm his wife. I don't know why I've put it off for so long, especially after the wedding. I am not worried that he will get angry. Mostly. But I do worry about the pressure Papa may put on him to keep things from me. I just have to be more persuasive.

I paste a smile on my face as the door swings open and my handsome husband enters with a gust of cool air. The days are warmer, but the nights are still chilly. Glen closes the door and spins, a grin covering his face.

"Is that pot roast?" he asks, sniffing the air.

"Yup," I say, walking over to take his coat as he shrugs it off his shoulders. "Mama's recipe. Potatoes and beans to go with it."

Glen catches me around the waist and spins me around, backing me into the door. He leans down and gives me a kiss that causes my knees to go wobbly. "How about we start with dessert?" he asks before claiming my lips again.

Laughing, I push against him, giving him a playful swat as he backs away. "Strawberry shortcake for dessert," I say, making sure to swing my hips as I sashay back to the stove. I give him a coy look over my shoulder. "First dessert, anyway."

His laugh is loud and happy, and the butterflies still wiggling around in my belly calm down. He will be reasonable, I am sure of it. A husband and wife can have difficult conversations. I don't know why I have been nervous at all. We risked everything to be together. Certainly a conversation is not much of a risk.

I bring the food to the table and Glen eats with gusto, exclaiming over every bite.

"Really, babe," he says, sitting back and patting his stomach. "Don't tell Mama, but I think your roast is even better than hers."

My cheeks warm with pleasure as I set dessert in front of him. I watch him dig in with as much enthusiasm as he's shown the rest of the meal, and a smile plays at my lips even as I gather up the courage to speak.

"Glen," I say, my voice wavering slightly.

"Yeah, babe," he says, his focus on his cake.

"I was wondering if I could ask you something."

He looks up at me then, smile still in place, eyes twinkling. "You can ask me anything, Clara, you know that."

I nod, exhaling. "I know. I just . . . I don't want you to be angry."

Glen's eyes tighten at the corners, the twinkle replaced with suspicion. "Why would I be angry?" He takes another careful bite, but the levity of a few minutes ago is seeping away, replaced with growing tension.

Breathe, Clara, I tell myself. No going back now.

"I just wanted to ask about . . . about Macy."

Glen's fork clatters to his plate, and his hands ball into fists, knuckles white. He squeezes once, then flexes his hands, stretching his fingers. His voice is unexpectedly calm when he speaks. "What did you want to know?"

This feels dangerous, but I push forward anyway. I have his attention. My words tumble out of my mouth so fast, I am worried he won't understand them all. "I wanted to know where she is and if she's okay and if there's a way I can see her."

Glen's fingers tap against the wooden surface of the table, and the sound seems louder than normal, magnified by the silence of the room. "I thought it was clear that Macy no longer exists, Clara. She is no longer a part of your life, and you need to forget about her."

"But, Glen," I say, rising and going to crouch in front of him. I take his hand from the table, silencing the tapping, and sandwich it between both of mine. "You brought her to the wedding. I thought . . ."

His other hand moves to stroke the side of my face, pushing my hair out of the way. "That might have been a mistake. I thought it would bring closure."

"It did," I say quickly. "It was a lovely gesture, not a mistake at all. I've just been thinking that—"

The hand I'm holding moves to envelop both of my hands, squeezing to the point of pain before releasing me. He stands, knocking the chair over in his rush.

"There will be no more talk of Macy, Clara. That part of your life is over. You will not think of her or speak her name. There is only me, and Mama and Papa, and the girls. That's it. Do you understand?"

Gone is the man who came in the door a half hour ago. In his place is a statue, a copy of Papa that frightens me. He is showing up more and more, sucking my Glen away a little bit each time. I fear someday my Glen will be gone completely unless I do something. I stand and reach for him, imploring.

"Please, Glen, if I could just see her once more. Talk to her—"

Without warning, Glen's hand lashes out, striking me across the face. I cry out, covering the stinging spot on my cheek and staring at him through the fuzzy edges of my sight. The entire room seems to be tilting. His face, horrified for a moment, settles into a look of derision and rage.

"I can't believe you made me do that, Clara," he says. He grabs his plate from the table and throws it at the wall, leaving a patch of sticky strawberry juice and whipped cream on the surface above the plate. "Dammit!" He grabs his coat and storms out into the night, the door slamming hard enough to shake the entire house at his exit.

Tears leak from the corners of my eyes, and I stare at the door in disbelief. I cannot believe that just happened. My cheek is tender to the touch, but I refuse to look at it. Instead, I busy myself with cleaning up dinner. Glen will have plenty of leftovers to snack on over the next couple of days. I sweep and mop the floor, and scrub the wall, eliminating all evidence of Glen's anger.

All evidence except the bright red mark on my cheek, which is rapidly turning yellow. It will be a bruise. I dread facing Mama tomorrow and having to explain.

When Glen hasn't returned by ten, I get ready for bed and cry myself to sleep. It is late when he finally creeps into the house and slides under the covers. He gathers me close, kissing my tender skin, whispering apologies. His cheeks are wet with his regret, and I do not resist as he pulls me under himself. I absorb him. We are one. Always.

Now

When I sit down next to Tori at the next support group meeting, my hands are trembling. After my talk with Dr. Mulligan, she suggested that I share my experience with the group, just to gauge their reactions. I need to sort through my confusing thoughts before I agree to meet my family. All these years I have known that they didn't want me, that they gave me away. Now it appears that may have been a lie . . . which makes me wonder what else in my life has been a lie. In my dreams the past several nights, two little girls play, one blonde, one brunette. They are not new players in my dreamland, and I am beginning to wonder if these little girls are not just figments of my imagination, but snatches of memory, buried deep, only surfacing in the innocence of sleep. Who are they? What were they like? Did they get along? In my dreams, they laugh and play together, but then the blonde fades away, leaving the brunette in the dark. I want to share my dream with Dr. Mulligan, but she has a way of making me see things in ways I am not always prepared for.

If what I've been told is true, if I was taken from a loving family, what does that mean for the girls I raised? Were these girls all taken as well? Glen had to know. There's no way that I've been able to work it out in my mind that he didn't. I want to talk to him, to ask him why, but part of me is terrified of the answer. Terrified to know the truth, because if he knew, if he orchestrated all of it, then what does that make me? What did he make me?

I look around the circle at the girls who have bared their souls, shared their deepest hurts over the past weeks. I'm even more aware now of how different we are, but now I see the differences in an entirely new way.

Heather is on time for once, talking in low tones with a girl I do not recognize. I have grown accustomed to many of the faces in the group, but they come and go from time to time. I take deep breaths to calm myself as I question whether this is a good idea. What if they tell me that my family really doesn't want me? What if I tell them what I've done and they hate me? I think that is what terrifies me the most. That what I am beginning to suspect about myself and what I have done will be true. That perhaps in the fairy tale of my life, I'm not the princess, but the villain. And there are no happy endings for villains. A soft hand brushes my arm. "You okay?" Tori asks, her eyes filled with concern when I look over at her.

Words escape me, so I just nod. I will tell the group a short story if I cannot make my mouth form sentences. I clear my throat and take a deep breath. "I'm a little nervous, I guess." My voice is steadier than I expected, if a bit higher pitched than normal. "I just . . . I don't know. Maybe I'm not ready."

This time Tori grips my hands, which I have twined together in my lap. "You're ready, Clara. I know you may not believe it, but just being here shows you're stronger than you think."

My smile is rueful. "I am here to make Dr. Mulligan and Connor happy so I don't have to give birth in a cell."

Tori looks at me, her eyes appraising. "I can see it in your eyes, Clara."

"See what?"

"The light. It's coming." With one more squeeze, Tori turns away to greet the girl on her other side, leaving me once again at a loss for words.

What does she mean, "the light"? Everything has felt dark since the moment they tore Daisy from my arms. Everything except Nut. My hands go to my stomach. Maybe that is the light she sees. My light in the darkness. My angel. My son. My savior. I take a deep breath, drawing strength from the small life inside of me as Heather calls the group to order.

"I understand that Clara is ready to share with us today," Heather says, lifting her eyebrows in question. I appreciate that she gives me a chance to back out, but I feel a sudden burst of nervous energy. I stretch my fingers, one by one, preparing myself.

"Okay," I say, nodding. "Okay. I . . . I don't know how much I want to share." The nerves are back. I can feel the eyes on me, so I concentrate on Heather, on the piece of frizzy hair sticking straight up from her messy topknot. "I am a little scared," I admit to the hair.

"What are you scared of?" Tori's voice makes me jump, and the rest of the room comes back into focus.

My eyes drop to my knees, and I study the fabric of my loose pants. "I just don't want you to hate me," I whisper after a few beats of silence. I look up, meeting the gazes of those in the circle. "My story is very different. I think it might make you angry."

Tori's hand finds mine again. "No one is judging you. Just talk. We'll listen."

"Thank you, Tori," says Heather from across the circle. "That's something for us all to remember, especially since Clara's story may be triggering for some of you. Despite her unique circumstances, I want you to remember that she is a victim as well."

I bristle at the term. I still find it difficult to identify myself as a victim. At least in the same way as the other women are. Until recently, I had felt like a victim of the agents, of this place, even Dr. Mulligan at times. But after hearing these stories, learning about the family I may have come from . . . the villain role feels more apt all the time.

It is a sign of my growing restraint that I do not call Heather on her use of the word. Instead, I take another steadying breath and begin to speak.

"I don't remember going to live with Glen and his parents." I shake my head, dispelling the image of the two little girls that has been dancing through my head. "That's part of the reason I'm sharing today. I guess I used to belong to another family. They want to see me, and I don't know if I'm ready." I have the full attention of the group now. "My earliest memories are of doing lessons with Mama Mae . . . Glen's mother . . ." By now I have admitted to Dr. Mulligan and Connor that I was raised by Mama and Papa. Dr. Mulligan accepted it with little comment, and Connor seemed unsurprised, only saying it was about time I was fully honest with him.

I tell them about life with Mama and Papa, about the lessons we had, our "purpose," as it was presented to us. That we would adopt a role in the lives of our clients that only we could fulfill. That after being unwanted, cast away, we would be the perfect piece to add to another family, a family we were chosen for. I relay the excitement over getting a client, and then the drama of falling for Glen instead. To everyone else, Glen is the bad guy. Telling these women about my life, I try to explain to them how I could never see Glen as bad, despite how he acts at times. I give them just an overview of what my role was, that I raised the girls and prepared them for the next phase of their lives.

Some things I leave out. I know eventually I will need to share with them about Joel, about Harrison, about so many things that I have buried deep inside. But for now, for today, I tell them enough to see if they can still accept me. Their reaction will help me determine whether my family will be able to see me and accept me.

There is an uncomfortable silence when I finish. The last thing I talked about was the raid. I do not go into detail about the time I have spent in the hospital in the custody of the agents. That is something they cannot understand. As victims, they were never subjected to incarceration as I have been.

A dark stain marks the center of the circle. I think they use it as a focal point when they set up the chairs each week. I have been staring at it since I began speaking, and now it resembles a cat stretching across the carpet. Or perhaps a rocking horse. It begins to morph again when Erin speaks.

"Holy shit."

The tension eases a little, and a nervous wave of laughter makes its way around the circle. Even the corners of my mouth lift without my permission as I glance up at Erin. She has proven to be one of the most outspoken of the group, even if she is one of the youngest.

"So, you were, like, my age when you decided you wanted to be with Glen forever?"

I nod. There is another beat of silence. I brace myself, waiting for the anvil of judgment to come crashing down, for someone to start berating me and telling me what a horrible person I am.

The next question, from a quiet girl named Sara, surprises me. "Do you . . . Are you still in love with him?"

There is no judgment in her question that I can detect, and I take special care as I formulate my answer because I know she is being sincere. "I am," I say, releasing my words slowly. "I have loved Glen from the moment I met him. I cannot imagine existing and not loving him." Several of the girls shift in their chairs, but no one interrupts as I continue. "But I think, maybe . . ." I look at Heather for reassurance, and she smiles and nods for me to go on. "I think that you can continue to love someone but still realize that what they have done is wrong. It's easy to look at someone and see them in simple terms, good or bad, right or wrong, but I know Glen too well, every facet of him. I think there will always be a part of me that loves him."

"I get that," Erin speaks up again. "I mean, Brady was a dickweed, but I still had this need to please him. I wanted him to be happy with me. And there were times when he acted like a real decent guy. I hate him, but I don't. And I was only with him a couple years. You've known Glen for, like, ever."

Relief rushes through me. They don't hate me. They understand me. They accept me. They—

"Are you kidding me?" A woman around my age speaks up. I think her name is Pam. She was sold into the sex trade after accepting a modeling job overseas. "I knew people like her." She shoots me a scornful look, but speaks about me as if I am not here. "Women who somehow got lucky and got on a power trip. They had opportunities to help the rest of us, but chose to save themselves instead. Couldn't risk ending up as one of the underlings again."

"Now, Pam, that's not what Clara did." There is warning in Heather's tone.

"Bullshit! It's absolutely what she did! She could have found a way to save those little girls. Instead, she *trained* them, or whatever, and turned them over to be sex slaves." She turns to me, jabbing a finger in my direction. "And don't try to tell me you didn't know exactly what purpose those little girls would be serving for those sick fucks. You can play innocent, but you're too smart for that."

"Pam!" Heather's voice is sharp. "I need you to take a break."

Pam knocks over the chair in her haste to stand. "Where are all those little girls now, Clara? Scattered around the world? Most of them probably dead. All of them miserable. You did that to them. You say you thought you were training them for a better life, but if you truly believe that, you're lying to yourself. And when you finally wake up . . . well, I wouldn't want to be you."

Heather and Tori both stand to shield me from Pam, but the damage is already done. Pam has said everything that I feared, everything that I suspect the others are probably thinking as well. Why didn't I save the girls? Did I really think they were being sent to a better place, or did I just want to save myself? Would I have done anything to win Glen's favor?

And what would have become of me if I had never been with Glen?

Then

The drive to Papa's side establishment is short. I have not been here since Glen and I ran away all those years ago. Papa G and Glen have decided that I need to understand the other branches of the business in order to be a good partner for Glen. After three months of marriage, I am glad to be trusted with this information. I'm also hoping to have a chance to speak with Macy.

In the daylight, the long log building looks run-down. Without the flashy lights, it looks like what it is: a dirty brothel in the middle of nowhere. Glen taught me the word "brothel," and then cautioned me never to use it to describe Papa's business. He prefers terms like "pleasure palace" and "angels' playground." Any implication of anonymous sex is discouraged. It is actually called the Treehouse. I have already developed a healthy disdain for this side of the business, but I am led to believe it is quite profitable and important.

We enter the front door and are enveloped by a haze of smoke. Though it is the middle of the day, there are some customers at tables, watching girls dance at poles. The girls' makeup is piled on, and the bags under their eyes hint at sleepless nights, but I am sure the alcohol has dimmed any imperfections in the eyes of their clients. Sure enough, almost as soon as we arrive, a man stumbles to the cashier and points to one of the dancers. Money changes hands and the couple disappears down a long hallway.

"This is the main stage area," Papa explains, sweeping his arms to encompass the entire room. "This is where the girls hang out for men to make their choices. Most of the girls are sleeping now, as they had long nights." Papa winks. "But we always have some on the day shift."

I cough and wave the smoke away from my face. My skin feels dirty after only a few minutes in here. Glen clutches my hand and sends me a warning look. I try to breathe through my mouth, though that is not much better. The air is thick and rancid, and not only with smoke.

Papa leads the way down the hall. Some rooms have a red circle by them. Others are green. Papa knocks and opens the door to one of the green rooms.

"Kara?" Papa calls into the room. We follow him inside. The room is small, a double bed taking up most of the space. There is a tiny closet and a washbasin. Another door leads into a bathroom barely large enough for a toilet and a shower. A woman sits up in the bed, rubbing sleep from her eyes.

"Glen?" she asks, squinting. A smile works its way across her face.

"Ahh, Senior *and* Junior. Must be my lucky . . ." She trails off as she sees me. "And you are?"

"This is my daughter-in-law, Clara," Papa says, gesturing toward me. "Glen's wife."

Kara's lip curls. "Oh yes. The wife. Nice to meet you."

"Clara," Papa says. "Glen and I need to talk to Sonny for a moment. Why don't you stick around here while we take care of business?"

This trip is far less interesting than I had hoped. Still, with Papa and Glen leaving, maybe I can ask Kara some questions.

The men leave, and Kara crawls out of bed. She is completely nude and not ashamed. My face heats, and she grins. "Amazing. Girls around here don't blush. Do my boobs bother you?"

I don't answer, but she dons a robe anyway. I search for words. I feel awkward, but Kara is the picture of ease, as if she always has strange people in her room. And she does, I realize with a start. In fact, this is probably less weird, because I'm not trying to have sex with her.

"How long have you and Glen been married?" Kara asks, startling me.

"Um, a few months," I say.

"How sweet."

"How long have you been here?" I estimate her age to be about twenty-five.

"I came when I was sixteen," she replies. "So about three years."

My mouth drops open. "You're nineteen?" I ask before I can stop myself.

Kara is in the middle of lighting a cigarette, and stops to look at me. "Yeah. I guess. Why?"

I shake my head. "No reason. I thought you were at least . . . twenty." I scramble to cover up my mistake.

Kara laughs. "Let's be real here, Clara. I look like shit. This job ages you pretty quick."

"Then why do you do it?"

She stares at me in disbelief. "It's not like I chose it, bitch."

I have offended her. I hold up my hands. "I'm sorry," I say, and rack my brain for a new topic. There is something I want to know, but I am afraid to ask. Kara is watching me with a strange look on her face, so I plunge forward.

"Do you know a girl named Macy?" I ask. If Kara has been here for three years, she should know her. Maybe we can sneak over to her room and say hello.

Kara's face softens. "Yeah, I knew her."

Wait. "You *knew* her? Did she leave?"

"She a friend of yours?"

"My best friend," I say. "Until she messed up and got sent here. I haven't seen her since my wedding."

A muscle ticks in Kara's jaw, and she takes a deep drag of her cigarette. "Shit, I hate to be the one who has to let you know."

"Let me know what?"

Kara bites her lip, as if deciding how to word her response. "She . . . she ain't here no more. She . . . ahh . . . she got shipped outta here a couple months ago. Don't know where."

My hand flies to my mouth. Macy is gone? How could that be? How could Glen have kept that from me? Because surely he knew. He is his dad's right-hand man now. He knows everything that goes on. A girl cannot be moved without his finding out.

"I'm sorry," Kara says again. "She was real nice. Helped me out when I got in a bad spot."

My hands are shaking, and I sit down on the edge of Kara's bed, forgetting my aversion to touching anything in this godforsaken building. The building Macy lived in for two years, just minutes from where I have been living my dream. It feels so empty now that I know she's not here. That the tenuous connection I felt has been leading to nothing for months. Two months ago was just after the wedding. Did they send her away because she talked to me? Because I pressed for information? I feel myself losing it and I cannot get control. I have worked so hard on keeping myself composed, but knowing she is gone, knowing that dear piece of my childhood has been swept away, proves too much.

I am sobbing when Glen rushes back into the room. I hear him yelling, and I hear a smack and a thud as Kara falls to the ground under Papa's hand.

"Take her out the back door," Papa hisses, and Glen sweeps me into his arms, putting a hand over my mouth to muffle the sobs.

When we are back in the car, Glen holds me in his lap, rocking me and whispering words of comfort. I know I will pay for this breakdown later, but for now, Glen cares for me and lets me cry. As I come down from my loss of control, I realize that while I have lost Macy, I have not lost all of my childhood. Glen is still here. Glen is my tether, keeping my heart and my soul close to his own.

Now

Pam's words echo through my head as I stare at the cracked floor of my room. Connor brought me a letter from Passion this morning, but I have not read it. I clutch it to my chest, terrified that I will open it to find the same condemning words inside that have been bouncing through my skull since the last group. One of these days Passion is going to wake up, too, and realize that I could have saved her and chose not to.

Is she coming to the same realizations I have been? I always thought I was happy. I was living my dream with Glen and our daughters. And our daughters were happy, too. For the most part. Of course, the adjustment to living with us was always a little difficult, but I loved each of them, and I believe they came to love me as well. Passion and I were especially close. She reminds me of Macy in so many ways, a little wild, unafraid, but also of myself, eager to please, quick to help. Is it possible that I was so caught up in trying to please Glen, trying to please Mama and Papa, even trying to please the numerous clients who were in and out of our lives in a flash, that I missed something? Missed that it wasn't right, that the girls weren't okay?

A tear rolls down my cheek. What kind of mother sells her daughters? It was how I'd always lived, how I believed I came to live with Mama and Papa. But when I look back now, there is a dark shadow over my entire life, as far back as I can remember. Playing with the girls, while Glen plotted to sell them to whoever gave him the best offer. I am starting to wonder if he ever cared about them the way he claimed. His eyes certainly never lit up the way they did when I told him about Nut.

When I really think about it, there were times when I knew things weren't right. When things felt a little off. An itch I couldn't quite scratch. But I trusted Glen more than I trusted myself. Each time I spoke up, talked back, I was taught that my thoughts and opinions were wrong, and I stopped believing any doubts that popped into my head.

Dr. Mulligan claims my family still wants to meet me. We talked about some of the things she could share with them, so they know the basics, but I'm not sure they fully understand. If they did, they wouldn't want to meet me. They wouldn't want me to taint their perfect lives. I imagine them living in sunshine, happy, smiling like in the pictures I was shown. I will bring nothing but darkness and heartache into their world.

I flop onto my back, letter still held over my heart, the springs on the bed squeaking in protest at the sudden movement. My family will be better off if we do not meet. I don't want them to know what I've done. It will be better if they just move on, and I can start fresh with my precious Nut. And maybe when Glen gets out, he can start fresh, too. We can find a house far away, where no one knows us, and there is no "business." Just us. Together. As we were always meant to be.

My daydreams lull me into a light sleep, and I wake when I hear the door creak open. I roll my head to the side to peek at the intruder.

"You have a visitor, Clara," Jay says, poking his head into the room.

I groan. I don't think I have the patience to deal with Mama today. "Tell her I'm sick," I say, and it's not entirely untrue. I have felt ill since Pam lobbed her verbal assault.

"Connor says you need to go."

"Connor says," I mimic, knowing I'm being difficult, but finding it hard to care. With a dramatic sigh, I heave myself into a sitting position. "Fine. Yes, sir. Whatever you say, sir."

Jay frowns, and I feel a small stab of guilt. He has been nothing but kind to me and doesn't deserve my mocking, but he's the only available target at the moment, and it feels good to release my anger at someone. I am being selfish again. Perhaps it's just who I am. Selfish.

"Let's get this over with," I say, standing to follow Jay down the drab hallway to the visitor room. I brace myself, preparing to put on a happy face for Mama. I don't know how I am supposed to react to her now, so I decide to pretend nothing has changed.

Jay opens the door to the visitor room and I freeze. Tori leans on one of the tables, studying her nails. She looks up when Jay clears his throat. "You have fifteen minutes," he says, pulling the door shut behind him.

Tori smiles and nods toward a table. "Care to sit?"

My feet carry me forward before my mind can catch up with the action. None of the girls from the group have visited me before. No one even really mentions the fact that I am being held here, that when the group disperses at the end of each hour, I head back into protective custody while they all head to their homes, their friends and family. I flush in embarrassment that Tori is seeing me like this, in this place, even though we are in the same building where we normally meet.

"How are you, Clara?" Tori asks when I finally slide into the chair across from her.

"Okay."

Her brow wrinkles. "Let me try that again. How are you *really*?"

She's beginning to sound like Dr. Mulligan. "Do you really care?" I can hear the bitterness in my voice, again misdirected.

Leaning back in her chair, Tori crosses her arms. "Of course I care. I wouldn't be here if I didn't. I had to get special permission from that agent and your therapist. Would someone who doesn't care go to all that trouble?"

I cross my arms over my chest, mimicking her position, and study her. Her face remains open, honest, and I see a glimmer of concern in her eyes. She really is here to see how I'm doing. Something inside me cracks.

"Everyone hates me, don't they?" I place my elbows on the table and rest my face in my hands. "You're here to ask me not to return to the group? It's okay. I won't be back."

"Oh, Clara." Tori sighs. "That would be a mistake, not to come back. Don't let Pam's outburst keep you away."

"She's right though, isn't she?" I don't know if Tori can understand my mumbling through my fingers. "I've done some terrible things."

Cool palms grasp my wrists, pulling my hands away from my face. "Clara, look at me." Tori's voice is firm, sharper than I have ever heard her speak. "Self-pity will get you nowhere. Blaming yourself for things you didn't do will get you nowhere. So snap the hell out of it and talk to me."

I'm shocked. Tori is always so gentle and affirming in group. She has always let me take my time in things, but now she is demanding and almost harsh. And it's just what I need. This sort of interaction is familiar. I know how to respond to commands. I pull my hands away and sit up straighter in my chair.

"What do you want me to say?" I ask. "I look back at the last seventeen years and all the beautiful memories I thought I had are shadowed by what-ifs. What if I hadn't been taken? What if I had listened to that part of me that wondered if what we were doing was right?" My fingernails dig into my palms. "There was always a part of me that wondered. Not until later. And I told myself it was fine, that Glen was good and kind, and that he loved the girls as much as I did, so he wouldn't put them in a bad situation."

Tori listens, her gaze never wavering from mine, steady and calm.

"As for his other . . . businesses, I always believed the women wanted to be there, or that they had done something that made them deserve that kind of life. Even when I lost my best friend . . . even when she was forced into that life, I still believed it was because she had committed an act awful enough to deserve it."

The tears come. They drip down my cheeks and onto the table, and I make no move to wipe them away. Tori says nothing until the streams slow, and I use my shirt sleeve to dab my eyes.

"Why did you decide to share your story?" Tori asks at last.

I shrug. "Dr. Mulligan said I needed to. I wanted to cooperate so I can get out of here."

"Bullshit."

My eyes fly to hers, startled. "What?"

"You heard me. That answer is bullshit. You forget that I've been in your place. Obviously not exactly, but I had no intention of being part of a therapy group or talking to anyone about anything when I got out. I hated the word 'victim.' But what I found out was that the best way to stop being called a victim was to stop acting like one and become a survivor instead. So, Clara, again, why did you want to share your story?"

The words fall out of my mouth before I can stop them. "I wanted to know if everyone would think I was terrible. I wanted to know if my family, the one that I was born into, would think less of me if they found out what I did. I wanted someone to tell me, one way or the other, if I am a bad person." I am breathing hard, my heart thumping with the exhilaration of being so honest with someone, with putting a name to all those feelings that I've been holding in.

"And what did you find out?"

My shoulders droop. "I am not a good person. I should not meet my family because they deserve better than a dark, used-up version of the girl they lost."

Tori taps her chin, lips pursed. "Who said that?"

Eyebrow raised, I stare at her. "Pam?" Tori was there. She heard everything Pam said.

"Okay. Who else?"

I search my memory for another hostile face, but come up empty. I shrug. "I guess that's it. But she said it all."

"So one person's opinion matters more than the other ten of us who were there? That seems a little harsh."

When she puts it that way, I feel a twinge of guilt. "But she said everything that I feared. It was like my worst nightmare coming alive."

Tori reaches out and grabs my hands. "Listen, Clara. There are going to be people who see you as the bad guy. They are going to question your choices. They are going to paint a crazy dark caricature of you and try to convince everyone, yourself included, that you purposely tried to hurt those girls. That you wanted them to be miserable."

"That's not true!" I say, yanking my hands from hers. "I loved those girls. Every one of them. I wanted them to be happy. I believed Glen when he said they would be. I mean, sometimes I questioned . . . but I never wanted bad things for them. Never."

"Then there's your answer." Tori leans back in her chair. "Everyone does things they're not proud of. Everyone makes bad choices. But your intentions were never bad. And no matter what, the only thing you can control is what you do now."

"But I should have—"

"Stop it." Tori sounds impatient. "I've mentioned the house I was kept in a few times during group. Did I ever tell you how I ended up in that house?"

I shake my head.

"I wanted to go to a concert and my parents wouldn't let me. I stayed over with a friend, and we hitched a ride into the city."

"And the guy who gave you a ride took you?"

"No." Tori laughed, but the sound was bitter. "A security guard. He told us we could go backstage to meet the band. Except once we were in the back hallway, some big guys jumped out and forced us into a van."

"I'm so sorry."

Tori shakes her head. "That's not the point. The point is that for years I beat myself up over my choice not to listen to my parents. I thought it was my fault. If only I had listened. If only I had told them where I was, since they didn't even know to look in the city for days. But it was never my fault. Sure, I made bad choices, but the guys who took me? They are the ones at fault."

"But I did things. I helped them."

"Clara. You have a choice now. Focus on what you did and how bad you feel about it, or focus on how you can start the process of healing, not only for yourself, but for your family, and for the families of the girls who were taken."

Jay taps lightly on the door frame. "Time's almost up, Clara." I nod at him.

Tori stands. "I hope you'll come back, Clara. And I hope you'll see your family. I was terrified the first time I saw my parents after I was rescued. I thought they would be angry. But they were just so over-joyed to have me back and be able to tell me how much they loved me."

I nod as I stand as well. "I'll think about it. Thank you."

She moves as if to hug me, but then steps back and smiles. "See you soon?"

"Sure."

She turns and walks to the exit, sending a small wave before slipping out the door. As Jay walks me back to my room, my mind is tumbling with a mix of confused emotions. I have a lot of thinking to do.

Then

Glen shakes out the blanket and snaps it so it floats to the ground, perfectly smooth. I clap in delight. "Nicely done, Mr. Lawson."

"I do what I can, Mrs. Lawson," he says, settling down on the blanket and pulling me to sit between his knees, my back to his chest. His arms wrap around me and I snuggle in, happy and content. This is the first time we have had the opportunity to be together like this since we moved into the house. There always seems to be something to do, another crisis Glen has to take care of. And Joel has brought in several new girls over the past few weeks, almost more than I can handle. Thank goodness Passion has been helpful, and Mama even came by to help get everyone settled.

But tonight, it's just us. Just Glen and me, by ourselves, enjoying a late picnic. The girls are asleep, Joel is keeping watch over the house, and Passion is in charge within. Glen brought me along the lake path to a small clearing away from the compound. It's like our own little world out here, and the stars shine even brighter away from the flood-lights around the house.

Glen kisses my hair and reaches for the picnic basket. I sit up and turn to face him, and we take turns feeding each other bits of chicken and fruits, all finger food for this very purpose. And we talk, as we have not talked in months. About the girls, about the future, about the past.

"Tonight is extra special, Clara," Glen says, glancing up at the sky. "Do you remember the first time we went out on the roof?"

Of course I remember. Everything changed that night. That's when our relationship really began, the obedient girl and the rebellious boy. I nod. "Yes, the meteor shower."

He grins. "The meteor shower." He takes my shoulders, his hands gentle as he turns me around and pulls me back against his chest.

Streaking through the dark sky, I see first one, then two, then countless shooting stars, blazing triumphantly for but a moment, then fading to nothing. The other stars, which I had before seen as bright and stunning, pale in comparison to their fiery cousins. I grip Glen's arms, which are wrapped around me, mesmerized by the show Mother Nature is putting on for us. It is glorious and exhilarating and also a little sad, watching those tiny lights pulse and die. I say as much to Glen.

"But what a gift their short lives are, baby," he whispers in my ear. "Their purpose has been served. What a way to go."

His breath tickles my ear, and when he stops talking, his lips remain, moving down to kiss just behind my ear and down my neck. I close my eyes and focus on the points where his skin meet mine. His hands stroke across my stomach, then divide and conquer as one moves up and one moves down. He guides me to lie down on the blanket as the kisses and caresses continue.

As Glen rises above me, his face framed by the falling heavens behind him, I see the boy I fell in love with. The boy who was eager for the future, who was excited about what the world had to offer. This is the Glen I remember, not the cynical man he has become, so much like the father he both revered and despised. I pull his lips to mine as we come together and I pour all my feelings into him, all the words I am not brave enough to say.

In the afterglow, I am afraid my Glen will disappear again, but as we lie entwined, sweat cooling on our skin from the breeze coming off the lake, he holds me close, whispering words of love. I want to stay in this spot forever, just the two of us, the way we both always wanted it to be. The way we were meant to be.

A rustle in the bushes startles me, and I curl into Glen, trying to cover myself. His body stiffens.

"Who's out there?" Glen growls, and I am fearful for whoever has interrupted our time.

"Sir, Mr. Lawson, I'm sorry to bother you . . ." A timid voice floats out from the trees.

"Then get the fuck away," Glen says, pulling the blanket up over our bodies.

"Sir, there's been a breach at the training camp. Joel sent me to find you."

"Fuck." Glen mutters a few more choice expletives before responding. "Fine. Give me five minutes. Wait by the south guard station."

"Yes, sir." Hurried footsteps fade into the forest, and Glen rests his forehead on mine.

"I'm so sorry, baby," Glen says. "I hate to cut this short."

I manage a small smile. "Duty calls." I flinch, hoping Glen does not reprimand me for my flippant comment. I didn't mean for it to come out sarcastic.

Instead of getting angry, Glen turns thoughtful. "Why don't you come with me? See some of the other things I do? I know you don't see much of my other businesses. Maybe you should."

I wrinkle my nose. "I've seen the brothel."

He laughs. "No, I mean the training camp. If you promise to do as

I say and stay out of the way, you can come along and check it out." He pauses. "If you want to, that is."

Glen wants to show me the training camp, and he's giving me a choice. I'm not sure what has gotten into him tonight, but his mood is a gift I am not willing to waste.

"I would love to go."

We pull on our clothes, fabric and zippers rustling in the quiet night, and Glen grabs my hand and leads me along the path. A guard shack comes into view in minutes, and I realize that our picnic spot was not as private as I had first assumed. The young guard who interrupted us waits by the building, standing tall, but a flush creeps up his neck when he glances in my direction. My cheeks grow warm.

Glen looks between the two of us, smirking. I am thankful when he doesn't comment. Instead, he goes into commander mode as we climb into the jeep waiting along the dirt road that wraps around the lake. I know the training camp isn't too far, within walking distance, but the guards use vehicles to get between the cabins and the camp in a short amount of time.

The boys who are brought in go to the training camp and participate in a rigorous program to build their physical strength and train them to be obedient workers. When they graduate the program, they are sent to be laborers or bodyguards elsewhere. Those at the top of the class move into the cabins as part of Glen's guard. I know Papa had a similar program, and I shudder when I remember my few visits there.

When we pull up, it's clear that there is something going on. Boys are running toward a tight knot of men. I cannot see what they are guarding, but they all look down to the center of their little circle, arms crossed. Glen hops out of the van and strides toward the crowd, the guard who drove us scrambling after. I hesitate before climbing out, the rock in my gut telling me I should have stayed back at the picnic site.

Everyone grows quiet as Glen approaches, and the men part for him. His power here is palpable, and I have the throwaway thought that I wish Papa had lived to see Glen really step into his position and own it. I think Papa always believed in Glen, but Glen snarls if I ever mention Papa these days.

I creep forward, the only sound now the rustling of the trees, the insects chirping, and Glen's solid footsteps against the dirt of the clearing. As I move closer, I hear another sound, a whimpering. Glen is now part of the circle, hands on hips, staring at the ground. He moves to the right and I see it.

A boy, who looks to be in his early teens, though he is quite small, is curled into himself on the ground. He is covered in twigs and dirt, and I realize that he must have tried to run away. Quite brave. Some of the boys they bring in are not cut out for such a rigorous program.

Glen crouches, signaling to the men in the circle. As one unit, they grasp the boy's limbs and pry him out of his tiny ball. He struggles, and his whimpers turn into high-pitched screeches, his voice cracking.

Smack.

Glen's fist falls across the boy's face, and he is shocked into silence. I cannot hear what Glen says as he speaks in a low voice to the boy, but the boy's eyes grow wide, and fresh tears track mud down his dirty cheeks. Glen grabs the boy's shoulders and shakes him, and I swear I hear his teeth clatter. I gasp, and the boy's bright eyes snap to mine. There is pleading in them, and I start forward without thinking.

An arm snakes around my waist, yanking me to the side. The assailant drags me into the shadows of the trees until I can no longer see Glen or the boy. I can still hear the murmur of voices.

The thick arms release me, and I whirl on my attacker. Joel. Of course. The look on his face is serious this time, no hint of humor, and my sharp words die on my tongue.

"Not this time, Clare," he says. "This is Glen's domain. I don't . . ."

He runs a rough hand through his hair. "I don't know what he would do to you if you interfered here."

A caring Joel? Concerned for my well-being? Or saving his own skin? I search his face for signs of mirth, but find only sincerity. Perhaps the only time I have seen Joel so serious. I nod. "Okay."

Screams pierce the air, and I turn back, ready to run back to the camp despite my agreement to stay out of it. Joel grabs my arm.

"Let me walk you back. I'll tell Glen where you went."

I strain against his hold, but he is stronger. He pulls me away, and the wails grow quieter with distance, lost in the wind in the trees and the occasional hoot of an owl. Joel and I do not speak. He walks me to the foot of the stairs, and I go straight into the house and up to bed without looking back.

Sleep is hard to come by, but I pretend to be unconscious when Glen returns. He climbs into bed and pulls me close, and I will myself to forget how the evening turned out. Maybe it is better not to know all of Glen's secrets, because despite them, he is my home.

Now

I sit on my bed, staring at the picture of the smiling McKinleys, trying to place myself there, to dredge up any memory of their faces. As it has for the past several days, my head begins to ache as soon as I dig deeper into the past, the two laughing girls from my dreams the only memories I can conjure. I am almost certain now that they are memories, memories of my sister and of myself. My eyes are sticky. I haven't been sleeping. The lights brightened a while ago, so I know it's morning. They haven't brought my breakfast yet. I wonder if anyone is watching me unravel. I feel myself slipping to that place, the place where I do not think about things, do not answer questions, do not have my own questions begging to be answered.

Oblivion beckons, not the true oblivion of death—with my Nut I still have so much to live for—but the oblivion of not thinking, not caring. I can go through the motions. I can eat, sustain myself for the life growing inside me. But I do not have to talk anymore. I do not have to cooperate.

And yet . . . the smiling faces of the family in front of me pull me in a different direction. I am not that girl anymore. The one who arrived in this place so many weeks ago. I am stronger than she was. I am smarter than she was. I have more to live for than she did.

I jump off my bed and rush to the door, banging my fists against the metal until I hear a click on the other side indicating the lock has disengaged. I back up as the door opens and one of the regular night guards steps inside. I have never bothered to learn his name, but his badge reads "Tom."

He raises an eyebrow at me, and I realize I must look like a crazy person. They probably all think I'm a crazy person anyway, and I find it hard to care one way or the other what they think of me. "I need to talk to Connor."

"Agent Calhoun has not arrived for the day yet."

I frown. I'm not sure why I pictured Connor as constantly around, always ready to talk when I am. I never imagined that he might have a life outside of this place, despite our conversation about his girl-friend. Friends. Family. All the things that I have lost, available to him. The thought makes me angry.

"I need to speak with him. NOW." The last word is shouted. I do not want to fade into oblivion. I do not want to shut down. I have been swirling in a storm of confusion since I arrived, and now I want answers.

Tom's mouth tightens. "I'll see what I can do." He closes the door behind him with more force than necessary.

Rage flows through my veins. I am angry at Connor for having a life. I am angry at Dr. Mulligan for making me think about things I would have rather left alone. I am angry at all the members of the support group for making me question my own actions, angry I might belong there after all. I push that thought away. I am angry at Mama Mae and Papa G for keeping me in the dark, for never fully trusting me, for treating me like a child no matter how old I got. And, most of all, I am angry at Glen. He did not prepare me for this, with his confusing instructions to say nothing and to speak, and his cryptic messages demanding that I rewrite history. I am alone. He is not going to save me this time. It is time for me to save myself.

My feet are starting to blister from my pacing by the time Connor enters the room. I whirl on him, fists clenched. "It's my turn for answers." My voice is low, almost a growl, and it surprises even me.

Connor studies me, unintimidated and calculating. He nods. "Can you wait a couple hours until Dr. Mulligan is available?"

His calm response pierces my angry haze. I take some deep breaths, the oxygen bringing clarity to my brain. "Fine."

There is a knock at the door and Tom steps in with my breakfast. I take it and return to sit on my bed, where I pick at the food on the plate.

"Tell you what," Connor says. "Promise me you will eat everything on your tray and I will personally go speed things along with Dr. Mulligan."

Instead of responding, I pick up the apple and take an enormous bite. A smile tugs at the corners of Connor's mouth before he turns and leaves the room.

True to his word, Connor returns within the hour to fetch me. I have also fulfilled my part of the bargain and return an empty tray to Tom on the way out. We march through the quiet hallways. It's still early enough that there is little of the normal bustling activity.

I stop short when I see Dr. Mulligan, and Connor runs into me from behind, gripping my shoulders to steady himself. Dr. Mulligan is in jeans and a T-shirt, nothing like her usual business style. Her hair is pulled back into a ponytail, and her makeup is minimal. She looks younger, somehow. She smiles as I stare.

"I apologize for my appearance, Clara," she says. "It's Saturday, so I wasn't planning on being here."

Saturday? I count in my head. Of course it's Saturday. I lost track of the last couple of days. Weeks.

"I-I'm sorry," I stammer, guilt washing over me, eroding my anger even more.

Dr. Mulligan's smile is kind. "It's okay, Clara. It's just one Saturday, and when Agent Calhoun—Connor—called, I knew it must be important."

I nod and make my way to the couch. "I think . . . I think I'm ready to have some questions answered." I release the photograph I have been clutching and let it float to the table. "Tell me about my . . . about the McKinleys."

Dr. Mulligan sits next to me on the couch instead of in her chair as she normally does. She picks up the photo. "I have talked to Jane and Doug McKinley. I can tell you what they told me, but you'll learn more if you talk to them directly."

I swallow the lump that has already begun to form in my throat. "I want to know what they told you, and then I'll decide."

Connor remains quiet, but his presence is comforting. He has chosen to remain standing today, giving this moment to Dr. Mulligan, but the fact that he doesn't leave speaks volumes. He knows that I want him to stay. He has become a constant for me, here since this whole ordeal began. Drawing strength from him, I take a deep breath and turn to Dr. Mulligan. "I'm ready."

"According to Jane and Doug, on July 14, 1980, their daughter,

Diana—you"—Dr. Mulligan points to me—"went to play at the park with their older daughter, Charlotte. Charlotte came back alone, and when they went to find you, you had disappeared."

It makes me uncomfortable how she tells the story as if it really was me, a fact of which I am not yet entirely convinced. "So this Diana . . . she just . . . disappeared?"

"Yes. They searched the entire town and the surrounding country-side. There was a large state park, heavily wooded, and lots of fields. The whole town showed up to help look. They put up posters. They alerted the news teams. There was even a special report on the national news. But no one had seen you. You were just gone."

"So they stopped looking? How long before they gave up on her?" I know my voice sounds bitter.

A gentle smile crosses Dr. Mulligan's face. "Clara . . . Diana . . . they never stopped looking for you. They still put your picture out every year." She stands and walks to her filing cabinet, pulling out a piece of paper and returning to the couch. She hands it to me. I see the same picture they showed me the other day, a smiling brunette with dark brown eyes. Under the picture the word MISSING is printed in bold letters. Beneath that was the pertinent information: NAME—DIANA McKINLEY, LAST SEEN JULY 14, 1980. WOULD BE 23 NOW. Under the words is a picture of a woman whose face looks just a little off, almost unreal. If I squint, she almost looks like me.

I cannot speak. "They said my parents didn't want me," I finally whisper. "They told me they paid my parents a lot of money because *they* wanted me so much." The memories are fuzzy, but that has stuck with me. I never wanted to be unwanted again. I was so obedient to prove to Mama Mae that I was worthy of her time and money. That is why I also felt guiltier than Glen when we ruined their plans for my future.

"It's okay, Clara," Connor says, speaking up for the first time. "You couldn't have known."

"But I should have." My voice is rising. "If my parents loved me so much, how could I not have known? How could I have believed that?" My vision blurs as tears rush to my eyes.

Dr. Mulligan's hand covers mine. "You're trying to make sense of what you did seventeen years ago, Clara." I appreciate her use of the name I am familiar with. Diana still seems foreign to me. "Children are impressionable. Maybe you argued with them. Maybe you didn't believe it right away. But with enough time, we can be led to believe just about anything."

I swallow, but ignore the tears spilling onto my cheeks. All my thoughts from the past several days swirl through my brain, the questions I've asked myself, the conclusions I've started to reach. The reality that I may have to accept sooner rather than later. I have to know, but the next question I must ask terrifies me more than anything else that has happened. Especially since I believe I already know the answer. "Can we be led to believe that what we're doing is right? Even if it's wrong?"

Connor shifts, and when I look at him, the intensity of his gaze takes my breath. "What do you mean, Clara?" Dr. Mulligan draws my attention back to her.

"The girls . . . the business . . . the clients . . . I think . . ." Another deep breath. "I think that what I was doing might have been wrong."

I have never seen Dr. Mulligan speechless. I can tell she did not expect this from me. Certainly not now, and maybe not ever. Perhaps she assumed it would take me much longer to draw this conclusion, or that I would always believe that the world I had grown up in was normal. But the group has achieved its purpose.

I only spoke in the group the one time, but the stories I heard are all the same when they are stripped down to the basics. Girls being held against their will. Girls forced into servitude, many of them into sexual roles. All brainwashed into believing that what they were doing was their only choice, that there was no escape, no life outside of their current circumstances.

If the McKinleys truly wanted me, if they had not sold me to Mama and Papa as I had been told, then maybe it was all a lie. No, not maybe. It *was* a lie. I have been lied to my entire life, by the only family I have known. I was loved and cared for before that life was stolen from me. Before I was taught that my only value was in what I could do for others. I missed out on so much, and it tears me apart to think about the life that I could have had if Mama and Papa hadn't taken me.

Even worse, I did the same thing to so many other girls. I believed I was saving them from lives of being unloved and neglected, but instead I stole their futures, trained them, convinced them that they would be happiest with greedy men who wanted to exploit them for their own gain.

My soul feels crushed under a weight of guilt, and the sobs breaking forth sound as if they are coming from someone else. I don't recognize the noises I am making, but when Dr. Mulligan's arms come around me, I do not push her away.

I don't know how long I cry. When I am able to focus again, I see that Dr. Mulligan's face is stained with tears, and even Connor's eyes are red-rimmed, his knuckles white from the effort of holding in his emotion.

On the other side of the storm, my thoughts are clearer. I know what must be done, and I know the first step I want to take.

"What can I do to help hold them responsible for what they've done?"

Then

I am listening to an old record of Mama's, washing dishes, when they bring her in. A little girl with a short dark bob and teary brown eyes. She is not wild like Passion, but she is just as stubborn. Glen carries her in because she is playing a game where her muscles are all limp. He heaves her into a chair with a growl and stalks out without a word. We size each other up as the last strains of a song fade out. *Life in the fast lane . . .*

"Hello, Lane," I say, smiling at the inspiration. "You have very pretty hair."

She squints at me, still not allowing the tears to escape from her eyes. "That's not my name, lady, and you better not call me that again."

"How old are you, Lane?" I ask, turning to the sink. She huffs, and I smile at the small sound. Usually they are too scared to be at all entertaining, at least right away. I school my features back to a neutral expression and glance back over my shoulder.

"I'm ten, and if you don't bring me back to my parents, they're gonna find you and punch your face." She crosses her arms and legs as tight across her body as she can make them, scrunching her nose at the same time.

"I don't think I would like that very much, Lane, but I'm not too worried about it." I dry the last plate and stack it in the cupboard before taking a seat across from the little girl.

Her lip quivers. "Why do you keep calling me that? My name is Maria."

I tsk. "Hush now, Lane. Maria was your old name. Now you get a new name. How exciting!"

"I wanna go home." One crystal tear snakes down the dark skin of her cheek.

Scooting my chair closer, I lean in. "This is your home now, Lane. Your parents . . . well . . . they wanted you to have a better home than they could give you, so here you are!"

"That's not true!" Lane shouts, color blossoming on her neck. "I heard them talking about my surprise party just yesterday!" A thread of unease weaves into her tone. She is beginning to doubt.

"Hmm," I say, placing my chin in my hand. "Do you think maybe *this* was the surprise? You coming to live here?"

"No." Her voice cracks. "My parents would never get rid of me. They asked me what I want for Christmas and my birthday and where I want to go for spring break. There's no way they would plan all that and then send me away."

The problem with the older ones is that they have a hard time believing my stories. Of course, these are all unwanted girls, but I have to make up the reasons myself. I try to keep the stories different, in case the girls compare notes, but they rarely do. No one wants to admit to being unwanted, even if they are all in the same boat.

"Well, Lane," I say, slapping my hands on my thighs, "whatever the reason, you're here now, and I am so excited that you are a part of our family. We will begin your training tomorrow."

"She went to buy me a book," Lane says stubbornly. "She said to stay in the car and she would be back in ten minutes. And then those guys came and they dragged me out and I couldn't even scream. And now I'm here. My mom didn't leave me. She was coming back. *She was coming back.*" She whispers the last part, whether to convince herself or me, I am not sure, but I am shaken.

Glen never talks about how he gets the girls. I assume the parents hand them off. In my fantasies, I picture some beautiful scene where he promises to watch over them and give them the best life possible, and maybe even mentions how his wife will take really good care of them.

That is not the picture Lane paints for me.

I reach to touch her arm and she stiffens. "It will be okay, Lane. You will have a good life here. And a wonderful future." The words sound hollow all of a sudden. I have said them countless times, to countless crying children, but for the first time they sound insincere, false.

"I wanna be a doctor," Lane says. "My parents say I'm smart enough. I wanna go to college and be a doctor. Can I do that here?"

The smile is a struggle this time, forced onto my face by a sense of duty and a longing to comfort. "No, Lane. Not here. But we can learn about some doctor stuff, if that is what you want."

"What am I going to do here?" Lane asks. She is very articulate for a ten-year-old.

"We'll save those answers for another day," I say, pulling my hand back and standing. "For now, let's get you changed."

Lane does not move. She pulls herself into a tight ball and stares at the wall. She is stone. Even her tears dry up, and her eyes shutter, closed off from any emotion or response.

"Lane?" I reach toward her, and she doesn't react. "I need you to come with me, sweetheart."

Nothing.

I finish tidying the kitchen, keeping watch over Lane, waiting for some break in her armor. Her muscles must be getting sore from being in the same position for so long, but still she sits. And stares. Around eight, I call Passion in. She responds immediately, coming to stand next to where I am leaning against the door frame, arms crossed over my chest.

"I will need you to take care of the girls tonight," I say, glancing at her only for a moment before returning my gaze to the statue that is Lane. I don't want to miss the moment she breaks her pose.

Passion shifts, hands behind her back, sneaking peeks at the new girl across the room. I can tell she wants to say something, but does not want to speak out of turn. It is a constant battle with Passion, and though I know Glen does not approve, this quirk of hers always makes me smile.

"Did you have a question?" I ask, my voice innocent, a smirk dragging up one corner of my mouth.

"Umm . . ." Passion hesitates. I frown. I wish she would not assume that she will be in trouble with me. I have rarely found occasion to punish her since those early days.

"What is it, Passion?" My tone is crosser than I intend it to be. I make an effort to soften and turn a quick smile in her direction. "I am a little busy here."

"I was thinking maybe I could try?" Her statement comes out as a question. We need to work on her confidence.

"I'm not sure I understand. Please try again." Every moment is a teaching moment when raising children, especially these girls. Every interaction must be perfect.

She takes a deep breath, squaring her shoulders, lifting her chin. "If it is acceptable to you, Clara, I would like to try to help the new girl with her transition into our home."

This time my smile is sincere. "Once the other girls are taken care of, if Lane has not chosen to comply on her own, you may talk to her. Thank you, Passion."

I see the glee she tries to hide before she nods and hurries away. I shake my head. The other girls will most likely have a shortened story time tonight. But maybe Passion can help. She was by far my most difficult girl to transition in, although her form of rebellion was more explosive, while Lane seems to be shrinking into herself more even as I watch.

Thirty minutes later, Passion returns. "They're all in bed, the music is on, and most are already asleep." Her words come out in a rush.

Saying nothing, I nod toward Lane. I am interested to see how this interaction will go.

Passion approaches Lane with small, slow steps, pulling a chair closer to where the girl sits. She lowers herself to the chair, near enough that her knees might be touching Lane's if the younger girl's legs were dangling off the chair as they should be.

"Hello, Lane," Passion says, using the soft, cooing voice she reserves for the younger girls. She took note of Lane's name when I said it earlier, I realize with approval. She really is very good. "My name is Passion."

Lane scrunches up her nose. "That's not a real name."

Rather than becoming offended, Passion smiles at Lane. "Of course it is. It's what everyone calls me, so it's my name."

Lane has not moved a muscle other than those in her face. "Was it always your name?" she whispers.

Passion shakes her head, her gentle smile still in place. "It's a very special name Miss Clara gave me when I came to live with her."

"What was your name before?"

A cloud passes over Passion's face. "I don't remember," she says. I can hear the lie, but I do not admonish her. That is one lie she is allowed to tell, since she must never use her old name or tell anyone what it was. "But I like Passion. It describes me well."

Lane makes a face. "Lane doesn't describe me at all. I'm not lines on a road."

"Hmmm." Passion ponders Lane's words. "Well, maybe not if you think of it as *just* lines on a road. But lanes do so much more than mark roads."

"Like what?" Lane shifts, her arms loosening their grip on her knees. I feel Glen walk up behind me, his familiar scent a comfort. I look over my shoulder and return his questioning gaze with a finger to my lips. He stands close and I lean into him, watching the girls interact.

"They keep people on the right path, right?" Passion says, her face becoming excited. "And they can direct people in a lot of different directions. Maybe with your new name, you will be a good guide for people, to help them find the right way."

Delighted, I look up at Glen again. The hard lines of his face are not relaxed as I'd hoped. Surely he sees how Passion is taking the lead. Maybe she will be ready for her own client soon. She has come so far.

Lane nods. "I like that, I think. But I'll have to talk to my mom—"

Passion's hand shoots out to cover Lane's mouth, and the younger girl's eyes grow wide. "No, Lane," Passion says firmly. "You are not to speak of your old parents. They didn't want you. That's why you're here."

Fat tears roll from the corners of Lane's eyes. She tries to talk against Passion's hand, but it comes out muffled. Glen stiffens. I try to stop him, but he strides over to where Lane sits. Passion's eyes turn fearful. I rush forward, but I know I cannot stop whatever Glen has planned. I reach for Passion as she reaches for Glen and stop her before she can put a hand on him. I know that would not end well for her. Glen glares at Lane.

"Enough. You won't be a spoiled princess while you're living here. You will not talk about the people who gave you away. You won't use your former name. You will listen to Clara, and you will listen to me, or you will be punished."

Lane opens her mouth and a high-pitched wail comes out. It is cut off as Glen grabs her with rough hands. "I think we have an example of what happens when girls don't listen happening right now down at the tree." He throws Lane over his shoulder and stomps out the door.

I chase after him, turning to look back at Passion. "Stay with the girls," I command, and I can tell it takes everything in her to remain where she is instead of following me. "Glen!" I call. "Please, she was opening up, she was almost there—"

He whirls, and I wince as tree branches cut across Lane's face. "Are you questioning me, Clara?"

"No." I take a step back, knowing that in this mood he won't hesitate to strike if I say the wrong thing. "I just think if we wait—"

"Why wait? She needs to know, and the sooner the better. If you come, you do not interfere. Do you understand?"

I nod. I would rather be close, where I can keep an eye on her. If we are going to the tree, there will be any number of men and boys of all ages. I do not wish for her to be alone among them. I follow silently as Glen hauls Lane down the rest of the path.

Now

I fidget with my hair, though my reflection shows that it has not moved since I fixed it five minutes ago. I step back and smooth my skirt and simple blouse, a gift from my support group for a special occasion. I wonder briefly if I will ever get my old clothes back. There are more important things to worry about now, though.

I am meeting my family today.

Over the past few days, I have begun to think of them as my family. I still have no solid memories of them, but I'm hoping with this meeting, I will get closer to that. I have not had contact with Mama Mae or Glen, but have continued corresponding with Passion, who is now going by Emily. It's hard for me to wrap my mind around her with a different name, but she has been moved into a foster home, and it is her wish. I hope to be able to see her again, hold her again, but for now, her words give me comfort.

Mixed with my anxious excitement is a pit of fear in my stomach. Dr. Mulligan says my family cannot wait to meet me, and I believe her, but I also wonder if they will still be so excited when we're face-to-face. Though I am working to atone for my many misdeeds, I feel dirty, as if anyone who comes too close will be able to sense the rot from inside of me. I spin bizarre scenarios in which my family takes one look at me and walks out of the room, heads held high, refusing to acknowledge that such a black-souled individual could be related to them. In my worst imaginings, they shout horrible accusations at me, even worse because they are so true.

There is a knock at the door, and Jay and Connor step inside. We exchange no words, just polite smiles, as we head toward the room where my group meets. I requested this. I do not wish to do this reunion in Dr. Mulligan's office, and the official visitation room did not seem appropriate, either. Connor worked it out to have this room available.

We stop in front of the closed door. There are soft murmurs coming through the thin wood, and I am dizzy with the realization of what little there is separating me from a mother, a father, and a sister. Charlotte has a family of her own now, I have been told, but for now, only the three of them are here. I raise shaking hands to pat my hair one more time.

Connor turns. "Are you ready, Clara?" he asks, concern creasing his brow.

I nod. "Yes."

He raps on the door and the sounds from the other side cease. Connor and Jay step aside and I place my hand on the knob, turn, and push. I see Dr. Mulligan first. She stands with the other three in the center of the room, but as we approach she moves into a corner where she can unobtrusively lend support. The smile I flash at her reflects the queasiness in my gut.

My eyes drag back to the small group huddled in the middle of the room. The woman, dark shoulder-length hair shot through with streaks of gray, steps forward. Behind her, a man with a shiny head and a goatee places his arm around a woman not much older than me, whose dark blond hair falls in waves down to her shoulders. My family.

Before anyone says a word, I see it. I see the way the artificial light catches the strands of the woman's hair, like mine in the sunlight. The way the man's green eyes twinkle, keeping them from being too dark and serious, as mine have become. The nose of the blond woman, a mirror of her mother's . . . and of my own. My hand goes to my nose, tracing the shape, and the woman's face brightens.

"You are just as beautiful as I expected," she says, eyes glistening. There is no hostility in her voice, though it cracks with emotion.

My throat tightens. Tears begin to fall freely as I gaze on these people, and I have the feeling that I have always known them. Yes, they are strangers, but there is a familiarity that I have never before experienced. The older woman steps forward, arms out, and before I know what I am doing, my feet carry me toward her, closing the distance between us until I am wrapped in her warmth. I soak her shoulder with my tears, and hers fall into my hair, but neither of us moves.

A throat clears, and I look up to see both the man and the younger woman, my sister, with tears in their eyes. I smile, and they walk forward, joining us. I am in the middle, and I have never felt so safe, so loved, so cherished. They lend me their strength, and I know without a doubt, without uttering a word to them, that they will protect me with their lives.

After a long moment, we shift away from one another, sniffling, and chuckle as we take in our matching tear-stained faces.

"Please, Diana, let's sit down," the man says, gesturing toward the small cluster of uncomfortable chairs. The woman does not release me even as we sit. When we're all settled, the man speaks again. "Now that we've cried all over one another, I suppose some introductions are in order."

More laughter, and the woman squeezes my hand.

"I'm Doug," says the man. "I'm your dad." His voice breaks on the last word, but not in a sad way. More like an "I can't believe I get to say this" way. He points to the blond woman, who has taken the seat on the other side of me. "This is your sister, Charlotte, and the woman hanging off your hand is Jane."

"Your mom," Jane supplies, grinning at me even as tears leak out from the corners of her eyes again.

I look at each of them, their expectant faces shining with hope and happiness. I don't want to break the moment. The time to talk about my past will come, but it is not today. "I'm so glad to meet you . . . I guess to meet you again," I add awkwardly.

A cough that sounds suspiciously like a laugh echoes through the room, and I look back at the agents, but Jay just shrugs at me. I relax, knowing that they've got my back. This is not a normal situation, and to try to pretend otherwise would be stupid.

"I-I'd really like to know more about you guys," I continue. "We have a lot to catch up on."

Charlotte jumps right in. "We all live in a small community just outside of the city," she says. "I'm married, and I have two young boys, Eli and Isaac. You'll meet them soon, and my husband, Jon. They're all very excited."

I smile at her enthusiasm, but my heart constricts. Charlotte is living the life I was supposed to live. The life I thought I was living. I realize that this will be my life now, hearing about the experiences others have had, comparing them to my own, coming up wanting. But

Dr. Mulligan has already warned me against this, and I do my best to focus on Charlotte's words and the fact that she desperately wants to share her life with me, and I let the bitterness melt away. I am sure it will be back, but for now I am able to relax into the conversation.

Doug talks for a while about his job as a high school principal, entertaining us with stories of the kids he works with. I am surprised to find some commonalities, even though the way I did school was very different from what Doug is talking about. Kids are the same in so many ways, and I nod along with some of his anecdotes, being able to picture one of my girls or another trying to pull the same sorts of antics.

Finally able to speak in a steady voice, Jane talks about the work she does in a women's shelter. Her voice warms as she talks about her job and the people there, both her fellow workers, who are all as passionate as she is about these women, and the women themselves, from a variety of diverse backgrounds. She speaks with pride about the women who have gone on to finish school or get jobs or even just get back on their feet. There is sadness in her voice when she talks about the children who are at the shelter with their mothers, no place else to go. Her desire to help those who are less fortunate is touching, and I hope that I have at least a tiny bit of that in myself.

I don't talk much, just listen and soak it all in, and too soon Connor interrupts and tells my family it is time to leave. We stand, and Charlotte reaches for me first.

"We'll be back soon. My boys can't wait to meet Auntie Diana." She pulls me close. "I'm so glad to have you back," she says, her voice strained with emotion.

Doug pulls me into a hug next, his voice rough. "I always knew you were out there, Dee-Dee," he says, and my heart warms at the nickname.

Last, Jane takes both of my hands and simply gazes into my eyes before pulling me close. I am taller than she is, and it almost feels like

I am hugging one of my older girls, except I am borrowing strength from Jane instead of the other way around. She stands on tiptoe to whisper in my ear. "I love you so much, Diana."

Doug wraps his arms around his wife's and daughter's shoulders, and they walk out as a unit, Jane taking one last look behind her before the door closes. I hold back the tears as they leave the room. As soon as they are gone, I collapse back into a chair, emotionally exhausted and feeling somewhat unsettled. Connor, Jay, and Dr. Mulligan claim the chairs that had been occupied by my family.

No one speaks for several minutes. I am the one to break the silence. "What's next?"

Then

It is auction day. The girls stand in a line from youngest to oldest, quiet but for anxious shifting. We have more auction-ready girls now than ever before. Eight of them, from ages twelve to seventeen. I will miss my girls, but I will be glad to have fewer of them around. They are all dressed in simple white dresses, hair pulled back from their faces.

"Please line up in the great room downstairs," I say to the oldest, Rochelle, who obediently turns and leads the way down the stairs. I tiptoe down the hall to peek in on the younger girls. My next generation. Not all the girls downstairs will be taken today, and those left will be trained to help with the little ones or shunted to the brothel.

The little girls are playing with dolls. There are five of them, the youngest just six years old. I cannot imagine how a parent would not want her, but as always, I have plenty of room in my heart for her. I christened her Chloe. Samantha, who is ten and the oldest of this group, is sitting by Chloe, trying to entice her to play. She will warm up eventually. They always do. Passion keeps the other three occupied, but I know she is paying attention to Samantha and Chloe as well. The girls who are being specially trained for their own clients are in another room, working on mending.

I slip out before they can spot me and ask me to play. I must be there for the other girls right now. I am thankful that Glen has agreed to let Passion stick around and help me. She will not listen to anyone else anyway. He threatened to send her to the brothel. It was our only major fight. I ended up with a broken wrist, but I won. Passion stayed. She will keep the little ones safe and quiet while our guests are here.

Downstairs, I find the girls standing as I have had them practice. Hands clasped in front of them, shoulders back, eyes straight ahead. Glen walks up and down the row, nodding. I pause at the bottom of the stairs and drink him in. He is so handsome. The dark blue shirt he wears complements his eyes, and his dark hair falls in carefully mussed waves to his ears. I have no trouble understanding how he is able to charm the clients. Just looking at him is enough to bring me a sense of safety and reassurance. He looks up and catches me watching him, and a smile flits across his face.

Glen walks over to me, wraps his arms around my waist, and lifts me off the step, spinning me before setting me down and planting a firm kiss on my lips. "You look perfect," he says, and I feel a warm glow in my belly. He pats my rear before turning back to the girls. I notice some of his guards stationed around the room, and the glow from Glen's compliments turns to anxiety.

"Is it dangerous to have an auction here?" I ask. It had been planned for one of the old warehouses by our old apartment, but a couple days ago Glen came home and announced that we were hosting it here at the house instead. He didn't give a reason. He never gives a reason, and I didn't dare ask.

"Nah." Glen shakes his head. "My guys are here mostly to make sure the clients keep their hands off the merchandise until it's paid for."

I blanch at the term "merchandise." Sometimes it almost seems like Glen does not see our daughters as people. I dismiss that thought, though. He loves them as I do and wants good things for them. Better than they could have had if they had ended up on the street. Or dead. I eye the large guns strapped to the backs of the guards.

"Where are all these guns coming from?" I whisper, and receive a pinch on the inside of my arm in response. I bite my lip to keep from squealing.

"You ask too many questions, Clara." Glen's voice holds a warning. "Just stick to what concerns you. These girls."

I nod, afraid to speak again, and Glen moves away to confer with his men. The doorbell rings, and the clients begin arriving.

Refreshments are placed all around. In the far corner of the room a table is set up to take the bids. It is a silent auction, with both clients and girls identified only by numbers. I hover near the line to make sure the girls comply with requests. The clients are not allowed to touch the girls, but can ask them to move this way or that. They are allowed to ask questions as well, to determine interests and intelligence. I am proud of my girls. They all answer their questions with great thought and articulation. Glen beams with pride from the other side of the room, and I know it is me he is proud of.

The auction moves quickly, and soon it is almost the end, and time for Glen to tally the results to find the highest bidders. Each girl has packed a small bag to take with her. Good-byes were said this morning. I search the room for Glen and find him having an intense conversation with a man who looks to be in his forties. Glen's forehead is wrinkled in concentration, and the corners of his mouth are turned down. The man is gesturing with his hands, making sharp stabbing motions in the air. I watch with interest until Glen nods. He looks up and immediately finds me. His frown deepens, but he strides toward me, purpose in his steps.

"Clara, please go and bring the younger girls down." Glen's voice is flat as he gives the instruction. I don't understand.

"Before the clients leave? Shouldn't we finish the auction first?"

A hand flashes and there is a loud smack as it falls across my face. My hand flies to my cheek and I gasp. The room has gone quiet. My daughters' eyes are wide when I glance at them, but my attention returns to Glen at once.

"Don't you dare question me," he hisses. Louder, he says, "Go get the girls. Now."

I fight tears as I stand up straighter. I nod and rush up the stairs. I pause outside the door to the bedroom. I can hear the playful tones of little voices through the wood, and I am afraid of what is ahead for them. They are not ready to leave our home. My gut tightens as I turn the knob. The girls look up at me in surprise.

"Mr. Glen would like you all to join us downstairs," I say, trying to keep my voice upbeat. Passion stares at me, eyes wary, but she helps the little girls put their dolls away and takes the hands of the two nearest girls. I take one of Chloe's hands, and Samantha takes the other. The last girl, just seven years old, clings to my free hand. We march down the stairs in a glob, no order, nothing like the girls earlier.

The open stairway allows our guests to watch our progress, and I feel the weight of all their eyes on us. I line the girls up by age in front of the older girls, and then take Passion's arm and step back. When I see some of the clients eyeing Passion, I nudge her. "Go wait upstairs." My voice is quiet, but I see Glen look at me. He does not contradict my order, and Passion backs away and skirts up the stairs.

I am not surprised when the gentleman I saw talking with Glen earlier is the first to inspect the younger girls. He bends down to their level and talks to them in a low voice. When he gets to Chloe, he says something, and she giggles. I am in shock. He stands and nods, and Glen begins reading off the winners of the auction.

Each client goes with Glen into his office to settle his debt and comes out to collect his girl. Eight of the older girls find new homes. The man who made Chloe laugh is last. He and Glen are in the office for a long time, and the girls grow fidgety. Glen's men keep a watchful eye, stoic and unmoving. I suck in a breath when Glen emerges.

The man takes Chloe. And Amanda, the seven-year-old. Amanda screeches and cries, and the man slaps her across the mouth. I cannot help myself. I rush at him, shoving him away.

"Clara! No!" Glen shouts at me. He yanks my arm and throws me across the room. My head comes into contact with the railing to the stairs, and everything goes black.

Now

We reconvene the next morning to discuss strategy now that I have decided to cooperate fully with the investigation. We're back in the questioning room, but it doesn't feel as oppressive or intimidating as it has in the past. I am no longer resisting this process. I am no longer holding anything back. Meeting my family was the last piece of the puzzle. My emotions are still raw over my decision, but I do not doubt that I am doing the right thing for me and for my child. For our future.

Connor pulls out one of his many file folders and opens it, sliding it across the table. I gasp when I see Mr. Harrison's face staring up at me. In my mind, since South Dakota, his face has been permanently etched, and I cannot think of him without a wave of nausea crashing over my body. This picture, however, was clearly taken when he was a bit younger. He still has the creepy vibe, even through the picture, but there are fewer lines around his mouth and his eyes are not as dull as when I knew him.

"I take it you recognize this man," Connor says, raising an eyebrow when I look at him.

I nod. "Mr. Harrison. Yes."

"Richard Harrison was one of his many aliases. His given name was Fred Mundy. He had many dealings with shady individuals and organizations, a hand in many different jars, so it was no surprise when he turned up dead about a year ago."

My fists clench. This must be what Glen was afraid of from the beginning. That somehow they would connect Mr. Harrison to us. His warnings make even more sense now.

"We have several guys undercover in this area, checking out various questionable organizations. A few months after Fred Mundy was found, one of them was following a lead on an illegal brothel. He went to investigate, and the girl he talked to had very distinctive markings behind her ear."

He slides another photo across the table. It is a close-up of a small tattoo, an X with a star on each point. "This was Mundy's mark. He would tattoo his girls as soon as he got them, we think as a safeguard. Sometimes he told his business partners about them, but more often he would only bring that piece of information out when it suited him."

I stare at the photo. I don't remember seeing this on any of the girls, even Genevieve, but it seems as if it was designed that way. I look back at Connor. "So your guys, what, figured out this was one of Harris—Mundy's girls? Why didn't you bust them right away?"

Connor makes a face. "Many wanted to, but we knew the brothel was only the tip of the iceberg. We wanted more. We'd heard about an auction going on that the big boss was running, so we waited. And planned. But when we got to the location, there was nothing."

Auction day. The last-minute change in location. "Someone must have tipped them off," I say, staring at the table. "We had the auction at the house. I lost a lot of good girls that day." Young girls. Tears prick my eyes when I think about those girls, and the fact that they might have been saved if the auction had gone as planned at the warehouse. I shake my guilt off and pull my shoulders back. I won't be any good to them if I let this information crush me. I relay the details of the auction, which are still fresh in my mind. The agents scribble frantically.

Connor looks up when I finish, and his face is brighter than I've seen it since I've known him, though I feel a thousand years older. "What else?" Might as well get this all over at once.

Connor and Jay look at each other. "We've been building a case against Mae Lawson," Connor says, clearing his throat nervously. They are not sure what my feelings are toward Mama anymore. I am not sure I even know how to feel about the woman who raised me and lied to me for my entire life. "We need your help."

I nod. "I'll do whatever I need to."

"We are also hoping to find documentation of all the businesses," Jay says, and Connor shoots him a look. "What? She might know something."

"Papers?" I ask. I think for a moment. "I got very good at listening and storing information," I say. "I didn't ask a lot of questions, but many were answered if I stayed quiet."

Connor looks eager. I know this is what he has been waiting for since they brought me here. At this point I am willing to do whatever I need to in order to make up for everything I have done. Or at least begin to atone for my sins, and the sins of the family who raised me.

"I might be able to help find what you are looking for. But you will have to take me back to the house."

Connor frowns. "I'll have to check on that. Let's focus on Mae first, and we'll go from there."

I know Connor wants to protect me, but I am done being protected. He wants answers, but I refuse to give them passively. I'm standing up for myself. Starting with Mama.

"How soon can you get her to visit?"

Jay grins. "We'll call and invite her as soon as we're done here. Tell her you've had a change of heart and want to see her."

I nod. "Good."

They watch me, gauging how much more I'm willing to give today.

Leaning back in my chair, I cross my arms, my mind wandering back to our original conversation. "So finding Mundy's mark on some of Glen's girls led to all of this?"

"Sort of." Connor clears his throat. "We were onto the brothel already, but we had no idea how deep it went when we were making those early plans. If we can get those records, we might have enough evidence to shut down more organizations like Glen's, and make more connections to Mundy. We're trying to trace back his dealings to figure out who turned on him, though right now that's secondary to Glen's case."

I tap my fingers on my arms and purse my lips, then lean forward. "What if it isn't secondary?" I ask.

Connor's brow furrows. "What do you mean?"

"I can tell you exactly how Mundy died."

Then

Joel drives up to the lodge in one of the rented SUVs. I climb in the back as Glen takes the seat next to Joel. They speak in hushed tones, and Joel glances back at me, but I pretend to be absorbed in the bright starlight filling the sky. This may be the last time I have such an unobstructed view of the night sky, and I want to enjoy it.

Soon the starlight is dimmed by the bright spotlights surrounding Mr. Harrison's mansion. The gate is already open, and we continue to the front of his house. It looks dark, but for a crack of light shining through heavy curtains upstairs. The curtains twitch, and I know we are being watched. We exit the car, and I immediately glue myself to Glen's side, remembering my promise not to leave his sight. The door opens as we reach the bottom steps leading to it.

A sallow-faced man I do not remember seeing earlier holds the door open for us, not speaking a word, only casting furtive glances between us and the floor. The door clicks shut behind us, and the man engages the lock.

"Never know who's lurking in the dark," he says, his voice rasping through a mucus-filled throat. "Can't be too careful." He says nothing more as he leads us up the familiar staircase. The room we enter is the same as before, but only Mr. Harrison sits within, Genevieve perched on the edge of his chair. I can see now that the room is lined with bookcases and appears to be a study of some sort. There are many chairs scattered throughout the large room, and Mr. Harrison sits behind a large desk, writing as Genevieve runs a finger back and forth across his shoulders in lazy movements.

The man who let us in clears his throat, and Harrison looks up. He is not startled, and I sense that he was only pretending not to notice that we had entered. Genevieve's mouth curls into a smile as she watches us, and there are rocks in the pit of my stomach.

"Hello again, Glen," Harrison says, standing and walking around the desk. Genevieve is dethroned, and I can't help but smirk as she rights herself. Harrison looks at me, his small eyes scrutinizing. "A pleasure to see you again, Clara."

I incline my head in his direction, but say nothing.

"What is the reason for this meeting, Mr. Harrison, sir?" Glen asks, his voice calm. "I was under the impression that we had concluded our business earlier."

"Yes, yes, well, my boy," Harrison begins, and Glen bristles at the term. He handled it with grace earlier, but I can tell he is struggling to keep his cool this time. "I was going over our deal after your man"—he indicates Joel with a tip of his head—"left with the girls, and I have to say, I don't feel like the deal we struck was quite fair."

Glen clenches and unclenches his fists, the movement subtle enough that it escapes the attention of Mr. Harrison, but not Genevieve. She raises an eyebrow at me. I ignore her and watch Glen.

"I understood that you were happy with the terms." This time anger creeps into Glen's voice. I brush my fingers across his back, willing him to calm down. He releases a silent breath.

"But the girls you chose . . . Clara chose," Harrison corrects, "they were some of my best."

"Yes, I understand that," Glen says. "I gave you more than a fair price."

"I'm not so sure."

Glen takes a breath. "Given the history between you and my father, I am willing to give you a little more, sir, as a gesture of good faith. Tell me your price."

"It is not money I want, son." There is a gleam in Mr. Harrison's eyes. "In fact, if you give me what I want, I will throw in two more girls."

I do not like where this is going.

"What is your price?" Glen asks, and I feel his arm tremble.

"Her."

Glen turns horrified eyes to me, and I tear my gaze from his to look at Mr. Harrison, who is pointing a gnarled finger at me.

"You're fucking joking," Glen says, his voice strangled. "She is not on the bargaining table."

Harrison drops his hand. "So put her there. She is well-spoken, is nice to look at, and my girls were gushing over her. I think she could be an asset to my operation."

"She is not for sale." Rage creeps into Glen's voice.

The door opens behind us. Harrison sighs. "I was afraid you would take that stance, my boy." A click, and I turn to see a gun pointed at us. "I will just have to take what I desire."

Glen swallows hard, his throat bobbing. He exchanges a look with Joel, and Joel nods, almost imperceptibly. They have their own language, their own way of communicating that does not require words. They have grown up together. There are times when I am jealous of their bond, but in this moment I am grateful.

"Genevieve, take Clara to her new quarters." Genevieve walks around the table and grasps my arm, her long, talon-like nails digging into my skin. She tries to pull me toward the door, but I resist. I promised Glen I would not leave his side, and there are consequences for broken promises.

I am surprised when large hands plant themselves in the middle of my back and I am shoved from behind. Unable to stop my forward motion, I topple into Genevieve, and we both collapse to the floor. I hear a loud grunt and a crack, and when I look up, the sallow-faced man is dead, staring at the ceiling with blank eyes and a neat hole in his forehead, and Joel has Mr. Harrison by the arms. Glen is holding the gun.

I hear a whimper beneath me and look down to see Genevieve, her eyes wide, staring at Harrison. I jump up and back away from her, fitting myself into a corner, but she makes no move to stop me. She has forgotten I exist.

"My apologies, Mr. Lawson," Mr. Harrison says, his tone pleading. "I tried to take advantage. Please . . ."

"You underestimate me, just like my father always did," Glen says through clenched teeth. "But for you there will be consequences."

Joel forces Harrison to his knees. Harrison begins sputtering, his words incoherent. I watch Glen, astonished. Will he really go through with it?

And he does. The gunshot echoes through the large room, and Harrison slumps to the ground. Genevieve shrieks and backs into a bookcase behind her. Glen turns the gun on her. A quick pop and she slumps to the floor, tears still leaking from unseeing eyes.

Glen doesn't pause. He holds his hand out for me, and I take it without hesitation. Joel is rifling through the desk, shoving things into a bag I hadn't noticed before. "Let's go, Joel," Glen says, his voice urgent.

We flee from the house, and Joel takes us on a nightmare ride through the unfamiliar back roads. As we rush to the interstate, freedom, and home, I try to erase the images of the last thirty minutes from my mind. One thing I hold on to.

Glen will protect me with his life.

Now

I am in a new room today, a small lounge of sorts, with large windows and comfortable couches. It reminds me of Dr. Mulligan's office, except there is no desk or file cabinet and the frames on the walls are filled with flowery pictures instead of certificates and diplomas. My mother sits in the chair perpendicular to the couch I am on. It is just the two of us today. My father is working, and Charlotte had to take one of her boys to the dentist. But I'm grateful for this time alone with the woman who would have raised me, had things turned out as they were supposed to.

She fidgets in the chair, and I realize she is just as nervous as I am.

The realization calms me, and I smile at her. "I'm sorry . . . I'm not sure what to call you."

Laughing, she relaxes a bit. "Whatever you're comfortable with. Maybe you could start with Jane." She moves her hand to cover mine. "Not that I don't want you to call me Mom, but I thought maybe it would be easier . . ."

"Jane is good." I hadn't been sure what I wanted to call her until she suggested Jane. It feels right, for now.

"And . . ." Jane sounds hesitant. "Would you like me to call you Clara? I know that's what you've gone by since . . ."

Surprised, I take a moment to think. I assumed they would call me by the name they knew. It hadn't occurred to me that they would consider calling me by the name given to me by the people who took me. What do I want? How often have I even considered that question?

"Of course you'll want to go by Clara," Jane says when I do not respond. "It was silly of me to ask." She digs in the bag she brought. "I was wondering if you might want to paint your fingernails?" She sounds uncertain, treading such an unfamiliar situation. "I guess I thought it would be nice to have something to do instead of just staring at each other. Or we could just talk." She spills a handful of polish bottles onto the coffee table. "Whatever you like."

I reach forward and run my fingers over the rainbow of colors on display. I find a pale yellow that reminds me of the fields of flowers where I used to play with my daughters at the compound. The memory stings only a little. Dr. Mulligan has encouraged me to hold on to the happy memories, despite the sadness and pain that might be attached. After all, as she pointed out, I don't want to lose seventeen years' worth of memories.

"Would you paint them for me?" I ask, extending the bottle toward Jane. Her entire face lifts with her smile, and the uncertainty vanishes from her eyes.

"I would be happy to, D—" She clears her throat. ". . . dear. Right hand first, I think."

Her palms are smooth and dry as she holds my hand steady. The skin is soft and warm, and even though we have very little contact, that safe feeling comes over me again. We sit in silence for a few minutes, both concentrating on the shiny yellow polish sliding over the surface of my nails. The coolness of the liquid is a contrast to the warmth of the woman applying it.

"Jane," I begin, and there is a small tremor in my voice that causes her to look up, a question in her eyes. "I was wondering . . . could you tell me what I was like as a little girl? I don't remember much before . . ."

Pain slices through her eyes, but they clear almost at once, and the corners of her mouth quirk up before she returns to her task.

"Of course." She takes a deep breath. "Where to begin . . . You were always an individual. From the time you were born, you wouldn't let Charlotte boss you around. All my friends said you would walk later, talk later, do everything later than Charlotte, because she would be around to do them for you. But you weren't having any of that." She laughs. "You took your first steps at ten months. And you were smart, but not smart enough to be walking so young!" Her hand leaves mine for a moment and travels up to my face. I flinch as she brushes her fingers across my hairline. "This scar is from when you were eleven months old and tried to run after our cat, Freckles." She traces the thin white line that has always been a part of my features, so much so that I hardly noticed it. "The top half of your body got ahead of your little legs, and you toppled right into the piano bench. It was the first of many bumps and bruises, but you learned." She returns to her task, bending over my fingernails once again.

I bring my free hand to the scar, feeling the raised line that I had wondered about from time to time, but never given much thought. The enormity of what I've missed out on threatens to crush me. Had

I grown up with Jane and Doug and Charlotte, the story of my scar would have been repeated, year after year, on holidays, on birthdays, whenever I was being particularly clumsy. Perhaps it would have become a family joke, a warning to others. "Don't pull a Dee-Dee!" But instead, I am twenty-three years old and learning about it for the first time. A tear escapes, and I brush it away before Jane notices.

"What else?" I am hungry for more information, more clues about the girl I was before I was Clara.

Jane places my hand on the table to let my nails dry and reaches for the other. "You had quite the imagination. You drove your sister *crazy* with your stories." A small laugh escapes. "She would trade you play time for quiet time, but she would spend most of the play time 'setting up' her area. Of course, you didn't much follow her quiet time rules, either."

All my nails are painted, and I admire the buttery color as Jane puts the cap back on the bottle. "Did Charlotte and I like each other?" I ask hesitantly.

"You were sisters." Jane smiles. "You had your fights, but you loved each other. Lottie was always more serious, especially after . . . Well, you balanced each other out." She stares out the window, wistful. "I always dreamed of seeing you two as teenagers, sharing clothes, talking about boys . . ." Her voice begins to wobble, and my eyes fill again.

"I'm sorry," I whisper. My life wasn't the only one affected by Mama and Papa's actions. I know this, but each time I talk to my family, I realize it more. "I wish . . ."

Jane reaches out to grip my wrists, careful not to smudge my manicure. At first I recoil. Her strength surprises me, but it is not overpowering. I force myself to relax. She is not trying to dominate me, as Glen would if he made the same move. She just wants me to listen. I look straight into her eyes as she speaks, eyes that are so familiar though we were only recently reunited.

"Listen to me, C-Clara." She stumbles on my name, but her voice remains strong. "This is not your fault. None of this is your fault. Those people stole you from us, stole you from yourself. You did what you had to do to survive all these years, and . . ." Her voice cracks as she chokes on a sob. "I am so thankful that you did." Her hands release my wrists to cup my face. "I don't want to waste any more of our time on misplaced apologies or unnecessary guilt. You are my daughter. And I love you. I have always loved you."

My cheeks are wet. "But there's so much you don't know. About me. About what I've done."

Jane is already shaking her head before I finish. "I don't care. Do you hear me? I. Don't. Care. I want to know you. I want to know what your life has been like. It's going to hurt like hell, for both of us, but I *need* to know. And you need to trust that nothing—*nothing*—you can tell me will change how I feel about you. I won't let you go again. I promise."

My mother pulls me into her lap, though I have grown taller than her, and she holds me as I cry, and as she cries with me. She holds me as if she has been holding me for twenty-three years, and she holds me as if she will never let me go.

I believe that she won't.

Then

It's dark and I don't like it. Those people said they would come back, but it's been forever and I don't want to stay here forever. My throat hurts from crying. I miss my mommy and daddy, but the lady said that they didn't want me anymore and that I had to go with them. I wonder if they got rid of Lottie, too.

I'm really hungry. We were gonna get McDonald's tonight, but I don't think these new people know that I like chicken nuggets and not cheeseburgers. I hope they have a TV. And I hope Mommy gave them Theo. I can't sleep without my little stuffed puppy. I start crying again because I really need Theo.

The door opens and that woman is standing there. I can hardly see her because she's all dark and the light is behind her, but she is scary, so I scoot closer into the corner. She reaches down and grabs my arm, and it hurts.

"Ow!" I say. "That hurts. Don't do that."

She shakes me. "You will remain silent, child."

"My name is Diana."

I don't see her hand coming, but she hits me across the face and it stings and I taste blood. It tastes like metal and it's gross. I always taste it when I lose a tooth, but this time I just bit my cheek. I cry harder. Even if Mommy and Daddy don't like me, they are nicer than this lady. I want to go back to them. Maybe if I clean my room more they will let me stay.

The woman drags me into another room, a kitchen, and shoves me into a chair at the table. There is a sandwich on a plate. "Eat," she orders. I pick up the sandwich. Just cheese and butter. Gross. I put it back down.

"No, thank you," I say, trying to use my polite voice. "Do you have any macaroni and cheese?"

The woman walks over and pinches my arm, hard. "Don't!" I yell, drawing the word out. She is meaner than Lottie. She doesn't say another word, but picks up my sandwich and throws it in the garbage.

"You won't be eating tonight, Clara."

"My name is Diana."

"Not anymore, it isn't," she says. "My name is Mama Mae, and you will call me Mama Mae."

"You are not my mom."

Another slap across the face, and I feel one of my baby teeth wiggle. I only have a few left. I start to cry again.

"You will watch your mouth around me, Clara. You will speak only when asked a question. You will do exactly as you are told, or you will be punished. We will begin your training tomorrow."

The man who was driving the car earlier walks into the room. "She giving you trouble, Mae?" he asks.

"No. Nothing unmanageable," Mama Mae says. "Did you find Glen?"

"Yeah, he and Joel were down by the creek again."

Mama nods, then turns back to me. "This is Papa G. You will do what Papa G says. He is in charge first, and then me. His punishments are harder than mine, so you would be smart to behave. Your old parents said you were smart. Are you smart, Clara?"

It is on the tip of my tongue to correct my name again, but instead I nod. I am smart. Mrs. Weisser says so. I am going to be in the gifted program next year. My heart feels sad when I think about school. I wonder if Mama Mae will let me go to my old school. We have a concert next week that I don't want to miss. Maybe if I'm really good they'll let me go.

"Good girl," Papa G says, his voice gruff. "She's a pretty one, Mae. She'll bring in a good price in a few years."

"And very trainable. That didn't take long at all for her to stop talking back." Mama Mae is watching me with a strange look in her eyes. "She is going to do big things for us, Glen."

Papa looks at me again and leaves. Mama grabs my arm, leading me out of the kitchen and down a dark hallway. She takes a key from a necklace and unlocks a door at the end of the hallway. She pushes me into the room ahead of her.

"You'll share a bed with Macy," Mama says, nodding toward a girl sitting cross-legged on a double bed, already in a nightgown. "Here is something to sleep in. The bathroom is over there. Any of the girls can answer your questions. I will collect you in the morning." With a whirl of skirts, Mama Mae is gone, locking the door behind her, leaving me clutching the nightgown she shoved into my hands.

I do not look at anyone, but go in the bathroom and change. The tiny room holds a gross sink with brown spots all over it and a toilet that wiggles when I sit on it. There's a bathtub, too, but I hope I don't have to use it. The nightgown I have been given is thin, and I scurry across the cold tile back into the other room. I do not know where to leave my clothes, so I take them back to the bed with me and ball them up to put under my pillow. I don't want to let them out of my sight.

The other girl, Macy, is already under the covers. I climb in, and she turns to face me. "Hi."

"Hello," I say. I am feeling scared again. I want my mommy. The sheets are scratchy and the blanket has holes all over it.

"What's your name?"

"Which one?"

Macy smiles, and I am surprised there is smiling here. Everyone seems so mean and serious. "Both."

"My name is Diana. But they keep calling me Clara."

Macy nods. "I'm Macy. My old name was Ella."

"How long have you been here?"

She shrugs. "A few weeks?"

"Did your parents give you up?"

A sad look crosses Macy's face. "Yes. Mama and Papa told me they didn't want me anymore and wanted money instead. I still miss them, though."

"Me too." A tear escapes my eye, and I was trying really hard to stay brave. "Is it always so scary?"

"Yes, but you get used to it."

A sharp rap on the door interrupts our conversation, as well as the other whispered conversations of the other girls in the room. "Quiet time, lights out!" Mama's voice says. The lock clicks, and Mama pokes her head in. "You," she says, looking at me. "You figured out where everything is?"

I nod, afraid to answer her. I don't want to get hit again.

"Where are your clothes?"

Before I can answer, her eyes shoot to the side of me, where my brand-new Strawberry Shortcake T-shirt is sticking out from under my pillow. She stalks across the room, rips my clothes from under my pillow, and shakes them at me. "You always put dirty laundry down the chute," she scolds.

"I-I was wondering if I could keep them," I say, my voice shaking.

"No."

Without another word, Mama stomps into the bathroom, and I hear a whooshing sound as my clothes are tossed in with the rest of the laundry. I hide my tears until Mama turns out the light and locks us back in. No one even tries to make me feel better. I cry myself to sleep.

Now

I stare at the ceiling tiles in my room, waiting for Connor to retrieve me for Mama's visit. I was allowed to call to ask her to visit, since I had denied her last several visits. I rub my rounded abdomen, taking comfort from Nut. I am doing this all for him. I have to be sure of my decision. If I follow through, Mama will be in prison. Glen will be in prison. Nut and I will be free.

Is being free from Glen what I want? I haven't yet decided. That step will come later. By helping implicate Mama, however, the dominoes will begin to tip. And with the information I've already given them on Glen, his fate is almost certain. All they need is a little more proof to put him away forever. A wave of nausea runs through my body. Can I be without him? Before this, I never would have thought so. He has been my world for almost half my life, but I am learning that it doesn't have to be that way.

I never expected to be in this position. But after learning all the things that Glen has done . . . I can't help but think that he deserves whatever consequences they come up with. Part of my heart breaks at that knowledge. But the other part breaks for all the families he has destroyed, all the lives ruined, lost, because of his decisions. They deserve justice. I want to help deliver that, even if it means putting Glen away.

A part of me cannot help but wonder what kind of man Glen could have been if he had lived another life, if he hadn't inherited this legacy. I remember him as that excited boy, the one who convinced me to run away from the only home I'd ever known with only his love and promises of a better life. What if we had succeeded that day? What if we'd gotten on that bus and disappeared? It's almost painful to imagine what our lives might have been. We might have had our own family, kids we would have raised to be even better than we were. He might have been different. I know I would have been. I tamp down the guilt threatening to rise. Now is not the time for "could have beens."

My parents came to see me again, and watching them together was like magic. Two people in love, but as equals. Doug attended to Jane, made sure she was comfortable, but not for show. Jane did not look over her shoulder, waiting to see how Doug would react to a misstep. She was confident on her own, while still being connected to Doug. I can't stop comparing their relationship to mine with Glen.

Connor knocks on the door and enters, but says nothing. He knows I'm ready. I sit up as he enters and struggle to my feet before he can cross the room to help me. He takes my elbow anyway and leads me toward the door.

"Are you okay, Clara?" he asks, concern lacing his tone. "Are you sure you want to do this?"

I laugh. "I thought you wanted me to do this weeks ago."

"Not if you're not ready." He runs a hand through his hair. "You are strong, Clara. You have nothing to prove."

My head is already shaking before he finishes the sentence. "I do, though. To myself. It is time for me to stand up to Ma—to Mae Lawson."

The look on Connor's face is proud, and once again I am allowed into the visiting area without cuffs. "Will it look suspicious?" I ask. "Will she think there is something wrong?"

"No," Jay jumps in. "You've been unshackled before. It might seem weird if we decided to start again."

That makes sense. I take a deep breath as Jay opens the door, admitting me to the room. No one else is using the area today. There are extra recording devices set up around the room, and Mama has signed a document saying she understands that what she says and does will be recorded. This is not a change from her other visits, but she doesn't know about the microphone I am wearing this time. Nor do I plan on telling her.

Mama stands as I enter, holding her arms out. I go into them and close my eyes, trying to imagine them as the comforting arms of my family. They feel cold and lifeless, and I am relieved when she releases me after a brief moment. Her hand goes to my stomach.

"You're starting to show," Mama says, eyes shining. "That's my grandbaby in there."

I force a smile. "Yes. On track and healthy, according to the doctor." I move away and her hand falls back to her side. "How are you, Mae?"

Her smile is tense. "Not great, Clara." She leans forward. Good. My microphone will pick her up that much clearer. "They've been asking me questions, acting like I should have known about everything."

I frown. "But you did know. It was Papa's business first."

Mama swats my hand, hiding the gesture with her body. It does not hurt, but it's a reminder of my place. "Quiet, you silly girl. Of course I know that. I trained you, didn't I? But they aren't supposed to know." She pauses. "You haven't said anything to them, have you?"

"Of course not." I pretend to be offended by the question. "You trained me better than that."

Mama doesn't look convinced. "You know it is Glen's wish that I stay out of this. Even if he ends up in prison, he wants me to live the rest of my days as a free woman."

"What if it is between you and me?" I ask. I am going off script, but I'm curious. "If there was a choice between me going to prison and you, who do you think Glen would choose?"

Her eyes narrow. "Why would you ask such a question?" In her eyes, I see the truth. Glen would send his mother to prison if it meant I could be free. The guilt I have been trying to ignore lessens. I am doing this to earn my freedom. Mama has had years of freedom. I have not been free since before I can remember.

I pretend to be hurt. "I just don't know if he cares anymore," I say. "It has always been about protecting the Lawsons and the Lawson name, and you never really considered me one of you."

"Of course we did!" Mama's voice rises. She closes her eyes and takes a deep breath. She lowers her volume again. "They have those listening devices all over this room, so keep your voice down." She still speaks to me as if I am a child.

"I'm sorry, Mama," I say, my voice contrite. "You're right. I am being careful. It's just spending so much time alone . . . I keep thinking back on things and wondering . . ."

Mama's eyes soften, but I see her fists clench. "What do you wonder, child?"

"What . . . what would have happened to me? If Glen didn't love me? If the client didn't want me?"

"That was never going to happen. If you and Glen had not been together, you would still be living happily with the client we chose for you. He would have treated you well."

"What would I have done?"

An exasperated sigh tells me that Mama is already tired of my questions. I must be smart. "You know what you would have done. What I trained you for. You would have been his confidante. You would have lived in luxury, gone on exotic vacations, and fulfilled the role his wife could not. If Glen had not been in the picture, you would have been trained fully to succeed in your role."

Pursing my lips, I act hesitant. "And . . . what about the other girls? Like . . . like Macy?"

Mama's face clears. "This is what you've been thinking about? All this time and you still think about that girl?"

I nod, not trusting my voice. Despite knowing this is supposed to be an act, I am desperate to know more about what happened to Macy. I did not realize how much I still thought of her until Mama said it. She is always there, living in the back of my mind.

Mama's face contorts into an expression of derision. "Clara, I know you loved her, but Macy was never special. Not like you. She died of a dirty disease and was put with all the other girls."

"If I wanted to say good-bye . . . if I ever got out of here . . . could you tell me where?"

"Clara . . ."

"Please, Mama." I reach across the table and clutch her hand.

She falters. "I'll take you when you're out."

I squeeze her hand tighter. "In case it's a long time, Mama, please, just . . ." I allow a tear to escape and Mama's posture slumps. I know I have won.

"There is a site, a few miles away from the old compound . . ." Mama continues, but I tune out. Connor will take down all the instructions. I cannot stop thinking about Macy, and all those like her, dying alone, being left to rot. It tears my heart in two, and I know I cannot handle being in the same room as this woman any longer. When she has finished, I lean over.

"Mama," I gasp. "I don't . . . I don't feel well . . . Call the guard."

She jumps up. "Help! Someone help her, please!" She rushes to my side of the table. "Oh, Clara, you can't lose this one, too. There aren't supposed to be any lasting effects."

I look up at her. "What do you mean?"

She claps a hand over her mouth. Through her fingers she mutters, "The special tea . . . He said you weren't ready."

"Ready for what?" My ruse is forgotten for a moment as I focus on what Mama is saying.

"A baby is such a big responsibility. 'Wait until she's at least twenty-five, Mae,' he told me. 'Then maybe they'll be ready.' Even on his deathbed, he knew what was best, what he thought was best." Mama talks as if I am not even there, bringing her hands to her lap and wringing her fingers together.

"Mama, please. What are you talking about?"

"The tea . . . the morning sickness tea. It . . ." She cannot continue, and buries her face in her hands.

The truth crashes over me, and I no longer need to feign illness. I lose what little I have eaten today all over the visitation room floor. Black spots dance in front of my eyes, and I focus on Connor's voice as he helps me limp from the room.

"It's fine, Clara. You're going to be okay. You did great." This last sentence as he deposits me back in my room. "I'm going to go fetch the doctor. You'll be okay."

I may never be okay again.

Then

We are folding laundry when there is a commotion in the front hall. "Keep going," I say to the girls helping. I hurry toward the noise, picking out the sounds of men grunting and a child crying. I burst into the entryway just as Glen emerges from his study.

"What's going on?" he asks, annoyed.

Joel is at the front of the group, as he always is. He moves aside and, from the back, one of the other men pushes a girl forward.

"Rose!" I gasp, moving toward her. Glen throws out an arm, stopping me. Rose is shaking, tears streaking her face. I want nothing more than to gather her close and take her away from these men, but I stop.

Rose is one of our newer girls. She has only been around for a few months, but she is older than the girls I usually get. Older girls are usually brought to one of the other branches, but Rose was timid enough that Glen saw the potential for a quick turnaround. He had hoped that years of training could be compressed for her. She was a test, to see if we could train the right kind of girl in less time.

She had acclimated well. A quick learner, she showed a lot of promise. She already had clients interested in her after our last tour. Now she looks nothing like the lady I have been cultivating. Her hair hangs in strings on either side of her face, interlaced with twigs and leaves. Her clothes are torn and dirty, as if she was caught in some trees. The realization hits me at the same time as Glen seems to understand.

"She ran." It is not a question. With this presentation, there's no mistaking what has happened. "How far did she get?"

"Almost to the road." Joel is the one who responds. "She found a hole in the fence. It's already being repaired."

Glen nods. He walks forward until he is right in front of the trembling girl. Despite her fear, she stares up at him defiantly. "Why did you leave, child?" he asks, and he sounds so much like Papa G that it makes my skin crawl.

"I was going home." Though Rose tries to keep her voice level, a tremor at the end gives her away.

Glen clasps his hands behind his back and begins to pace in front of her, a solemn look on his face. "Are your accommodations not to your liking?" he asks, his tone conversational. "Is there anything we could have done to make your stay more pleasant?" He is mocking her. It is a new side of Glen. There is no warmth in his eyes when he looks at Rose, only calculating menace.

"I just want to go home," Rose says, and the tears begin falling again.

Glen laughs. He *laughs*. "Oh, my dear girl. That will never happen." He stops and turns to her, standing close, and grabs her chin between his thumb and forefinger, forcing her face up. "It's a shame you made this choice, Rose. You could have been happy here. Your future could have been bright, like the other girls Clara trains." He turns to smile at me, but there is a chill in it that prevents me from returning it. "Instead, I'm afraid your introduction into your new life begins tonight."

He releases her and steps back. Rose sobs, the fight gone from her body. Without warning, Glen winds up his arm and backhands Rose across the cheek. She screams. Another scream mixes with hers, and I realize it is mine. I rush forward, grabbing his arm as he raises it for a second hit. Glen turns to me, enraged, and the blow meant for Rose lands on my face instead. He shoves me into the wall.

"Miss Clara?" A small voice sounds from the hallway behind me. Livvy has come to see what the commotion is about. "We're done with the folding."

Glen is breathing hard. He swipes a hand across his mouth, where spittle has gathered at the corners. "Go take care of the girls, Clara, and then wait for me in my study."

I hurry away, my hand covering the spot on my cheek that met the back of Glen's hand. I take the girls to the library and begin them on some study materials.

"What happened, Miss Clara?" Livvy asks. She is always curious. It's something I've been working on with her.

"Nothing for you to worry about, Livvy."

"When will Rose be back?"

"Rose will not be coming back, girls." Though Glen has not said as much, I know what he meant by starting her new life. His brothel has been very successful, one of the most successful aspects of his business. That is where the girls Rose's age end up. I wish she had been the exception. Another failed experiment.

"Did a client come for her already?" Jealousy laces Livvy's tone. She is twelve and has looked up to Rose since she arrived. She is eager to please and looks forward to having a client of her own. She understands her place and what an honor it will be. It is for this reason that I cannot punish her for her curiosity this time.

I lie to my daughters. A necessary part of helping them feel secure. "Yes, she will be with her client tonight."

Maggie, who came at the same time as Rose, but is much younger, sticks out her bottom lip. "But who will read to me at night?"

"Passion can do that. She's a great reader."

Maggie frowns. "Passion is scary."

A little. But she loves her younger sisters.

"We didn't even get to say good-bye." Livvy again.

"Tell you what, girls. Tomorrow we will have the good-bye ceremony for Rose, even though she cannot be with us. And I will take all your cards and gifts and make sure she gets them, okay?"

"Can we work on them now?" Maggie wants to know.

"Of course." I smile at them as they become excited. Livvy finds the craft box in the corner and they dive in, eager to create the best good-bye cards they can manage.

"Clara." I turn to find Glen lounging in the doorway. "You were supposed to meet me in my office."

"I'm sorry, Glen. The girls had questions, and I thought it would take you longer to . . ." I trail off. In fact, I am not sure what Glen was going to do with Rose before bringing her to her new assignment.

"Joel is taking care of her while we talk. I will go over with her later to get her settled in."

I nod.

"Where is Passion?"

"She was in the garden. Why?"

"I need her to take care of the girls for a while."

My stomach clenches. Whatever Glen has planned will not be quick. He has not lost the cruel mask he wore while dealing with Rose, and I am frightened. "I'll get her." I slip past him and call for Passion out the back door. She cleans up and goes to help the girls with their projects. "Cook will have dinner in an hour," I tell her. "And you know how bedtime routines run."

Passion takes all my orders without question. She is my sidekick, the one I know I can count on. She takes over when I am . . . indisposed. And never asks for an explanation. I think Glen has not found a client for her for that reason. I worry about what will happen to her as she gets even older, but for now I am grateful that she is here.

When I knock on the door of the study and enter, Glen is standing in front of the window, staring out at the mountains, arms crossed over his chest. When he turns around, the cold fury in his eyes stops me in my tracks. "Lock the door, Clara."

Now

Charlotte shifts next to me, and her hands clasp and unclasp in an anxious rhythm. I glance in her direction, and she gives me a small, nervous smile. I want to reach out and squeeze her hands, give her some sort of reassurance, but I am not sure where our relationship stands yet. She has agreed to attend the group with me today, which is a good step, but I wonder as I watch her fidget whether it's too much, too soon. Talking with Jane helped, but I still fear hearing what Charlotte's life has been because of me.

That is why we're here today. Heather suggested that I invite my sister to sit in, maybe talk about what life was like after I was taken. She suggested having the support of the group might help me feel more comfortable sharing some more of the things I went through as well. I do not want my family to know how I spent my years away from them, but even Dr. Mulligan agrees that we need to be open. I see her point, but the habit of secret-keeping is proving a difficult one to break.

I have been to the group a couple of times since Pam's outburst and have shared meeting my family. It is nice to have these other women along on my journey, and I have discovered that they really are rooting for me. Pam has not been back, though Heather assures me that she was not kicked out, but has chosen to undergo more individual treatment before returning to the group. I hope she does. She needs, and deserves, the support as much as I do.

When it seems we are all settled, Heather gets the ball rolling. There is no one new today, and I feel a surge of strength as I look around the circle. One hand rests on the mound under my shirt. Charlotte and Jane brought me some maternity clothes last week, and I have been allowed to wear them instead of the clothes I was issued when I arrived.

"As we discussed last time, Clara has brought a guest to our meeting today." Heather nods at Charlotte, who gives a little wave. "Sometimes we will ask family to sit in and maybe talk a bit about the other side of things. Charlotte has agreed to talk about her life after Clara was taken. First, though, I want to go around and just give a small bit of information about your story. Obviously we don't have enough time to go into everyone's, but I think it will help Charlotte feel more comfortable sharing about her life if she knows a little about yours."

Tori starts, and even though I have heard each story before, I feel a stab of emotion with each retelling. The girls only speak for a couple minutes apiece, but I can tell their words are affecting Charlotte as well. This time I do reach over and squeeze her hands. She gives me a shaky smile, and then it is her turn.

"I . . ." She clears her throat. "I'm not really sure what to say? Where to start?" She looks between Heather and me, seeking guidance.

"Just . . . whatever you feel comfortable with. Start with the day Clara disappeared. Or earlier, if you like. What it was like both before and after."

Charlotte breathes in deeply through her nose. "Okay." She looks at me. "Are you sure you want to hear?"

I nod, although her question makes me nervous. "Please. Just be honest." My attempt at a smile feels sickly, but Charlotte's shoulders straighten and she takes another deep breath.

"Diana was three years younger than me . . . still is, I suppose," she adds with a nervous chuckle. "And I felt equal parts adoration and annoyance for her most of the time." A ripple of laughter travels around the group. "The day she . . . well, I was really mad at her that day. She was being more annoying than usual, and then she got Mom to make me take her to the park. I was so angry at her . . . I left her." Her voice becomes choked, and red splotches appear on her neck. I can tell she is holding back tears, but one escapes and travels down to her jaw, dripping onto her blouse and leaving a perfect circle of dark blue.

"I snuck in so Mom wouldn't know I left Diana . . . though I knew she'd come bursting in to tattle on me soon enough. I waited. And waited. And heard Mom and Dad talking about driving down to the park to pick us up. I went to confess to them that I left her behind, and I've never seen them move so fast.

"We drove up and down the route between the park and home. Searched all the equipment and the woods around the park, in case she got hurt. There was nothing. No sign that she had even been there to begin with. And the whole time, this feeling grew in my gut, this terrible, awful knowledge that it was my fault."

"No, Charlotte—" I begin.

She spins to face me, shutting the rest of the group out. "Yes, Diana. I left you. If I hadn't, they wouldn't have been able to get you."

"You don't know that." A flash of memory. "They knew my name, Charlotte. They had been watching me. Planning. Maybe if you had stayed, they wouldn't have gotten me that day. But maybe they would have gotten both of us. Do you really think you could have fought them off?" I feel sick when I think of Charlotte being put in the same position. "No. I will not let you blame yourself. You were a kid."

It is clear that Charlotte is not convinced. Heather clears her throat. "Go on, Charlotte. What happened after?"

Charlotte nods. "After. Yes. After you were reported missing, search parties were out for weeks, looking for some sign of you, hoping to find you alive." She looks away, focusing on the floor. "Then looking for a body. They thought you might have wandered into the big national park, but no one could figure out how you'd gotten so far that we couldn't find you.

"Of course, Mom and Dad never believed you just wandered off.

You weren't stupid. Unfortunately, the stretch between our house and the park was deserted. No houses. Very little traffic. That's why Mom always made us go together. There was no proof you'd been taken. You were just gone. Poof.

"Life was different after you were gone. Less colorful, like it lost its sparkle. We couldn't really mourn you, because we didn't know if you were dead." Tears fall more rapidly now, raining down over Charlotte's cheeks, splashing onto our linked hands. I don't even remember grabbing hers again, but I hold on tight. "There were times that I wished we would find your body. Wished you would be dead so we could just move on."

I gasp, and I hear the sound echoed through the group, but no one says anything. I wanted to hear this, and I want to be supportive for Charlotte, who is struggling to continue. I rearrange my face into what I hope is an open expression and lean in. "Go on. Please."

Tear-filled eyes find mine, and I begin to lose my hold on my own emotions. "Everything was tainted after you disappeared. Holidays. Birthdays. Family gatherings. Everyone asking if there was news, talking about how old you would be, speculating about what you would be like. 'Diana would have gotten her license this year. I'd buy her a car if she'd just come home.' Meanwhile, I was trying to live my life in the shadow of your disappearance.

"I missed you, Diana. But there were times that I hated you, too. That I was so angry at you I could hardly hold it in. One bad Christmas I found an old drawing you'd made for me and I ripped it to shreds. I wished you'd never existed."

My tenuous hold on my emotions has collapsed, and I feel the sobs rising in my chest. I tamp them down, allowing only the tears to hint at the storm inside. Each word is like a knife, but at the same time, each word is healing. I can see it in Charlotte's face, what admitting this is costing her, but also what she is gaining.

"I carried the guilt of losing you. And then I carried the guilt of hating you and wishing you dead. I-I think I still carry that guilt. And anger." Charlotte's voice has fallen to a whisper.

"That's not fair," Erin chimes in from across the circle. "While you were pouting on Christmas, Diana was being raised to be someone's sex toy."

I shook my head. "No." Sending a smile Erin's way to soften my admonition, I say, "Charlotte deserves to have any emotions that come. There is no right or wrong." I turn to Charlotte, thinking I sound an awful lot like Dr. Mulligan. "I don't blame you," I say. "I'm glad you told me. We have a lot of work to do, I think. But I never want you to hold back, okay?"

Charlotte tries to speak but can't, and her mouth opens and closes. Her eyes squeeze shut, and I reach for her, pulling her close, letting my own sobs loose. I don't care who is watching, or what they think. I hold my sister until our tears slow and our hands grow sweaty from clutching each other.

A sniffle echoes in the room, and I look up to see that all the women in the circle have been affected. Tears stain pale cheeks, and red-rimmed eyes fight to hold back emotions. I release a small laugh.

"So, who's next?"

Then

Glen closes the safe, twirling the dial and pocketing the key. I sit on the bed, watching him, wondering what it is he has to file away so securely when he has an entire file system downstairs. It is not my place to wonder. But still, I hate that Glen keeps things from me. More and more I feel like there are secrets building up between us, erecting a wall that did not exist before. I have heard Harrison's name whispered, and it never fails to make my blood run cold. Nothing can connect Glen to Harrison. He assured me of that. Still, I worry. I would ask, but the last time I spoke out of turn, both my eyes ended up blackened. Glen has become more tense lately. It began not long after he got rid of Joel, but it has been escalating. I see more of Papa in him every day, as if the old coot has come back to inhabit his son's body.

I must remember not to allow those thoughts in our bed.

"I'll be gone only a few days this time, Clara. I don't like leaving you here alone."

"I'm not alone," I say, waving a hand. "Mama is just down the hall, and you're leaving some guard behind. We'll be fine."

His face does not relax. "Just make sure to keep your activities to the backyard. Don't go far on your walks. Stay inside as much as possible."

It is in these moments that I wish I were permitted to roll my eyes. Glen is being ridiculous. It is as if we have jumped back in time to the first trip he took. He was nervous leaving me then, too, but this seems worse, somehow, as if he knows something will happen.

"I promise," I say, standing and walking over to him. I rise up on my toes and kiss the tip of his nose, which earns me a small smile. He leans down and captures my mouth, deepening the kiss. His hands roam down my back and up my skirt. When I start to hope his plans might be postponed, he tears himself away, leaving me gasping for breath.

Glen grins. "Baby, I wish I could stay and finish that, but I need to go. We'll pick this up when I get back."

I pout, but he knows it is for show. Rising up one more time, I allow my lips to brush against his ear as I whisper, "Hurry back."

He groans and hurries out of the room. I chuckle to myself, pleased that I can still affect him like that. Despite his intensity, and my feelings of growing apart, there are some things that have not changed between us.

The next day, the girls and Mama take their afternoon rest in their rooms while I sit on the porch to read. I've only been out for a few minutes when one of the guards approaches me.

"Miss Clara?"

I look up, shading my eyes from the sun. "Yes?"

"Mr. Lawson requested that you and the girls stay inside as much as possible."

"For heaven's sake, I'm only on the porch. This is hardly outside."

The guard shrugs. "I'm sorry, ma'am. Orders are orders." There is warning in his voice, but I do not care. Usually the guards are required to take my orders, not give them to me. I stand up, indignant.

"What is your name, guard?" I ask, planting my hands on my hips. "I'll be talking to my husband about you."

"Shawn, ma'am, and please, I'm only trying to follow Mr. Lawson's orders." There is true fear in his tone. I soften, but only on the inside. I won't talk to Glen about him, but I'll let him sweat it out.

"I'm going in, Shawn. Expect to hear from Glen at his return."

"Yes, ma'am." The guard uses a shaky hand to touch his forehead. No wonder they left him back.

Entering the coolness of the dark house, I wander the halls, trying to find an appealing spot to read. I really enjoyed being outside. Faint giggles float down from upstairs, and I smile, remembering the days when Macy and I would muffle our laughter in hopes that Mama would not barge in and yell at us for disturbing rest time. I pause as I pass Glen's office. If I cannot find a comfortable place to read, maybe I can find another activity to keep me occupied.

Another change Glen has made is hiding the key to his office from me. But this might be my only chance to get the answers I still long for. Before I can change my mind, I slip a pin from my hair, crouch in front of the door, and wiggle the pin in the lock. Nothing happens. I sit back on my heels, frustrated, thinking, trying to imagine what my husband might consider a suitable hiding spot. I know him better than anyone. Surely I can figure this out. Then I remember. The library. I hurry to the room down the hall and pray the liquor cabinet is unlocked. It is, and, just as I hoped, I find a key tucked into the top corner. I have noticed Glen drinking more lately, another reminder of his father that I wish he would not take on.

I return to the office and let out a small victory cry when the door opens without a sound. I slip in and close the door behind me, just in case any nosy guards enter the house, or Mama rises early from her rest. I'm not too worried. She has been spending more time in her room this stay than normal. I get the sense she is avoiding me, but I can't say I am upset that she isn't interfering with the girls as much as she usually does.

I spend the next fifteen minutes riffling through the drawers, careful to keep things in their places. Glen cannot know I've been in here. I find the client files and flip through, looking for one name, but these files are coded by numbers. Sitting in Glen's desk chair, I spin, trying to decide how far I will go to find out what happened to Macy. I do not want to break Glen's trust, but I also owe it to my friend to learn where she is. I haven't thought about what I'll do with the information once I have it. But where else would Glen keep that information?

The safe upstairs. I sit up. Of course. I close my eyes and imagine myself sitting across from Glen, watching him. He never opens a drawer before he goes for the key. I would hear that. In my memories, I remember a small click. It takes another twenty minutes of pushing on every available surface under the desk, but I find it. The key to the safe.

Standing, I make my way to the door, listening for footsteps above. All is still quiet, and I climb the stairs on light feet, making as little noise as possible. My heart beats an erratic rhythm as I cross the room to the safe, hidden behind the vanity in our bedroom. Spinning the dial, I smile at Glen's combination. The lock clicks, I turn the key, and open the safe.

Papers are stuffed into every available corner. I have not paid attention when Glen has opened it before. It never occurred to me that I would do something so rash as to break in. I groan, overwhelmed at the volume of information in front of me. The girls will be up soon, and there will be no chance to look later. I grab what looks like a ledger and quickly scan through the pages. It is organized by year, and I recognize some of the names. The information is basic, but enough. I flip to the front of the book, but it doesn't go back far enough. I grab for another one, my fingers eager as they run down the columns of information.

I bounce on the balls of my feet in excitement when I finally find what I'm looking for.

Name: Macy
Assignment: ~~Angels~~ Treehouse
Status: ~~Active~~ Deceased 11/22/91

Macy didn't leave the brothel as I had been told. She died. She has been dead for years and no one bothered to tell me. I look at the date again. Just over a month after my wedding. She was living, breathing, warm, *alive*, and then she wasn't. All these years . . .

The room is spinning and I have no control over legs that will no longer hold me up. The ledger falls to the floor as I curl up, my sobs silent as they take over my entire body. I do not know how long I lie there in silent misery, wishing for the peacefulness of oblivion, before small hands are running across my arms, tugging, trying to pull me loose from myself.

"Miss Clara? Miss Clara, are you okay?" I do not know which of my daughters is speaking, only that I cannot answer. I want to. I know I cannot shut down, but after so many years of wondering, cataloging things to tell her in case I ever got to see her again, learning of her death hits me like nothing has before.

"Move, girls. Get out of here. Go start your chores." Mama's gruff voice overpowers the smaller ones, tinged with concern and something else. Apprehension?

The door closes, cutting off the chatter of the worried girls, and a blanket of silence descends over the room. I can feel Mama's presence, feel her eyes on me, but still I lie curled into myself, wishing I had never gone snooping. Glen has been protecting me from this.

An unexpected wave of anger hits me when I think of Glen. He has kept this from me. All this time, avoiding questions about Macy, knowing I was holding out hope, and he knew she was gone. I have never felt this much anger toward Glen, and it frightens me enough that I unfold myself in shock, sitting up and blinking at Mama, who is standing at the door, arms crossed, an unreadable look on her face as she stares at the ledger on the floor, still open to the page declaring Macy's death.

"What have you done, child?" she asks, her voice surprisingly soft.

I don't answer. I pick up the dropped ledger and stuff it back into the safe, cursing its existence. I slam the door of the safe shut, twirl the dial, and conceal the safe back into its hiding spot. Mama moves as I storm toward the door. I return the safe key to its spot under the desk, lock up the office, and return that key to the library. My entire body vibrates with energy that must be released, but I don't know how to get it out. Perhaps this is how Glen feels when I make him angry. It would feel good to hit something. Or someone.

Mama, who has followed me to the library, takes a seat in one of the high-backed chairs. "Come, have a seat, child," she says, gesturing to the chair across from her.

"I'm no child, Mama, even if you and Glen insist on continuing to treat me like one."

Her lips purse at my tone, but she does not react otherwise. "Please sit down, Clara."

I consider for a moment. I don't want to sit. I want to run. I want to scream. I want to break something. I want to cry. Still, Mama may have the answers I'm looking for. She can't deny it anymore. Her reactions have proven that she knows exactly what I found in that safe.

"Why?" I ask, choosing to pace back and forth instead of sitting. "Why would you keep this from me?"

Mama sighs, the exhausted sigh of a woman tired of keeping secrets. "We thought it was best that you let it go, Clara. Macy was not a part of your life anymore."

"She will always be a part of my life."

"You had moved on. It was just best not to bring it up."

My heart squeezes at the callousness of her statement. I'm surprised it still responds to anything. I thought it would be numb by now. "You still should have told me."

"No. I stand by our decision. You didn't need to know. If anything, this little tantrum proves that."

I spin to face her. "Tantrum? Macy was my best friend. We grew up together. She was torn away from me."

"She made her choices."

The urge to scream is almost overwhelming. "She was the last link to my childhood! The only one left who really knew me!"

Mama looks scandalized. "The last link? What about me? What about Glen?"

Glen. My pacing starts back up, faster than before.

Of course it always comes back to Glen. Glen, who charmed me from the moment I met him. Glen, who wanted to hate me, but couldn't bring himself to do so. Glen, who would have given up everything for me. Glen, who is always trying to protect me.

My steps slow, and I sink into the chair across from Mama. "I miss her," I whisper, and a fresh wave of tears washes down my cheeks.

Mama leans forward, taking my hands in hers, squeezing them as the tears roll faster. "I know, child," she says. "But now you can truly move forward."

I nod, unable to speak. There are still so many questions unanswered, but maybe Mama is right. Maybe it's best to leave them in the past and focus on the future.

"I won't share this little spell with Glen, okay? This will be our secret." Mama's voice is soothing, but there is a warning in it. If Glen finds out what I have done, I'm not the only one who will be held responsible. For the first time, I wonder if Glen didn't ask Mama to stay just to keep an eye on the girls, but also to monitor my behavior. I shake the thought loose almost as soon as it pops into my head. Glen trusts me.

The guilt washes over me then. I have broken that trust. But he doesn't need to know. He will never know. And from now on, I will trust him implicitly. Until death.

Now

My pulse beats faster as the van moves along the gravel drive toward Glen's brothel. This is the first time I have been granted a pass to leave the facility other than my visits to Glen and my field trip to the prison. After Mama's information about the graveyard proved to be valuable, they decided that I might be able to help with more than just information. I agreed to help them look for documents. The agents have brought me here first to see if anything is salvageable, but my heart sinks as I spy the blackened skeleton where the building used to stand.

"Someone sent up the alarm here before we could get to them," Connor explains. "They torched the place."

"What about the girls?" This is the first time I have given much thought to anyone besides Glen, myself, and my daughters. What happened to the rest of Glen's men? To the women who lived here? Connor's face is grim, and I already know before he speaks that I do not want to know that answer.

"There were many deaths, Clara." Everyone continues to use the name I am used to, even my family when they visit. "Some survived, but no one made it out without injuries." Connor takes a deep breath. "It appears they didn't plan on anyone getting out. The doors and windows were locked. Our men were lucky to get the ones they did."

Panic threatens to overcome me as the van stops. I don't want to get out, but it's something I need to do. Connor helps me from the backseat, and I walk toward the ruined structure. The scent of a campfire is on the breeze, mixed with something more sinister, and I breathe through my mouth to avoid inhaling the stench of death. I walk closer and see that in a couple of the rooms, the doors, though blackened, remain in their frames. Long scratch marks mar the wood beneath the ash and soot, and I can almost hear the desperate screams of the women trapped inside.

I wonder if any of them welcomed death. If the heat and smoke and flames were like friends, coming to free them from a weary life, to bring them to a new place and time. I'm not sure I would have survived in a place like this. I have Glen to thank for keeping me out of it. It is a strange dichotomy of emotions, and one I am still not ready to tackle. I turn to Connor.

"Can we go to the house now? There's nothing here."

He nods. "Of course."

We climb back into the van and travel the few miles down the road to the beautiful house that Glen bought for me. For us. For our family. For his business. I am gripped with unexpected emotion as the house comes into view. It is as gorgeous as the first day Glen brought me here. Unchanged, except for an overgrown lawn and a general atmosphere of abandonment. Yellow police tape flutters in the wind where it has come loose. I take a deep breath and exit the van.

It is as if the entire world has been holding its breath for this moment. All is silent. No one moves as I step forward. They all seem to realize what this means. I walk up the steps, my feet echoing across the wood of the porch. Connor reaches around me to remove the last remnants of the police tape blocking my progress. I had not even realized he was behind me, and when I look back I see that I am at the head of a sort of macabre parade. Everyone looks solemn as they survey the house. It's a small group, and I wonder how many of them were in the original raid, when this house was bursting with children.

I step inside and am transported back to that day. Everything is almost as we left it, although there are signs of a search here and there. A pile of clothes sits in the side hallway, where Elaine dropped it when the men entered the house. My chair, where I sat brushing Daisy's hair, is still pulled out at the same angle, though they took the brush as evidence. I walk through the rooms, running my hands over objects, memories, vestiges of a life that seems so long ago, yet like it happened yesterday. I gaze out the giant windows in the great room, the mountains unchanged, and look down on the rows of cabins, almost expecting to see the normal bustle of activity as men rush from one assignment to the next.

"Clara." I jump as Connor appears beside me. "I don't want to rush you, but . . ."

"Of course. The papers." I turn left and head toward Glen's office.

"We searched in here," Connor says, keeping pace with me.

I enter the room without replying, but stop short in the doorway. This room looks very different. It has been searched thoroughly. There are open drawers and broken knickknacks everywhere, and the empty file cabinets show that every scrap of paper in here has already been taken. I force my feet forward and around the desk.

Kneeling, I reach to the far back portion under the desk, finding a small knot and pressing to reveal a secret compartment. From the compartment, I withdraw a key. Connor's eyes widen with interest when I stand to show him.

"Glen doesn't know that I know about that, but I did some exploring of my own from time to time." My hands tremble slightly as I recall sneaking into the office in Glen's absence and what I learned from that exercise.

"So where does that key fit?" he asks. His eyes are bright, cheeks flushed with excitement. It gives me a certain degree of satisfaction to be holding all the cards, but also to be able to make Connor happy.

"This way," I say, heading out of the room.

"Not in the study?"

"Glen's too smart for that," I say, wincing at the worship I still hear in my own voice for him. Glen is smart. It's part of what drew me to him so strongly. Part of what still draws me. I lead our small parade up the stairs and to the master bedroom. This room, too, has been searched thoroughly, and I frown when I see that our mattress has been sliced open, springs jutting out at odd angles. "You sure you checked everywhere?" I ask, trying to keep my tone light to detract from the heavy atmosphere. Connor doesn't respond.

The vanity in the corner has been searched, but not moved. Not surprising, since it is made to look like it is part of the wall. I feel along the mirror for the handhold and pull the vanity easily from its niche in the wall.

"Holy shit," I hear Connor gasp from behind me, and I smile. The safe is in the wall behind the vanity, with both a lock and a combination.

"The combination is 10-6-91. Our wedding date." I insert the key, spin the combination, and pull the lever to open the door. I barely glance at the stacks of paper and money stuffed into the compartment before stepping back to let Connor examine it. I do not care what is in the safe. With that final act of betrayal, I have sealed Glen's fate. And possibly my own.

Then

I am on my side in bed, facing the wall. I feel nothing. Nothing but empty. Glen has given up on me. He left hours ago after pleading with me to talk to him. He doesn't understand. How could he? It isn't his fault.

I am the one who lost our baby.

This is the third time I have woken up to find blood on the sheets. The third time I have felt the cramps that signal the demise of our miracle. The third time the doctor has come to remove what is left. Empty. Lost. Alone in my body once again.

The door opens. The footsteps that enter are not Glen's. They are lighter, more graceful than his clomping gait. Too heavy for one of the girls. In a distant corner of my mind, I wonder how the girls are doing. Who is taking care of them. If they are doing their lessons. But I cannot find it in myself to care in this moment. This moment is mine to grieve, to crawl into that black hole. I am not sure I will emerge this time.

Springs squeak as the mattress lowers. "Clara?" Mama's voice is soft, soothing, unlike her usual brisk tone. "You need to eat something, dear."

Eat. The idea would almost make me sick, if I could feel anything. I continue to stare at the wall, not really seeing the grimy paint. Wondering what my baby would have looked like. If she would have had Glen's nose. My eyes. Or if it was a boy, Glen's strong jaw. Glen would make such a good father to a boy. He deserves a boy. And I cannot give him one. Again I have failed him.

"Clara. You need to get up. Glen needs you." I can hear the struggle in Mama's voice as she admits that. Though we have been married for four years, Mama still cannot give her full blessing. At least she is kind to me most days. Today more than ever. Today she talks as if I am dying. Maybe I am. "Glen doesn't know how to help you, Clara. He is drinking. I've never seen him drink this much."

That catches my attention. As a rule, Glen has never been a big drinker. He doesn't like the way alcohol dulls his senses. He blames Papa's drinking for his botched deals, the ones that put us under for a while. I don't know details, but Glen gets chatty in bed sometimes. I learn a lot if I stay quiet. I turn to face Mama. "How much has he had?"

"Too much to be of use to you tonight. He's passed out in the study."

I sit up. Passed out? I have never known Glen to pass out. "Is he okay?"

"He'll feel like hell in the morning. The best you can do to help him is get yourself cleaned up and be ready to go when he comes out of it."

Swinging my legs over the edge of the bed, I nod. Glen is hurting, and I need to be there for him. I stand on shaky legs, and Mama grabs my arm. She helps me toward the bathroom, and even assists in removing my nightgown and stepping into the shower. She is there when I emerge, still feeling empty, but slightly more human. There is a cup of tea waiting for me.

"It's medicinal," Mama explains, handing me the mug. "Recommended by the doctor."

I take a sip, and the liquid tastes like honey and cinnamon, sweet and spicy. Much better than the morning sickness tea Mama has been giving me. I won't be needing that anymore. I sit in one of the chairs in the corner of the room, unwilling to crawl back into bed yet. Mama takes the second chair. She watches me carefully.

"I'll be fine."

"I know." Mama takes a breath. "It's not right, you losing your babies."

Shocked, I can only stare at her. I expected more of a "buck up" statement. Even after all these years, Mama can surprise me. "Thank you for saying that."

She studies me again. Her expression changes, as if she has made a decision. "I told you once about Glen's sisters." It is not a question. She assumes I remember, and of course I do. It is the sort of information that I dared not ask about, but that I stored away to examine every once in a while, to try to find my own meaning or explanation. I nod.

"You never asked me what happened to them," she continues.

"No," I say. "It wouldn't have been proper."

"Smart girl," Mama says. Another compliment. Sort of. She is on a roll tonight. "It's time you knew." She closes her eyes, as if it will be easier to tell me her story if she can't see me. "I always wanted girls," Mama says. "And when I married Papa, I got more girls than I had ever dreamed. Papa G, he wanted boys. Strong boys to help with the business, to take over when he couldn't handle the load anymore. So when I got pregnant, he was over-the-moon excited.

"Back then, you didn't find out ahead of time if you were having a boy or a girl. At least most people didn't, and we didn't have the means anyway. So after eighteen hours of hard labor, we learned that I'd been growing a girl for almost ten months. Papa walked out without a word."

Mama looks so sad. I feel for her, though I can imagine Papa doing just that. Glen would have stayed by my side, but Papa and Mama's relationship was very different. I do not interrupt. I need to hear what happened next, and Mama might change her mind. Her face is tight and her knuckles white where they grip the arms of her chair.

"The next morning, Papa G came in with a fellow he knew from another side of the business. This is the guy Papa went to when one of his other girls got into trouble. They had already come to a deal, and in minutes, my darling baby was out of my arms and out the door with the man. I was promised she would have a good home, a loving family." Mama laughs bitterly. "As if she were a dog they needed to get rid of. My husband, Glen's father, sold my babies. All three healthy little girls. I don't even know what happened to them, though Papa said they went to nice families who could give them what we couldn't." A humorless laugh escapes her lips. "It's ironic, if you think about it."

I don't know how to process what I've just learned, so I reach over and place a hand over hers. She flips her hand to grip mine. "Clara, Glen was my last chance, and I told you why he is so important to me. It kills me to see him hurting. I know that you're hurting, too. I know what it feels like. The empty womb, the empty arms. But if you can be there for him, you'll both get through this. The men pretend they are the strong ones, that they protect us." Mama smiles. "But we are the ones holding them up, keeping them afloat. We are their anchors.

"I had my doubts about you, Clara, but I can tell that you are the one who can be Glen's anchor. It took me a while to get here, but seeing you weather these storms, seeing you lose three babies and get up and move forward . . . it's proven that you will stand by Glen through anything. Remember that: As long as you hold each other up, you will make it through anything."

Now

I flush the toilet after losing my lunch yet again. I can no longer blame Nut. His contribution to my stomach issues has long since passed. No. Today there is another reason.

Today I see Glen. It has been many weeks since our last visit. So much has changed. I am no longer the girl he knew. And I am more terrified of this visit than I was of starting therapy, or going to the support group, or even meeting my family. I walk to the sink to wash out my mouth, rubbing my rounded abdomen in the way that has become unconscious habit.

Without thinking about it, I begin to pace. I don't know what Glen will think of the changes in me, and it bothers me that I still care. I worry that I will be susceptible to his charm, as I always have been. That he still holds power over me, despite the revelations of the past few weeks. That I will take back everything I have done.

But I cannot take back all of it. The documents in the safe are proof enough to nail Glen for countless transgressions. I know now what it is called. Human trafficking. Buying and selling and trading humans. And I helped. I do not yet know what my punishment will be.

Jay walks into the room, interrupting my rapidly declining thoughts. He raises an eyebrow. I must look frightful. "Ready?"

I nod, not trusting my voice. I must save it for Glen. We set off down the hall. I do not really need him to lead anymore. I know the way by heart. Into the van and through busy streets to the prison. As we enter the building, I trail Jay, my feet feeling heavier the closer we get to the room where Glen waits. Connor is outside the door.

"We'll be right in there, Clara," he says, pointing to a door adjacent to the one I will enter. "We're watching and listening to the whole thing. As soon as you need to get out of there, just say so. You can have as much time as you need."

Smiling, I squeeze his arm. I remember his time limits from before. I would have abused them then. I would have stayed until someone pried me away. This time, I will not have that problem. But just in case, I know that he will be there. "Thank you."

Taking a deep breath, I nod at the guard, who unlocks the door and opens it for me. Glen is the only one in the sparse room. He looks strong, healthy, but his face is drawn, with more lines than I remember. He jumps up as I enter the room, rushing around the table to embrace me. I stiffen in his grasp and pat him on the back before stepping away from the circle of his arms.

"Clara?" His voice is laced with confusion. This is not the reunion he expected.

"Let's sit down, Glen," I say, and I am surprised at the strength in my voice. I move to the table. Glen remains where he is for a moment, and then follows, sitting beside me. I scoot my chair a little farther away from his so I can look at him fully. He leans forward and grips my hands, and I do not pull free.

"How are you, Clara?" One of his hands moves to my stomach. "How is our baby?"

"We're both good, Glen." I am not sure how this conversation will go. I will let him lead for now. "How are you?"

"How do I look, Clara?" Glen's eyes flash. "I am in hell." He runs a hand through his hair, still maintaining his grip on my hand with the other. "And they arrested Mama. Found all sorts of stuff in her house.

She should have gotten rid of all of Papa's records as soon as he died." He sighs and looks at me. "It's not looking good, Clare."

"I know." Connor has kept me updated. Mama put up a fight when they went to arrest her and search the house, but she is in custody now, being held at the same prison I visited. I hope she is eating the food and playing nice with the others.

Glen looks at me. "You know?" He is curious, but not suspicious yet. I glance at the mirror, where I know Connor and the guards are monitoring our conversation. Glen's face hardens. "How do you know, Clara?"

I look him straight in the eye as I say, "Because I helped get the information."

He recoils, dropping my hand as if it has burned him. "What the hell are you talking about?" He stands and begins to pace.

"I told them what they needed to know," I say, my voice even, calm. "And then I wore a wire when Mama came to visit."

Without warning, Glen flies at me, grabbing my shoulders. The door crashes open and guards pour into the room, pulling him off of me. Connor is close behind them and comes over to me, helping me to my feet. I wave them all off. "It's fine. Let him go." The guards comply, but stay close, and Connor does not leave my side. Glen looks between the two of us.

A brittle smile cracks his face. "I see. You're fucking him, aren't you? A little bed action and a little information? How could you betray me like that, Clara?"

To Connor's credit, his only reaction is the muscle jumping in his jaw. He lets me run the show.

"No, Glen. I'm not sleeping with Connor."

"Right." Glen's body is tense, ready to spring, and I'm glad that the guards remain in the room with us now. I had hoped to do this without a visible audience, but instead I tune them out and focus on Glen.

"You lied to me, Glen. My whole life, you lied."

He crosses his arms, staring me down, refusing to speak.

"All those girls were told the same lie. Their parents didn't want them. They didn't have a home. They were alone in the world, and you could give them a place to call home, a family that loved them." I laugh, but there's no joy in the sound. "But it was all for money, wasn't it? And prestige in your sick little community."

"You don't understand, Clara."

"I understand, Glen. You lied to me, pretended to love me, and screwed other girls while I waited at home, while I did everything you asked. EVERYTHING." I shout the last word, my calm façade crumbling beneath the weight of my emotion. I take a step forward, ignoring the small sound Connor makes. "I wanted to give you the world. I wanted to give you a family. But instead, you let your mother poison me, kill my babies, keep me feeling inferior in every possible way."

Glen's reaction is immediate. His entire body wilts. "My mother did what?"

And I realize that he didn't know. He has no reason to lie at this point.

"The tea she always gave me . . ."

Realization dawns on his face as he puts the pieces together. "She's the reason . . ."

I nod and watch as tears fill his eyes. I gaze into his shattered expression, and my heart breaks. It breaks for the life we could have had, if we were both different people. For the life I thought we had. For the babies I will never meet. For the last bit of innocence that was lying hidden within Glen, now eradicated by news of his parents' treachery.

"I am going to continue to cooperate with them, Glen," I say as I begin to walk toward the door. "You are no longer anything to me." The words stab me as surely as they must stab him, and I pray that someday they will be true. "I wish for you a long life of captivity, just as you made happen for all those children."

A strangled cry comes from behind me when I am almost to the door. "Clara." I have never heard Glen make a sound like that, and I turn around. Behind me sits a broken man, his power over me gone. "I always loved you, Clara," he says, his voice barely loud enough to carry to me.

My smile is gentle. "Maybe you loved Clara," I agree. "But Clara no longer exists. Good-bye, Glen."

Head held high, I exit the room to the sound of Glen's sobs. Once the door closes behind me, I sink to the floor of the hallway, heedless of whatever dirt and grime I might be resting in. My head cradled in my hands, I break.

Connor lets me cry for a few minutes, then helps me to my feet. Jay is on the other side. As I stand, I feel a weight falling from my shoulders. My heart is shattered, but my soul, which has been dark and twisted for so long, is starting the long process toward healing.

Then

Kelly is perfect. Her short bob is brushed to shining, and her simple jeans and T-shirt are exactly to the specifications of her client. She is my first daughter to go out into the world, and she will be taking care of children herself. She is sixteen, but looks older, at least eighteen or nineteen. Old enough to be a nanny traveling with a family.

Only her face does not match the image I am trying to portray. Tears stream down her cheeks. "I don't want to go, Clara," she whimpers. "Please, let me stay and help you."

"Don't be silly," I say, brushing imaginary lint off her shoulders.

"You get to go and travel the world. Mr. Green and his family do business in Europe and Asia and South America . . . and you will get to take care of his two children. They are adorable." I realize I am rambling, nervous in my own right that she will not perform. Glen will not be happy. Though Papa made the initial contact, he's sitting this part out, since the training has been primarily a joint effort between Glen and myself. He will be waiting to hear how things go. And to give his judgment.

"But . . . have you seen him?" Kelly asks, her voice trembling. "He's old, and I know what you said about—"

"Hush," I say, sharper than I intend. I gentle my tone. "He is your life now, Kelly. Simple as that. Don't forget it, and you won't have a problem."

Kelly continues to sob quietly, shoulders shaking. I am grateful that the client requested no eye makeup. It would be a disaster by now. I hand her a tissue. "Calm down, Kelly. He'll be here soon."

Glen taps on the door and walks in. "What's going on?" He does not look pleased to find such a mess of a girl waiting for him.

"Just some nerves," I say, standing in front of Kelly, shielding her from his view. "She'll be fine."

"Mr. Green just called from the front of the building. He's on his way up."

Kelly begins to sob louder, covering her face with her hands. Glen pushes me aside and walks up to stand directly in front of her. "Kelly." She lowers her hands and looks up at him. Without warning, he slaps her across the face with his open hand. "Snap the fuck out of it," he says. His voice is low, but menacing. "Your client will be here soon. If you don't perform as promised, you'll end up at one of our other . . . establishments."

The fear in Kelly's eyes is clear. None of the girls here are fully informed about the other branches, but they know they do not want to be a part of them. She wipes her eyes and nose and squares her shoulders. Glen turns and stalks out of the room without another word.

As soon as he is gone, I rush to Kelly's side to inspect her face. There is some reddening, but I do not believe it will bruise. I cover it as best I can and finish as the bell sounds through the apartment.

"To your beds, girls," I order, and the other girls move to sit on their beds, silent as they watch Kelly with expressions varying from anxiety to envy. We wait.

"Clara, bring Kelly out," Glen calls. I brush my hands across Kelly's shoulders one more time before opening the door and leading her out. I plaster a bright smile on my face for the intimidating Mr. Green, who stands waiting, briefcase in hand. I assume it holds his payment. Papa and Glen deal only in cash.

My eyes are still on Mr. Green when I see his eyebrows vee as he looks over my shoulder. I turn to see that Kelly has stopped. Her eyes are wide as she stares at her client, and then her face crumples.

"I'm sorry," she wails. "I can't . . . I can't . . ." She backs up, her intent to flee back to the bedroom clear. Glen is there before she can take a step.

"You can and you will," he hisses, his grip tight on her wrist. He yanks her forward, and she stumbles. I rush forward to catch her, but Glen reaches out and shoves me away. I run into the table, and I feel a bruise begin to blossom on my hip. "No, Clara. The time for soft words is over. She's been trained for this." He leans forward and whispers something in her ear that I cannot hear.

Mr. Green has been watching the entire exchange with interest. "Is there a problem?" He sounds almost amused.

"Not at all, Mr. Green," Glen says. "Kelly just cares so much for her sisters and Clara, she's having a hard time leaving."

"Should I worry?" Mr. Green's voice is laced with suspicion.

I jump in. "Of course not," I say, laughing a little. "Kelly is loyal. As soon as she meets your children, she will never want to leave them. And I know you can offer her things we cannot." I raise an eyebrow and he grins.

"That is true." He turns to Kelly. "Girl. Get over here." He tosses the briefcase on the table next to me. "You belong to me now." He grabs her from Glen and pulls her forward until her front is flush with his. He grips her chin and forces her face upward. "This place does not exist. These people do not exist. Only I exist. Are we clear?"

Kelly nods, a difficult gesture with her chin firmly in his grasp.

"Good. We are leaving then," he says. With a tip of his head toward Glen and a wink in my direction, he drags Kelly out of the apartment. Glen locks the door behind them.

"How could you let that happen, Clara?" he asks without turning around.

"I'm sorry, Glen, I told you she wasn't—"

He slams a hand against the door. "You don't *tell* me anything! When I have a client, I expect the girl to be ready! Or are you not able to handle simple instructions?" He spins to face me and stalks forward. I try to back away but the table is there. He stops in front of me and places his hands on either side of my hips. Our lips are a breath apart. "If you can't handle this, then maybe I need to find someone who can."

His words hit my heart like an arrow, piercing my soul. "You don't mean that."

"Screw it up like that again and you'll see how serious I am." His words leave no questions as to his meaning. He grips my arms, squeezing tight, till it hurts, then throws me to the floor before stomping off to his study. I understand his anger. Papa found Kelly, and Mama gave me some help with the training, but Glen handled the transaction on his own. He needed it to go smoothly so that Papa will trust him to handle part of the business independently, with his own clients.

When Papa stops by later to check in, Glen is all smiles. "It went great, Pop!" he says. "Smooth sailing." He flashes me a grin. "Clare was brilliant, as I knew she would be."

I manage a smile back before heading to put the girls to bed. Glen is closing the door behind Papa when I return.

"We did it!" he crows, and grabs me around the waist, spinning me around. He carries me to the bedroom, and soon I forget all about the bruises on my arms and hip as we celebrate. There is only Glen, who gives me pain sometimes, but also takes it away.

Now

I am surprisingly calm as I wait in an antechamber, counting the minutes until I will take the stand to speak against my husband. Ex-husband? We found out that the marriage between Glen and myself was never even legal. How could it be, when Clara did not exist? They could have gotten documents, as they did for the South Dakota trip, or for any of the other girls when they were sold, but it was one last cruel joke from Papa, who had never forgiven Glen for screwing up and falling in love with the wrong girl.

The room echoes with the ticking of the clock. I asked my family to give me some time alone. I have not seen Glen since our confrontation at the prison. He has tried to call, though I have no idea where he has found numbers to reach me. There is an extensive network of people within the prison system who can get almost any bit of information, apparently even information protected at the highest levels of government. He has sent letters as well, and those I have not been able to bring myself to throw away. I hope that after this day is over, I can find the strength to release him for good.

The door behind me creaks open, and I stand and follow the deputy into the courtroom. The benches are packed, and I resist the urge to search the room for the faces of my daughters. I know some of their families are attending, but I was told the girls were not allowed to come. Despite my avoidance of eye contact, I can feel the weight of the audience's stares. I do not know what they think of me, nor do I want to know. I have thought every terrible thought about myself, probably more than they have, and dwelling on it will only set me back. Unable to help myself, I glance at the front row. As promised, Dr. Mulligan and Connor are sitting there. My focal points. My resolve strengthens, and I walk with purpose to the witness stand, where I am sworn in.

When my eyes finally find Glen's, it is as if the entire room has disappeared. No one else exists but us, for a few seconds at least. Even after I break our gaze, I feel his stare, his eyes like lasers boring into my forehead. I don't remember all the questions I am asked. We have rehearsed this so many times, I can answer automatically. I'm glad there are no surprise questions, not even from Glen's lawyer. I know the evidence is damning, and my testimony, as an accomplice and a victim, is very convincing.

As I step down, I take one last glance at Glen. I drink him in, the blue eyes, dulled by his months in prison, the normally tousled hair, now cropped close to his scalp. He is thin, but I can tell he has been making use of the prison gym. I wonder if he has set up his empire there yet.

I walk from the room feeling lighter, the weight of my guilt some-what assuaged, and the corners of my lips tip up of their own accord. I am ready to move forward. I rub my rounded belly, the life inside almost ready to join the world. It's time.

Then

"Good night, angels," I whisper, flipping the light switch and pulling the door closed behind me. The last of the girls are in bed, though it is still light out. Glen insists on a seven o'clock bedtime for all but the oldest girls. I wander downstairs to find Passion in the kitchen, finishing the dishes.

"Anything else you need, Clara?" she asks, and waits obediently for my answer.

"No, thank you, Passion," I say. "Just keep an eye on the girls for me, okay?"

She nods and leaves the room. I rummage through the cupboards and refrigerator, coming up with a few items for a snack. Glen is working late at the brothel again. It was opened a year ago, and though it took a while for business to pick up, things appear to be running smoothly now. Lately Glen has been working a lot of hours over there. He always comes home very late, and exhausted. I wince as I bump a bruise on my arm, a remnant of my question about whether he should take a few days off.

Since Glen did not appreciate my suggestion of a break, I will bring a break to him. He should have time to have a small snack, even if he works while he eats it. I will slip in, drop the snack off, and be gone without interrupting him. Although, if he has time for a quick kiss, or more, I am always ready for him. I smile as I remember how we tested out the various rooms before the brothel was open.

Ted is waiting with the car when I leave the house. He was dubious when I asked this favor, but I promised I would take all the blame if Glen was angry. He will not be angry. The drive to the other building is short, and business is good tonight, if the cars packing the small lot are any indication. Loud music and laughter float through the air, disturbing the peace of what could be a beautiful night. I make a face. I rarely come here, and never when they are busy. I find the entire practice distasteful, but I know that Glen knows what he is doing, and it is a successful business for him. This new location has done well.

Glen used to keep the girls at a separate location and drive them to hotels that would look the other way as needed. When we bought the house and property, he was able to purchase this plot of land as well. A "one-stop shop," he calls it. I remember Papa G using a similar phrase.

I step out onto the gravel and wave at Ted. "I'll be right back," I say. I go to the side door and knock. I refuse to walk through the main part of the establishment. The door creaks open a few inches, a surly eye peeking out from the crack. The eye widens when it recognizes me, and the door swings wide. "Hello, Miss Clara," stutters the man. His face is familiar, but I do not know his name. I step inside.

"I brought something for Glen to eat," I say. "Is he around?"

There are three other men in this dimly lit and smoke-filled back room. The first man glances at the others, tugging at his collar. His Adam's apple bobs as he swallows hard. "He's uhh... indisposed right now, Miss Clara," he says. "Would you like to... errr..."

"I can just leave it," I say, smiling to put the man at ease. All the men are nervous around me, especially after what happened with Joel, when he disappeared. I don't believe they know much, only that Joel crossed a line with the girls. Still, they do not like to have much interaction with me and avoid even looking at me if they can. I wonder if they have guessed at what other lines Joel crossed.

A door at the far end crashes open, and the man steps in front of me, hiding me from view. I do not protest, but peek over his shoulder.

Glen stumbles in, each arm slung around a topless woman. He is clearly intoxicated, as I have never seen him before. I shrink back further, though with the darkness of the room, the man in front of me, and Glen's drunkenness, I am practically invisible.

"We're gonna be in my office," Glen slurs, pulling one of the women closer and giving her a sloppy kiss. It looks like he is trying to eat her face, and I feel sick to my stomach. He gropes at the other woman's breast, and she moans as if she is enjoying it. Glen breaks away. "Hold my calls!" He laughs and gives an exaggerated wink to the men in the room, then stumbles to a door on the opposite wall, the one that leads to his private office. It is difficult to tell who is holding whom up, but the women appear to be doing most of the heavy lifting. The door slams shut, and though the sounds are muffled, it is obvious what is going on behind the wall.

I step out from behind the man. "Thank you," I say. "I think I'll just head home."

He nods and doesn't attempt to speak. I yank open the door to the outside, welcoming the cool rush of mountain air on my flushed face. I don't look back as I pull the door shut, blocking out the last of the sounds of Glen's drunken tryst. I lean against the side of the building, trying to catch my breath, but my lungs will not pull in enough oxygen. I feel light-headed.

How long has this been going on? Is this what Glen does on his nights of "working late"? Am I not enough? What am I doing wrong? I stumble to the edge of the trees and vomit in the grass. How often has he come home from an evening like this and touched me? Touched me with those hands that were roaming all over other women? Kissed me with the lips he used to devour cheap lipsticked mouths?

And this whole time I thought I was better than them. Disgust fills me, but also shame that I am not giving Glen what he needs, that he has stooped to trying to find it here. I remember when I learned about Papa's indiscretions, the pity I felt for Mama. And she just accepted it. Not me. From now on, I will do everything in my power to make sure that Glen has no reason to seek out fulfillment elsewhere. I will be everything he needs, just like he is everything I need.

After several minutes, I am able to stand again. I throw my shoulders back and walk back to where Ted waits with the car. Nothing can be done about my red-rimmed eyes, but I put on a mask of cool indifference before sliding into the backseat.

"He wasn't hungry?" Ted looks at the basket I only now realize is still hanging from my arm. It's probably for the best. I do not want Glen to know that I was there.

"I couldn't find him," I answer.

Ted nods and turns back to start the car. He doesn't believe me, and I don't care. It's not his business to decide whether I tell the truth or not. His only job is to drive me home.

"Ted?"

"Yes, ma'am?"

"Best not to mention this to Glen."

"Yes, ma'am."

Now

The halls of the courthouse echo with the sounds of people going about their business. I focus on snippets of conversation as women in clicking heels stride past, discussing lunch plans, and men in suits speak in hushed tones, strategizing for their next case. Concentrating on them helps me to ignore the thoughts running through my head. Anything to keep from dwelling on what the next hour of my life will mean.

Connor leans against the wall opposite my bench, his casual stance not quite hiding the tension radiating from his body. He checks his watch every few seconds, and his fingers tap an uneven rhythm onto the pleats of his pants. Dr. Mulligan sits next to me, her legs crossed, the picture of ease. She told me in our last session that she is confident that the judge will come to a decision that will benefit everyone. My parents wanted to come, to show their support, but this is something I need to do without them. Even in their absence, I feel their support to my bones. They haven't wavered from my side since we reunited, despite knowing more about what I have done. I am slowly learning that unconditional love does exist.

Dr. Mulligan looks over at me, her lips turning up in a smile. "How are you feeling, Clara?" I wonder if she gets a bonus every time she asks that question. Maybe I'll have it embroidered on a pillow for her office when this is all over.

I attempt a return smile, but my lips don't quite cooperate. "Okay," I lie, looking away, knowing Dr. Mulligan will see through me.

A soft hand covers mine, and my eyes dart to meet her gaze. "You can do this," she says. "The hardest part is behind you."

Chills run across my body as I remember my testimony at Glen's trial. The last desperate look in his eyes before I opened my mouth and sealed his fate. The indefinable emotion that crossed his face when I glanced back at him that last time. I shake my head, dispelling the images from my mind, and rub a hand across my swelling stomach.

"Sorry I'm late!" Tori's shoes clatter down the hallway as she rushes to join us. My body sags in relief at her appearance. Tori has been an incredible support over these past months, and having her here, along with Dr. Mulligan and Connor, reminds me that I'm not alone. Confidence swells in my chest as I stand to embrace the older girl. "You doing all right?" she asks, her breath tickling my ear.

I nod. "Better now."

As if Tori's arrival signals the start of the meeting, the heavy wooden door at the end of the hall opens, and a smiling clerk addresses us. "Please come in. Judge Riebe will be in momentarily."

Connor pushes off from the wall, trailing the group as we file into the large chambers. Inside, a slight woman rises from her spot in one of the chairs settled in front of a large desk. She steps forward, offering her hand.

"Diana? My name is Carmen Sanchez, and I'm the state's attorney for your case."

I grasp her hand, grateful that mine remains dry, the trembling barely noticeable. It has become less startling to hear people refer to me as Diana, though those closest to me still use the name I have known for so many years.

"Nice to meet you, Ms. Sanchez," I say, my voice quiet, but clear. My other hand rests on my stomach, taking comfort from Nut, an unconscious habit I have developed. He reassures me with a kick, and I straighten my shoulders. "Thank you for agreeing to do this."

"Of course, and please call me Carmen." Her voice is warm and friendly, nothing like the attorneys I encountered at Glen's trial. Carmen releases my hand and gestures to one of the high-backed chairs. "Please, have a seat."

I glance back at Connor, who has taken up his usual stance at the back of the room, and Dr. Mulligan, who is also keeping to the background. They have come to be witnesses for me. Tori remains close at my side, taking post beside my chair as I sink into it.

Carmen perches on the other chair. "This should be pretty straightforward, but are you sure you don't want representation, Diana? It's your right."

I look up at Tori, who gives me an encouraging smile, and shake my head. "No. I am ready to take whatever consequences you deem fit for my part in Glen's business."

This is my penance. Though I have been told by Connor, by Dr.

Mulligan, by Tori, by my family, that I am a victim, that I only participated because of my relationship with Glen and the lies I had been told, I have insisted that I be held responsible for what I've done.

A door at the back of the room opens, and a uniformed bailiff steps into the chambers first. "All rise for the Honorable Judge Martha Riebe."

My knees wobble as I struggle to my feet, and a warm hand steadies me from behind. I shoot a grateful smile back at Tori before turning my attention to the newest arrival to our little party.

Judge Riebe strides to her desk, her robes billowing around her. She wastes no time in pulling out her own chair and sitting down, gesturing for us to do the same. Her short blond hair curls loosely around her face, and despite her serious expression, laugh lines radiate from the corners of her eyes and mouth. She is probably around Mama's age, maybe just a bit older, but where Mama's face is covered with crags and valleys that tell the story of years of stress and anxiety, Judge Riebe's face radiates a sense of peace and contentment. Her eyes flick across the file in front of her, reviewing my case. Finally, she looks up.

"Diana McKinley?"

I nod.

"I understand that you are here because you wish to be held responsible for your part in the trafficking ring run by Mr. Glen Lawson, Junior."

"Yes, Your Honor," I reply, inclining my head in agreement.

"I also understand," she continues, "that Counselor Sanchez did not wish to press charges, but you insisted."

"Yes, Your Honor," I repeat. "I was a large part of the organization, in charge of training the girls who were . . . sold." I stumble over the last word.

"Did you have knowledge of what was going on?" Judge Riebe's voice is brisk, betraying little of her reaction to my answers.

"I knew the girls were being prepared to serve men who paid a great deal of money for the honor of having them join their households. I knew them to be runaways or unwanted children, as I believed myself to be." Inwardly I cringe as I say the words. Even though I believed it for so long, having spent time with my family, I can't fathom how I didn't remember the amount of love they had for me.

"I understand you knew of Mr. Lawson's other businesses as well."

My stomach sinks. Though I know I deserve it, I can tell by the judge's tone that she is disgusted by what I have done. She should be, of course, but I had hoped for at least a small amount of understanding. Judge Riebe's mouth thins into a straight line as she meets my eyes, waiting for my answer.

"Yes, ma'am," I say, sitting up straighter. "Though I had no part in those businesses, I knew they existed. Girls who were not placed out of my home were often rerouted to the brothel."

"And how did you feel about the girls you'd spent years training ending up in a place like that?"

"I didn't like it," I answer. "But it was how things were done."

Judge Riebe watches me for a moment before turning back to the file. "I also understand that you were integral in uncovering evidence and giving testimony that sent Glen Lawson, Junior, Mae Lawson, and several of their cohorts to prison for a very long time."

"Yes, ma'am."

"And I have character witness statements from your therapist and a support group member, whom I am assuming have come to back you up today." She glances at Dr. Mulligan and Tori. "And also from the lead agent on the case, which is a relatively unusual occurrence."

Connor stands to the side of the room, his gaze fixed on Judge Riebe. He doesn't flinch under her stare, though I can see his jaw working. I had no idea he'd gone out on a limb for me like that. Of course he has been with me through all of this, but for all intents and purposes we are playing opposite sides of this game. Perhaps not as much as I'd thought.

"In fact," Judge Riebe says, "there is nothing typical about your case. Most victims we rescue are happy to be sent back to their families to recover. But then, most victims have not also been perpetrators in these situations."

My blood runs cold at the word "perpetrators." Is that what I am? I suppose it is. I try the label on for size, the weight of it pushing my shoulders lower. Even a small kick from Nut cannot lift me.

"You have been involved in illegal retention and exploitation of minors, as well as an accessory to three murders."

It takes all my strength to stay upright. The blood drains from my face as I remember what it was like in prison, which is no doubt where I am heading now. I just pray that they will allow Jane or Charlotte to take Nut when he comes. They will at least help him remember me. He will have a good life with them.

Judge Riebe looks at Carmen. "Counselor, what is your recommendation?"

"Your Honor," Carmen says, standing up, "we believe that the best rehabilitation for Miss McKinley would not be achieved in a prison setting. We request that she be sentenced to time served in the psychiatric ward of the hospital, as well as a transitional period in a recovery home and community service."

Lips pursed, Judge Riebe looks between Carmen and me. I cannot read her expression. Nut flutters, in a hopeful way, I think, as time stretches on. Connor shifts in his spot, and it occurs to me that the judge didn't even ask my people to say anything. Of course, she's read their words in the letters they wrote, and my heart swells at the thought that they must have said enough positive things to garner at least this much deliberation.

After what seems like forever, but is probably only a few minutes, Judge Riebe lets out a breath of air and her lips turn up in a small smile. "I have been following this case closely, Diana," she says, and I jump when she uses my name. She says it with warmth, not the hostility or judgment I expected. "I have been impressed with the work of the agents, but even more impressed with you. I can't even imagine what your life has been, and how going through this trauma has affected you, and yet instead of playing the victim, you have come forward to accept the punishment you feel you deserve." She looks around the room, pinning each person with her gaze for only a moment. "You have managed to win the respect and admiration of many intelligent and sensible people, and I trust their judgment as well as my own. I believe you will do much more good outside the prison walls than you ever could within them."

My throat tightens at her words, and I suppress my reaction until I'm absolutely certain she is saying what I think she's saying.

"For your part in your husband's business, Diana McKinley, alias Clara Lawson, you are hereby sentenced to time served, plus at least one year in a recovery home. You will be required to complete ten thousand hours of community service and check in with your probation officer at regular intervals, to be established by the officer. Furthermore, you will continue to attend therapy with Dr. Mulligan until she deems it appropriate to discharge you, and you will also continue to participate in your survivors support group. If any of these terms are not met, you are at risk for immediate revocation of probation and placement in a secure facility."

Judge Riebe continues, but I tune out. For weeks I have been expecting to trade one form of captivity for another. I had almost resigned myself to a life behind bars, being told what to do, when to do it. Instead, I am being offered freedom. Limited freedom, to start, but with hope of more on the horizon. Hope of a better future for myself and for Nut. Hope that we can be a normal family. Whatever normal we choose to be.

When Tori's hand falls on my shoulder and squeezes, I reach up and squeeze her fingers back. No matter what comes next, I know I won't be alone.

Then

I am so bored. The sun is shining and all boring old Lottie wants to do is play with her stupid Barbies and make them kiss the Kens and other gross stuff. And how many times can they change clothes? I see Mommy do laundry, and I bet Barbie's mommy gets really mad at her for making so many dirty clothes.

"Lottie, pleeeeeeease?" I use my best whining voice, because it bugs her and she will do what I want just so I will leave her alone. "Mommy won't let me walk to the park alone!"

"No, Dee-Dee. I don't wanna go to the park."

"Moooooooommmmmyyy!"

Mommy comes in right before Lottie can hit me. I stick my tongue out at her, but Mommy doesn't see. I am sneaky. "What is it, Diana? I'm trying to get ready for the party tomorrow."

I show her my best frowny face. "Mommy, it's nice outside and I just want to go to the park for a little while, but Lottie just wants to play with her dumb old Barbies and she's making them kiss and stuff and it's gross."

Mommy does a big breath and makes her lips really small. She does that when she is busy and we're bothering her. "Charlotte—" she begins, and Lottie interrupts her.

"No, Mom! Please! Dee-Dee is old enough to go to the park without me! It's only a few blocks!"

"Just for a little while, Charlotte. Please. It would help me out a lot." Mommy looks at me. "And I know Diana won't bother you for the rest of the day if you take her to the park for an hour."

I nod my head really fast so she knows that I am serious, but probably I will bother Lottie later. She's really fun to bother. I will just have to be sneaky. Charlotte throws down her Malibu Barbie or whatever one that is and grumbles as she gets up.

"Lottie is saying mean things!" I sing.

Mommy closes her eyes, and I know she is counting, because she says when she needs to take a break before she talks she counts to ten. I tried it once when Lottie was being mean but I got bored. "Diana, your sister is being nice and taking you to the park. Please don't make it hard."

I stick my lip out. Why do I get in trouble when Lottie is saying mean things? Lottie starts to put on shoes and I cheer up. "Yay! We're going to the park! We're going to the park!" I make up a song as I pull on my tennis shoes and skip out the door. "Come *on*, Lottie!"

Lottie moves really super slow like a turtle, but as soon as she comes outside she starts walking really fast. "Wait, Lottie! I can't walk so fast!" I have to run to catch up to her.

"I'm not speaking to you, Diana Patience McKinley. Mom said I had to walk you to the park, but she didn't say I have to talk to you."

No fair! I look back to see if I can run back and get Mommy to make Lottie talk to me, but we're already out of sight of the house. "You just talked to me, though," I say, hoping she will argue with me at least. She is smart and keeps her mouth shut. "Why is that dog outside?" I ask. "Why did those people plant yellow flowers? I like pink flowers better. They should have asked me. I am very good at flowers.

Do you think that Daddy will let me plant flowers in his garden? I would choose pink ones." I yammer in Lottie's ear, but she doesn't budge, and she hasn't said another word to me by the time we make it to the park. I shrug and run to the swings. "Push me, Lottie!"

Lottie sits on a bench and crosses her arms. She is so mean. One of her friends, Jessica, is here, and she joins Lottie on the bench. They talk and soon they are pointing at me. I jump off the swing and run over.

"What are you saying, Lottie-tottie?" I ask, putting my hands on my hips. She better not be saying mean things.

"I was just telling Jessica how annoying you are and how I wish I didn't have a little sister."

Tears fill my eyes. I can't believe she just said that in front of someone else. Almost like she means it! "That's not true. Stop being mean, Lottie."

"It is so true. You're the worst little sister in the world." Lottie stands up and pushes me.

"Fine!" I yell. "You don't like me, just leave! Go back to playing with your BARBIES!"

Lottie's face turns bright red, and I smile. Ha! Showed her. Her friends don't know she still plays with Barbies.

"I hate you, Diana!" Lottie screams, and runs in the direction of the house. Jessica looks at me and makes a face, then runs the other way, back toward her own house.

I play until the park is empty and my tummy starts to rumble. I wonder how Lottie got in the house without Mommy checking to see if I was with her. I decide to head home to tell on her. I bet she'll be in really big trouble. Maybe even get her dumb Barbies taken away. And maybe she'll have to do all the laundry. I will change my clothes as much as Barbie does if Lottie is doing the laundry.

A car pulls up beside me, and a woman with dark hair leans out. "Hi there," she says, smiling. "How are you, Diana?"

I stop and cross my arms. "How did you know my name?"

"Your mommy sent me. Get in the car, sweetie."

"Nuh-uh," I say, and start walking again. "Mommy said don't get in the car with people I don't know."

"But we do know you! We're going to your house tomorrow. Jane, I mean, your mom, invited us."

She knows my mommy's name. And my name. That means she must be a friend. I open the back door and hop inside. The man driving the car does not turn around. When we turn the wrong way, I get nervous. "Hey, lady, my house is the other way."

She turns in her seat. "I'm sorry I had to lie to you, Diana. I do know your mommy, but not because of the party. She wanted us to take you. You're going to live with us now."

"What? That's not right. Can we please go back and talk to her?"

"I'm afraid not. Your mommy and daddy don't want you anymore. They said you are nothing but trouble. But we want you, Diana."

I start to cry. "It's not true! You're a liar! Take me home!" The car jerks to a halt, and the woman climbs out of the front seat and opens the back door. I look around for a place to run, but she blocks my exit. I scramble across the seat to the other door, but it won't open, no matter how hard I push.

"Calm down, child," she says, reaching for me.

"No! Nononononono! I want my mommy!" I scream. The man gets out and comes around the car to help the woman. We are in a part of the big park where there are no playgrounds or other people.

"Hold her still, Mae," the man barks, and pulls a bottle and a cloth from a sack he is holding. The woman's arms hold me tight and it hurts how she squeezes me. The man pushes the cloth in front of my nose and it smells sweet, and I'm afraid that I won't be able to breathe, but then I feel sleepy. My arms and legs can't move anymore. And everything goes dark.

Now

Butterflies dance in my stomach, right alongside Nut, who is doing the rhumba. I fidget as I sit on the bench at the park, brushing imaginary lint from my skirt. My mom and Charlotte sit at the other end of the park, watching Charlotte's children play on the playground. I rub my belly, talking to Nut. "Soon that will be us, angel," I say. "I can't wait for you to meet Grandma and Aunt Lottie and your cousins."

"Clara?" A timid voice comes from behind me. I stand and turn around. A girl with wild hair and bright eyes stands, her hands lacing and unlacing in nervous rhythm, flanked by a kind-looking older couple. My Passion. She doesn't use that name anymore.

"Emily," I say, and walk around the bench, holding out my arms. She looks to the woman, who nods and nudges her toward me. Her face breaks into a grin as she rushes at me. We cling to each other, the wetness on my cheeks matching the wetness pooling on my shirt from her tears.

We have been in regular contact since I moved into a recovery house for trafficking victims, but this is the first time we have seen each other. We have been kept apart because of the trials, first Mama's and then Glen's, and my own hearing as well. Emily gave her testimony at Glen's last week, and we have been granted permission to see each other again.

Emily steps back and her eyes widen at my pregnant belly. "Wow, Clare, you are huge!"

I laugh. "I'm about to pop any day. I can't wait to meet him."

She doesn't ask any of the normal pregnancy questions, like what

I'm going to name him. As she always has, Emily reads me and knows those are not questions for today. I take her hand and lead her to the bench.

"How are you? Really?" I ask, looking her in the eyes, not releasing her hands. She smiles.

"I'm really good." She motions to the couple she came with, still standing a few feet away. "Mary and Leonard have been great. They're helping me out a lot. I'm pretty far behind in school, but catching up fast. It's different, but I like it." Her face lights up. "They let me sign up for art classes. The teachers say I have a gift for seeing detail. I'm thinking about going to art school. You know, after I graduate."

My heart fills as I look at her, as passionate as ever, but over something she chose for herself. She deserves it. Through letters I have learned that Emily was a foster child when she was taken. She had been in the system for years, bounced from home to home. That's why no one claimed her that first day. Her current foster parents stepped up to take her in, and she has flourished with them. I stand again, walk over to the couple, and extend my hand toward Mary.

"Thank you," I say, and my voice catches. I can barely speak around the emotion in my throat. "Thank you for taking care of her."

Mary ignores my hand and pulls me into a hug. "You're welcome." No other words need to be said. There are too many and not enough. Emily joins our huddle, and Leonard pats our backs with awkward hands. These are the parents Emily deserves. I was her mother for a while, but Mary can be the mother I never was. And I am glad of it.

Emily and I walk around the park for a while, arms linked, talking about the future, but avoiding discussing the past. She asks about the other girls. I have not been allowed to see any of the rest of them, nor will I be allowed. Though my heart aches for them, I know it is for the best. Emily was a special circumstance, and rather than have her run away to find me, the powers that be made an exception. She will be eighteen soon anyway.

I introduce Emily to my family. She seems so grown up as I watch her interact with my nephews. I feel a pang as I realize that I stole that kind of childhood from her. I take a deep breath and correct myself. I didn't steal it. Glen did. Mama and Papa did. I am a victim as well. That's what Dr. Mulligan makes me repeat each time we meet. I hope I believe it soon.

I hug Emily good-bye and we promise to get together again soon. "I love you," she whispers, her words a balm to my soul. "You will always be my mother." And then she is gone.

Then

"Girls, start your chores!" I call upstairs. I can hear them giggling, and I smile at their antics. I'm glad Glen is not around. He has been in a strange mood all week. I've seen him carrying papers up to put in the safe in our bedroom, and he has burned boxes of papers in the fire pit every night. I hope we aren't moving again. I love this house.

Daisy stumbles down the stairs, her eyes sleepy, hair rumpled. "Cassidy says I have to help clean the toilet," she says. "I don't know how to clean the toilet."

I smile at her and take her hand. "Let's get you ready first, and then we'll talk about it, okay?" I find a brush in the bathroom and sit at the kitchen table. I feel Daisy relax as I begin to pull the brush through her long silky strands. "You have such pretty hair, Daisy," I say.

She doesn't reply, but I see her small smile in the reflection in the window. We sit in companionable silence until I hear gravel crunching on the driveway, announcing the arrival of visitors.

Now

I pat the last of the dirt in place and wipe my hand across my forehead. I cannot wait to see how these flowers bloom. I have added to the garden every season in the two years that I have lived in this small cottage. We are just down the block from my parents and across the street from Charlotte and her family.

Charlotte and I had plenty of things to work through, and I still see Dr. Mulligan two times a month. Charlotte carried the guilt of my disappearance for years, believing that if she had not used such harsh words, I never would have gotten into the car with Mama and Papa. It's strange to see guilt on someone else, and it helped me to realize that we are not just the sum total of our actions. Every choice is an intricate result of many different factors.

My probation ended three months ago, though I will spend the rest of my life attempting to atone for my sins. I work with the local human trafficking task force, volunteer at the women's mission in town, and speak to groups to raise awareness. I share my story in the hope that others will not go through what I did, and each time I share it, another piece of me is healed. I also took over running the support group that helped me so much when I needed it. In another year, I will earn my college degree, and after that I hope to go on for more schooling. Perhaps someday I will be a Dr. Mulligan for someone else.

Connor called last week to tell me that Mae Lawson had died in prison. She was found hanged in the bathroom, and they suspect foul play. It does not surprise me that Mae would make enemies.

I stand and brush the dirt off my hands. "Ella! Let's go wash up!"

My daughter stops jumping rope and skips over to me. She gazes up at me with bright blue eyes. Glen's eyes. "Okay, Mommy!" She kisses my hand and runs into the house.

Ella has been the brightest light in my life. No one was more surprised than I when Nut turned out to be a girl, but I could not have been happier. I dread the moment when she starts asking questions about her father. It will come soon, I am sure, but for now, I am enjoying watching her grow into a little person.

I have tried to hate Glen, but I cannot. He will always hold a part of my heart. My first love. My only love. The man who gave me Ella. For me, she was conceived in love. And I think, in his own way, Glen always loved me, too. He just didn't have a very good example of what love looked like. Perhaps that's why I can't bring myself to hate him. It wouldn't be worth the energy anyway. Between his trafficking and at least four murders, he will be in prison for life.

They were able to track down some of the girls we had sold throughout the years using the files in Glen's safe. Many men were brought to justice, and many girls were saved. For many others, however, rescue came too late. My heart aches every day for the daughters I lost, who will never again know true freedom.

"Excuse me?" A woman is on the sidewalk, staring at me. I have been so lost in my memories that I did not hear her approach.

"Hello," I say, walking to stand in front of her.

"Hi." She smiles. "My name is Carol, and we just moved in two houses down." I had seen a moving van there earlier, but hadn't paid much attention to who it was. "I have a daughter about your daughter's age, so I wanted to come introduce myself."

I smile back at her. Ella will be so excited to have a playmate. I wipe the remaining dirt from my palm and extend my arm to shake her hand.

"My name is Diana."

Acknowledgments

Making a book is hardly a solitary venture. It would probably take another book just to fully thank everyone who has been a part of this process.

First, I want to thank my parents. You always taught me to believe in myself and to be confident in my abilities. You were the ones who believed in me even when I struggled to believe in myself. To my mom, Martha Olsen, who read *The Girl Before* numerous times, in every iteration, sometimes in just a day: thank you for your tireless work and all the time you've dedicated to helping this book to be the best it could be. And to my dad, Tim Olsen, who has always been my biggest fan, even before the book was written: thank you for your boundless enthusiasm and infectious excitement, even through the more difficult stages.

Thank you to my siblings, both by blood and by marriage, Ben and Heather Olsen, Emily and Martin Moen, for your unwavering support and love. Ben and Emily, you are the best big brother and sister I could ask for. Thank you for being amazing examples in my life, and for pushing me to try new things, especially when one of those new things was trying to write a book. Heather and Martin, thank you for jumping into the family and treating me like a sister. You make our family whole.

To my incomparable agent, Sharon Pelletier, I am so thankful to have you as a partner in this crazy endeavor. You understood Clara in an uncanny way from the very beginning, and helped shape her story into something special.

Thank you to my incredibly talented editor, Sara Minnich Blackburn, who continued the work of shaping *The Girl Before* into the gem it is today. Every new suggestion, even the hardest ones, made my book even better, and I'm proud of the story we crafted together. And thank you to Liz Stein, who got the ball rolling in making those first changes.

The team at Putnam has been wonderful, and I feel so blessed to be a part of such a prestigious group. There are so many talented people who have had a hand in helping to make *The Girl Before* into something we can all be proud of. To all the readers, copy editors, the amazing cover designers, and the marketing team, I am forever and eternally grateful for the work that you do. It's an unbelievable feeling to have so many people believe in this story.

I have been so lucky to have a giant support system of friends that have been cheering me on from the start. Thank you to Andrea Gustafson, my Alpha Gal, who read some of my earliest work and told me years ago that she would see my name on shelves. To Kari Hunerdosse, Beta Babe extraordinaire, who was one of the first to read *The Girl Before* and tell me it was something special, and who also keeps me on my toes by demanding more words on a regular basis. To Jenny Moyer, who held my hand in the early days of this journey, who was there for the disappointments and the celebrations, and who continued to encourage me through countless lunches and frantic texts. You deserve all the cake, girl.

Kathleen Palm, thank you for being my best cheerleader, my sunshine on rainy days, and for the countless gifts of happiness. You have an uncanny ability to know when I need a pick-me-up, and I'm fairly certain you're made of magic. Margie Brimer, you are my soul sister. Thank you for your input on the early stages of *The Girl Before*, and in all aspects of my life, actually. Jamie Adams and Sarah Bales, thank you for hours in the Clubhouse, brainstorming with me and convincing me to keep going. Tana Haemmerle, thank you for your extreme honesty and for your unparalleled friendship and support. I wouldn't have made it here without you.

To Sara Burrier, I always thought you were just a bit too cool to hang out with me. Thanks for being one of my best friends, and for inspiring me in so many different ways to tell Clara's story. My life is better with you in it.

And Nicole Worthley, the other half of my brain, my person, and the one who first brought the important issue of human trafficking to my attention. You are a rare and precious gem, and God blessed me when He put you in my life all those years ago.

Thank you to all those who fight daily to bring freedom to the men, women, and children who find themselves in seemingly hopeless situations. You give me hope that someday slavery really will be eradicated.

Most importantly, I thank God for all the beautiful blessings He's given me. Everything listed above is only a small portion of what I've experienced. I truly wouldn't be writing this right now without Him.